# Scion

## DIVI
## LOYA

Publisher's Cataloging in Publication Data
(Prepared by The Donohue Group, Inc.)

Scion. Volume three : divided loyalties / Writer: Ron Marz ; Penciler: Jim Cheung ; Inker: Don Hillsman ;
Colorist: Justin Ponsor.

p. : ill. ;  cm.

Spine title: Scion. 3 : divided loyalties

ISBN: 1-931484-26-0

1. Fantasy fiction.  2. Adventure fiction.  3. Graphic novels.  I. Marz, Ron.  II. Cheung, Jim.  III. Hillsman,
Don.  IV. Ponsor, Justin.  V. Title: Divided loyalties  VI. Title: Scion. 3 : divided loyalties.

PN6728 .S35 2002
813.54 [Fic]

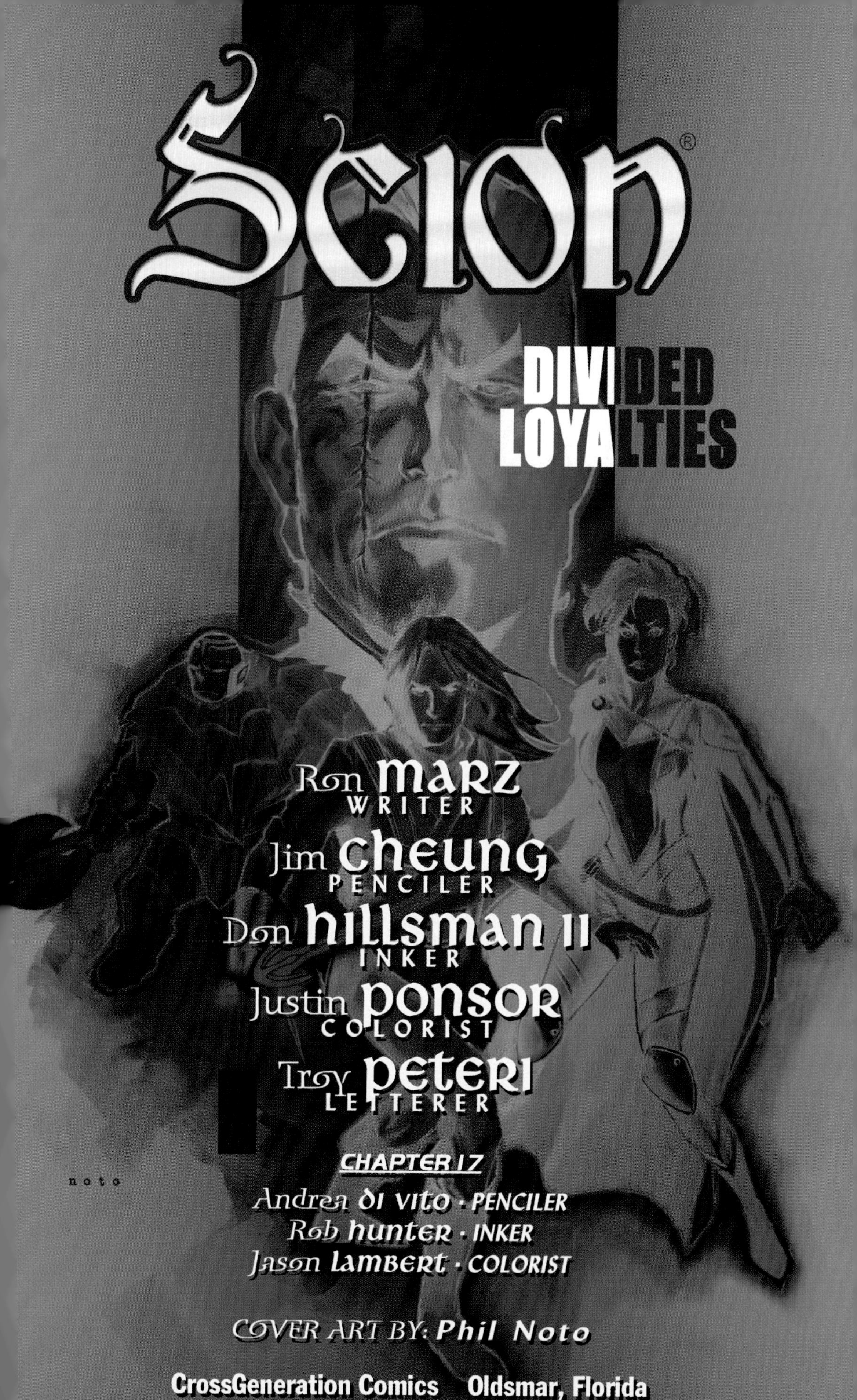
noto

# Scion®

## DIVIDED LOYALTIES

Ron **MARZ**
WRITER

Jim **CHEUNG**
PENCILER

Don **HILLSMAN II**
INKER

Justin **PONSOR**
COLORIST

Troy **PETERI**
LETTERER

**CHAPTER 17**

Andrea **DI VITO** · PENCILER
Rob **HUNTER** · INKER
Jason **LAMBERT** · COLORIST

COVER ART BY: **Phil Noto**

**CrossGeneration Comics Oldsmar, Florida**

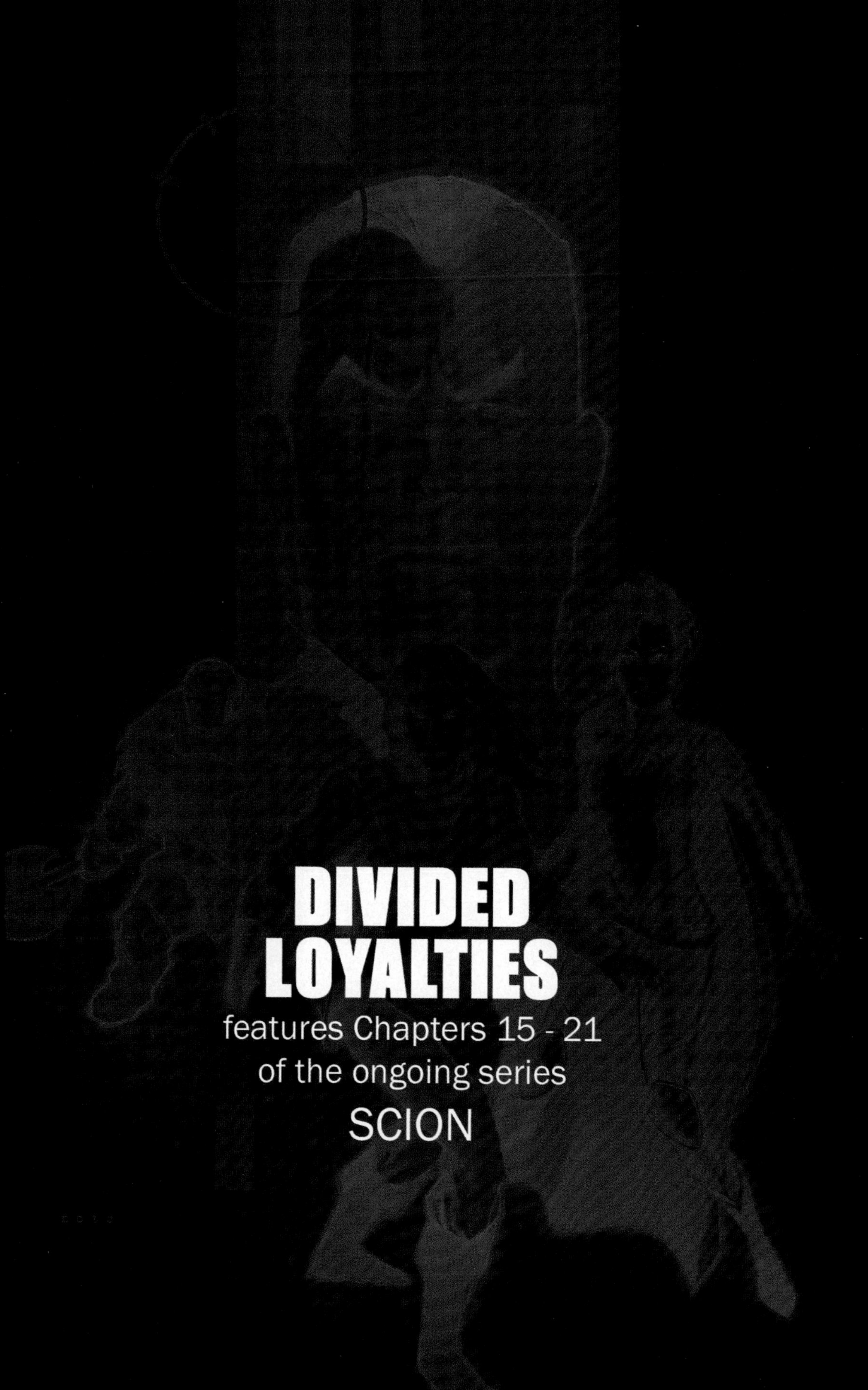

# DIVIDED LOYALTIES

features Chapters 15 - 21
of the ongoing series
SCION

# Thus Far in Scion

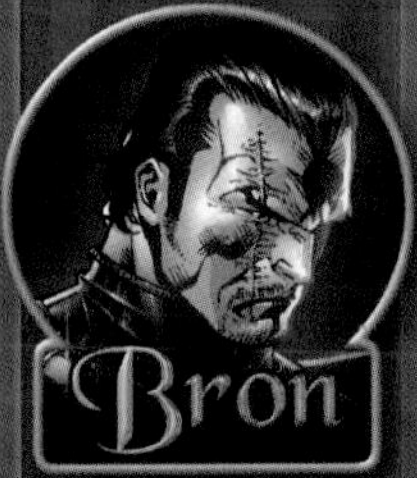
Bron

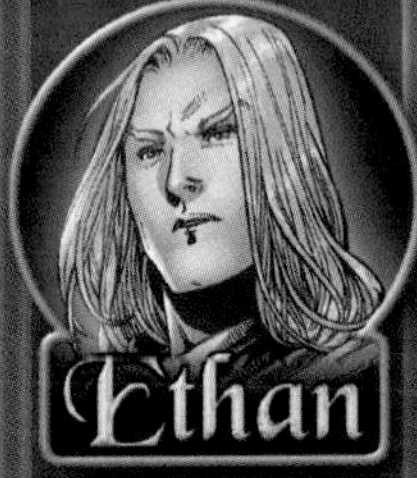
Ethan

What started with a mysterious sigil led to war. Prince Ethan of the West-ruling Heron Dynasty was graced with a mark granting him power, resulting in the accidental scarring of Prince Bron of the East-ruling Raven Dynasty during ritual combat.

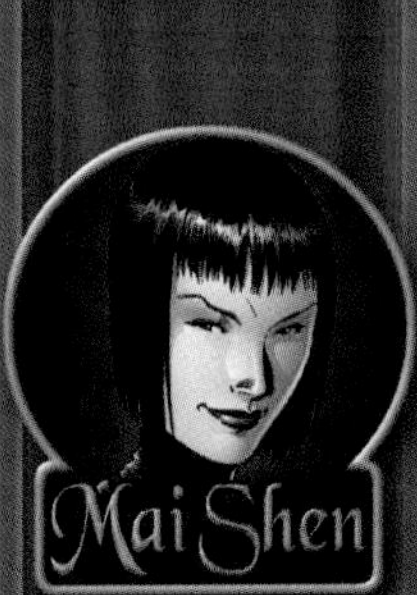
Mai Shen

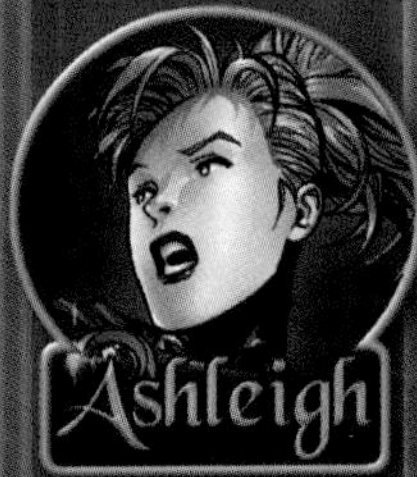
Ashleigh

Ethan surrendered himself to the Ravens but was soon freed from his imprisonment by a woman named Ashleigh who wanted Ethan to join the Underground cause of freedom for the genetically engineered Lesser Races. Ethan declined her offer and set off for home as war loomed.

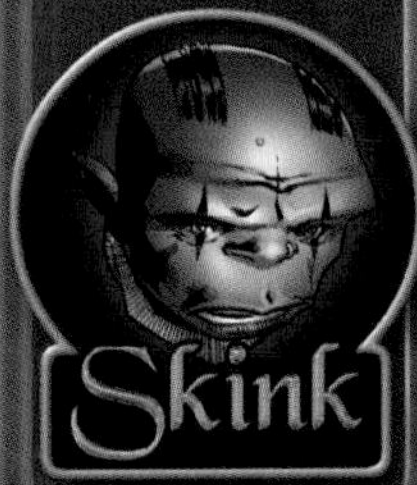
Skink

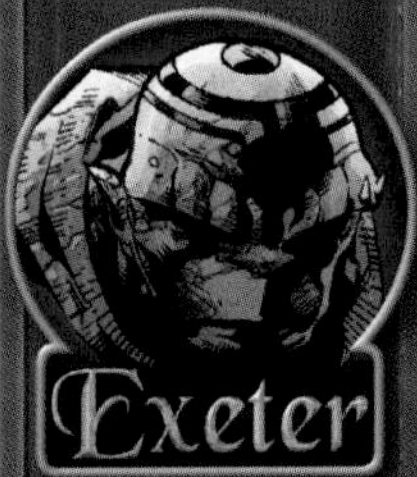
Exeter

When the battle was met, first victory belonged to the Herons, but Ethan's oldest brother and heir to the throne, Artor, was brutally slain by Bron. Ethan vowed to have his revenge and returned to Eastern lands.

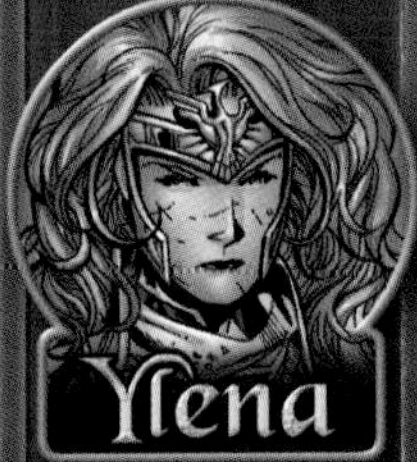
Ylena

The mysterious Mai Shen revealed herself as a member of the godlike First and imbued Bron with a portion of her power. Bron then murdered his father King Viktor, framed Ashleigh for the crime and took the throne for himself.

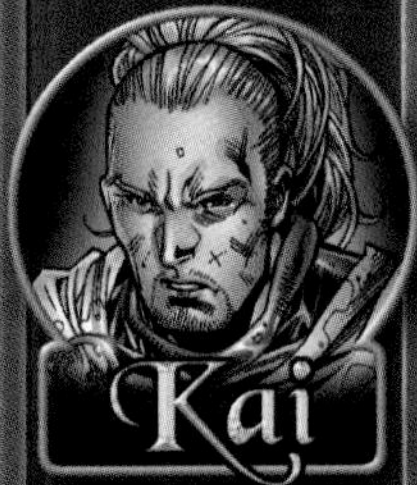
Kai

Ethan freed Ashleigh from the Raven dungeons, but learned her true heritage – she is, in fact, Bron's sister. Ethan met Bron in combat and was apparently slain, but rose again when his wound was healed by his sigil. Ethan, Skink and Ashleigh made a narrow escape from the Raven Keep and headed north toward the Underground's hidden sanctuary.

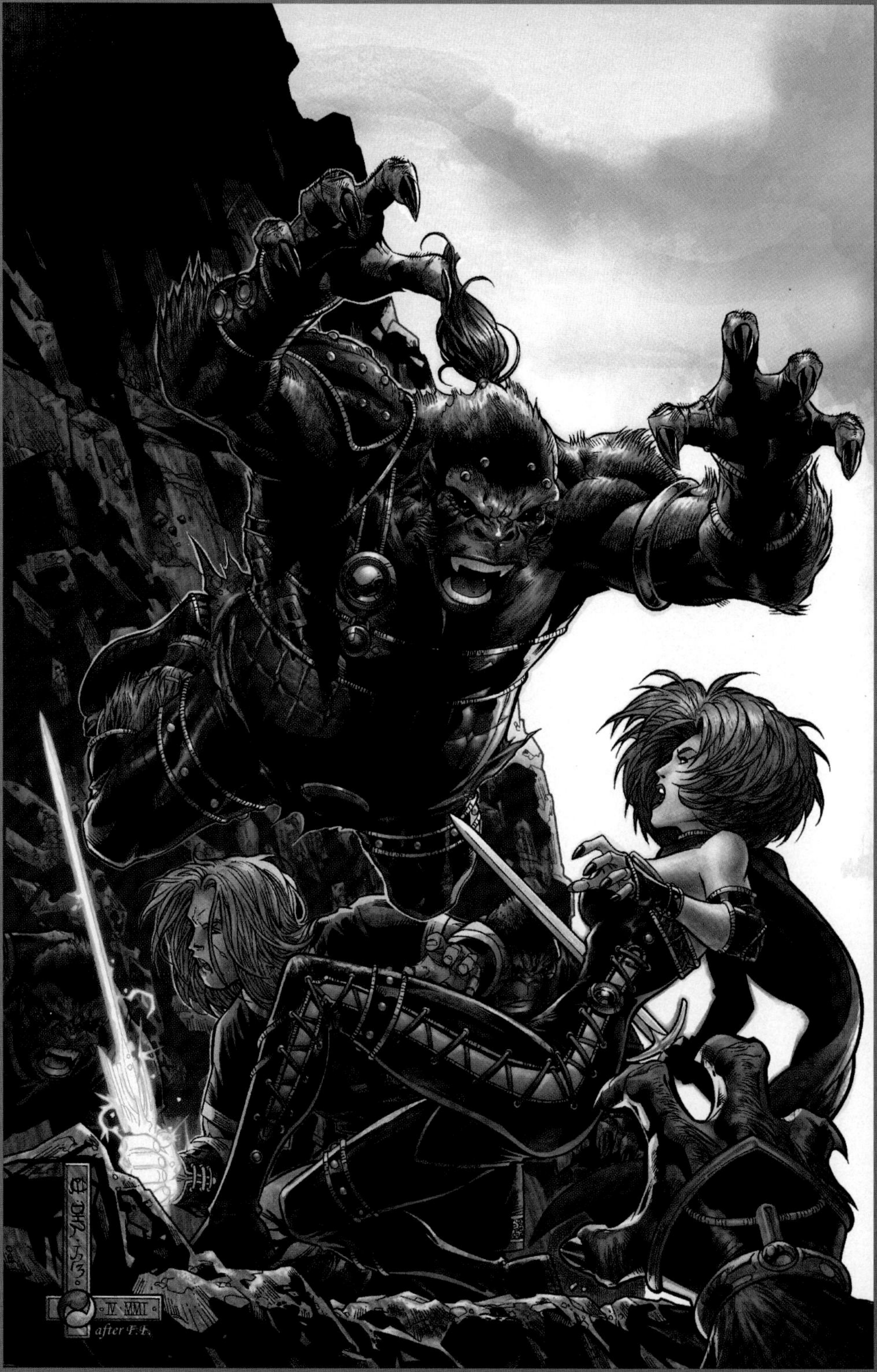
IV MMI
after F.F.

SCION • CHAPTER FIFTEEN

YOU WOULD HAVE ENJOYED IT.

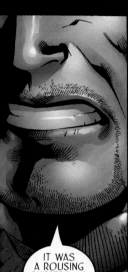

NO ONE SUSPECTS THE TRUTH, IN CASE YOU WERE WONDERING. MAI SHEN KNOWS, OBVIOUSLY. SHE HELPED TURN ME INTO WHAT I AM TODAY.

YOU NEVER HAD AN INKLING OF WHAT SHE WAS, DID YOU?

IT WAS A ROUSING SUCCESS, AS FUNERALS GO.

SUCH A GENUINE OUTPOURING OF GRIEF FOR THE SLAIN MONARCH. I EVEN SHED A FEW TEARS MYSELF...

...JUST SO THE PEOPLE COULD SEE THE HUMAN SIDE OF THEIR NEW KING.

"KING BRON." THEY'RE ALREADY GETTING USED TO THAT.

SHE'S OUT THERE NOW, THAT DAMNED HERON PRINCE WITH HER.

I ACTUALLY KILLED HIM, BUT HE WON'T STAY DEAD.

THEY MANAGED TO GET OUT OF THE CITY SOMEHOW, PROBABLY HER FRIENDS IN THE UNDERGROUND AGAIN.

AND THEN THERE'S ASHLEIGH. SHE MADE IT SO EASY TO PLACE THE BLAME FOR THE MURDER UPON HER SHOULDERS.

BUT SHE'S MANAGED TO SLIP THROUGH MY FINGERS.

BUT I PROMISE YOU, I'LL FIND THEM. AND WHEN I DO...

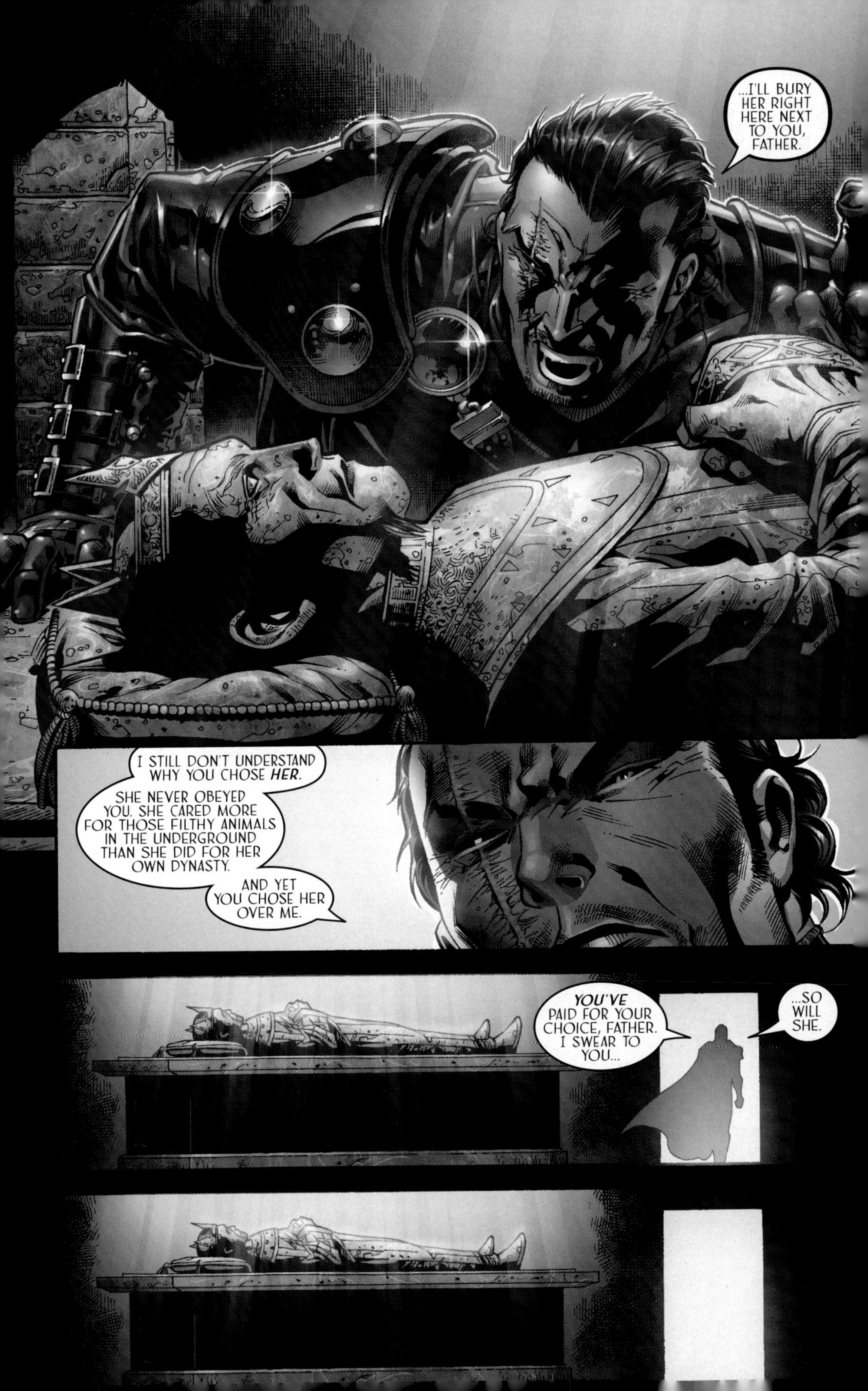
...I'LL BURY HER RIGHT HERE NEXT TO YOU, FATHER.
I STILL DON'T UNDERSTAND WHY YOU CHOSE HER.
SHE NEVER OBEYED YOU. SHE CARED MORE FOR THOSE FILTHY ANIMALS IN THE UNDERGROUND THAN SHE DID FOR HER OWN DYNASTY.
AND YET YOU CHOSE HER OVER ME.
YOU'VE PAID FOR YOUR CHOICE, FATHER. I SWEAR TO YOU...
...SO WILL SHE.

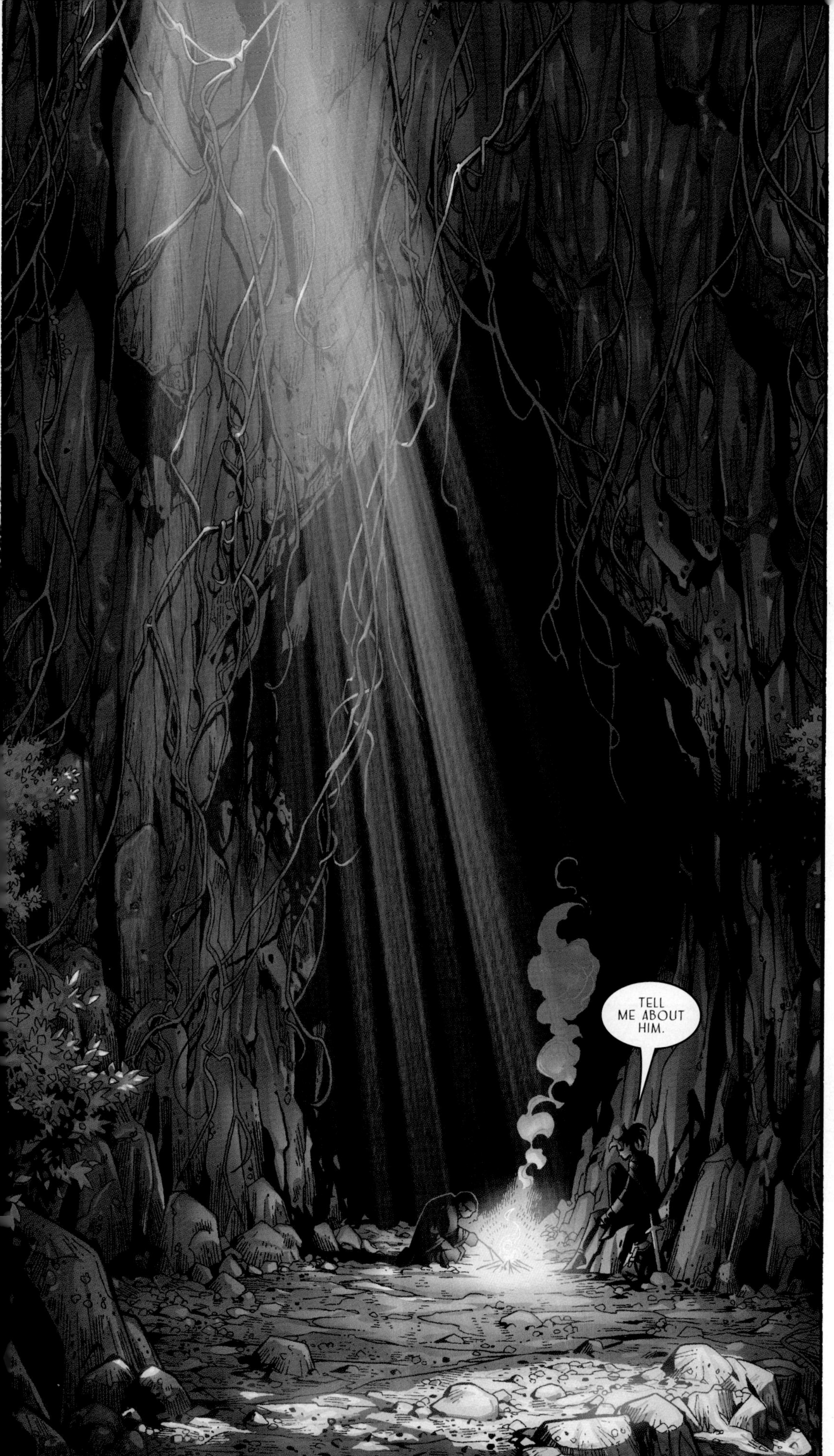
TELL ME ABOUT HIM.

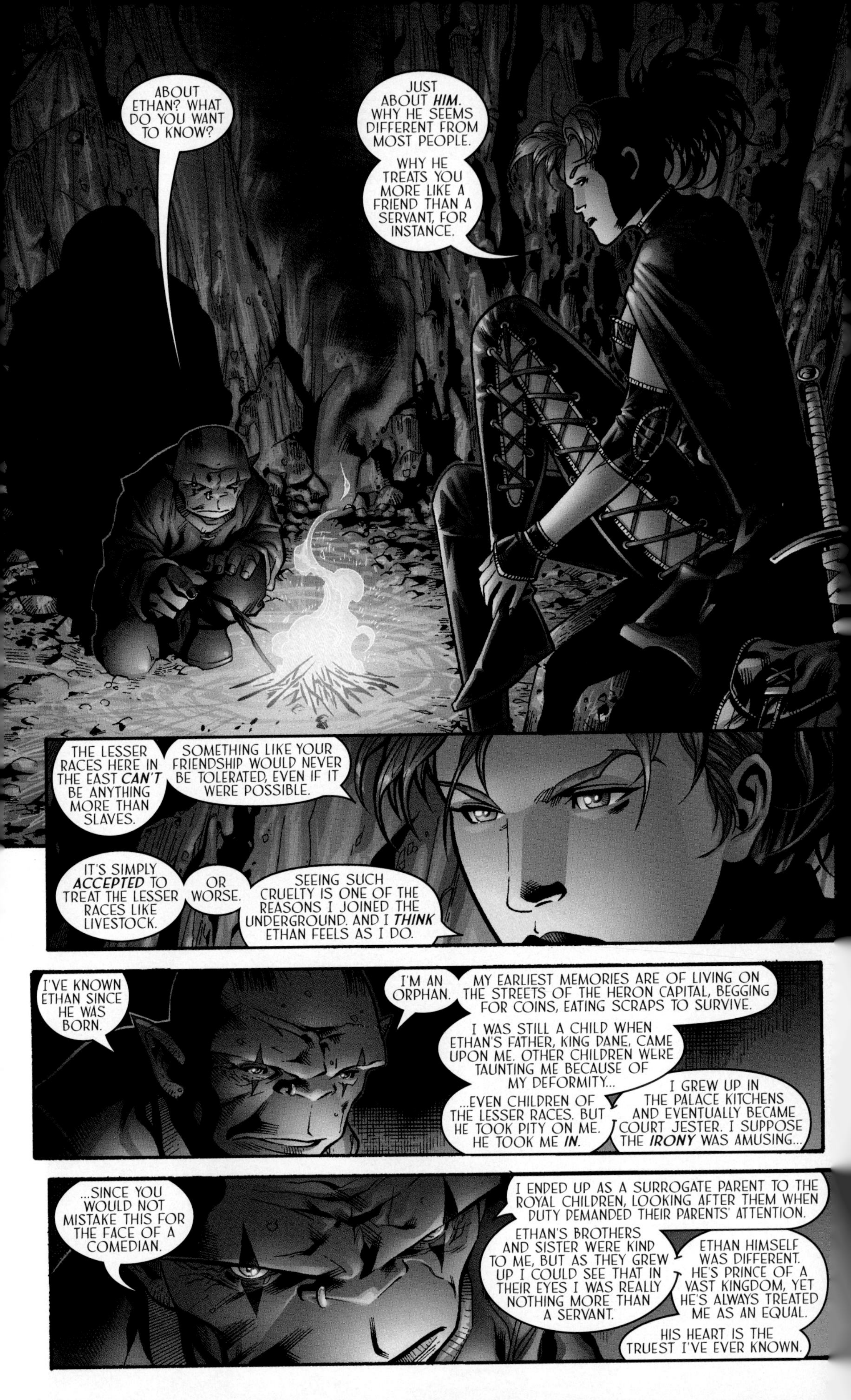
ABOUT ETHAN? WHAT DO YOU WANT TO KNOW?
JUST ABOUT *HIM*. WHY HE SEEMS DIFFERENT FROM MOST PEOPLE.
WHY HE TREATS YOU MORE LIKE A FRIEND THAN A SERVANT, FOR INSTANCE.
THE LESSER RACES HERE IN THE EAST *CAN'T* BE ANYTHING MORE THAN SLAVES.
SOMETHING LIKE YOUR FRIENDSHIP WOULD NEVER BE TOLERATED, EVEN IF IT WERE POSSIBLE.
IT'S SIMPLY *ACCEPTED* TO TREAT THE LESSER RACES LIKE LIVESTOCK.
OR WORSE.
SEEING SUCH CRUELTY IS ONE OF THE REASONS I JOINED THE UNDERGROUND. AND I *THINK* ETHAN FEELS AS I DO.
I'VE KNOWN ETHAN SINCE HE WAS BORN.
I'M AN ORPHAN.
MY EARLIEST MEMORIES ARE OF LIVING ON THE STREETS OF THE HERON CAPITAL, BEGGING FOR COINS, EATING SCRAPS TO SURVIVE.
I WAS STILL A CHILD WHEN ETHAN'S FATHER, KING DANE, CAME UPON ME. OTHER CHILDREN WERE TAUNTING ME BECAUSE OF MY DEFORMITY...
...EVEN CHILDREN OF THE LESSER RACES. BUT HE TOOK PITY ON ME. HE TOOK ME *IN*.
I GREW UP IN THE PALACE KITCHENS AND EVENTUALLY BECAME COURT JESTER. I SUPPOSE THE *IRONY* WAS AMUSING...
...SINCE YOU WOULD NOT MISTAKE THIS FOR THE FACE OF A COMEDIAN.
I ENDED UP AS A SURROGATE PARENT TO THE ROYAL CHILDREN, LOOKING AFTER THEM WHEN DUTY DEMANDED THEIR PARENTS' ATTENTION.
ETHAN'S BROTHERS AND SISTER WERE KIND TO ME, BUT AS THEY GREW UP I COULD SEE THAT IN THEIR EYES I WAS REALLY NOTHING MORE THAN A SERVANT.
ETHAN HIMSELF WAS DIFFERENT. HE'S PRINCE OF A VAST KINGDOM, YET HE'S ALWAYS TREATED ME AS AN EQUAL.
HIS HEART IS THE TRUEST I'VE EVER KNOWN.

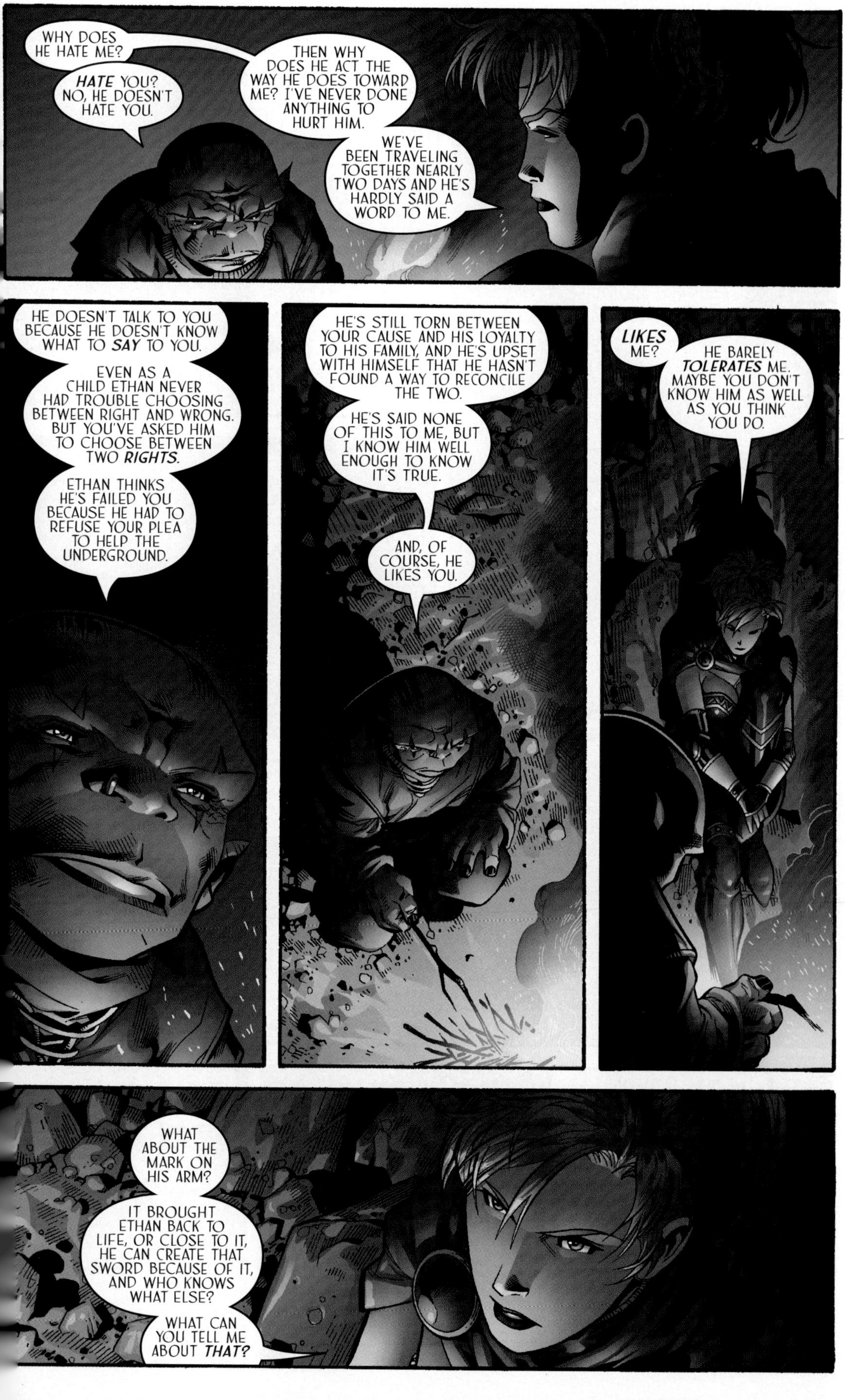
WHY DOES HE HATE ME?
HATE YOU? NO, HE DOESN'T HATE YOU.
THEN WHY DOES HE ACT THE WAY HE DOES TOWARD ME? I'VE NEVER DONE ANYTHING TO HURT HIM.
WE'VE BEEN TRAVELING TOGETHER NEARLY TWO DAYS AND HE'S HARDLY SAID A WORD TO ME.
HE DOESN'T TALK TO YOU BECAUSE HE DOESN'T KNOW WHAT TO SAY TO YOU.
EVEN AS A CHILD ETHAN NEVER HAD TROUBLE CHOOSING BETWEEN RIGHT AND WRONG. BUT YOU'VE ASKED HIM TO CHOOSE BETWEEN TWO RIGHTS.
ETHAN THINKS HE'S FAILED YOU BECAUSE HE HAD TO REFUSE YOUR PLEA TO HELP THE UNDERGROUND.
HE'S STILL TORN BETWEEN YOUR CAUSE AND HIS LOYALTY TO HIS FAMILY, AND HE'S UPSET WITH HIMSELF THAT HE HASN'T FOUND A WAY TO RECONCILE THE TWO.
HE'S SAID NONE OF THIS TO ME, BUT I KNOW HIM WELL ENOUGH TO KNOW IT'S TRUE.
AND, OF COURSE, HE LIKES YOU.
LIKES ME?
HE BARELY TOLERATES ME. MAYBE YOU DON'T KNOW HIM AS WELL AS YOU THINK YOU DO.
WHAT ABOUT THE MARK ON HIS ARM?
IT BROUGHT ETHAN BACK TO LIFE, OR CLOSE TO IT. HE CAN CREATE THAT SWORD BECAUSE OF IT, AND WHO KNOWS WHAT ELSE?
WHAT CAN YOU TELL ME ABOUT THAT?

I CAN TELL YOU I DON'T THINK IT BROUGHT HIM BACK TO LIFE. THAT MUCH, AT LEAST, SEEMS BEYOND ITS POWER.

IN A WAY, THE SIGIL *STARTED* ALL THIS. IT WAS AT THE TOURNAMENT ISLE...

...I IMAGINE YOU WERE EVEN THERE...

...JUST BEFORE HE FOUGHT BRON.

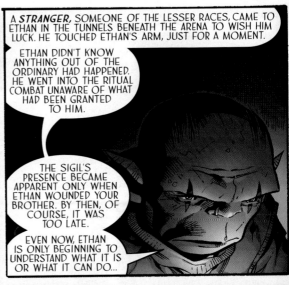

A *STRANGER*, SOMEONE OF THE LESSER RACES, CAME TO ETHAN IN THE TUNNELS BENEATH THE ARENA TO WISH HIM LUCK. HE TOUCHED ETHAN'S ARM, JUST FOR A MOMENT.

ETHAN DIDN'T KNOW ANYTHING OUT OF THE ORDINARY HAD HAPPENED. HE WENT INTO THE RITUAL COMBAT UNAWARE OF WHAT HAD BEEN GRANTED TO HIM.

THE SIGIL'S PRESENCE BECAME APPARENT ONLY WHEN ETHAN WOUNDED YOUR BROTHER. BY THEN, OF COURSE, IT WAS TOO LATE.

EVEN NOW, ETHAN IS ONLY BEGINNING TO UNDERSTAND WHAT IT IS OR WHAT IT CAN DO...

...BUT HE *ALREADY* UNDERSTANDS IT'S CHANGED HIS LIFE.

HIS DESTINY HAS BECOME... FAR DIFFERENT THAN HE IMAGINED IT WOULD BE.

I HOPE *PART* OF HIS DESTINY IS TO HELP THE UNDERGROUND.

WE NEED SOMEONE LIKE HIM IF WE'RE TO HAVE ANY HOPE OF CHANGING THE LOT OF THE LESSER RACES ON *EITHER* SIDE OF THE GREAT SEA.

THERE'S NOT MUCH OUT THERE...

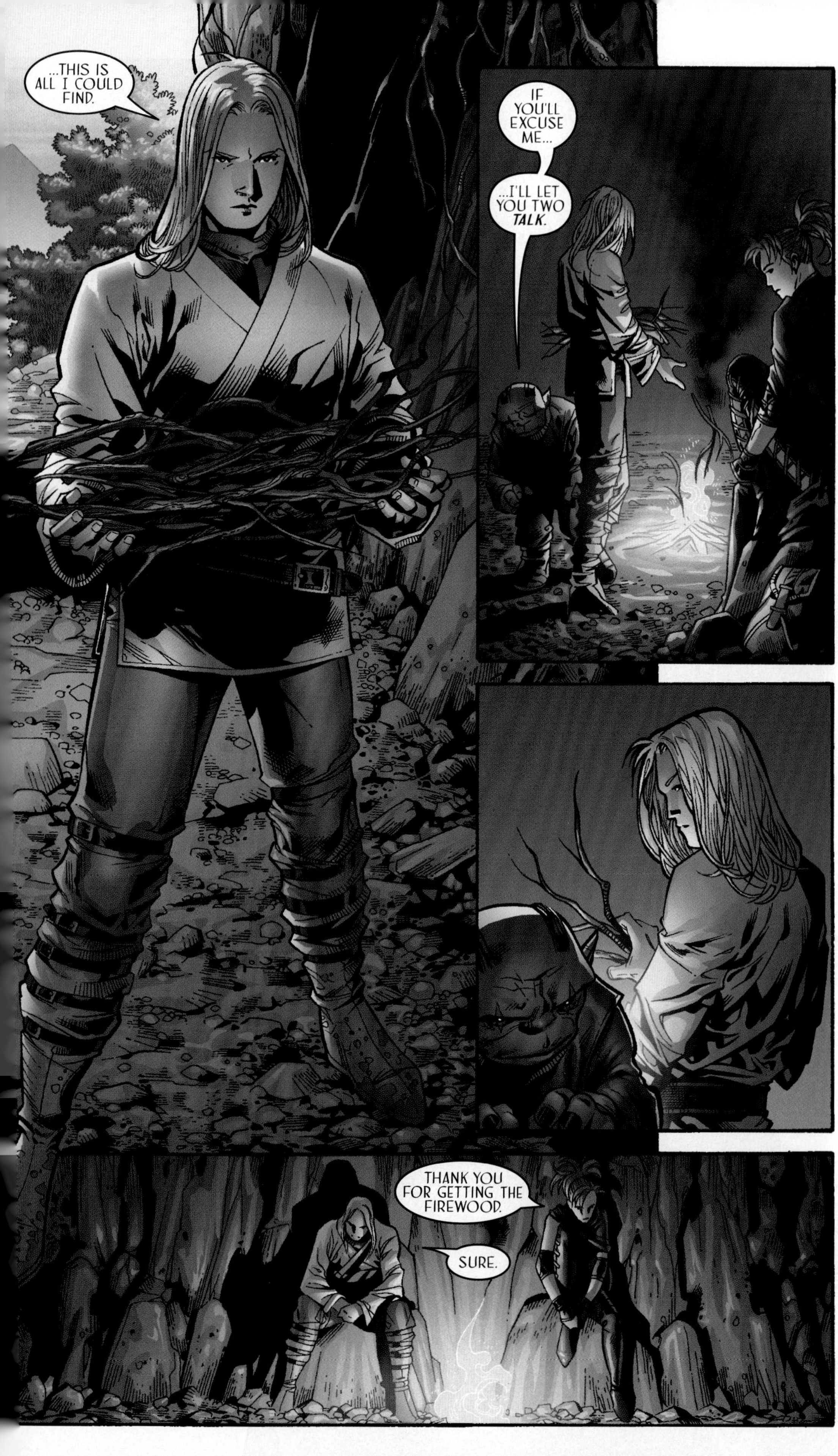
...THIS IS ALL I COULD FIND.
IF YOU'LL EXCUSE ME...
...I'LL LET YOU TWO *TALK*.
THANK YOU FOR GETTING THE FIREWOOD.
SURE.

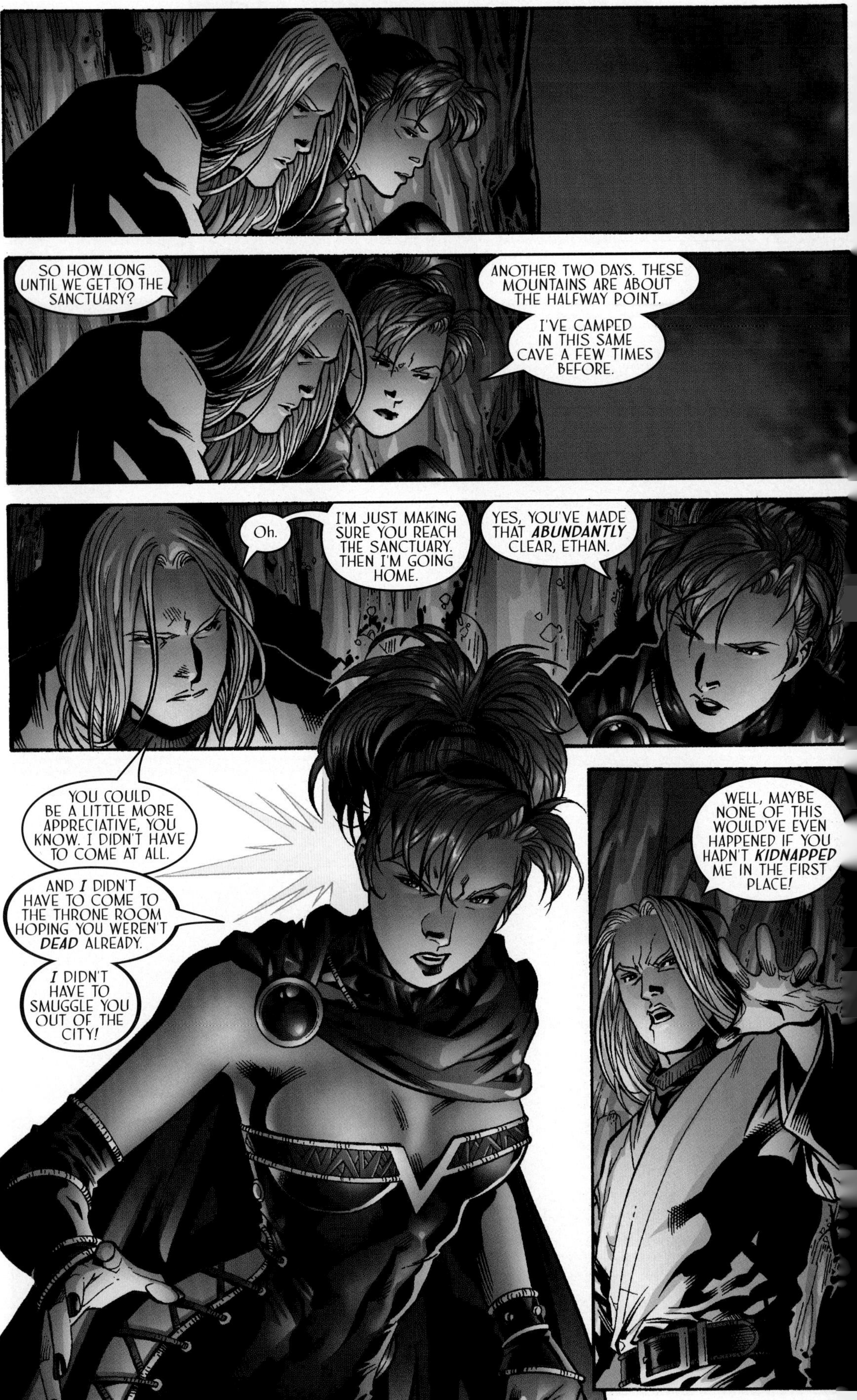
SO HOW LONG UNTIL WE GET TO THE SANCTUARY?
ANOTHER TWO DAYS. THESE MOUNTAINS ARE ABOUT THE HALFWAY POINT.
I'VE CAMPED IN THIS SAME CAVE A FEW TIMES BEFORE.
Oh.
I'M JUST MAKING SURE YOU REACH THE SANCTUARY. THEN I'M GOING HOME.
YES, YOU'VE MADE THAT ABUNDANTLY CLEAR, ETHAN.
YOU COULD BE A LITTLE MORE APPRECIATIVE, YOU KNOW. I DIDN'T HAVE TO COME AT ALL.
AND I DIDN'T HAVE TO COME TO THE THRONE ROOM HOPING YOU WEREN'T DEAD ALREADY.
I DIDN'T HAVE TO SMUGGLE YOU OUT OF THE CITY!
WELL, MAYBE NONE OF THIS WOULD'VE EVEN HAPPENED IF YOU HADN'T KIDNAPPED ME IN THE FIRST PLACE!

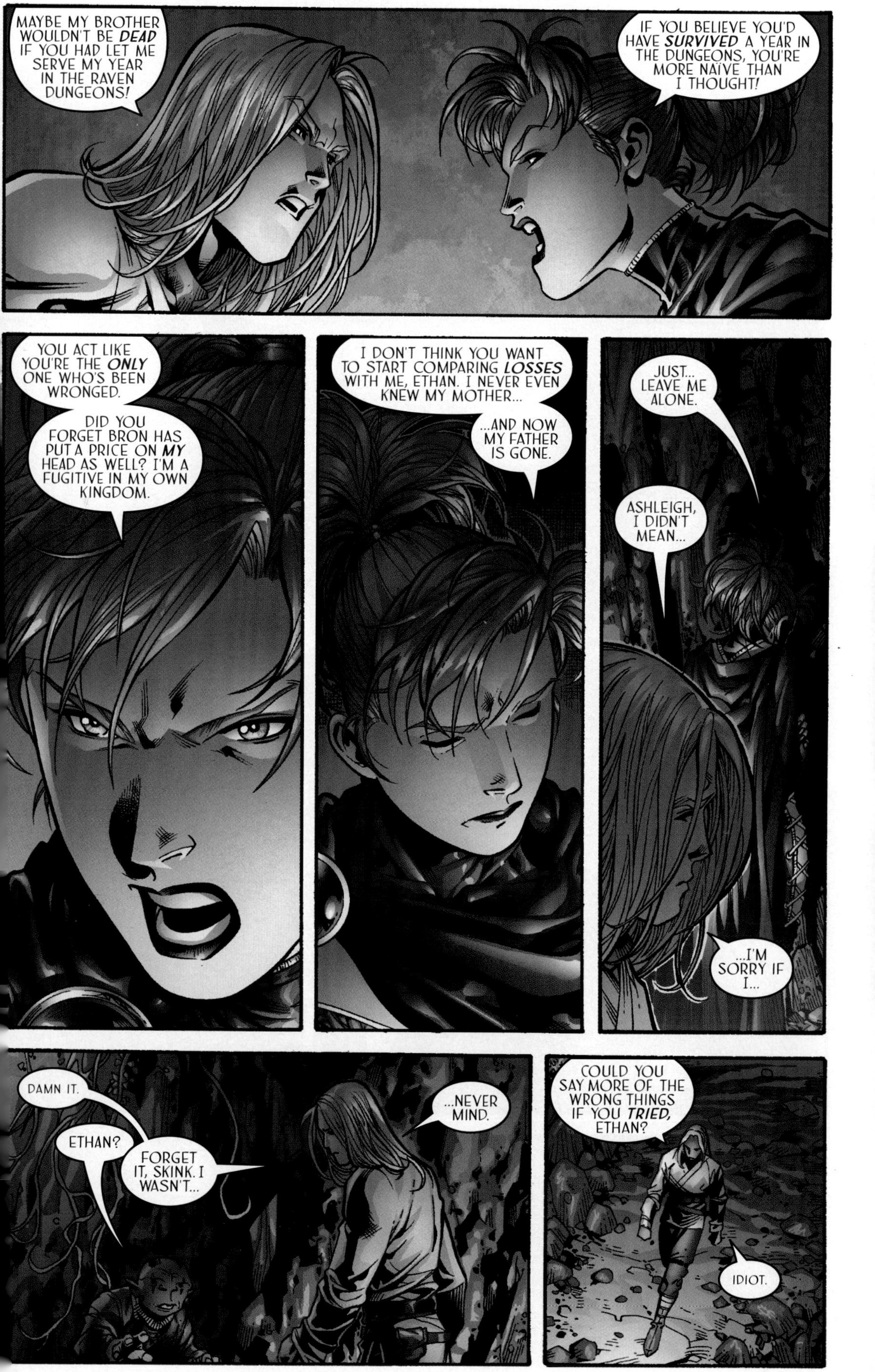
MAYBE MY BROTHER WOULDN'T BE *DEAD* IF YOU HAD LET ME SERVE MY YEAR IN THE RAVEN DUNGEONS!
IF YOU BELIEVE YOU'D HAVE *SURVIVED* A YEAR IN THE DUNGEONS, YOU'RE MORE NAÏVE THAN I THOUGHT!
YOU ACT LIKE YOU'RE THE *ONLY* ONE WHO'S BEEN WRONGED.
DID YOU FORGET BRON HAS PUT A PRICE ON *MY* HEAD AS WELL? I'M A FUGITIVE IN MY OWN KINGDOM.
I DON'T THINK YOU WANT TO START COMPARING *LOSSES* WITH ME, ETHAN. I NEVER EVEN KNEW MY MOTHER...
...AND NOW MY FATHER IS GONE.
JUST... LEAVE ME ALONE.
ASHLEIGH, I DIDN'T MEAN...
...I'M SORRY IF I...
DAMN IT.
ETHAN?
FORGET IT, SKINK. I WASN'T...
...NEVER MIND.
COULD YOU SAY MORE OF THE WRONG THINGS IF YOU *TRIED,* ETHAN?
IDIOT.

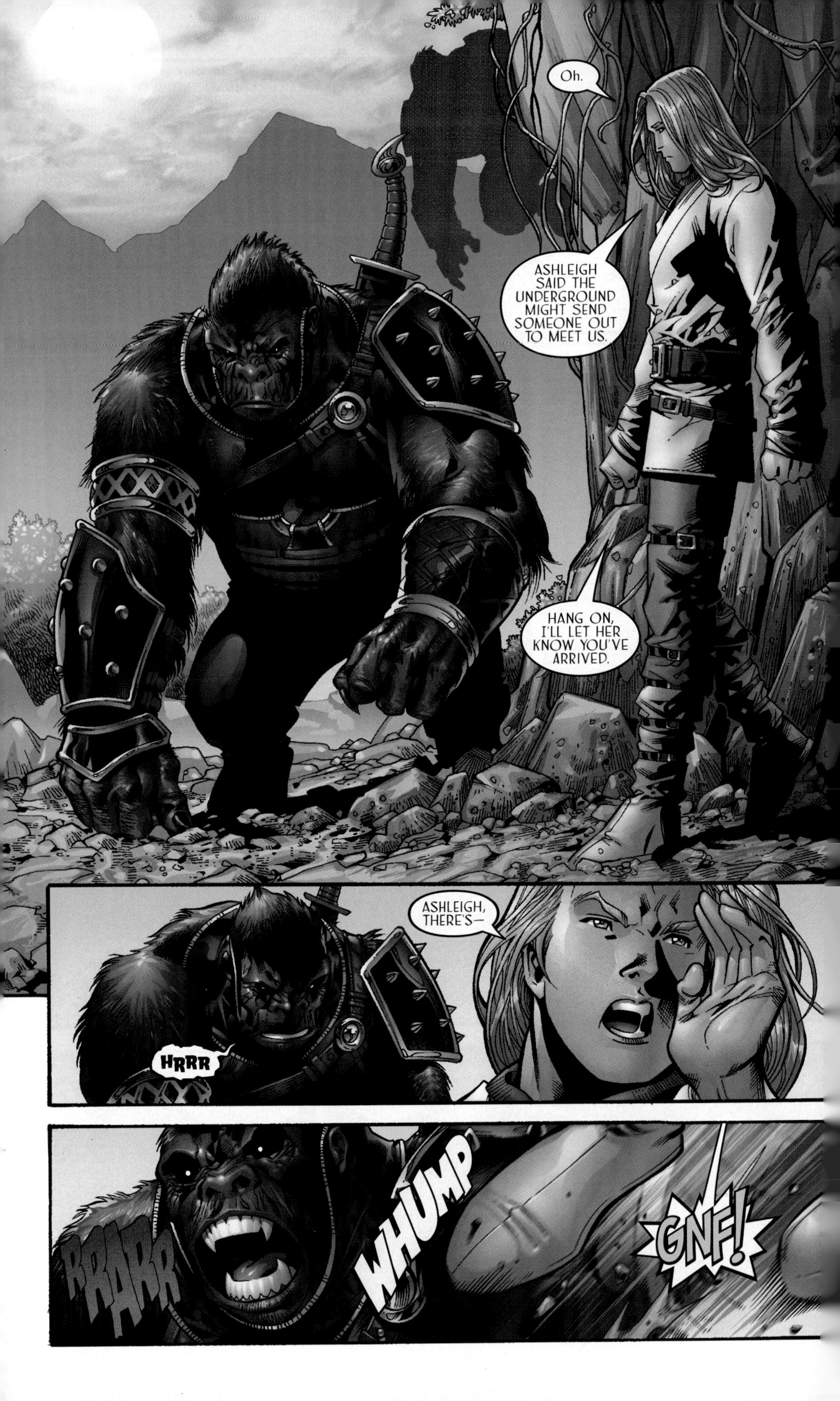
Oh.
ASHLEIGH SAID THE UNDERGROUND MIGHT SEND SOMEONE OUT TO MEET US.
HANG ON, I'LL LET HER KNOW YOU'VE ARRIVED.
ASHLEIGH, THERE'S—
HRRR
RRARR
WHUMP
GNF!

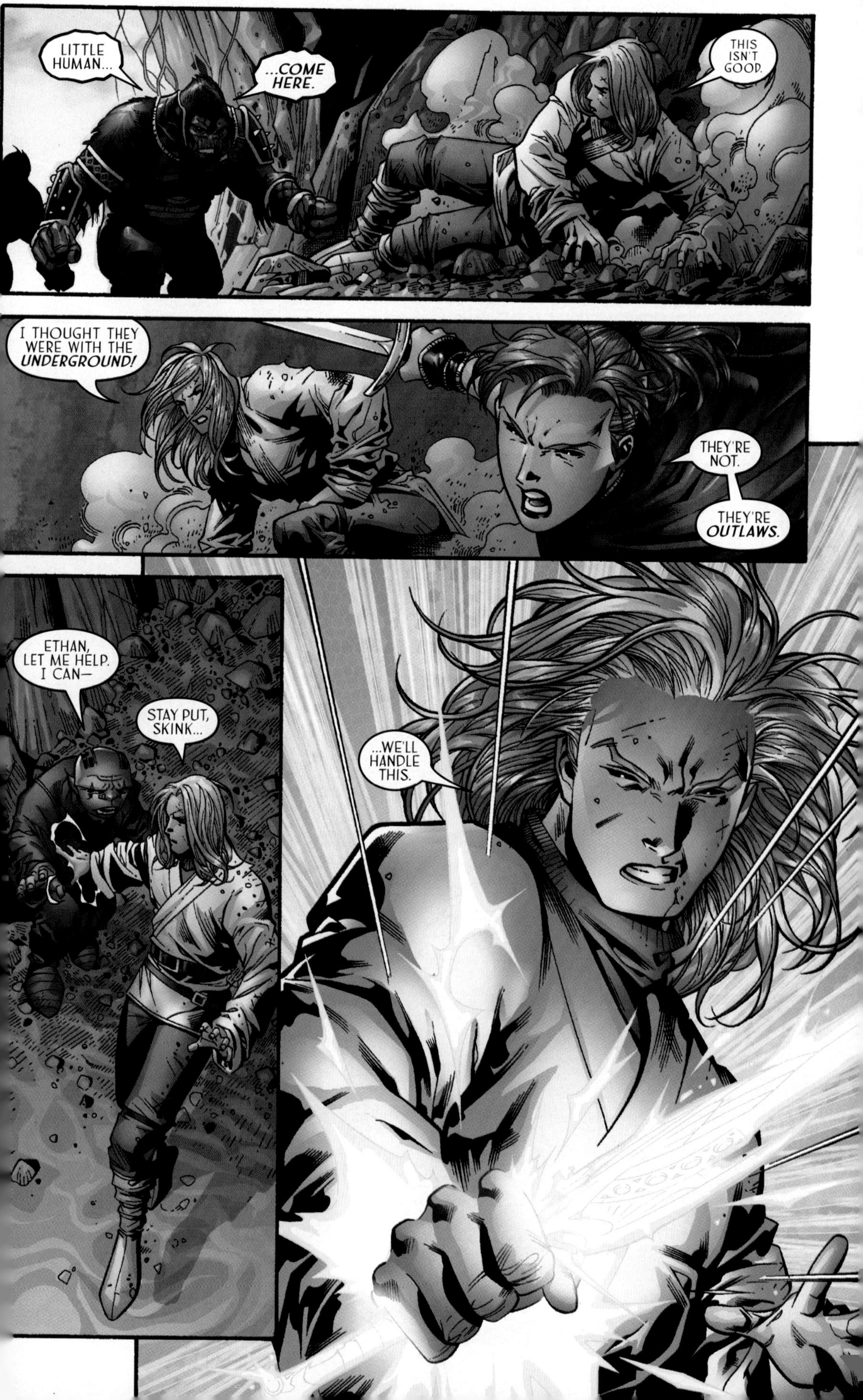
LITTLE HUMAN...
...COME HERE.
THIS ISN'T GOOD.
I THOUGHT THEY WERE WITH THE UNDERGROUND!
THEY'RE NOT.
THEY'RE OUTLAWS.
ETHAN, LET ME HELP. I CAN—
STAY PUT, SKINK...
...WE'LL HANDLE THIS.

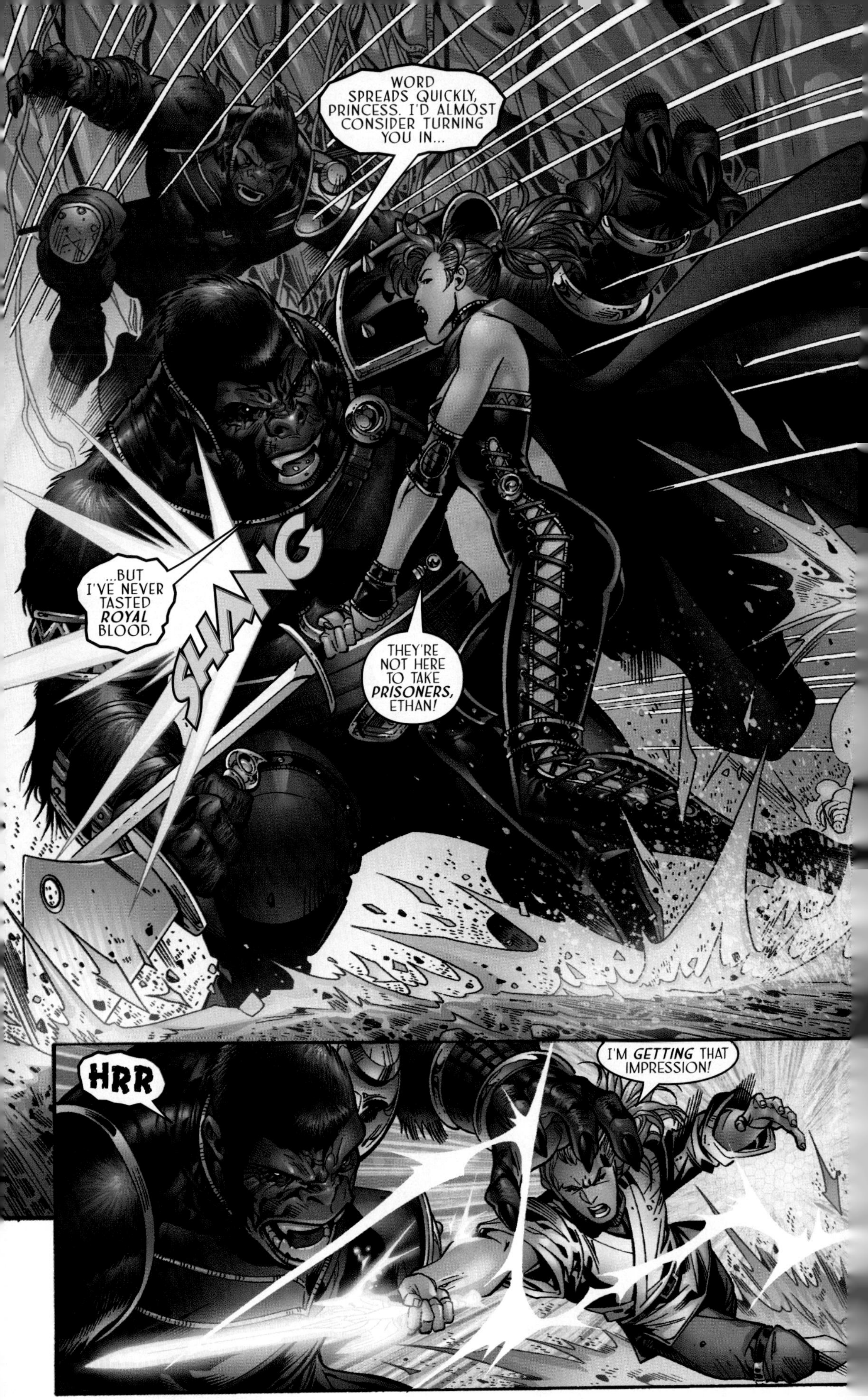
WORD SPREADS QUICKLY, PRINCESS. I'D ALMOST CONSIDER TURNING YOU IN...
...BUT I'VE NEVER TASTED *ROYAL* BLOOD.
SHANG
THEY'RE NOT HERE TO TAKE *PRISONERS*, ETHAN!
HRR
I'M *GETTING* THAT IMPRESSION!

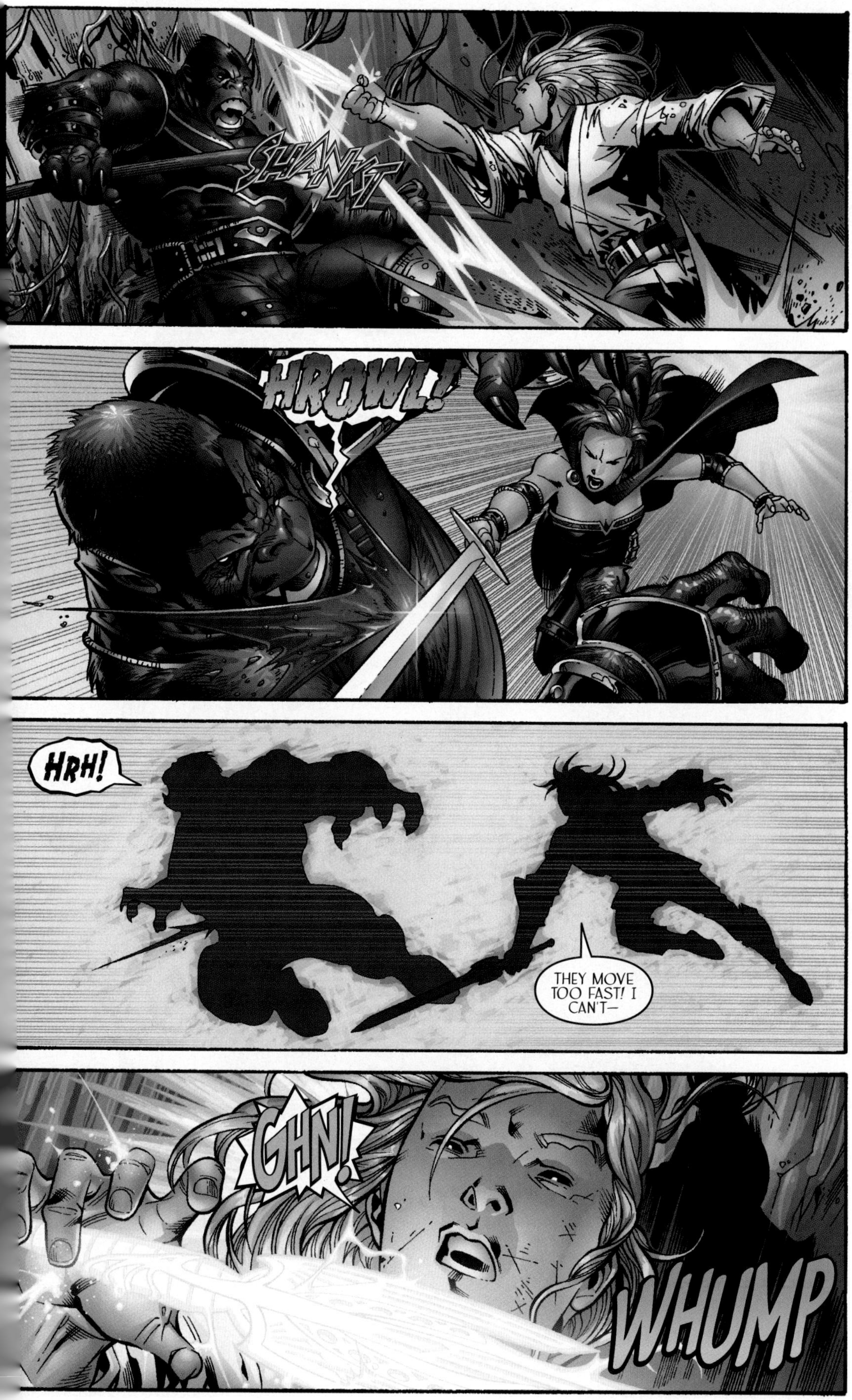
SHANKT
HROWL!
HRH!
THEY MOVE TOO FAST! I CAN'T—
GHN!
WHUMP

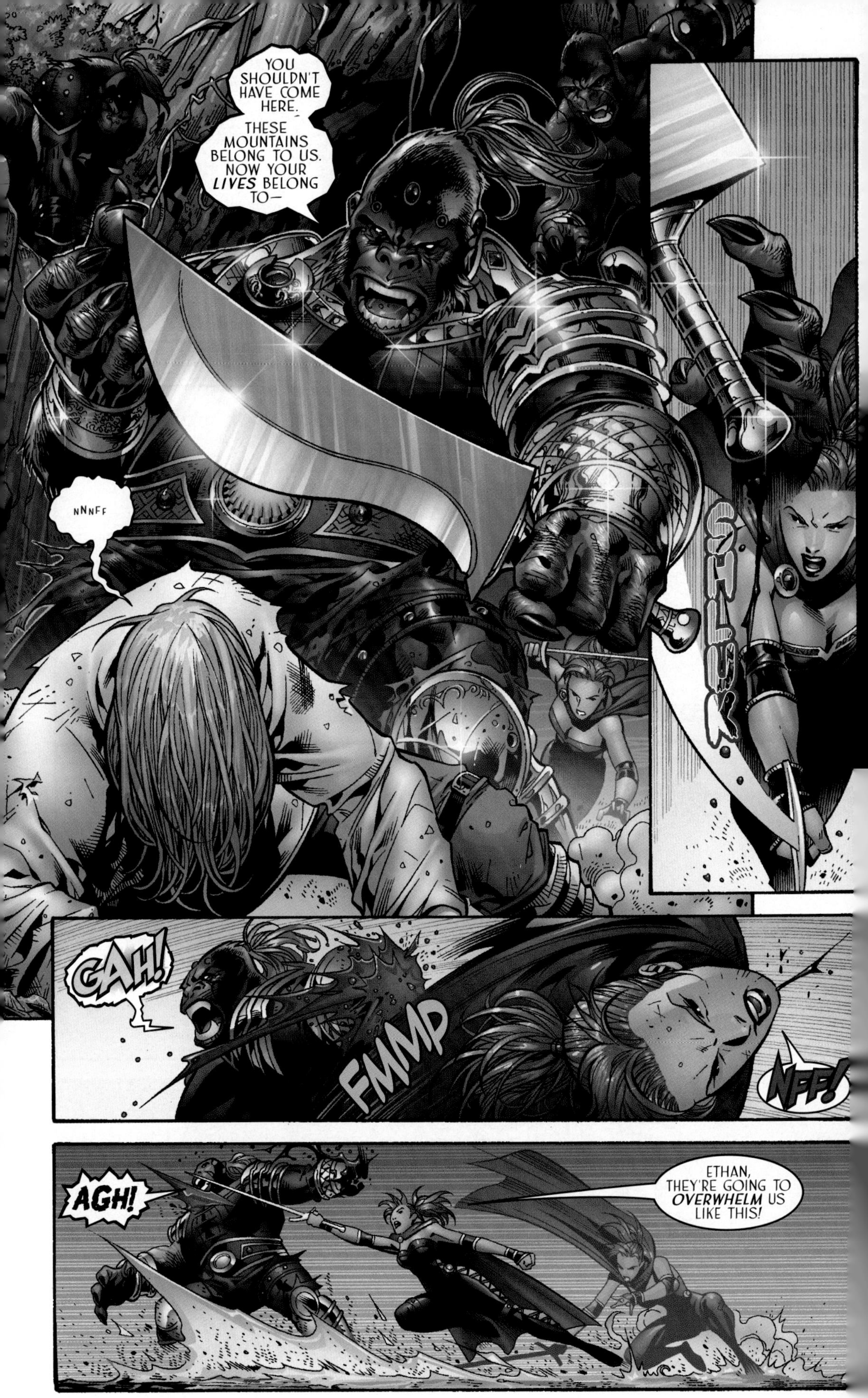
YOU SHOULDN'T HAVE COME HERE.
THESE MOUNTAINS BELONG TO US. NOW YOUR *LIVES* BELONG TO—
NNNFF
SHLUK
GAH!
FMMP
NFF!
AGH!
ETHAN, THEY'RE GOING TO *OVERWHELM* US LIKE THIS!

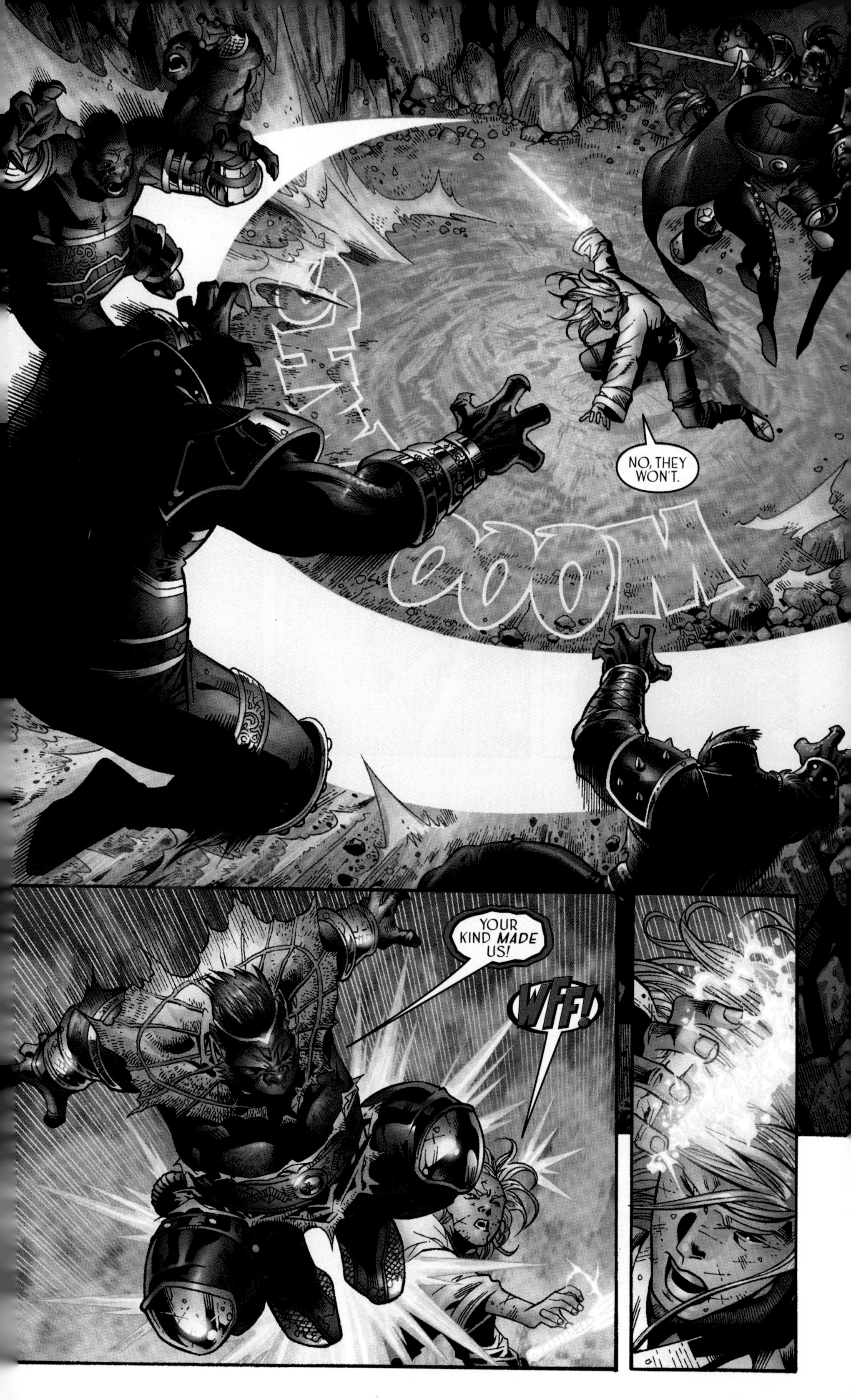

NO, THEY WON'T.
WOOOM
YOUR KIND *MADE* US!
WFF!

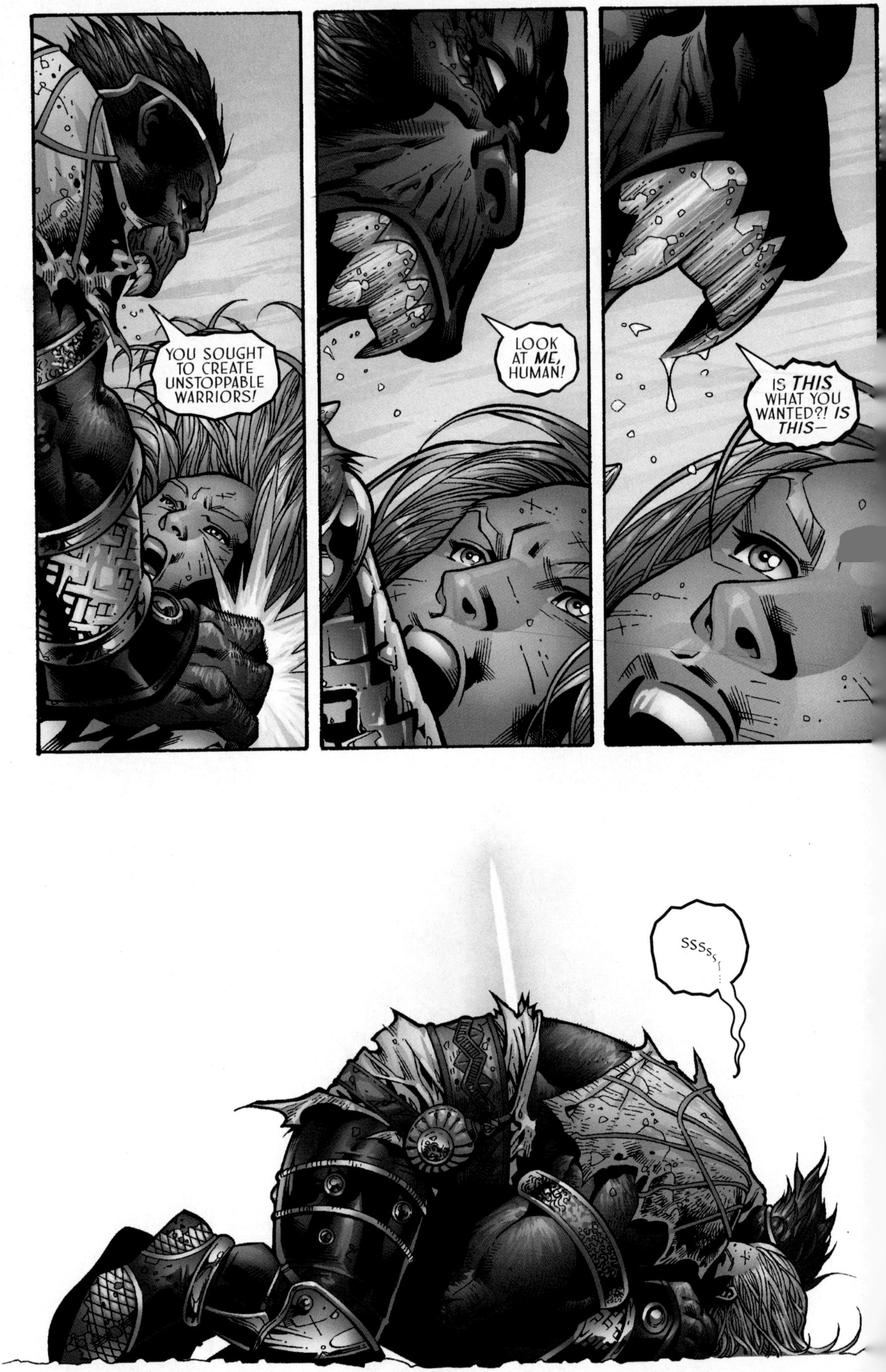

YOU SOUGHT TO CREATE UNSTOPPABLE WARRIORS!
LOOK AT ME, HUMAN!
IS THIS WHAT YOU WANTED?! IS THIS—
SSSs...

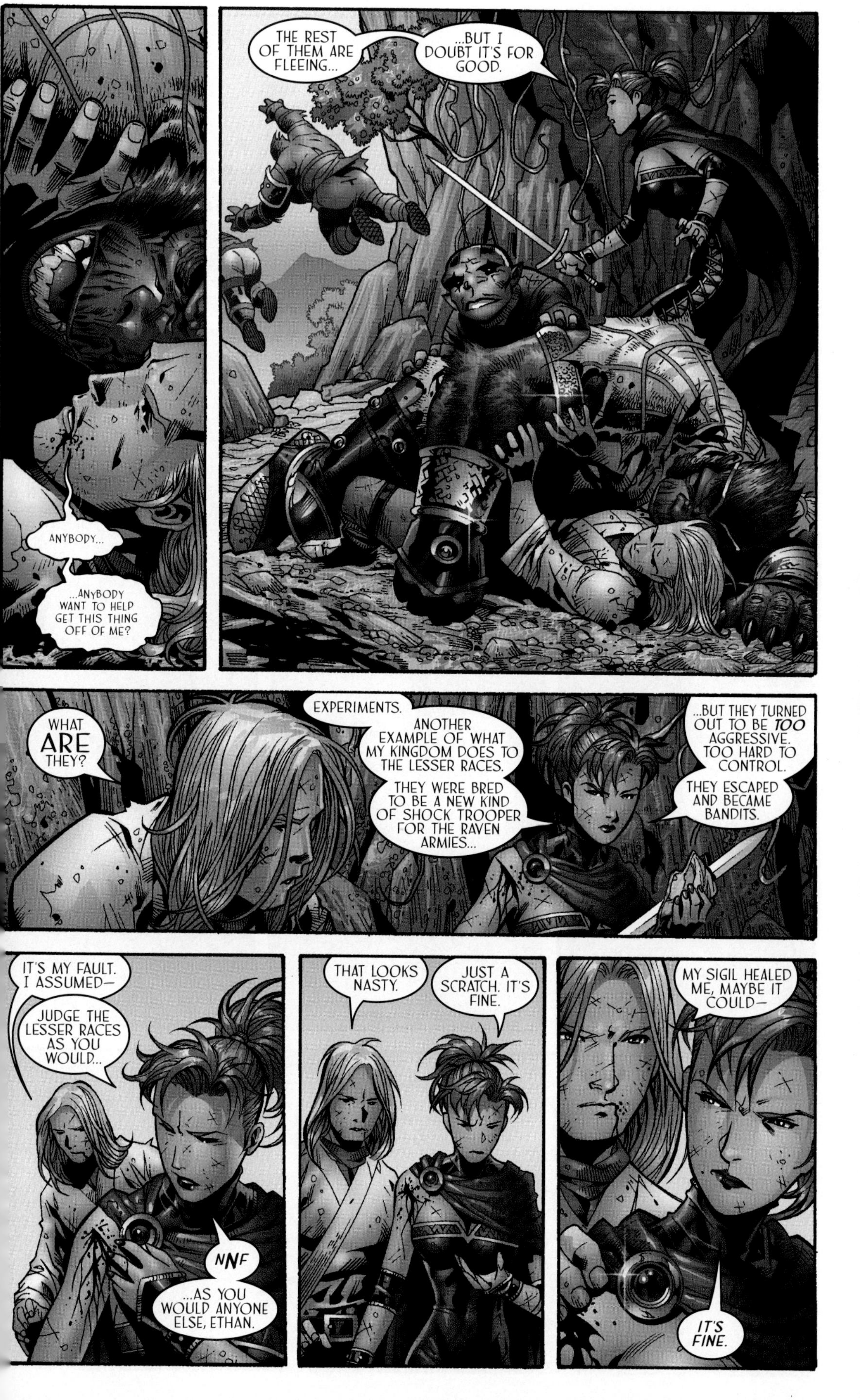
THE REST OF THEM ARE FLEEING...
...BUT I DOUBT IT'S FOR GOOD.
ANYBODY...
...ANYBODY WANT TO HELP GET THIS THING OFF OF ME?
WHAT ARE THEY?
EXPERIMENTS.
ANOTHER EXAMPLE OF WHAT MY KINGDOM DOES TO THE LESSER RACES.
THEY WERE BRED TO BE A NEW KIND OF SHOCK TROOPER FOR THE RAVEN ARMIES...
...BUT THEY TURNED OUT TO BE TOO AGGRESSIVE. TOO HARD TO CONTROL.
THEY ESCAPED AND BECAME BANDITS.
IT'S MY FAULT. I ASSUMED—
JUDGE THE LESSER RACES AS YOU WOULD...
NNF
...AS YOU WOULD ANYONE ELSE, ETHAN.
THAT LOOKS NASTY.
JUST A SCRATCH. IT'S FINE.
MY SIGIL HEALED ME, MAYBE IT COULD—
IT'S FINE.

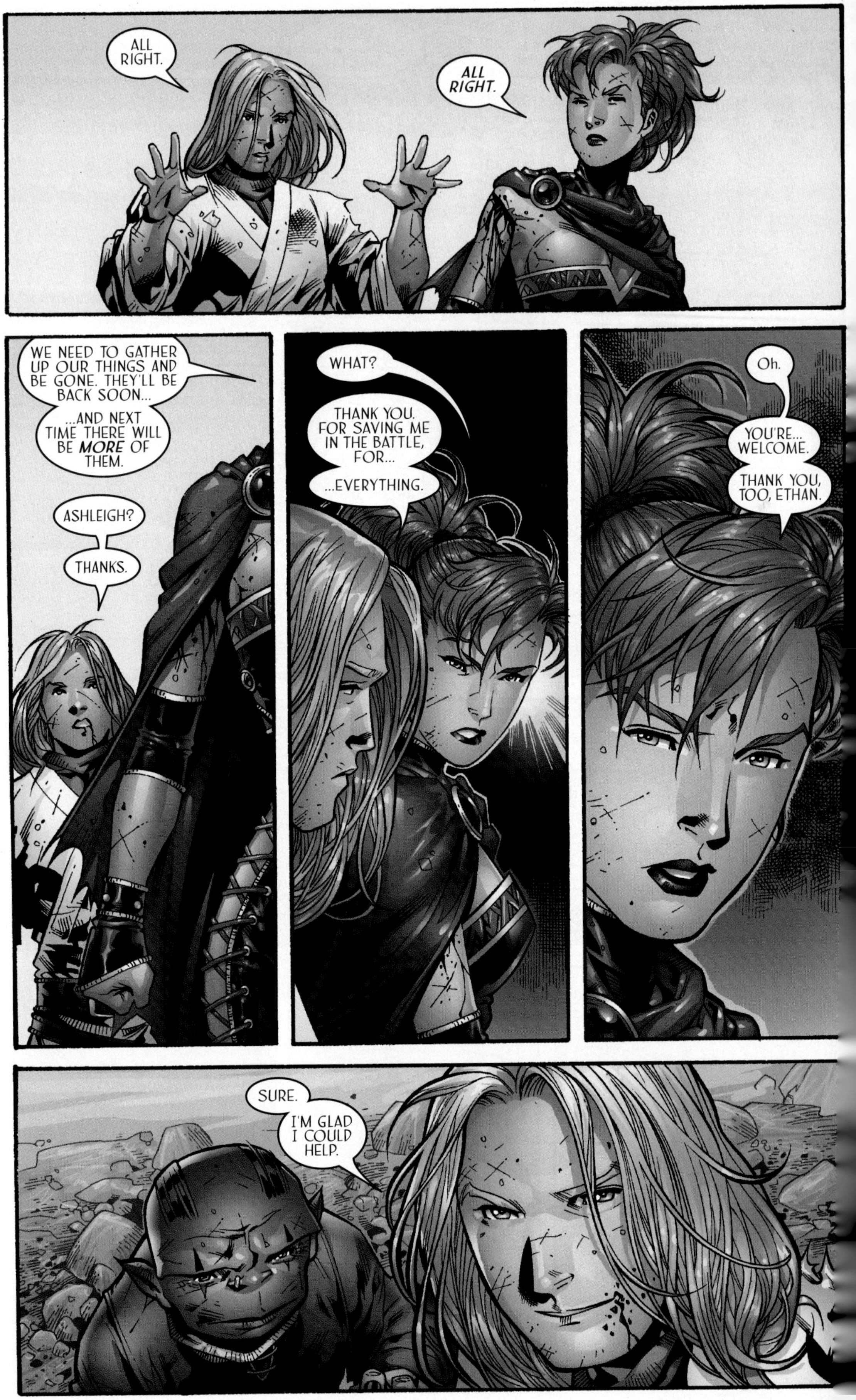

ALL RIGHT.
*ALL RIGHT.*
WE NEED TO GATHER UP OUR THINGS AND BE GONE. THEY'LL BE BACK SOON...
...AND NEXT TIME THERE WILL BE *MORE* OF THEM.
ASHLEIGH?
THANKS.
WHAT?
THANK YOU. FOR SAVING ME IN THE BATTLE, FOR...
...EVERYTHING.
Oh.
YOU'RE... WELCOME.
THANK YOU, TOO, ETHAN.
SURE.
I'M GLAD I COULD HELP.

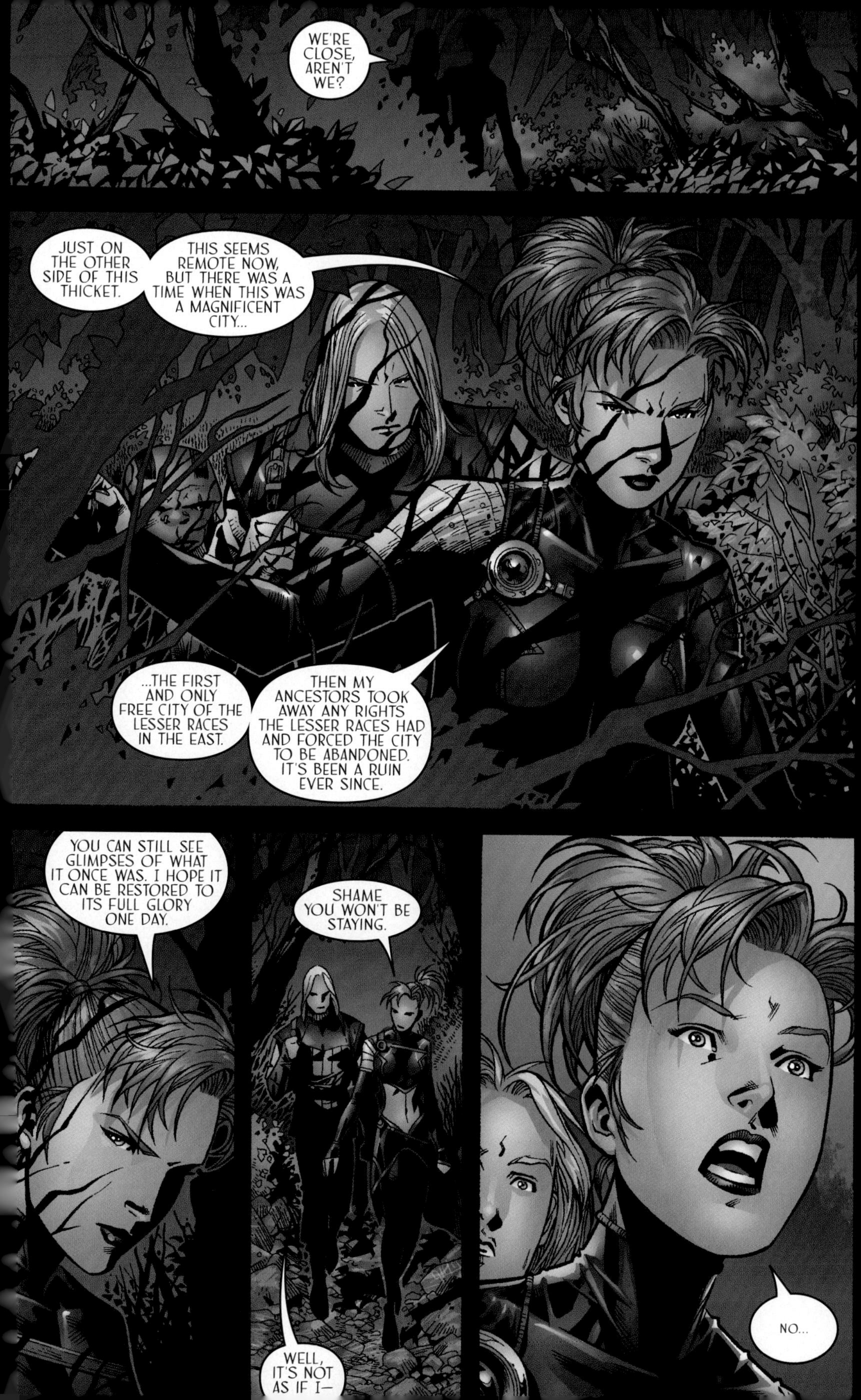
WE'RE CLOSE, AREN'T WE?
JUST ON THE OTHER SIDE OF THIS THICKET.
THIS SEEMS REMOTE NOW, BUT THERE WAS A TIME WHEN THIS WAS A MAGNIFICENT CITY...
...THE FIRST AND ONLY FREE CITY OF THE LESSER RACES IN THE EAST.
THEN MY ANCESTORS TOOK AWAY ANY RIGHTS THE LESSER RACES HAD AND FORCED THE CITY TO BE ABANDONED. IT'S BEEN A RUIN EVER SINCE.
YOU CAN STILL SEE GLIMPSES OF WHAT IT ONCE WAS. I HOPE IT CAN BE RESTORED TO ITS FULL GLORY ONE DAY.
SHAME YOU WON'T BE STAYING.
WELL, IT'S NOT AS IF I—
NO...

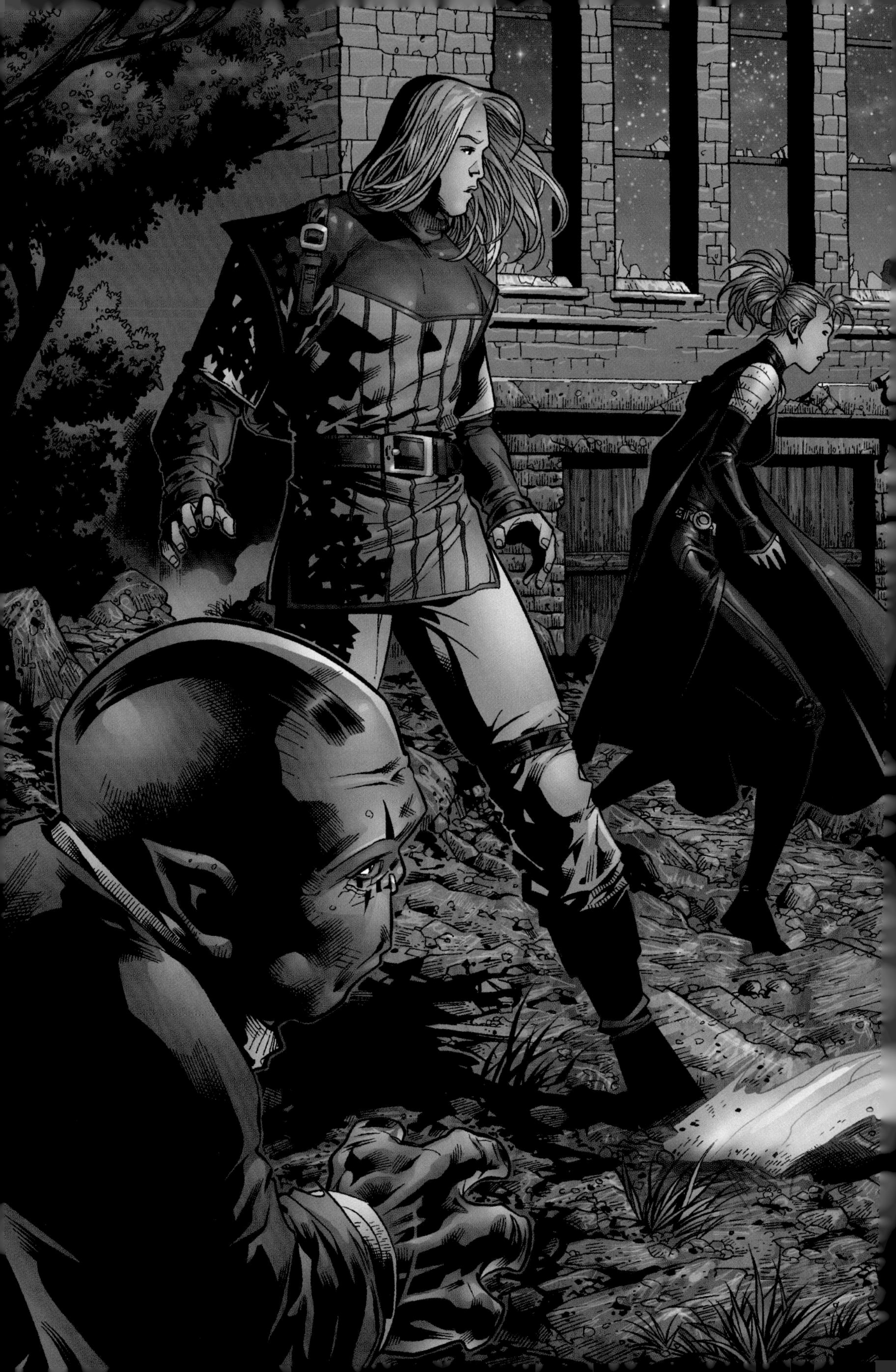

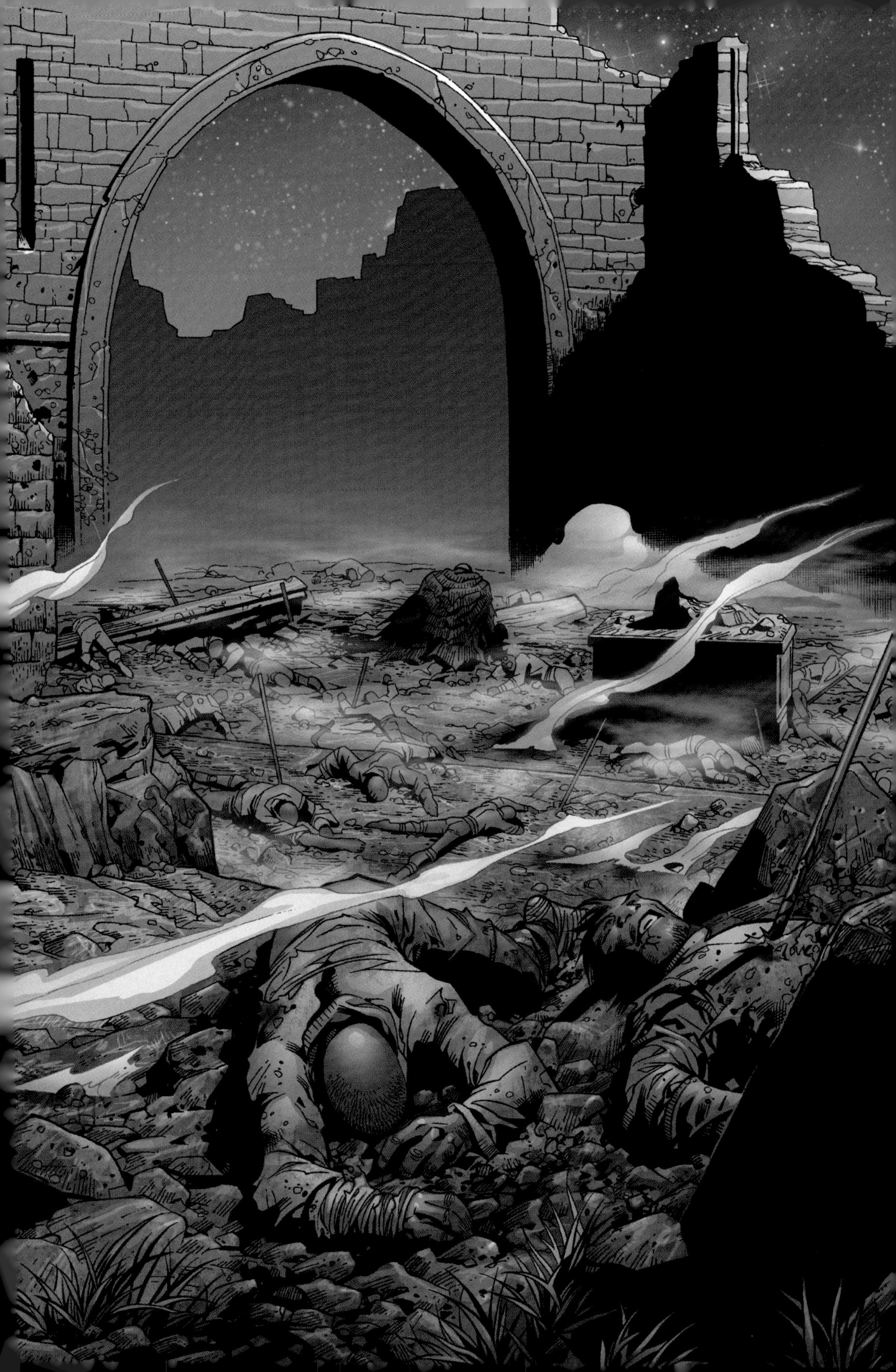

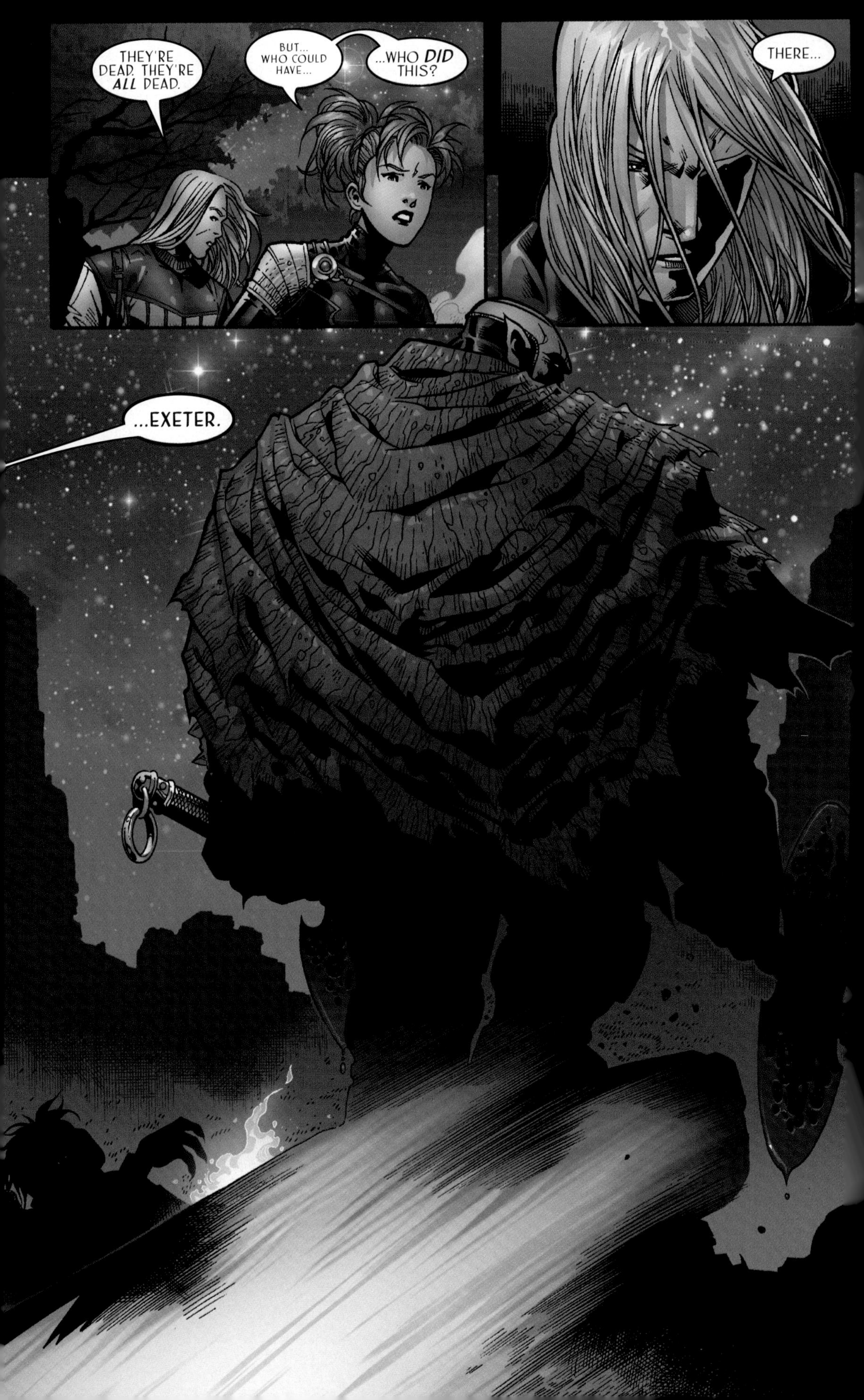
THEY'RE DEAD. THEY'RE *ALL* DEAD.
BUT... WHO COULD HAVE...
...WHO *DID* THIS?
THERE...
...EXETER.

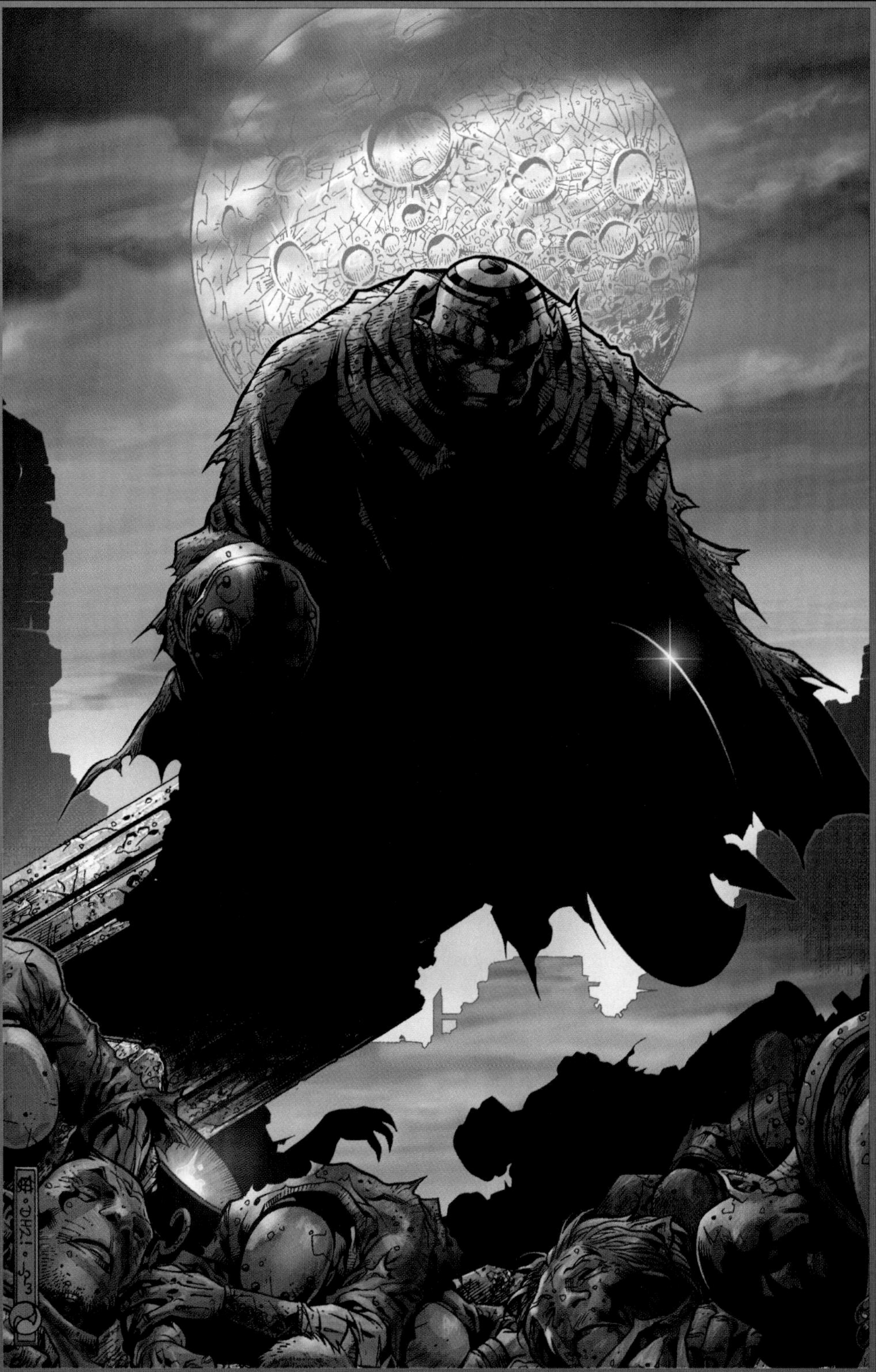

SCION • CHAPTER SIXTEEN

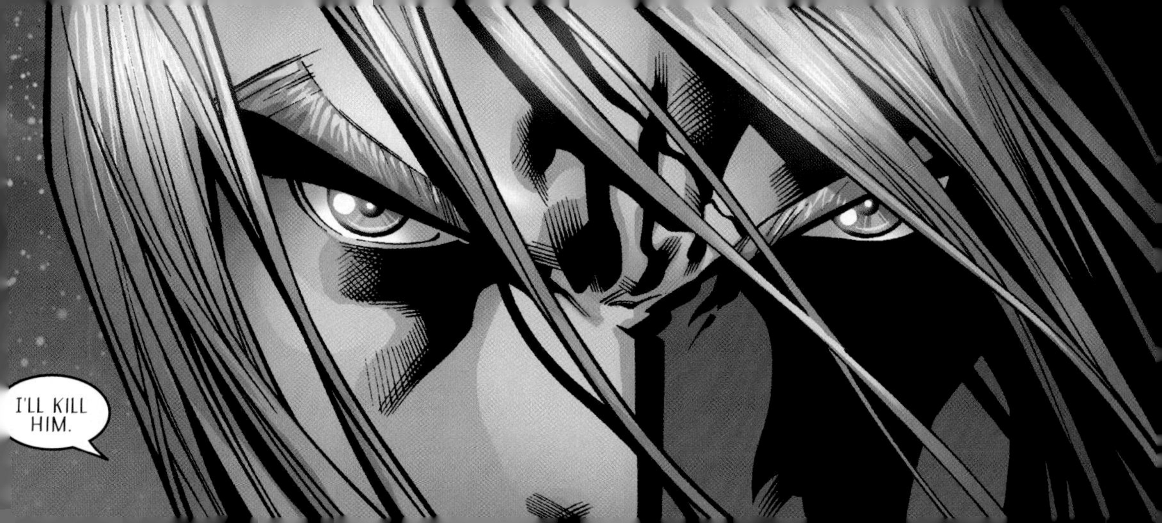
I'LL KILL HIM.

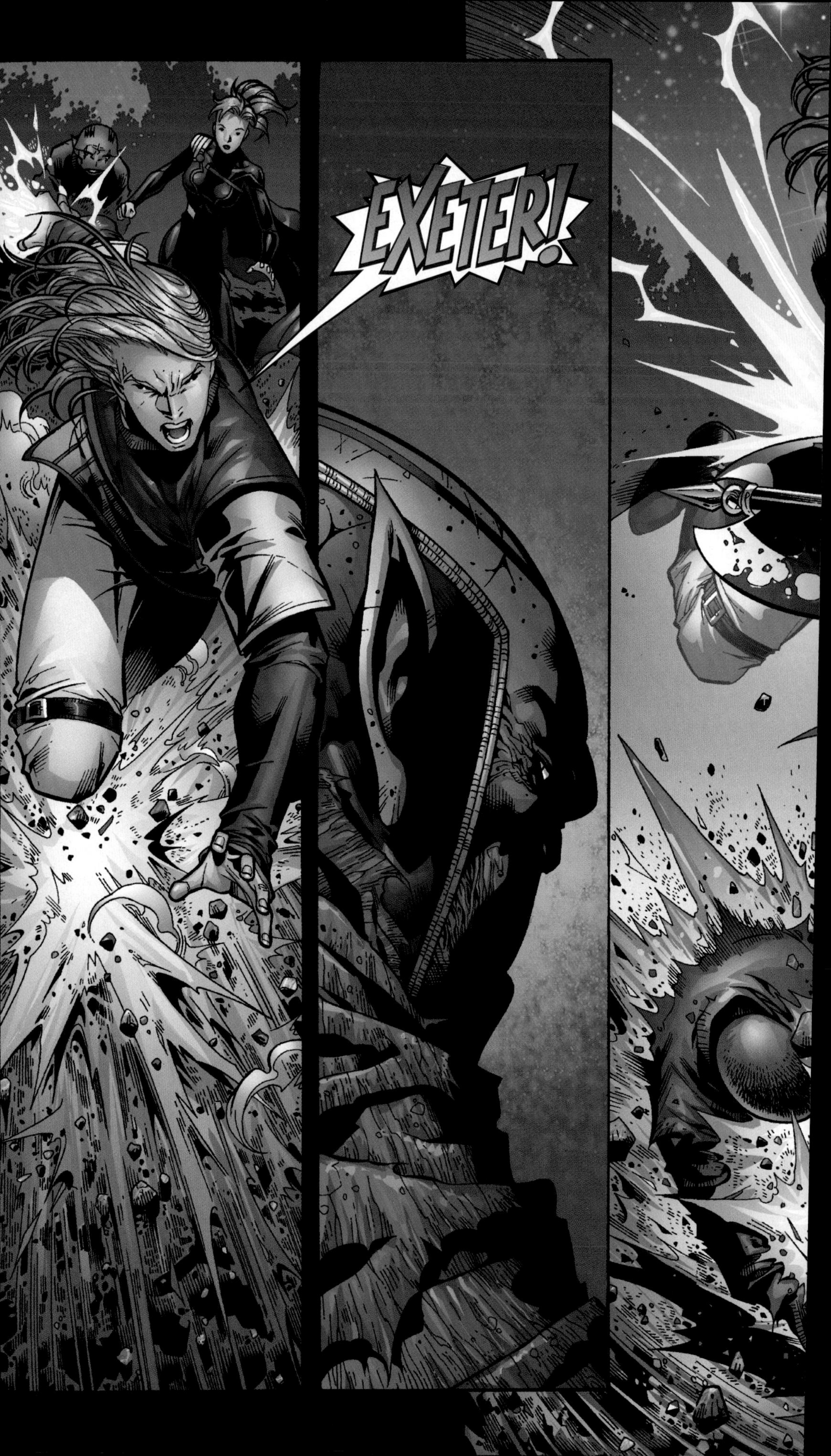
EXETER!

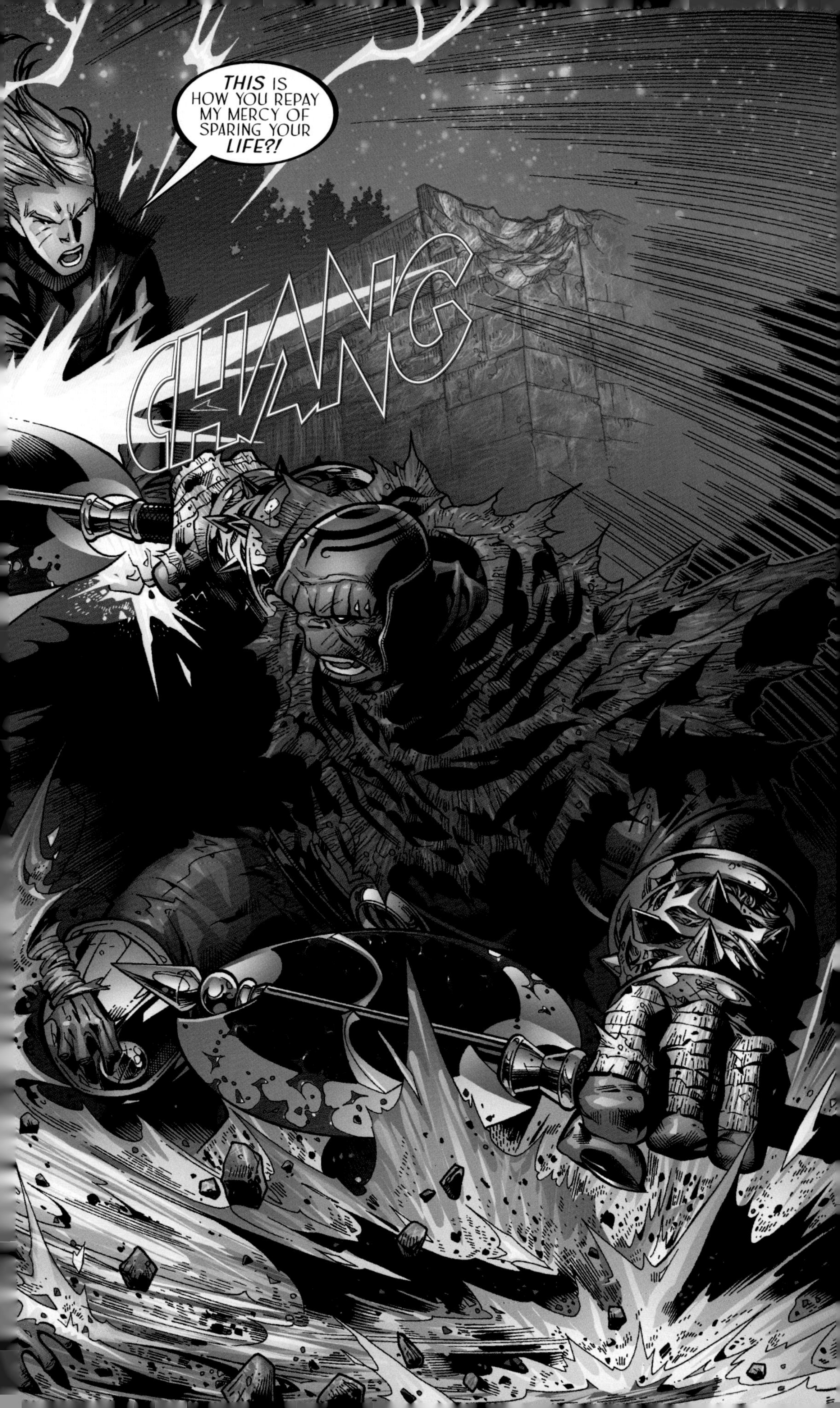
THIS IS HOW YOU REPAY MY MERCY OF SPARING YOUR LIFE?!
CHANG

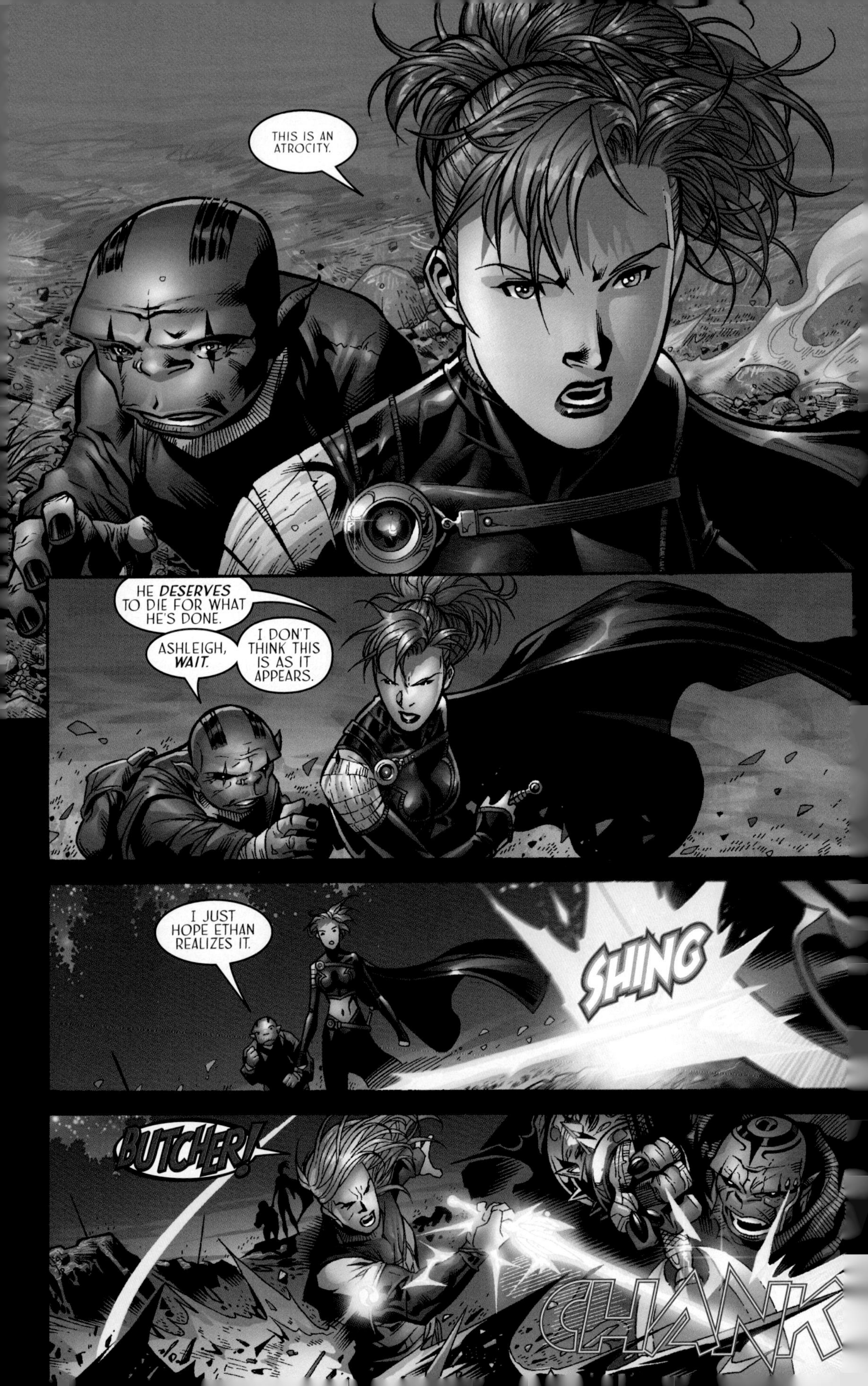
THIS IS AN ATROCITY.
HE DESERVES TO DIE FOR WHAT HE'S DONE.
ASHLEIGH, WAIT.
I DON'T THINK THIS IS AS IT APPEARS.
I JUST HOPE ETHAN REALIZES IT.
SHING
BUTCHER!
CHANK

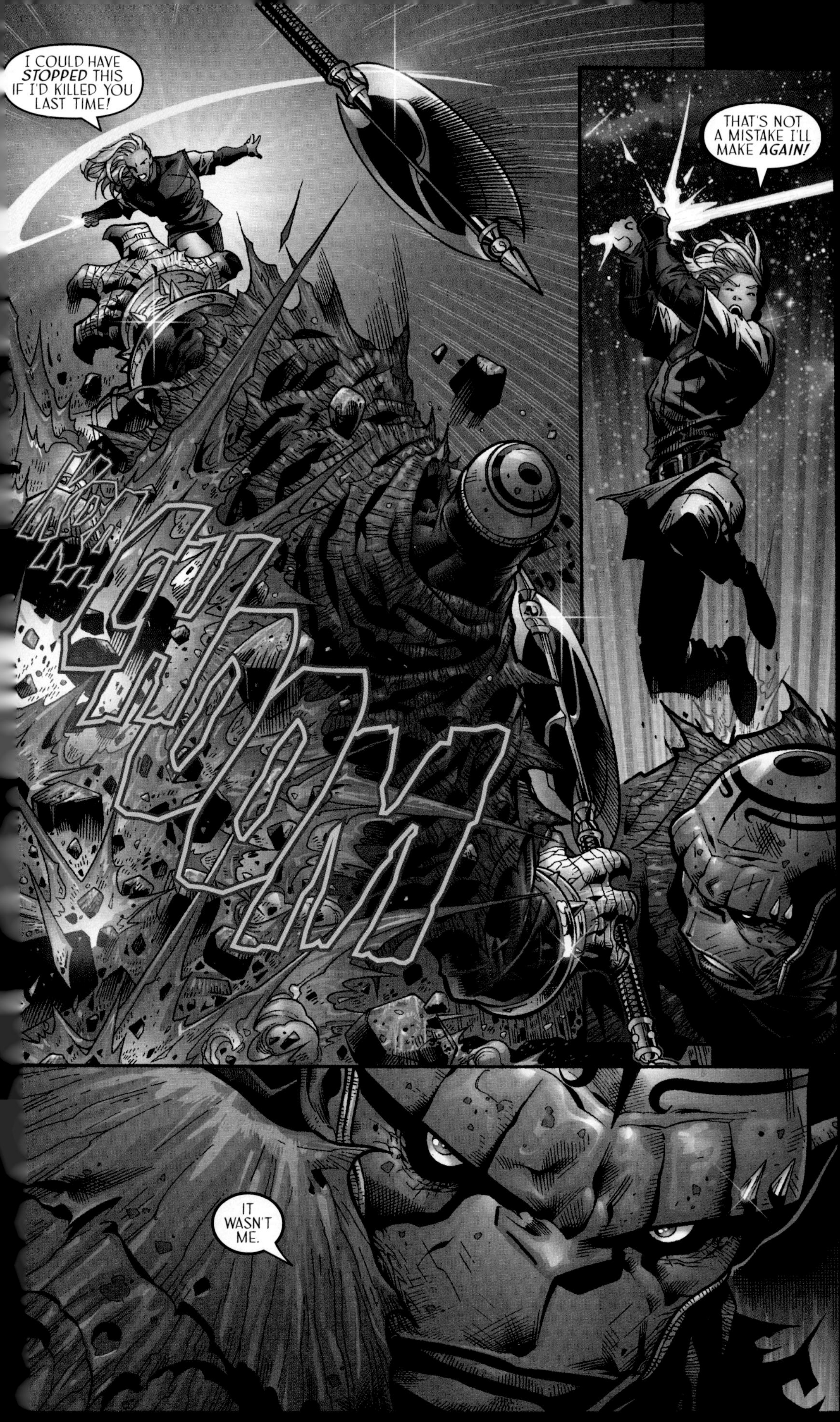
I COULD HAVE STOPPED THIS IF I'D KILLED YOU LAST TIME!
THAT'S NOT A MISTAKE I'LL MAKE AGAIN!
IT WASN'T ME.

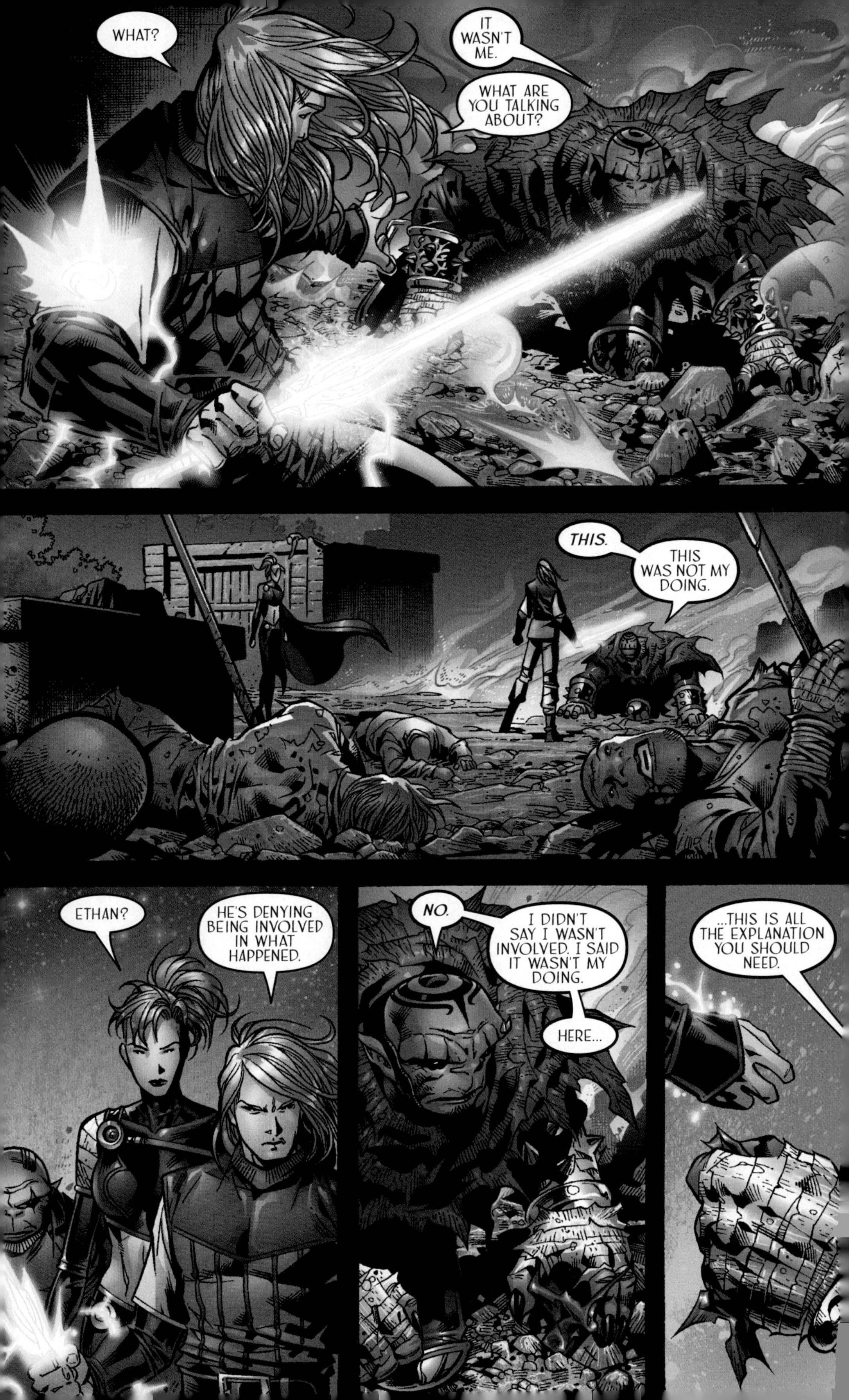
WHAT?
IT WASN'T ME.
WHAT ARE YOU TALKING ABOUT?
THIS.
THIS WAS NOT MY DOING.
ETHAN?
HE'S DENYING BEING INVOLVED IN WHAT HAPPENED.
NO.
I DIDN'T SAY I WASN'T INVOLVED. I SAID IT WASN'T MY DOING.
HERE...
...THIS IS ALL THE EXPLANATION YOU SHOULD NEED.

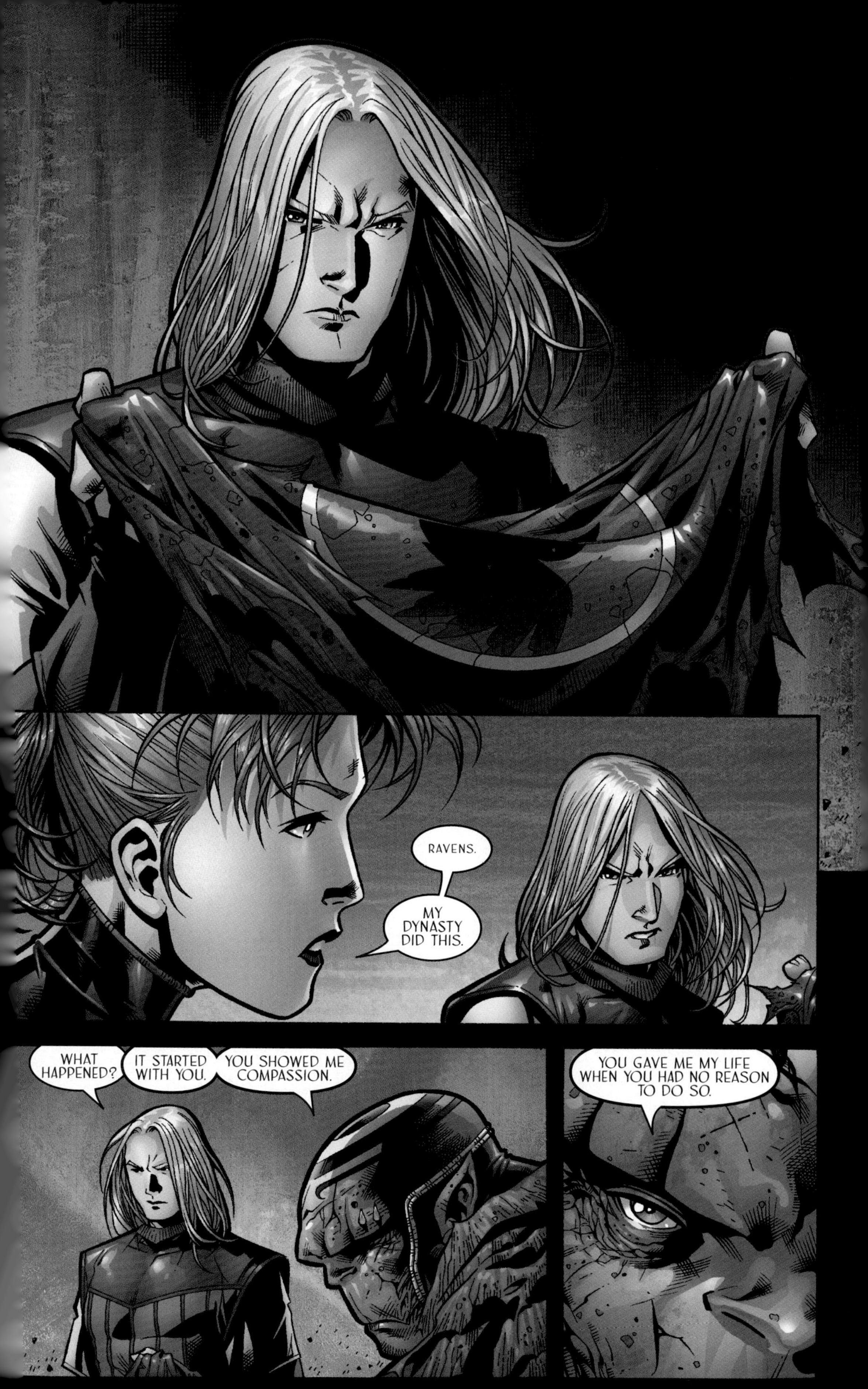
RAVENS.
MY DYNASTY DID THIS.
WHAT HAPPENED?
IT STARTED WITH YOU.
YOU SHOWED ME COMPASSION.
YOU GAVE ME MY LIFE WHEN YOU HAD NO REASON TO DO SO.

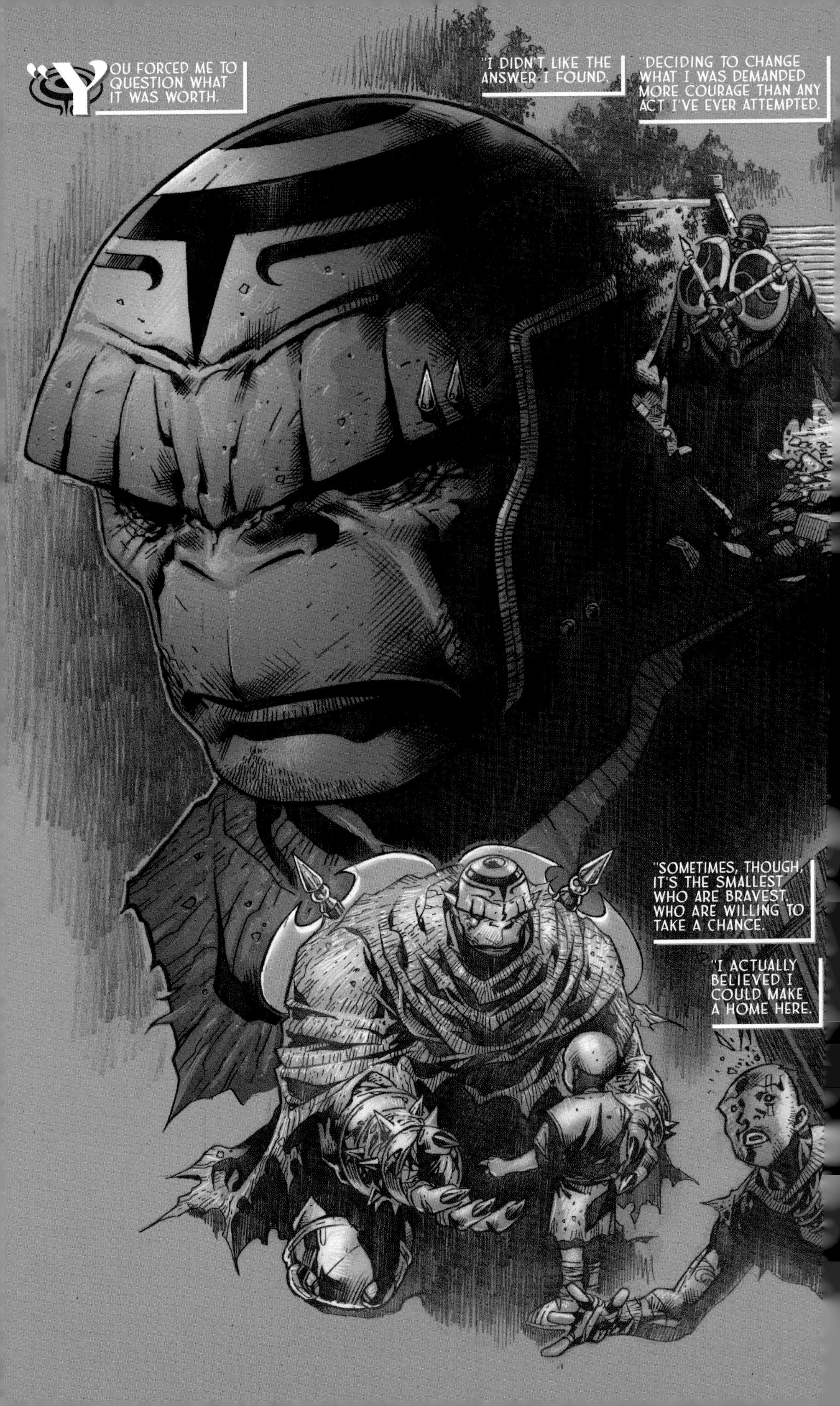
"YOU FORCED ME TO QUESTION WHAT IT WAS WORTH.
"I DIDN'T LIKE THE ANSWER I FOUND.
"DECIDING TO CHANGE WHAT I WAS DEMANDED MORE COURAGE THAN ANY ACT I'VE EVER ATTEMPTED.
"SOMETIMES, THOUGH, IT'S THE SMALLEST WHO ARE BRAVEST. WHO ARE WILLING TO TAKE A CHANCE.
"I ACTUALLY BELIEVED I COULD MAKE A HOME HERE.

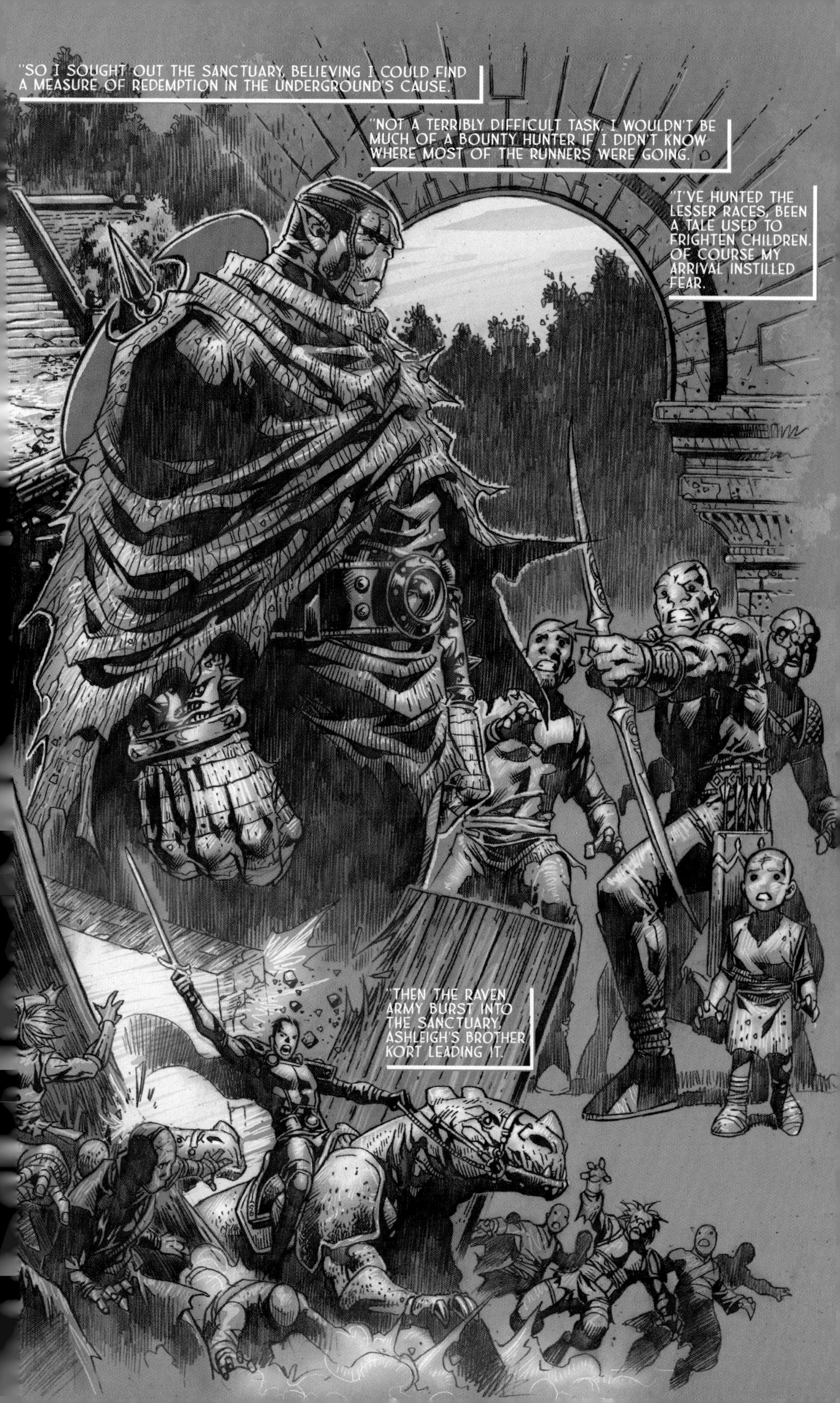
"SO I SOUGHT OUT THE SANCTUARY, BELIEVING I COULD FIND A MEASURE OF REDEMPTION IN THE UNDERGROUND'S CAUSE.
"NOT A TERRIBLY DIFFICULT TASK. I WOULDN'T BE MUCH OF A BOUNTY HUNTER IF I DIDN'T KNOW WHERE MOST OF THE RUNNERS WERE GOING.
"I'VE HUNTED THE LESSER RACES, BEEN A TALE USED TO FRIGHTEN CHILDREN. OF COURSE MY ARRIVAL INSTILLED FEAR.
"THEN THE RAVEN ARMY BURST INTO THE SANCTUARY, ASHLEIGH'S BROTHER KORT LEADING IT.

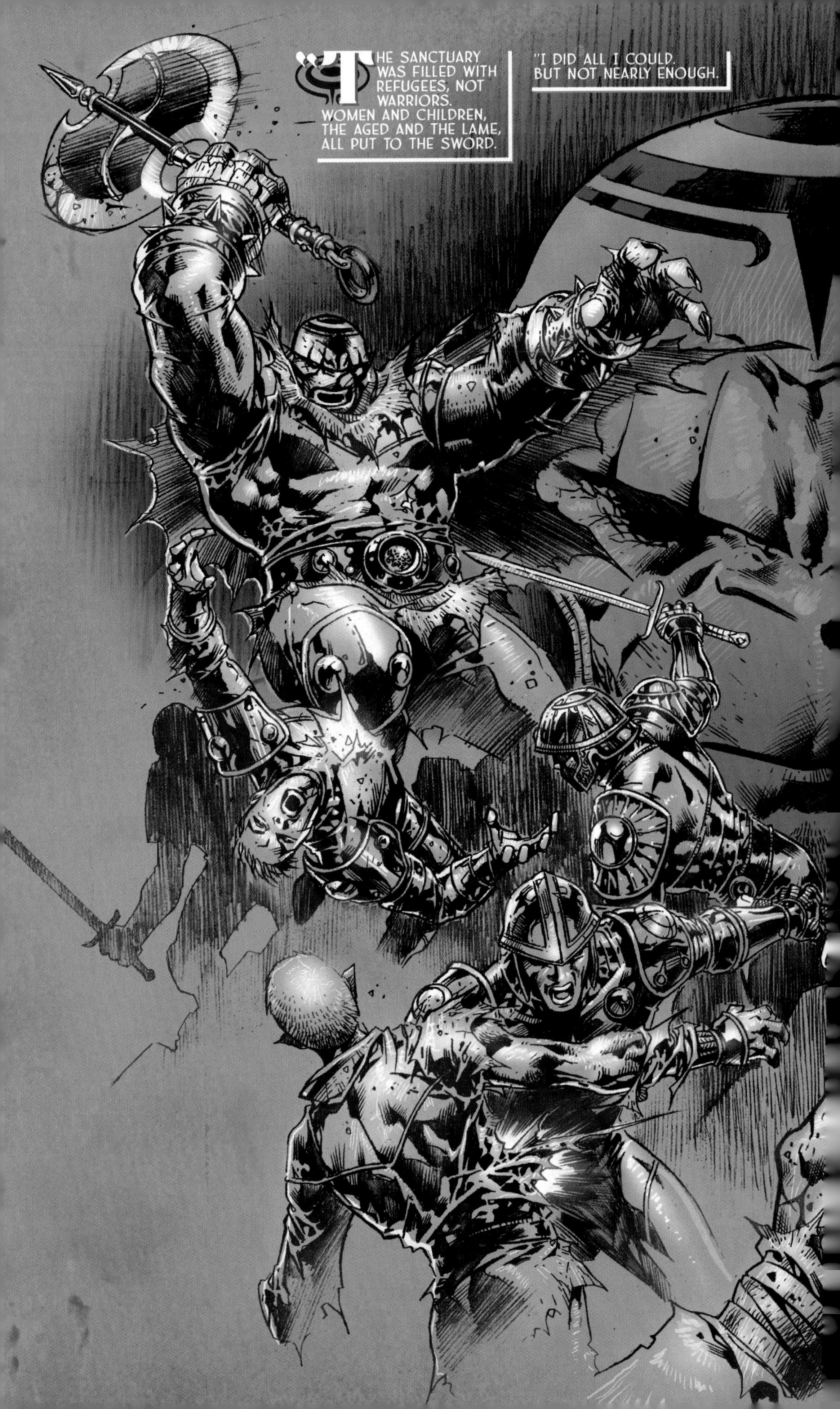
"THE SANCTUARY WAS FILLED WITH REFUGEES, NOT WARRIORS. WOMEN AND CHILDREN, THE AGED AND THE LAME, ALL PUT TO THE SWORD.
"I DID ALL I COULD. BUT NOT NEARLY ENOUGH.

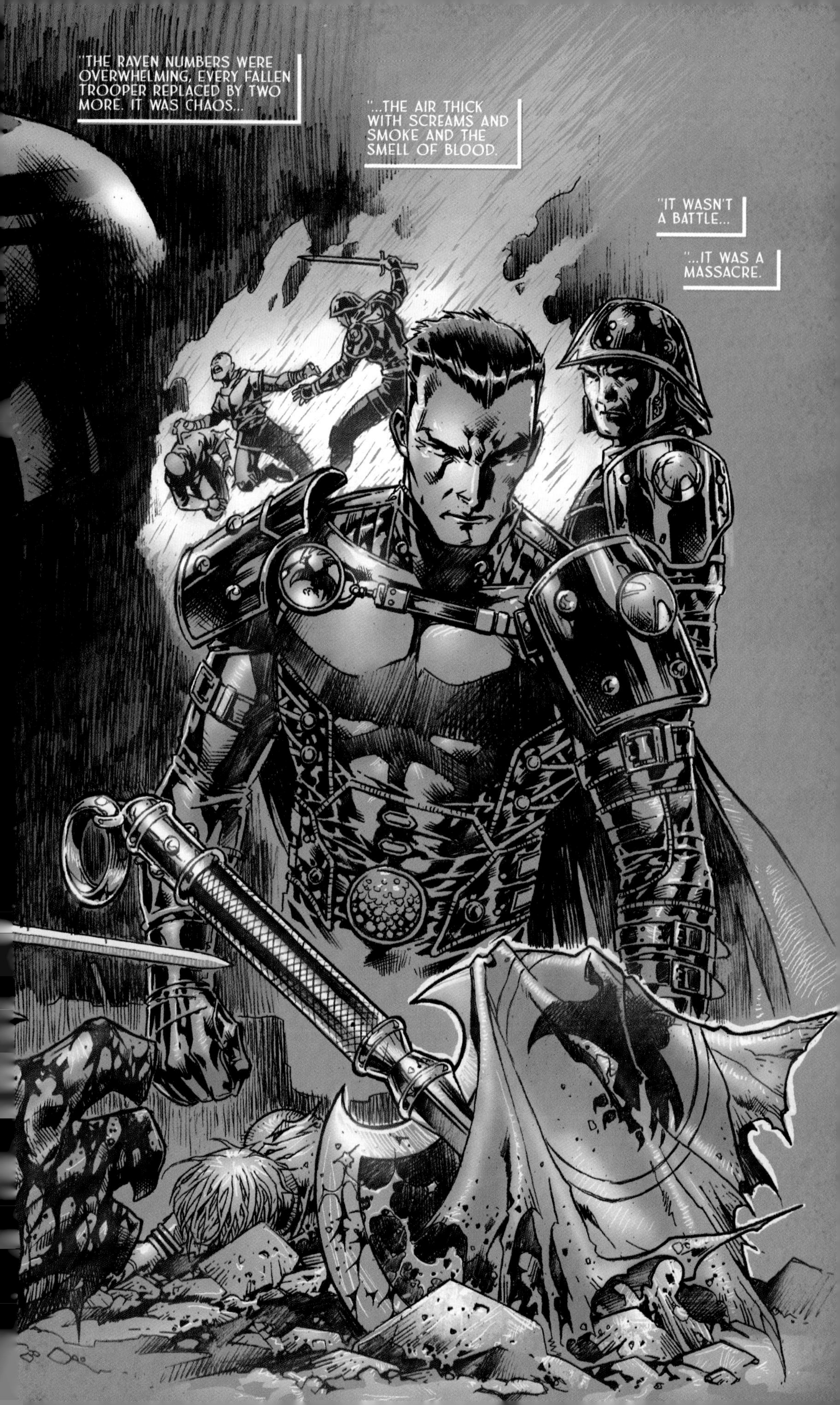
"THE RAVEN NUMBERS WERE OVERWHELMING, EVERY FALLEN TROOPER REPLACED BY TWO MORE. IT WAS CHAOS...
"...THE AIR THICK WITH SCREAMS AND SMOKE AND THE SMELL OF BLOOD.
"IT WASN'T A BATTLE...
"...IT WAS A MASSACRE.

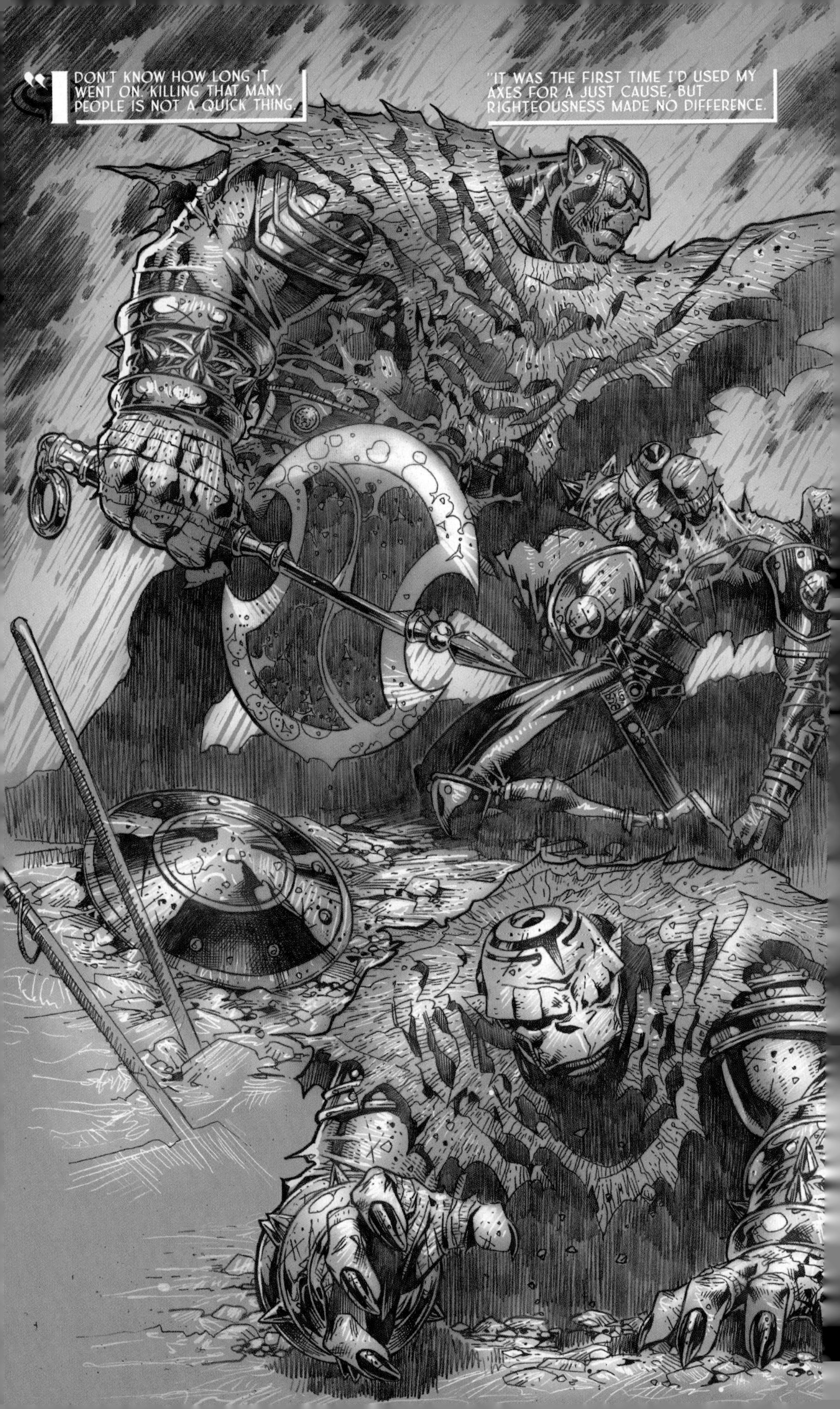
"I DON'T KNOW HOW LONG IT WENT ON. KILLING THAT MANY PEOPLE IS NOT A QUICK THING.
"IT WAS THE FIRST TIME I'D USED MY AXES FOR A JUST CAUSE, BUT RIGHTEOUSNESS MADE NO DIFFERENCE.

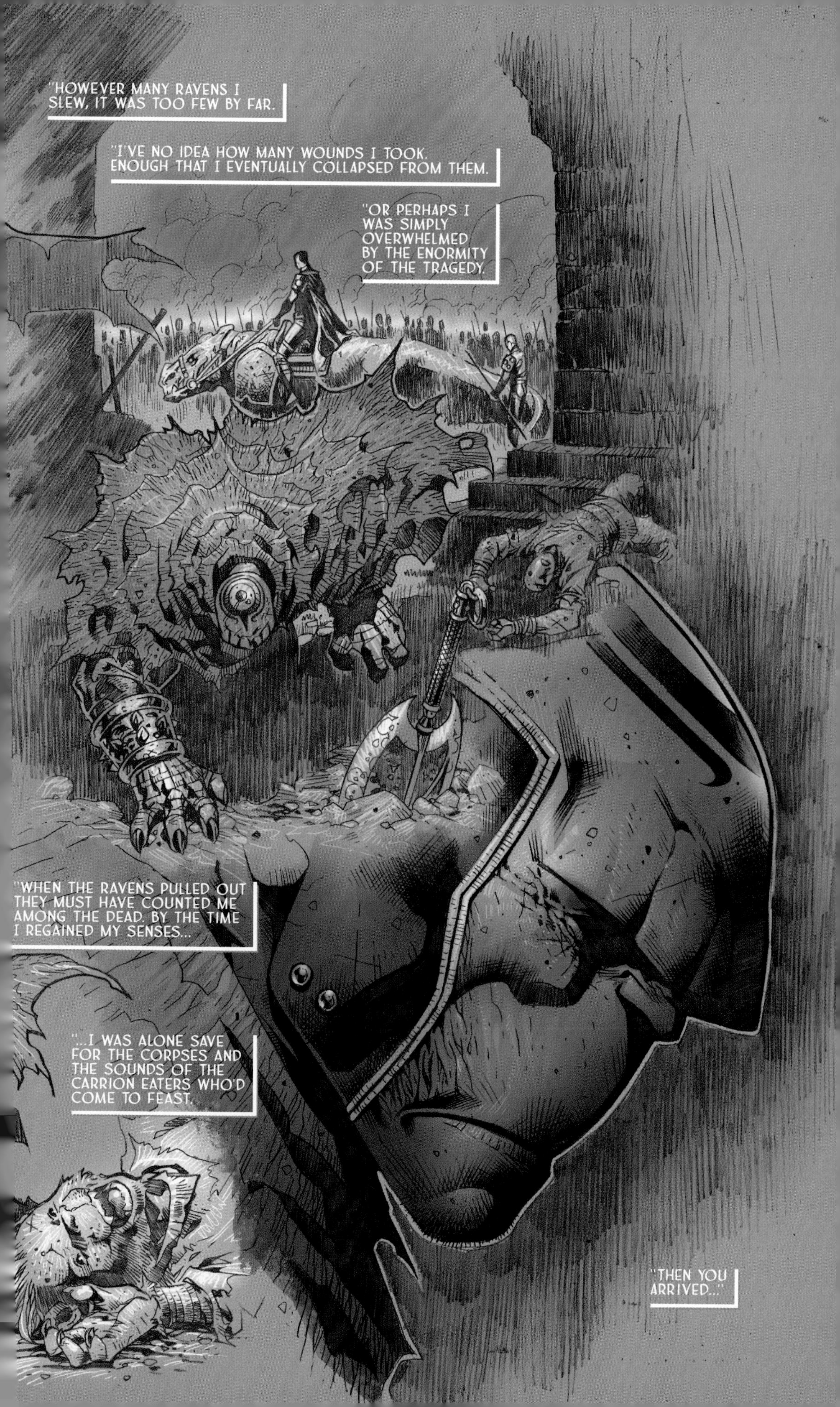
"HOWEVER MANY RAVENS I SLEW, IT WAS TOO FEW BY FAR.
"I'VE NO IDEA HOW MANY WOUNDS I TOOK. ENOUGH THAT I EVENTUALLY COLLAPSED FROM THEM.
"OR PERHAPS I WAS SIMPLY OVERWHELMED BY THE ENORMITY OF THE TRAGEDY.
"WHEN THE RAVENS PULLED OUT THEY MUST HAVE COUNTED ME AMONG THE DEAD. BY THE TIME I REGAINED MY SENSES...
"...I WAS ALONE SAVE FOR THE CORPSES AND THE SOUNDS OF THE CARRION EATERS WHO'D COME TO FEAST.
"THEN YOU ARRIVED..."

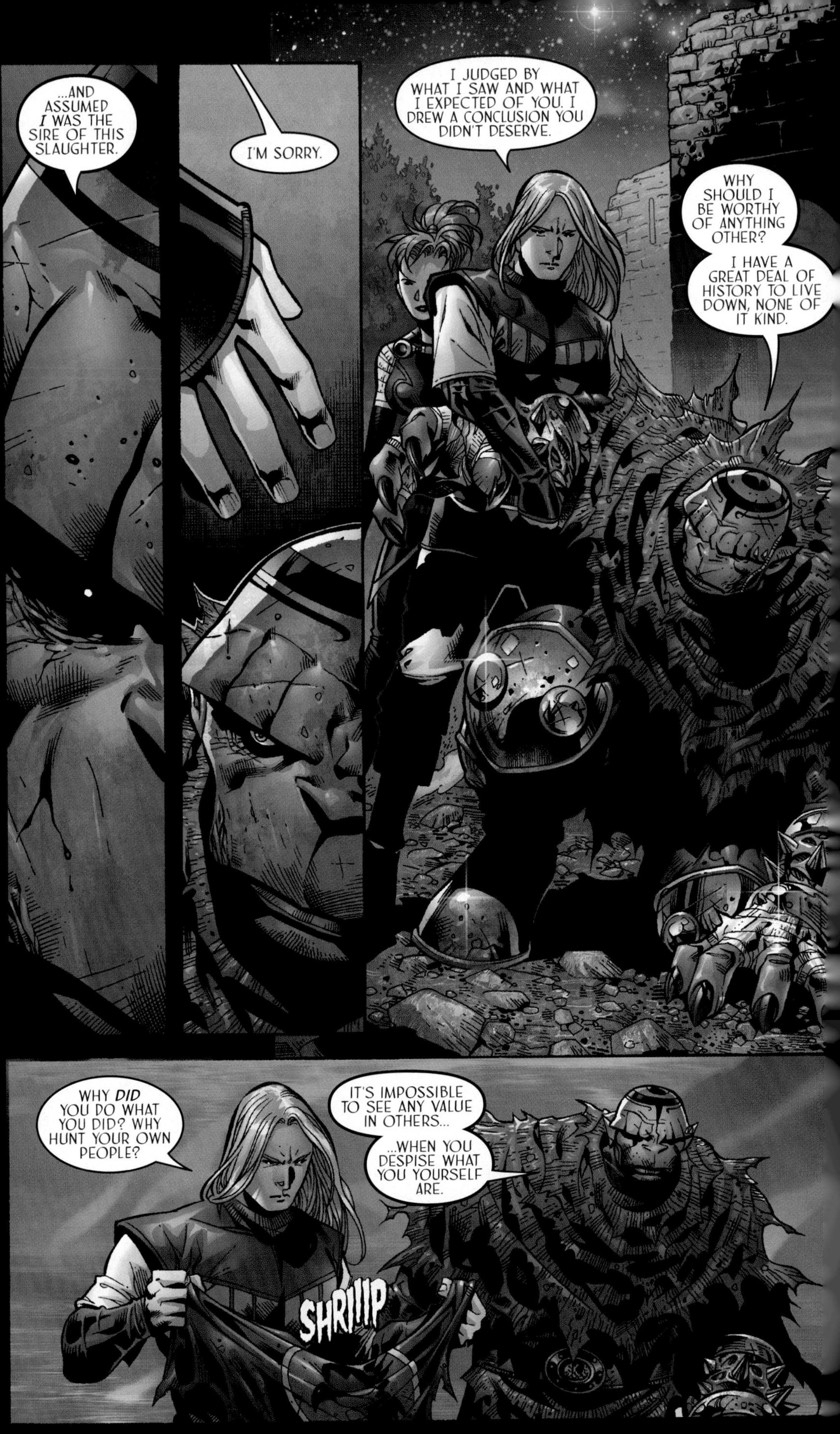

...AND ASSUMED *I* WAS THE SIRE OF THIS SLAUGHTER.
I'M SORRY.
I JUDGED BY WHAT I SAW AND WHAT I EXPECTED OF YOU. I DREW A CONCLUSION YOU DIDN'T DESERVE.
WHY SHOULD I BE WORTHY OF ANYTHING OTHER?
I HAVE A GREAT DEAL OF HISTORY TO LIVE DOWN, NONE OF IT KIND.
WHY *DID* YOU DO WHAT YOU DID? WHY HUNT YOUR OWN PEOPLE?
IT'S IMPOSSIBLE TO SEE ANY VALUE IN OTHERS...
...WHEN YOU DESPISE WHAT YOU YOURSELF ARE.
SHRIIIP

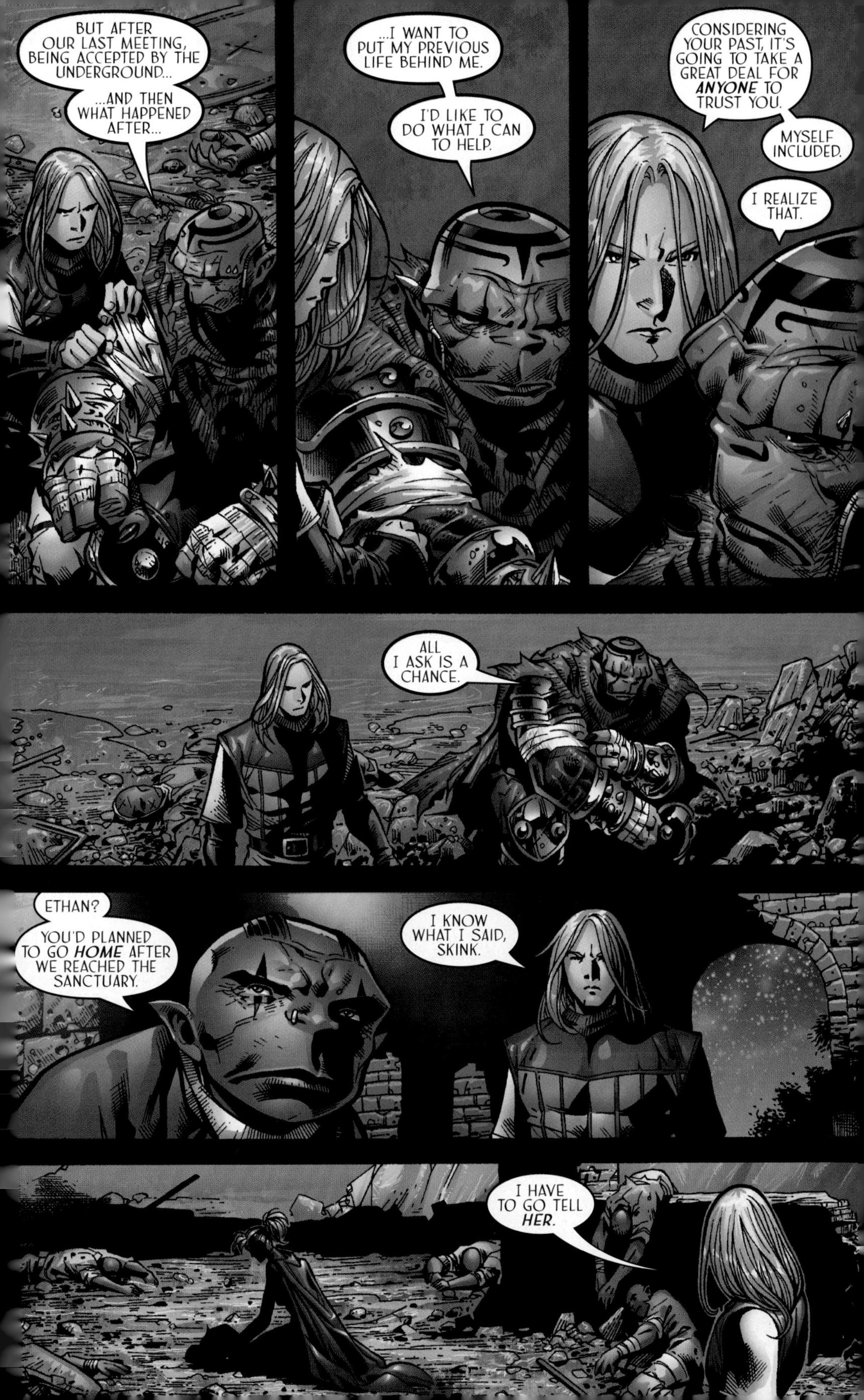
BUT AFTER OUR LAST MEETING, BEING ACCEPTED BY THE UNDERGROUND...
...AND THEN WHAT HAPPENED AFTER...
...I WANT TO PUT MY PREVIOUS LIFE BEHIND ME.
I'D LIKE TO DO WHAT I CAN TO HELP.
CONSIDERING YOUR PAST, IT'S GOING TO TAKE A GREAT DEAL FOR ANYONE TO TRUST YOU.
MYSELF INCLUDED.
I REALIZE THAT.
ALL I ASK IS A CHANCE.
ETHAN?
YOU'D PLANNED TO GO HOME AFTER WE REACHED THE SANCTUARY.
I KNOW WHAT I SAID, SKINK.
I HAVE TO GO TELL HER.

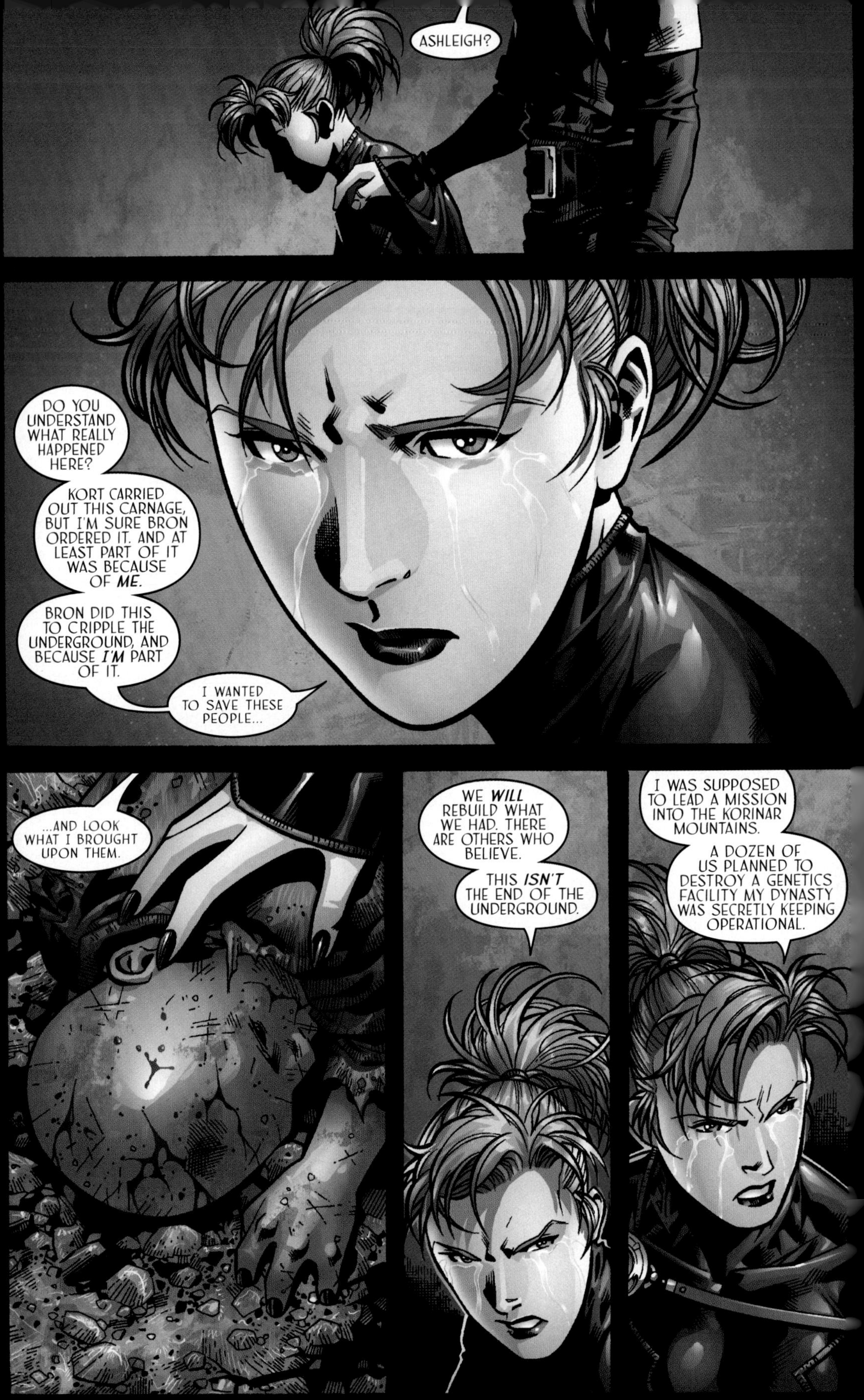
ASHLEIGH?
DO YOU UNDERSTAND WHAT REALLY HAPPENED HERE?
KORT CARRIED OUT THIS CARNAGE, BUT I'M SURE BRON ORDERED IT. AND AT LEAST PART OF IT WAS BECAUSE OF *ME.*
BRON DID THIS TO CRIPPLE THE UNDERGROUND, AND BECAUSE *I'M* PART OF IT.
I WANTED TO SAVE THESE PEOPLE...
...AND LOOK WHAT I BROUGHT UPON THEM.
WE *WILL* REBUILD WHAT WE HAD. THERE ARE OTHERS WHO BELIEVE.
THIS *ISN'T* THE END OF THE UNDERGROUND.
I WAS SUPPOSED TO LEAD A MISSION INTO THE KORINAR MOUNTAINS.
A DOZEN OF US PLANNED TO DESTROY A GENETICS FACILITY MY DYNASTY WAS SECRETLY KEEPING OPERATIONAL.

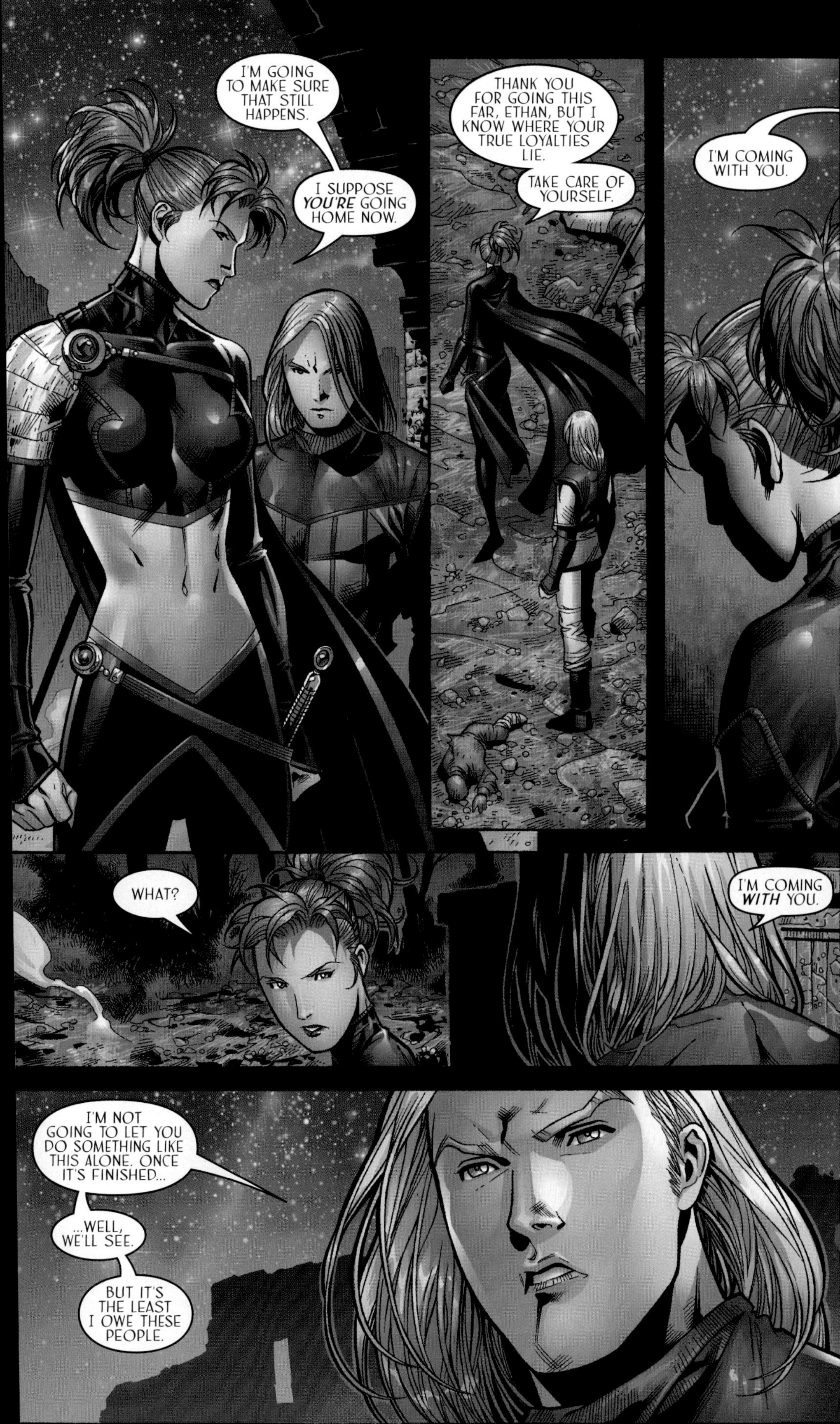
I'M GOING TO MAKE SURE THAT STILL HAPPENS.
I SUPPOSE *YOU'RE* GOING HOME NOW.
THANK YOU FOR GOING THIS FAR, ETHAN, BUT I KNOW WHERE YOUR TRUE LOYALTIES LIE.
TAKE CARE OF YOURSELF.
I'M COMING WITH YOU.
WHAT?
I'M COMING *WITH* YOU.
I'M NOT GOING TO LET YOU DO SOMETHING LIKE THIS ALONE. ONCE IT'S FINISHED...
...WELL, WE'LL SEE.
BUT IT'S THE LEAST I OWE THESE PEOPLE.

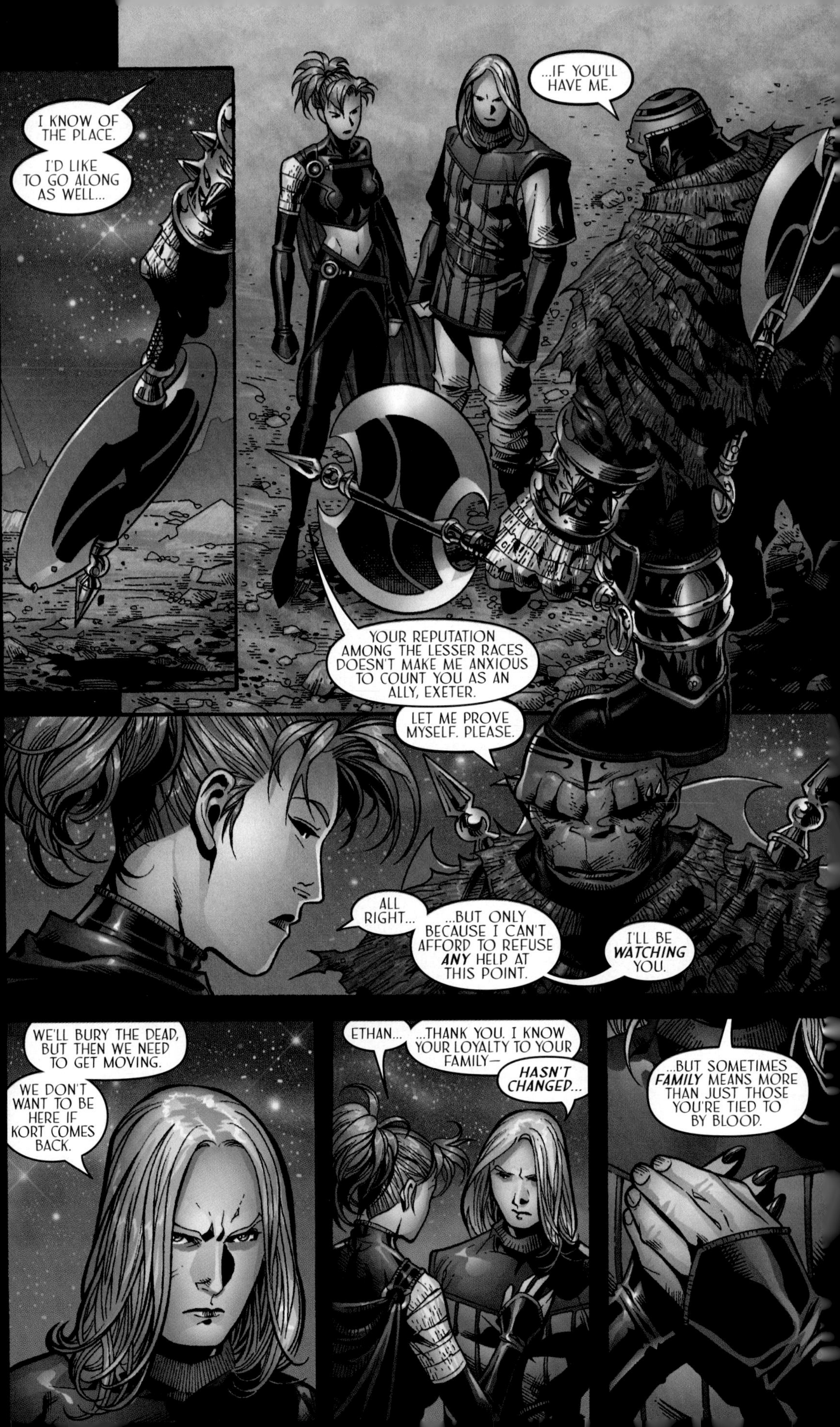
I KNOW OF THE PLACE.
I'D LIKE TO GO ALONG AS WELL...
...IF YOU'LL HAVE ME.
YOUR REPUTATION AMONG THE LESSER RACES DOESN'T MAKE ME ANXIOUS TO COUNT YOU AS AN ALLY, EXETER.
LET ME PROVE MYSELF. PLEASE.
ALL RIGHT...
...BUT ONLY BECAUSE I CAN'T AFFORD TO REFUSE **ANY** HELP AT THIS POINT.
I'LL BE **WATCHING** YOU.
WE'LL BURY THE DEAD, BUT THEN WE NEED TO GET MOVING.
WE DON'T WANT TO BE HERE IF KORT COMES BACK.
ETHAN...
...THANK YOU. I KNOW YOUR LOYALTY TO YOUR FAMILY—
**HASN'T CHANGED...**
...BUT SOMETIMES **FAMILY** MEANS MORE THAN JUST THOSE YOU'RE TIED TO BY BLOOD.

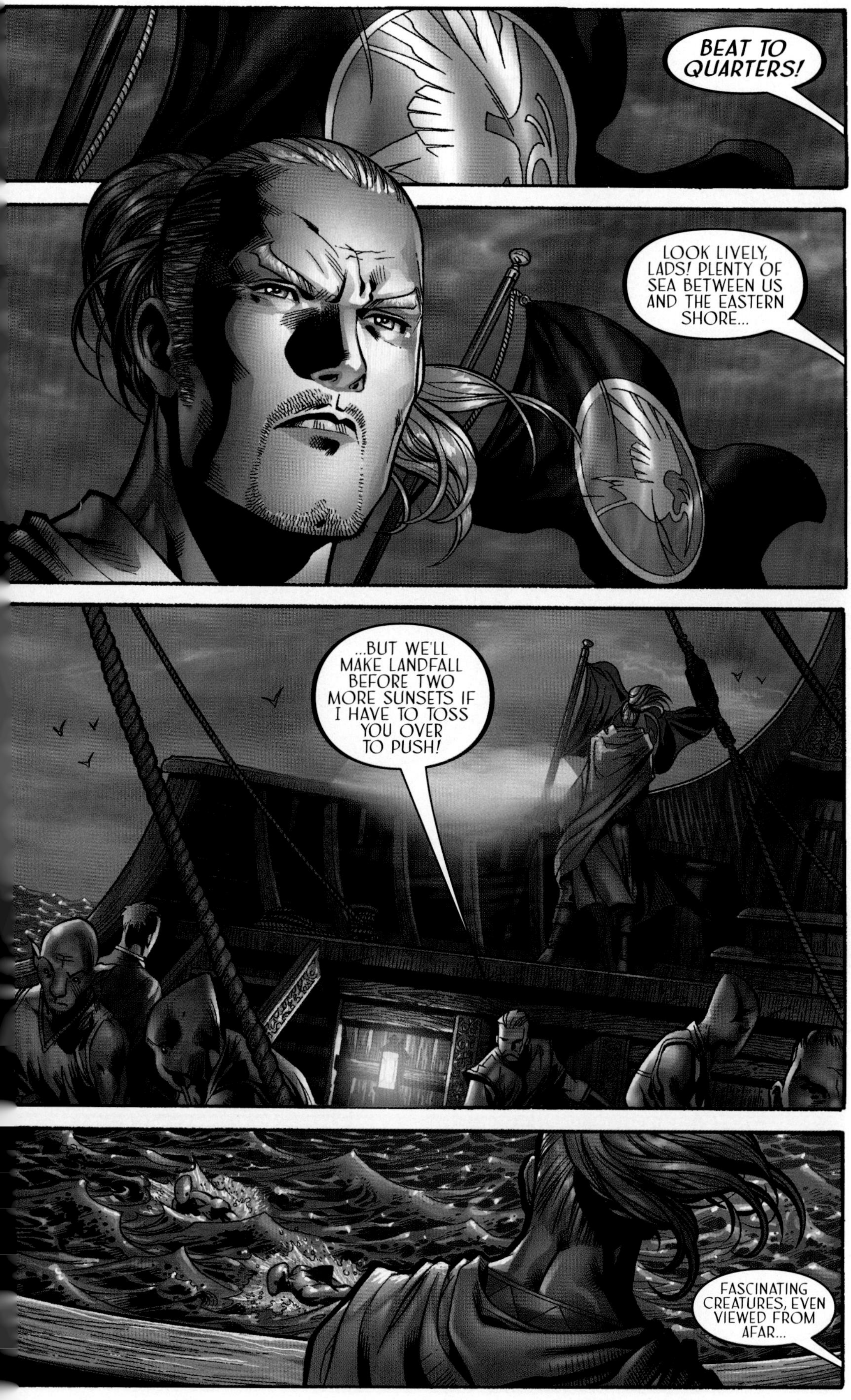
BEAT TO QUARTERS!
LOOK LIVELY, LADS! PLENTY OF SEA BETWEEN US AND THE EASTERN SHORE...
...BUT WE'LL MAKE LANDFALL BEFORE TWO MORE SUNSETS IF I HAVE TO TOSS YOU OVER TO PUSH!
FASCINATING CREATURES, EVEN VIEWED FROM AFAR...

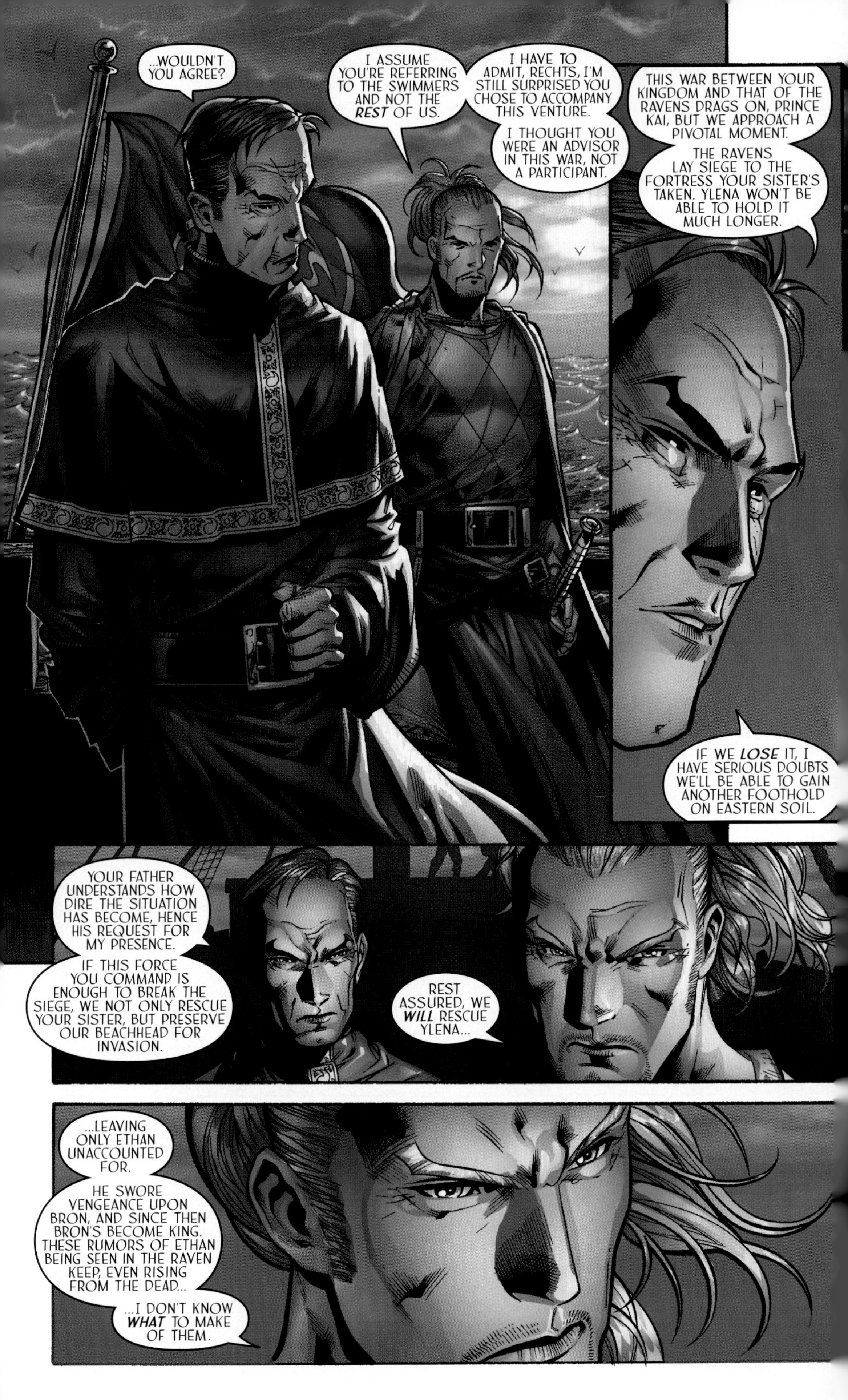
...WOULDN'T YOU AGREE?
I ASSUME YOU'RE REFERRING TO THE SWIMMERS AND NOT THE *REST* OF US.
I HAVE TO ADMIT, RECHTS, I'M STILL SURPRISED YOU CHOSE TO ACCOMPANY THIS VENTURE.
I THOUGHT YOU WERE AN ADVISOR IN THIS WAR, NOT A PARTICIPANT.
THIS WAR BETWEEN YOUR KINGDOM AND THAT OF THE RAVENS DRAGS ON, PRINCE KAI, BUT WE APPROACH A PIVOTAL MOMENT.
THE RAVENS LAY SIEGE TO THE FORTRESS YOUR SISTER'S TAKEN. YLENA WON'T BE ABLE TO HOLD IT MUCH LONGER.
IF WE *LOSE* IT, I HAVE SERIOUS DOUBTS WE'LL BE ABLE TO GAIN ANOTHER FOOTHOLD ON EASTERN SOIL.
YOUR FATHER UNDERSTANDS HOW DIRE THE SITUATION HAS BECOME, HENCE HIS REQUEST FOR MY PRESENCE.
IF THIS FORCE YOU COMMAND IS ENOUGH TO BREAK THE SIEGE, WE NOT ONLY RESCUE YOUR SISTER, BUT PRESERVE OUR BEACHHEAD FOR INVASION.
REST ASSURED, WE *WILL* RESCUE YLENA...
...LEAVING ONLY ETHAN UNACCOUNTED FOR.
HE SWORE VENGEANCE UPON BRON, AND SINCE THEN BRON'S BECOME KING. THESE RUMORS OF ETHAN BEING SEEN IN THE RAVEN KEEP, EVEN RISING FROM THE DEAD...
...I DON'T KNOW *WHAT* TO MAKE OF THEM.

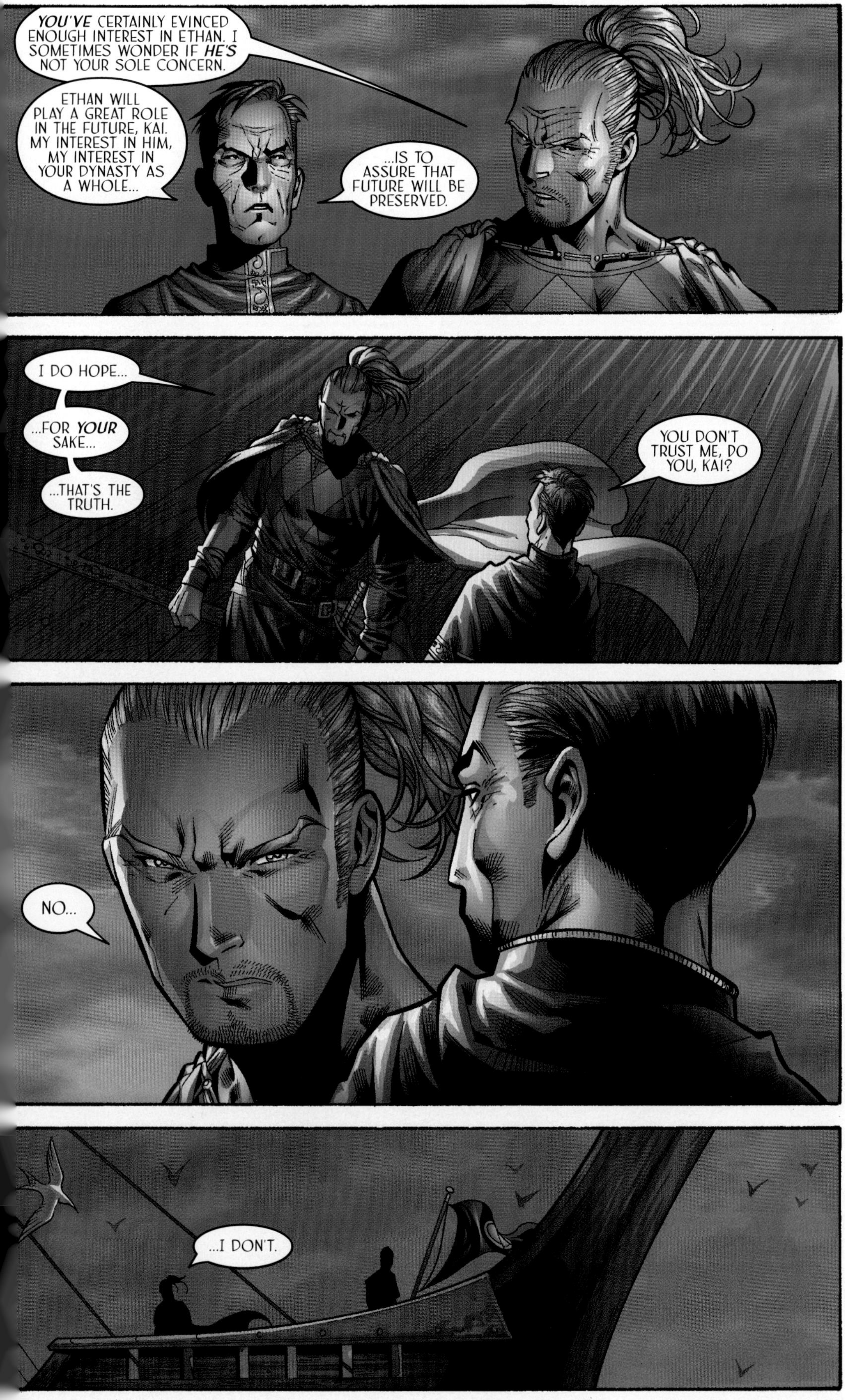
YOU'VE CERTAINLY EVINCED ENOUGH INTEREST IN ETHAN. I SOMETIMES WONDER IF HE'S NOT YOUR SOLE CONCERN.
ETHAN WILL PLAY A GREAT ROLE IN THE FUTURE, KAI. MY INTEREST IN HIM, MY INTEREST IN YOUR DYNASTY AS A WHOLE...
...IS TO ASSURE THAT FUTURE WILL BE PRESERVED.
I DO HOPE...
...FOR YOUR SAKE...
...THAT'S THE TRUTH.
YOU DON'T TRUST ME, DO YOU, KAI?
NO...
...I DON'T.

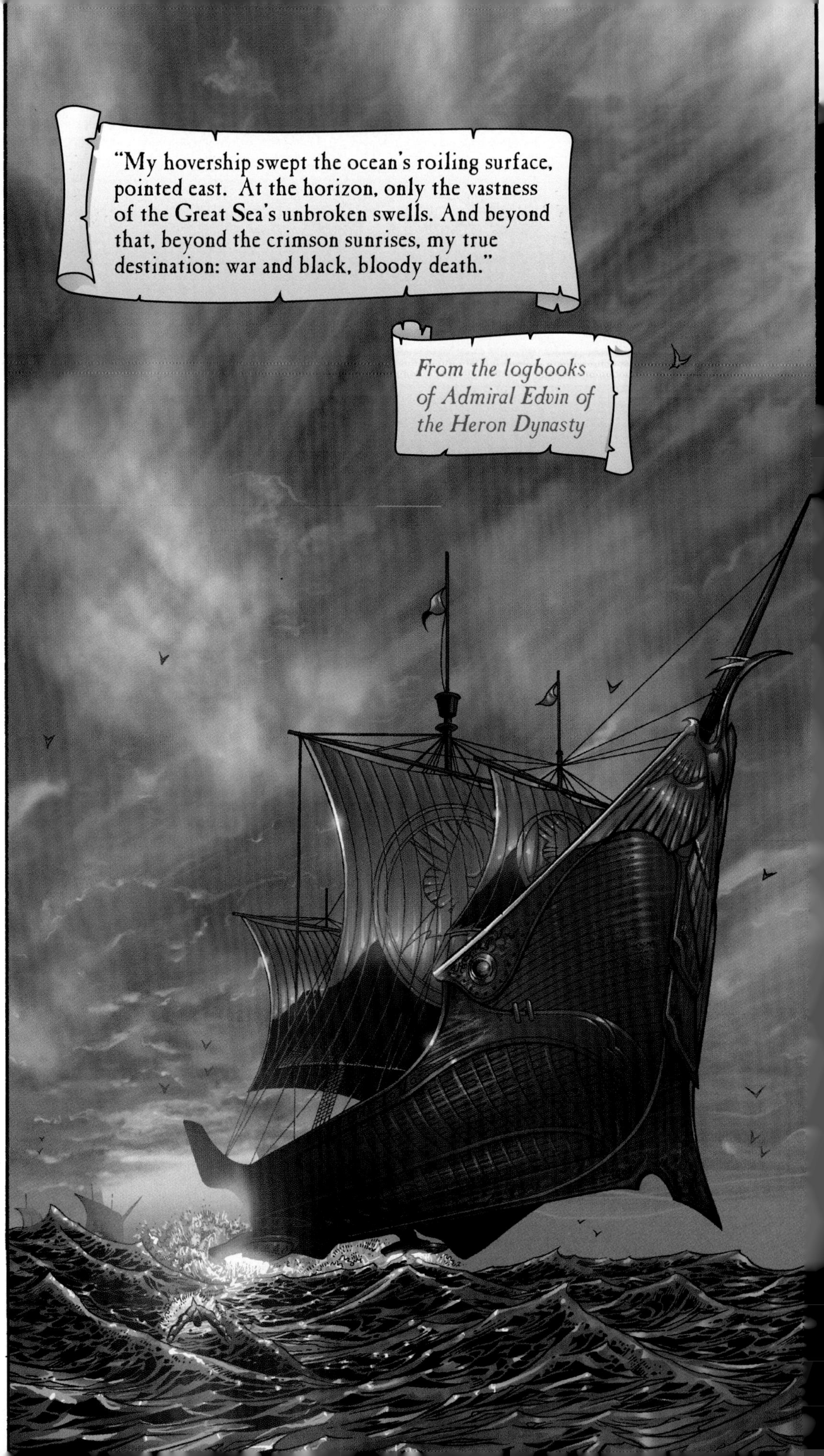
"My hovership swept the ocean's roiling surface, pointed east. At the horizon, only the vastness of the Great Sea's unbroken swells. And beyond that, beyond the crimson sunrises, my true destination: war and black, bloody death."
*From the logbooks of Admiral Edvin of the Heron Dynasty*

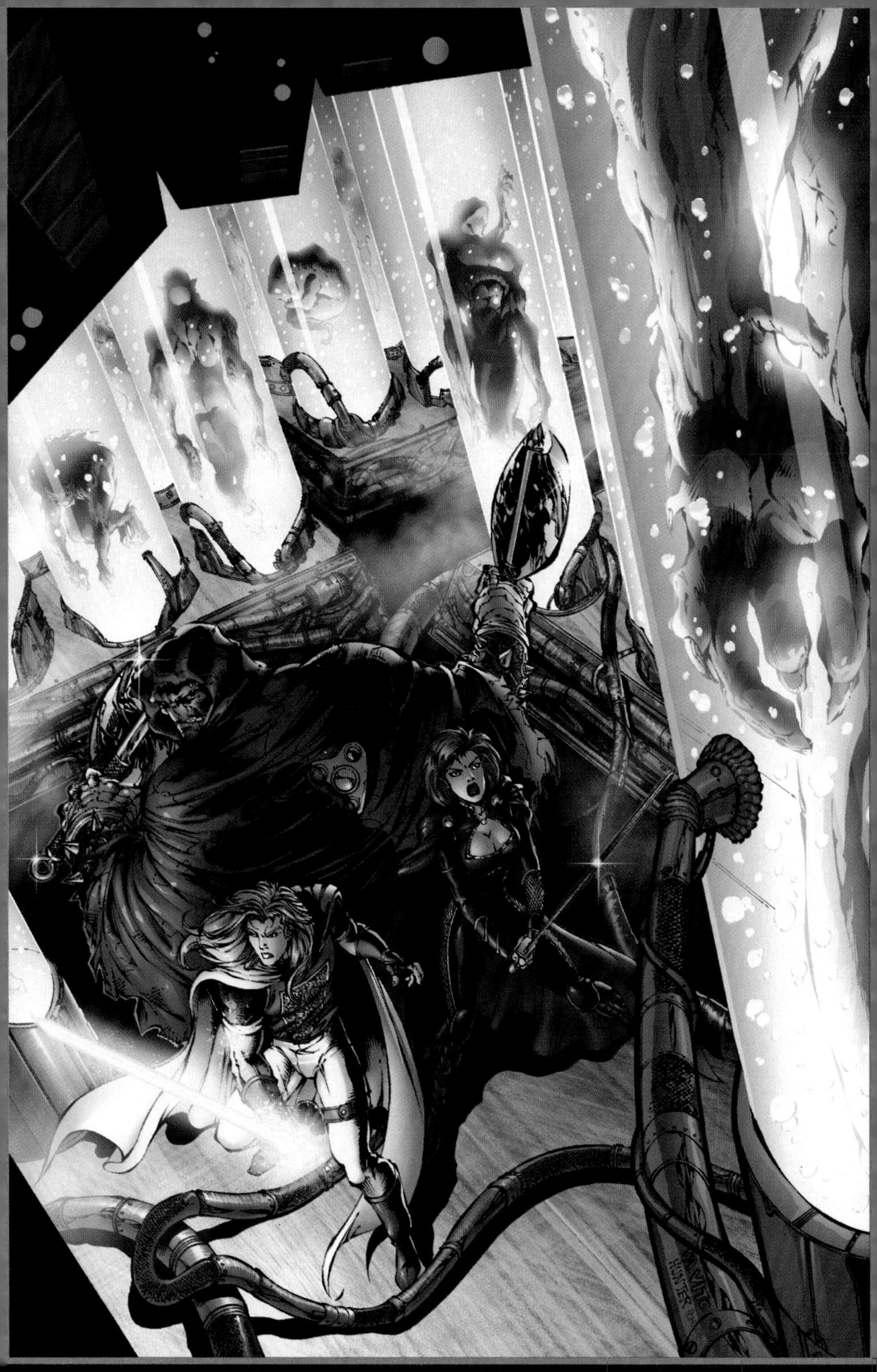

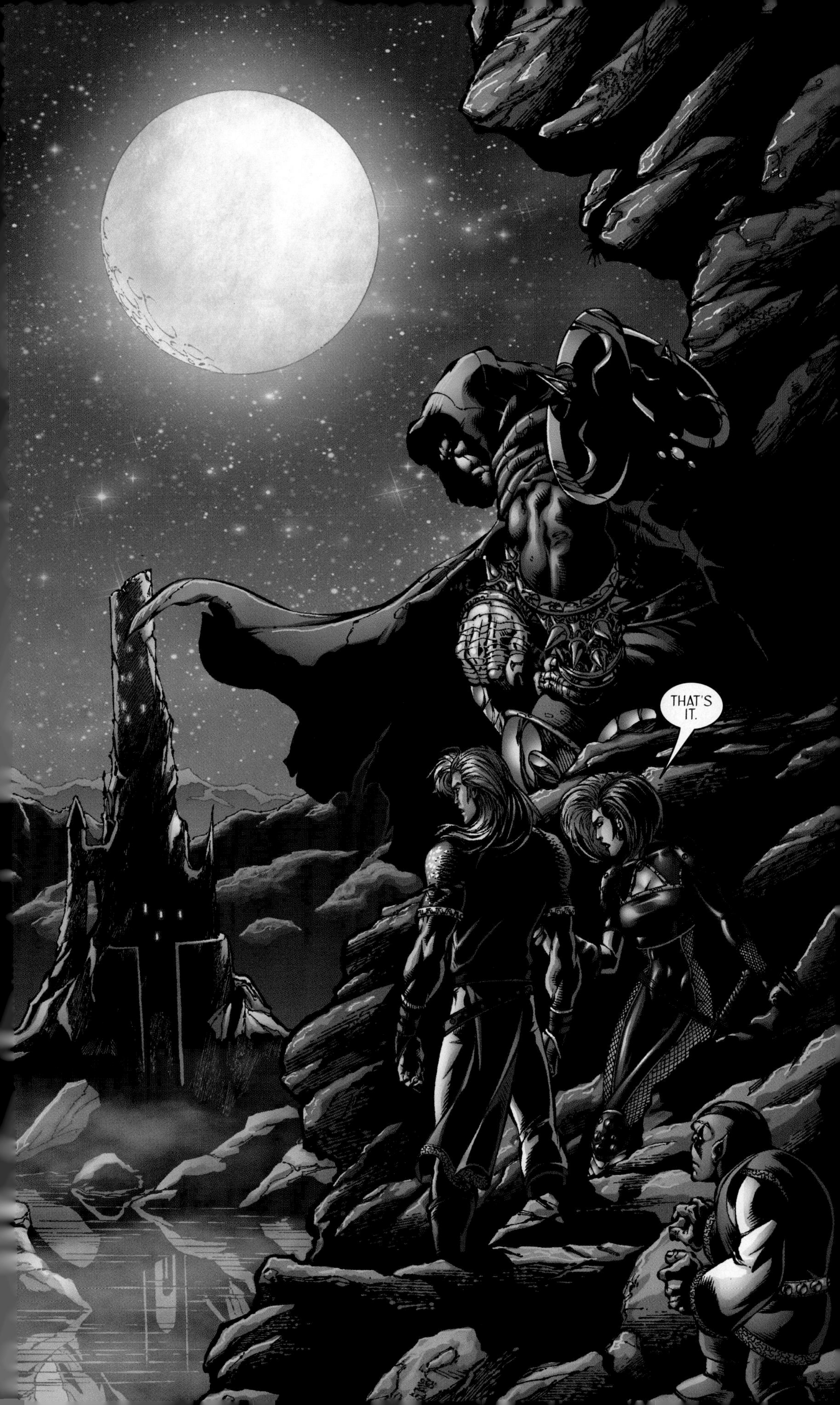
THAT'S IT.

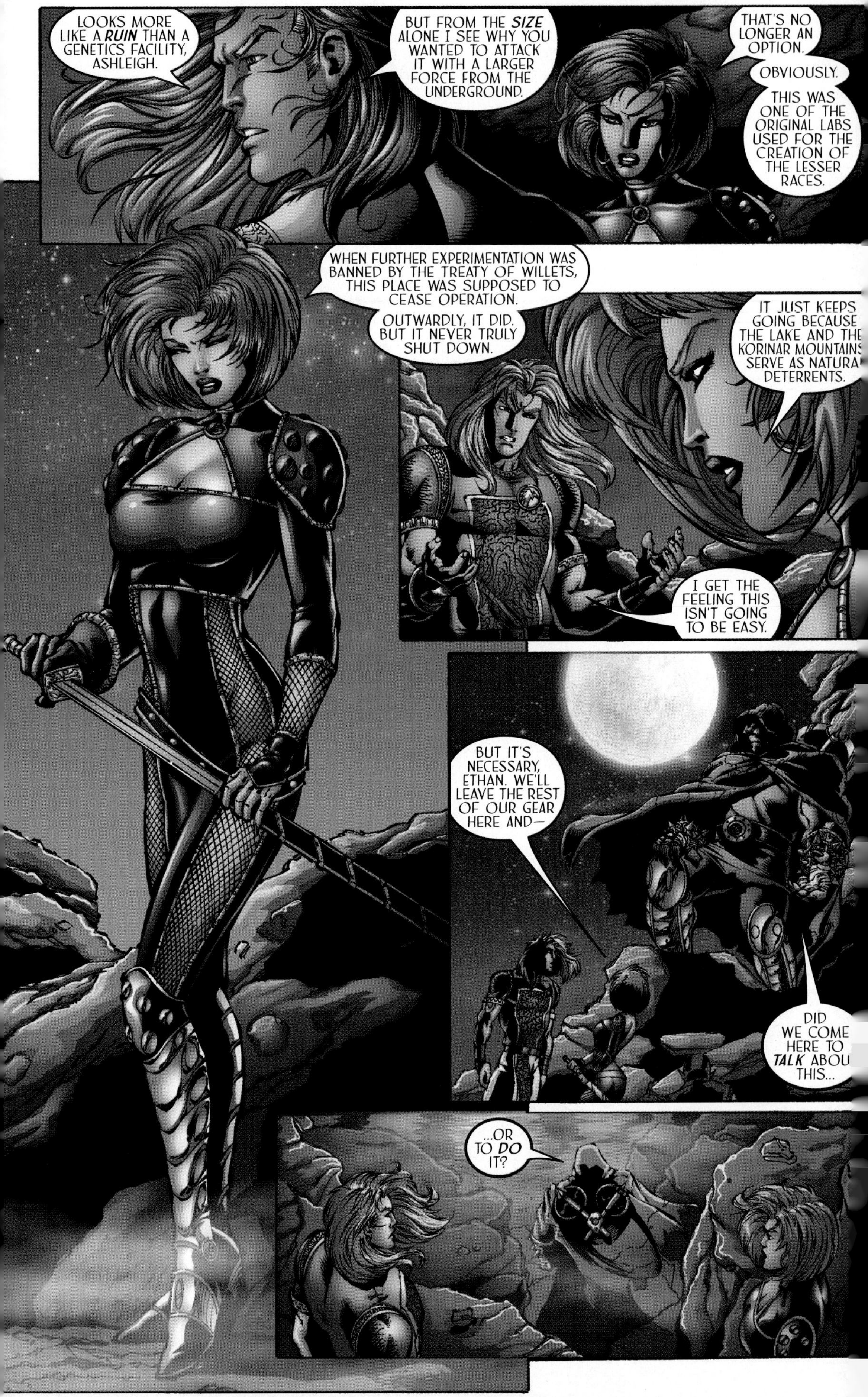

LOOKS MORE LIKE A *RUIN* THAN A GENETICS FACILITY, ASHLEIGH.
BUT FROM THE *SIZE* ALONE I SEE WHY YOU WANTED TO ATTACK IT WITH A LARGER FORCE FROM THE UNDERGROUND.
THAT'S NO LONGER AN OPTION.
OBVIOUSLY.
THIS WAS ONE OF THE ORIGINAL LABS USED FOR THE CREATION OF THE LESSER RACES.
WHEN FURTHER EXPERIMENTATION WAS BANNED BY THE TREATY OF WILLETS, THIS PLACE WAS SUPPOSED TO CEASE OPERATION.
OUTWARDLY, IT DID. BUT IT NEVER TRULY SHUT DOWN.
IT JUST KEEPS GOING BECAUSE THE LAKE AND THE KORINAR MOUNTAINS SERVE AS NATURA DETERRENTS.
I GET THE FEELING THIS ISN'T GOING TO BE EASY.
BUT IT'S NECESSARY, ETHAN. WE'LL LEAVE THE REST OF OUR GEAR HERE AND—
DID WE COME HERE TO *TALK* ABOU THIS...
...OR TO *DO* IT?

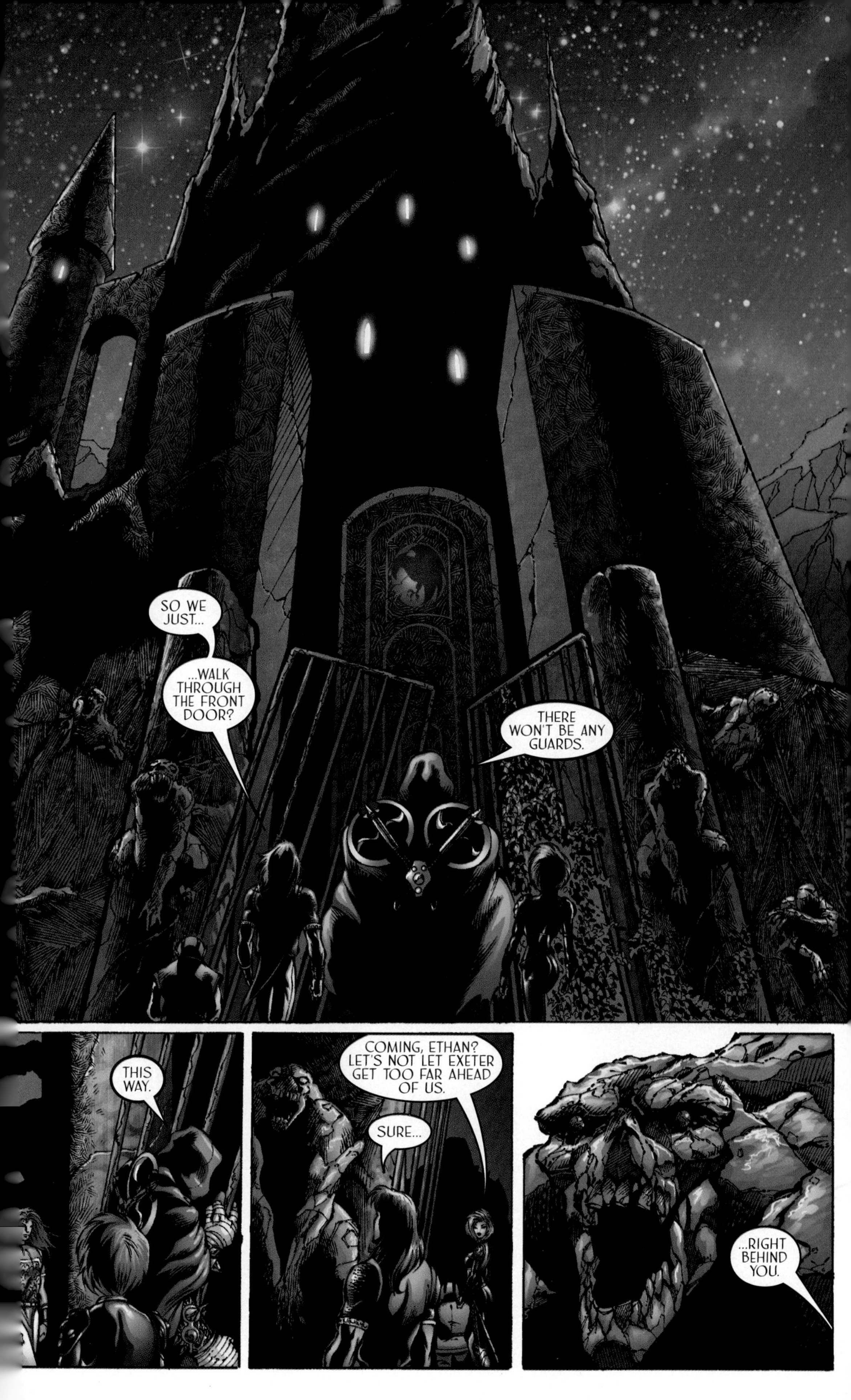
SO WE JUST...
...WALK THROUGH THE FRONT DOOR?
THERE WON'T BE ANY GUARDS.
THIS WAY.
COMING, ETHAN? LET'S NOT LET EXETER GET TOO FAR AHEAD OF US.
SURE...
...RIGHT BEHIND YOU.

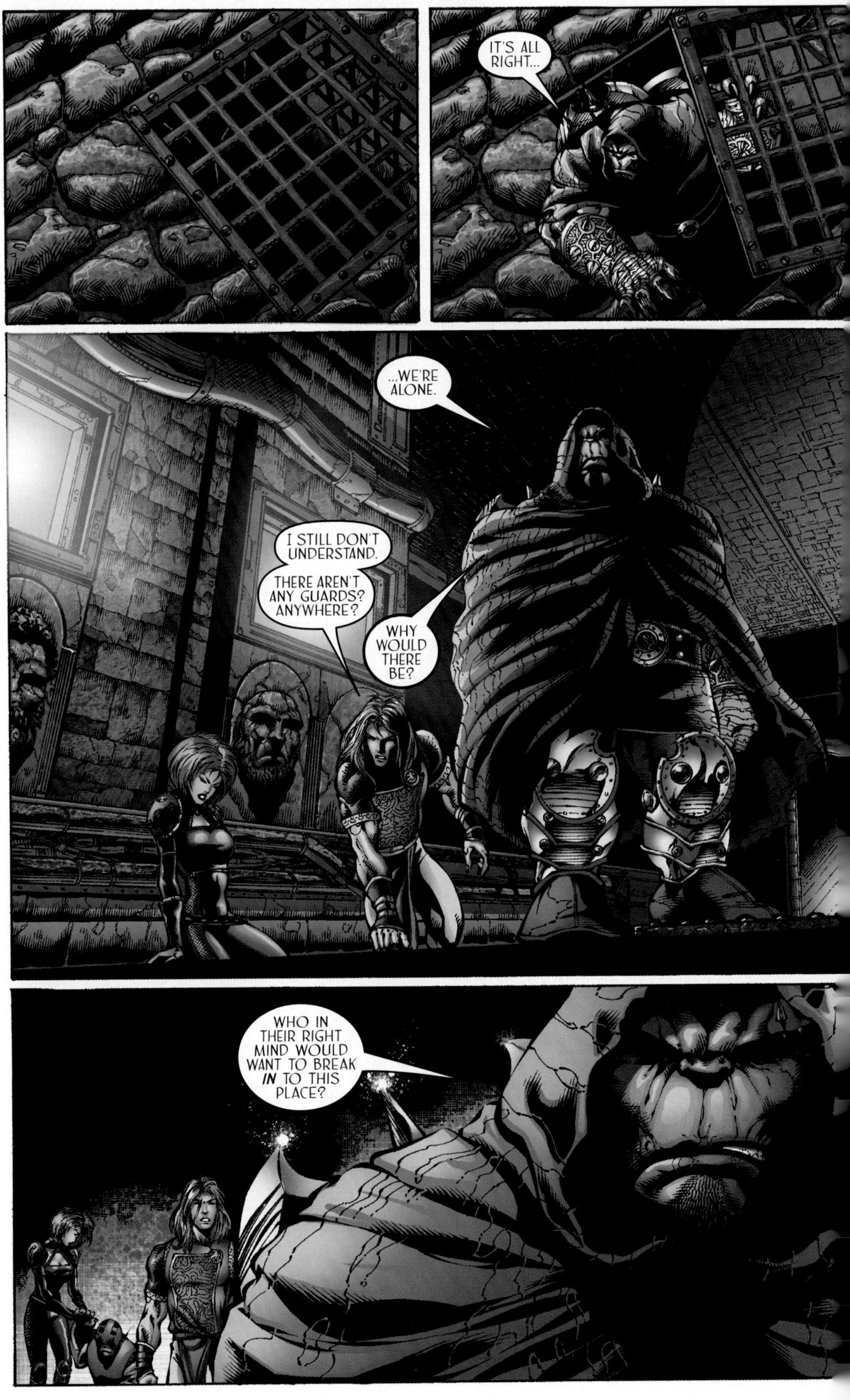
IT'S ALL RIGHT...
...WE'RE ALONE.
I STILL DON'T UNDERSTAND.
THERE AREN'T ANY GUARDS? ANYWHERE?
WHY WOULD THERE BE?
WHO IN THEIR RIGHT MIND WOULD WANT TO BREAK ***IN*** TO THIS PLACE?

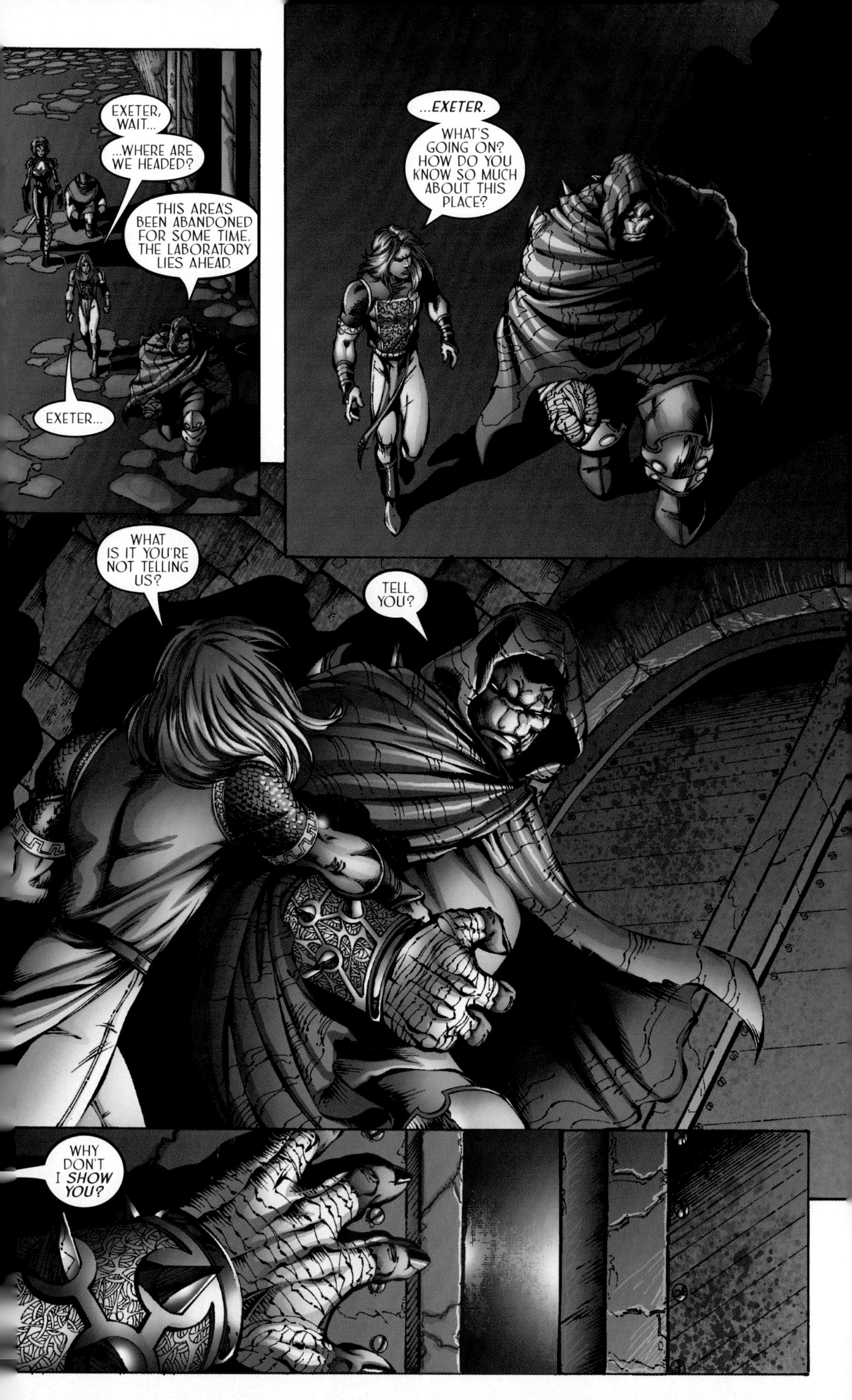
EXETER, WAIT...
...WHERE ARE WE HEADED?
THIS AREA'S BEEN ABANDONED FOR SOME TIME. THE LABORATORY LIES AHEAD.
EXETER...
...EXETER.
WHAT'S GOING ON? HOW DO YOU KNOW SO MUCH ABOUT THIS PLACE?
WHAT IS IT YOU'RE NOT TELLING US?
TELL YOU?
WHY DON'T I SHOW YOU?

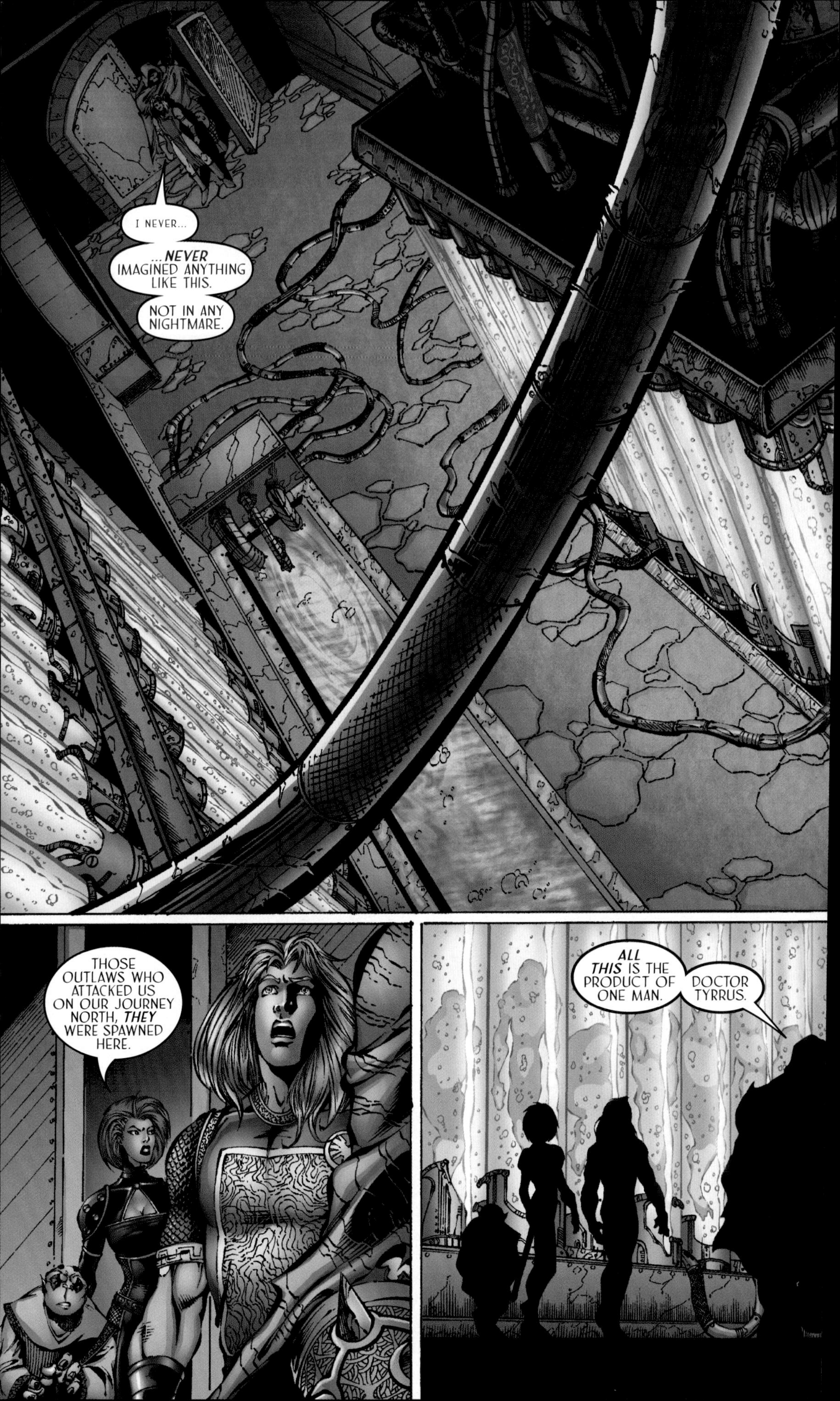
I NEVER...
...NEVER IMAGINED ANYTHING LIKE THIS.
NOT IN ANY NIGHTMARE.
THOSE OUTLAWS WHO ATTACKED US ON OUR JOURNEY NORTH, THEY WERE SPAWNED HERE.
ALL THIS IS THE PRODUCT OF ONE MAN.
DOCTOR TYRRUS.

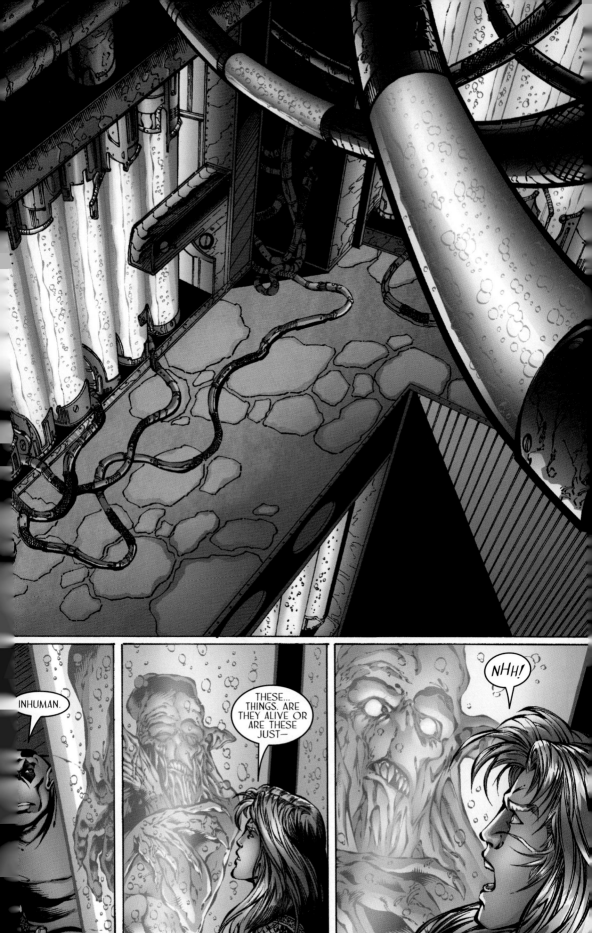

INHUMAN.

THESE... THINGS. ARE THEY ALIVE OR ARE THESE JUST—

NHH!

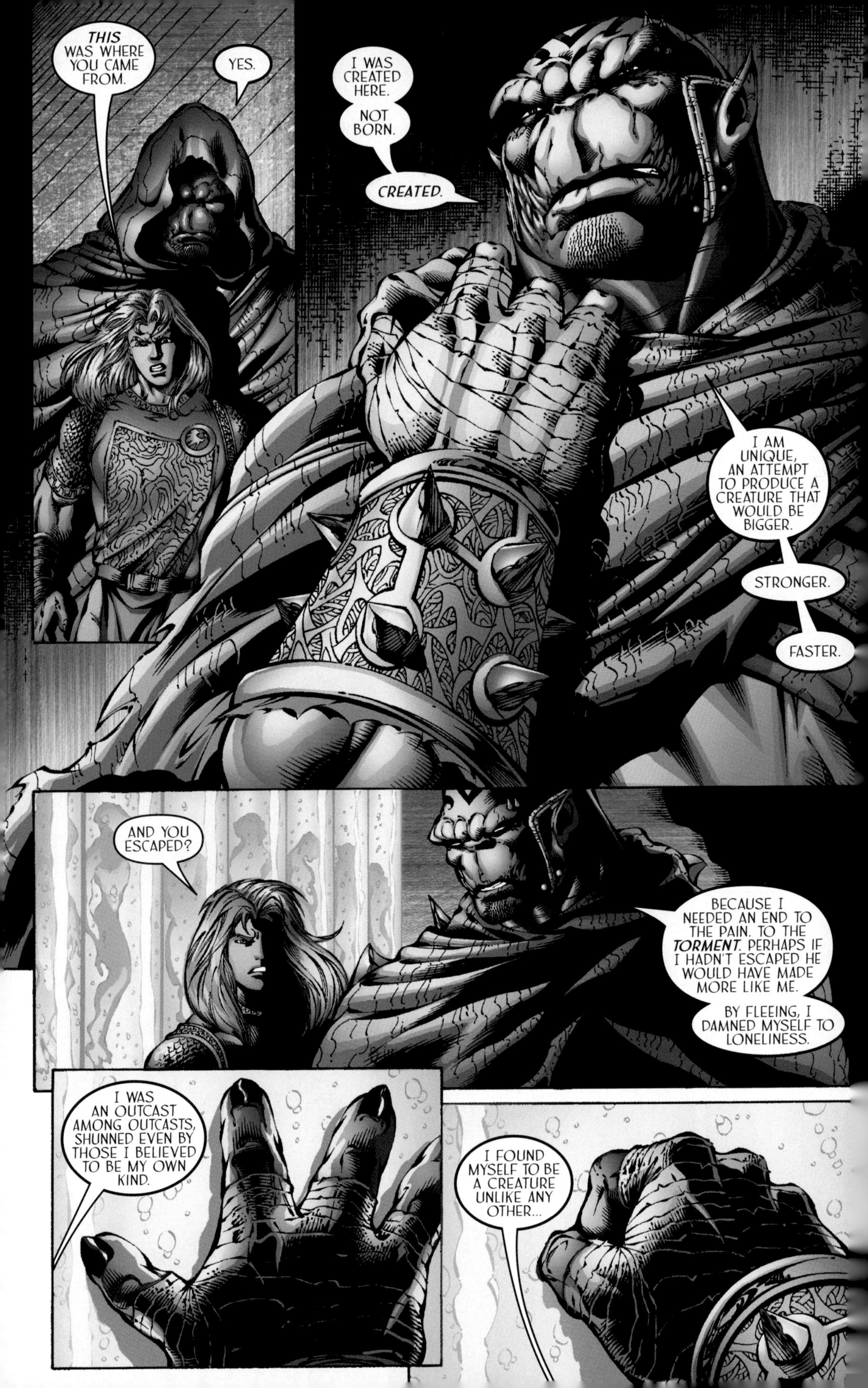
THIS WAS WHERE YOU CAME FROM.
YES.
I WAS CREATED HERE.
NOT BORN.
CREATED.
I AM UNIQUE, AN ATTEMPT TO PRODUCE A CREATURE THAT WOULD BE BIGGER.
STRONGER.
FASTER.
AND YOU ESCAPED?
BECAUSE I NEEDED AN END TO THE PAIN. TO THE TORMENT. PERHAPS IF I HADN'T ESCAPED HE WOULD HAVE MADE MORE LIKE ME.
BY FLEEING, I DAMNED MYSELF TO LONELINESS.
I WAS AN OUTCAST AMONG OUTCASTS, SHUNNED EVEN BY THOSE I BELIEVED TO BE MY OWN KIND.
I FOUND MYSELF TO BE A CREATURE UNLIKE ANY OTHER...

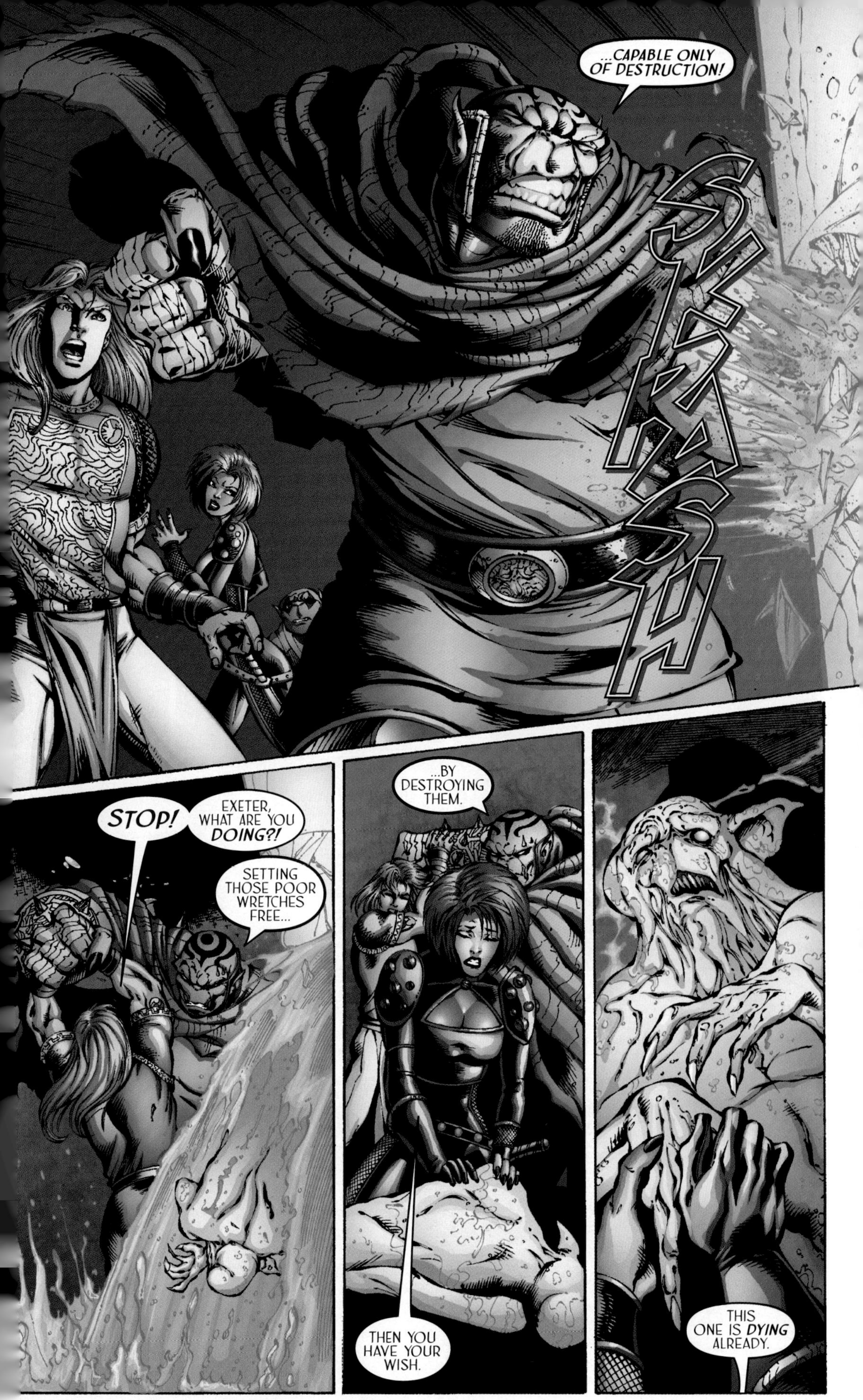

...CAPABLE ONLY OF DESTRUCTION!
STOP!
EXETER, WHAT ARE YOU DOING?!
SETTING THOSE POOR WRETCHES FREE...
...BY DESTROYING THEM.
THEN YOU HAVE YOUR WISH.
THIS ONE IS DYING ALREADY.

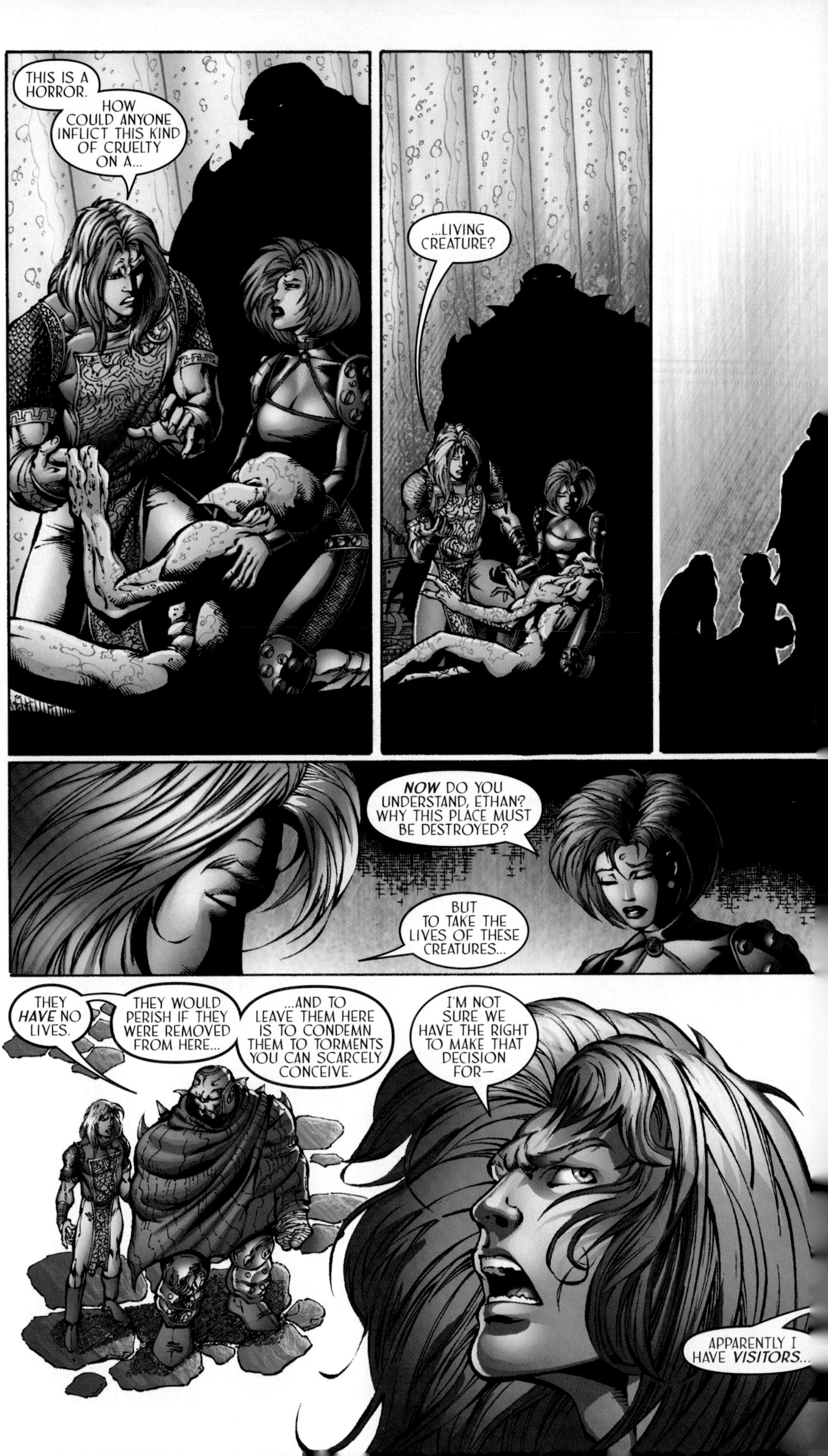
THIS IS A HORROR.
HOW COULD ANYONE INFLICT THIS KIND OF CRUELTY ON A...
...LIVING CREATURE?
NOW DO YOU UNDERSTAND, ETHAN? WHY THIS PLACE MUST BE DESTROYED?
BUT TO TAKE THE LIVES OF THESE CREATURES...
THEY HAVE NO LIVES.
THEY WOULD PERISH IF THEY WERE REMOVED FROM HERE...
...AND TO LEAVE THEM HERE IS TO CONDEMN THEM TO TORMENTS YOU CAN SCARCELY CONCEIVE.
I'M NOT SURE WE HAVE THE RIGHT TO MAKE THAT DECISION FOR—
APPARENTLY I HAVE VISITORS...

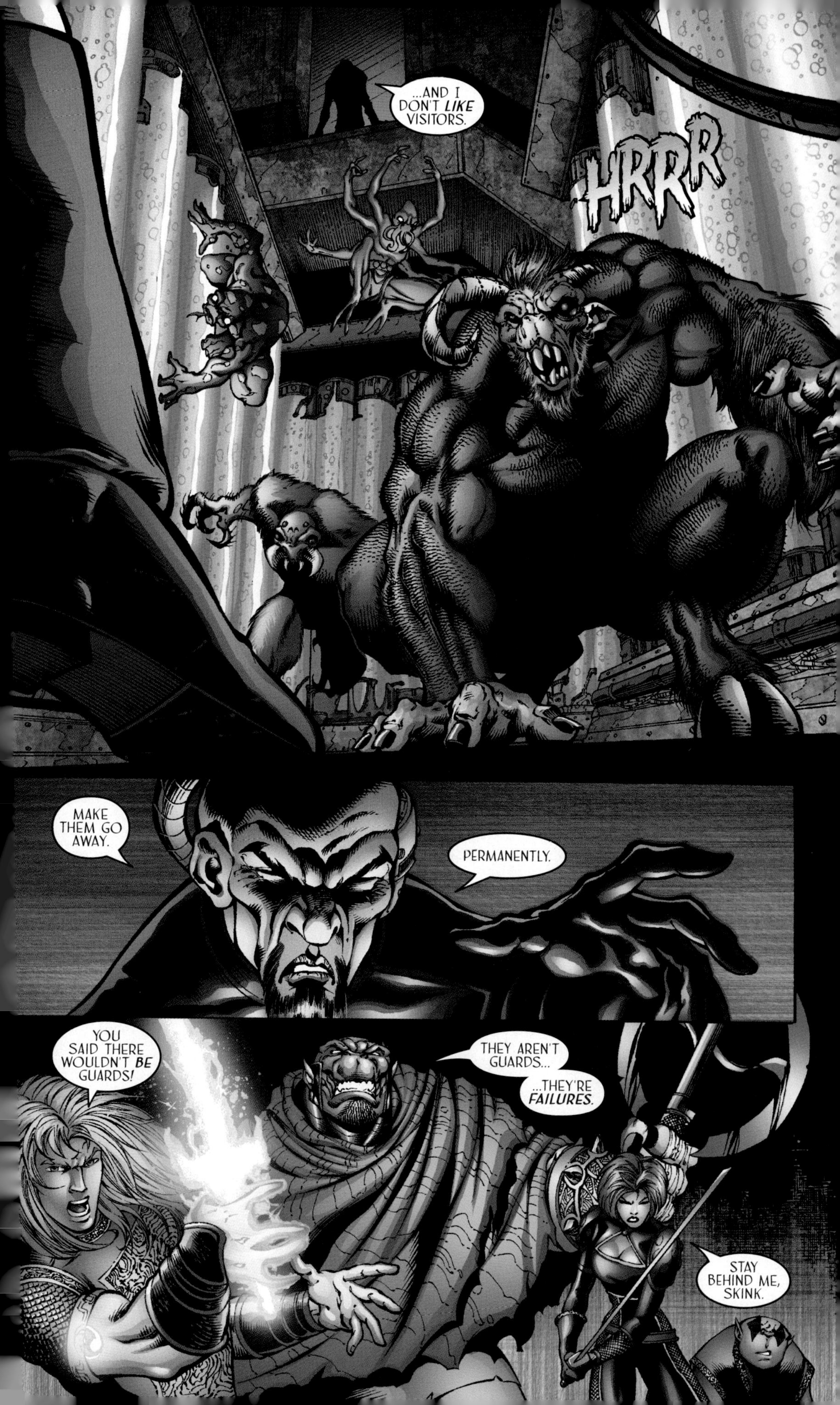
...AND I DON'T LIKE VISITORS.
HRRR
MAKE THEM GO AWAY.
PERMANENTLY.
YOU SAID THERE WOULDN'T BE GUARDS!
THEY AREN'T GUARDS...
...THEY'RE FAILURES.
STAY BEHIND ME, SKINK.

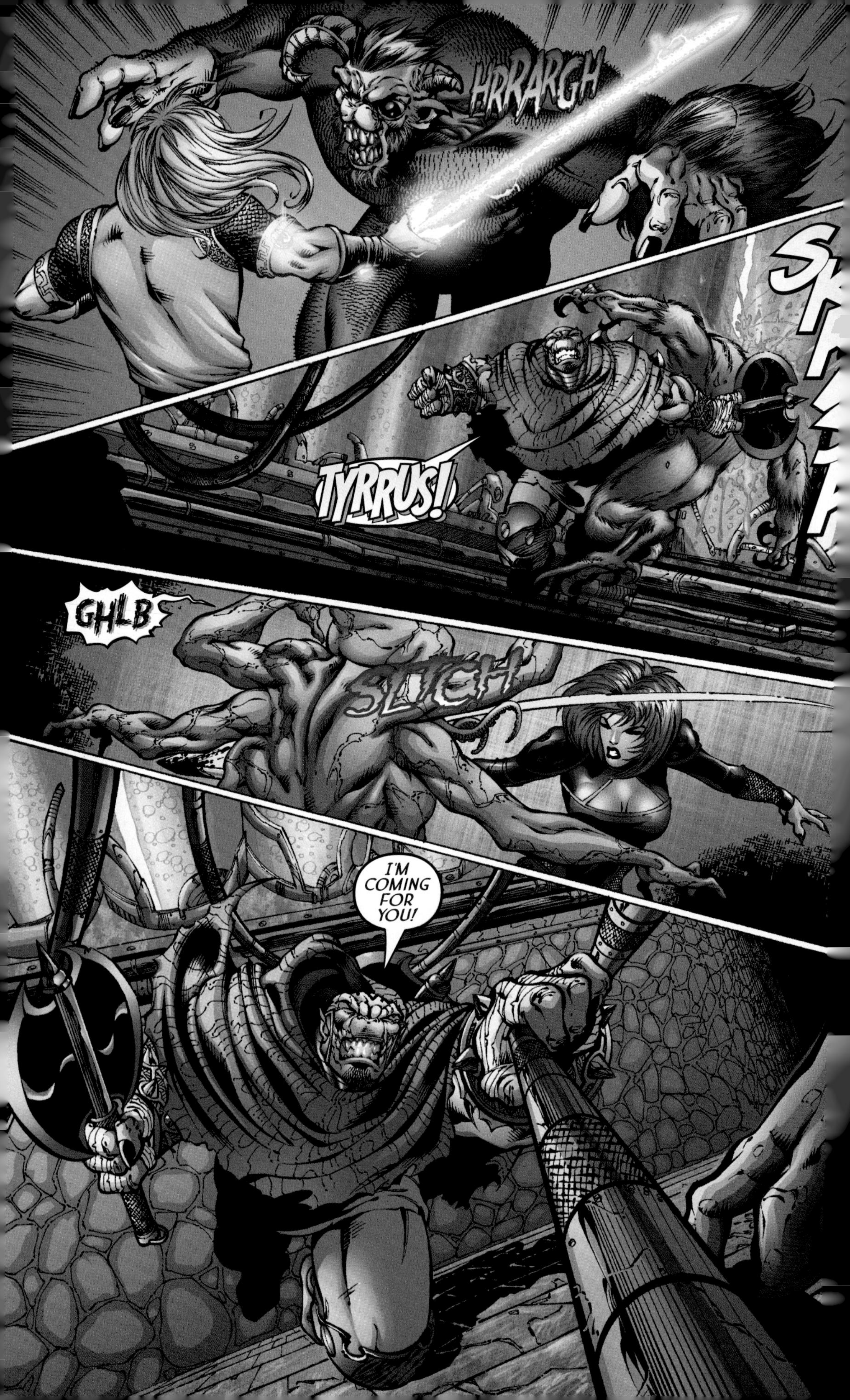
HRRARGH
TYRRUS!
GHLB
SLICH
I'M COMING FOR YOU!

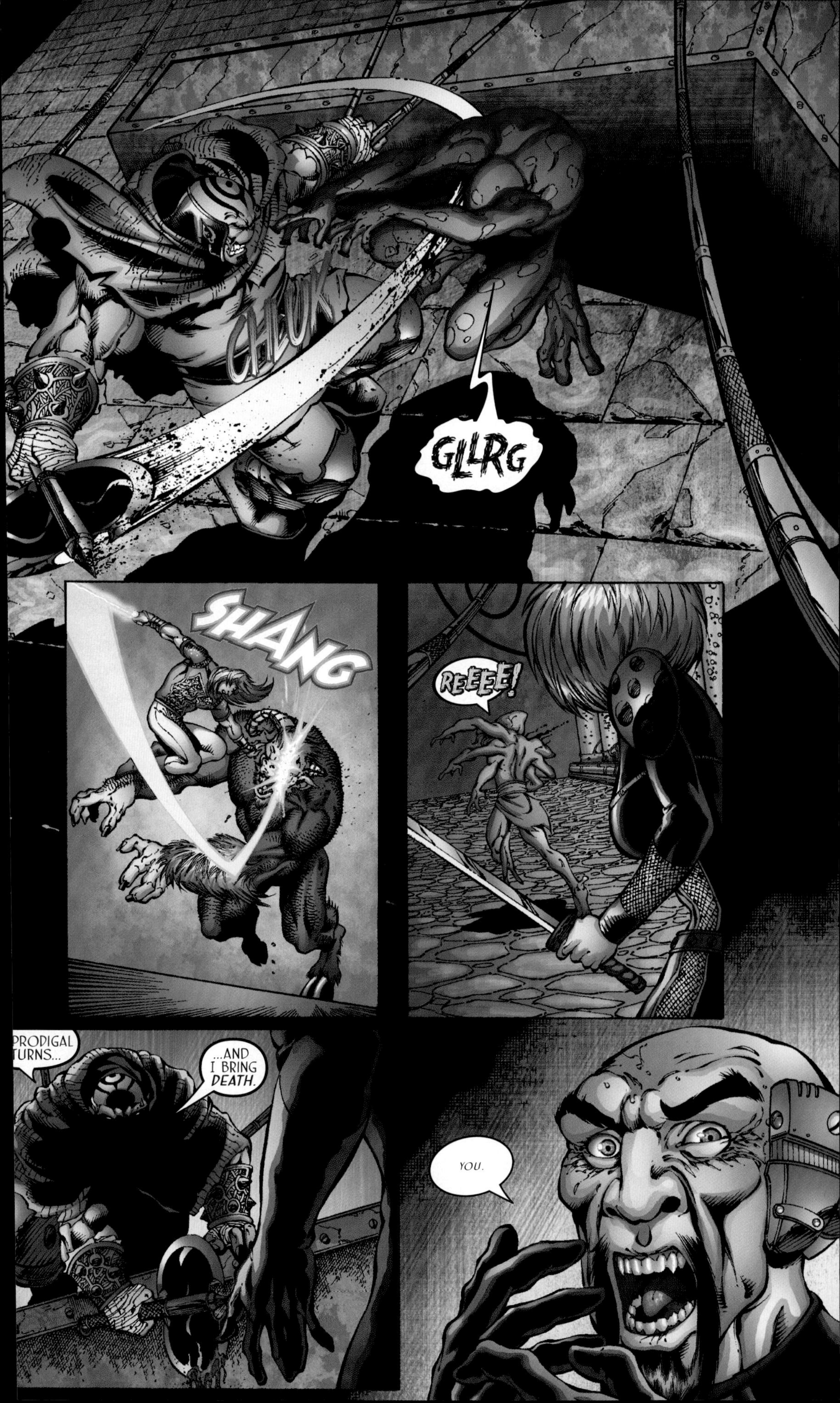
CHLUK
GLLRG
SHANG
REEEE!
PRODIGAL
TURNS...
...AND
I BRING
DEATH.
YOU.

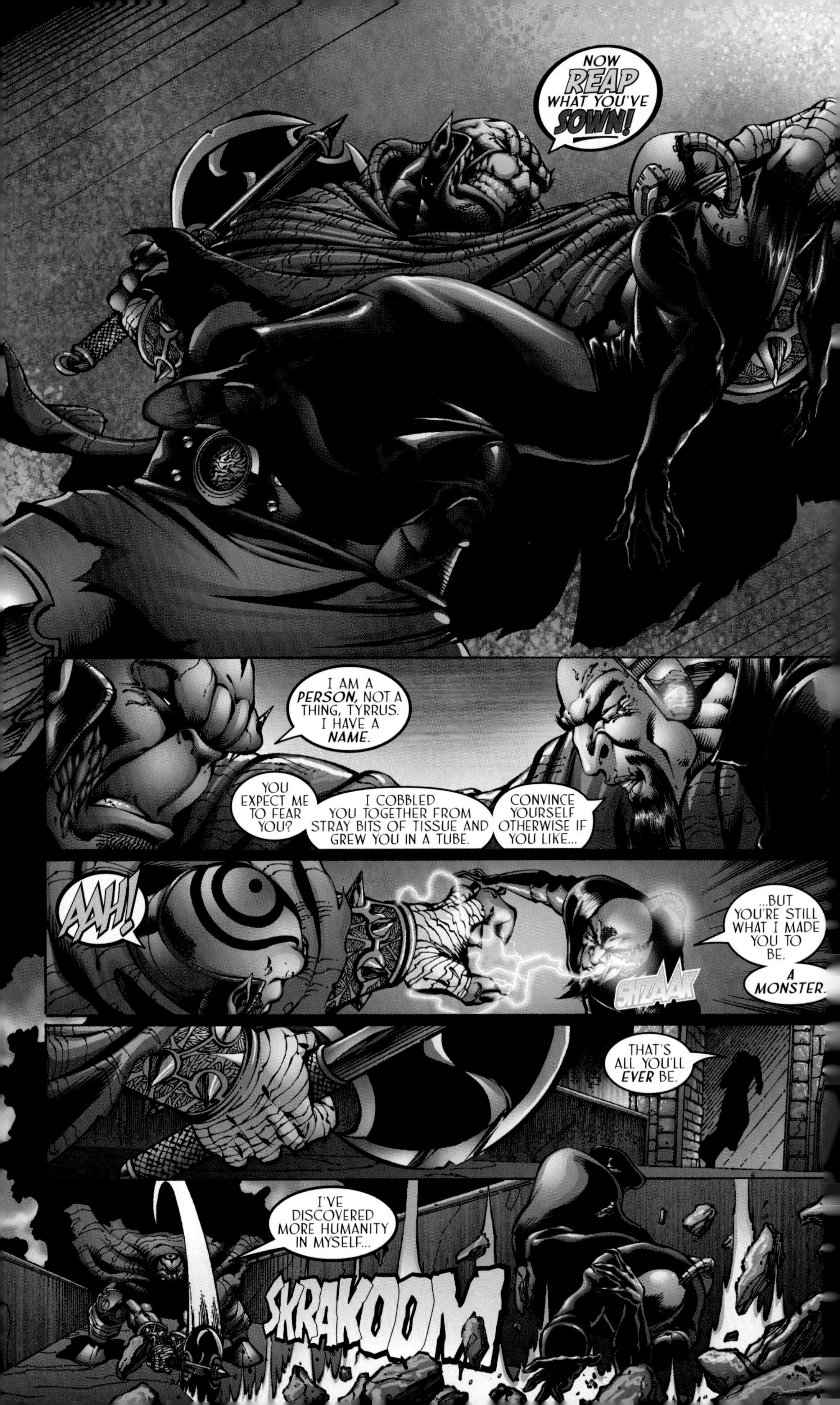

NOW REAP WHAT YOU'VE SOWN!
I AM A PERSON, NOT A THING, TYRRUS. I HAVE A NAME.
YOU EXPECT ME TO FEAR YOU?
I COBBLED YOU TOGETHER FROM STRAY BITS OF TISSUE AND GREW YOU IN A TUBE.
CONVINCE YOURSELF OTHERWISE IF YOU LIKE...
AAH!
...BUT YOU'RE STILL WHAT I MADE YOU TO BE.
A MONSTER.
SHZAAK
THAT'S ALL YOU'LL EVER BE.
I'VE DISCOVERED MORE HUMANITY IN MYSELF...
SKRAKOOM

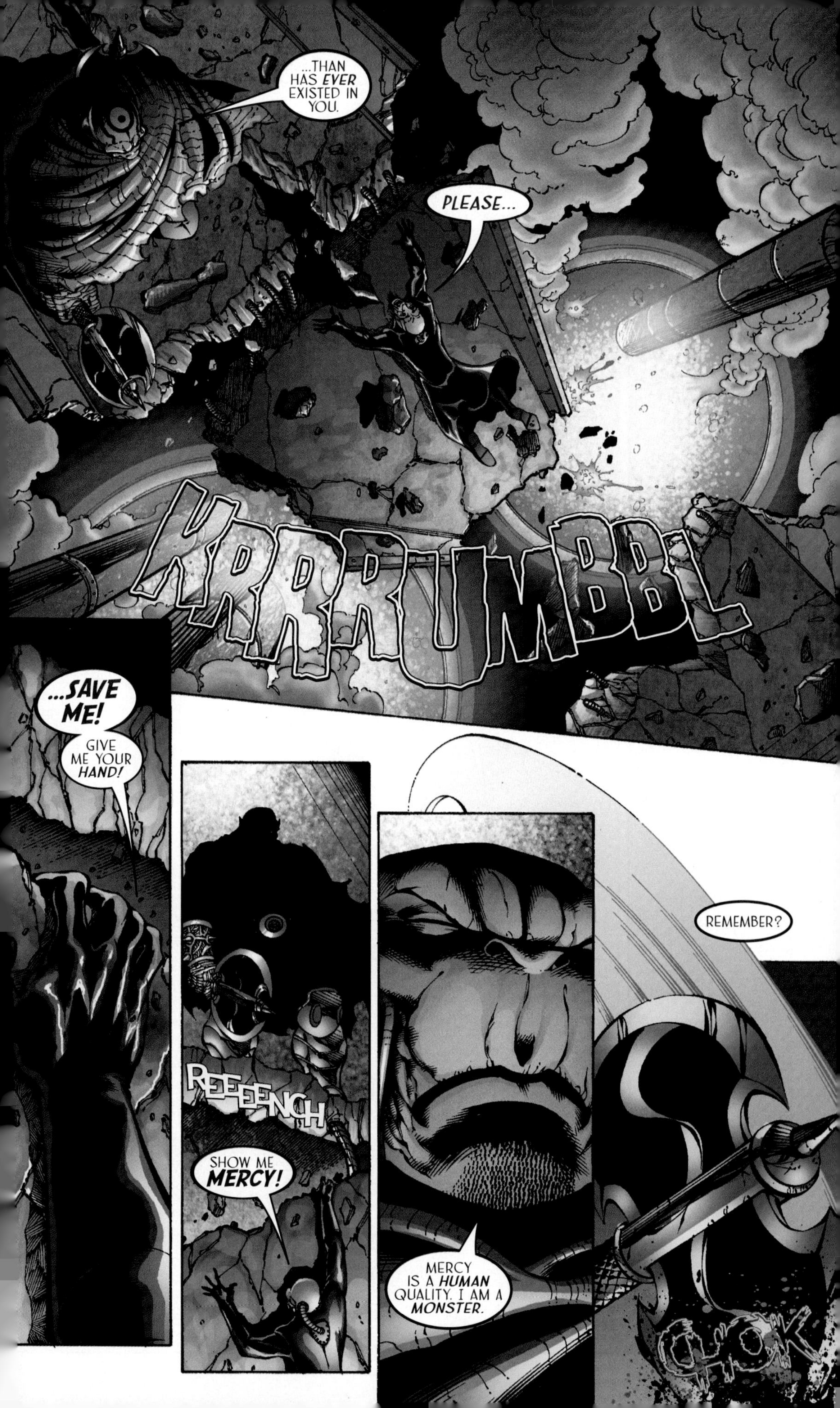
...THAN HAS EVER EXISTED IN YOU.
PLEASE...
KRRRUMBBL
...SAVE ME!
GIVE ME YOUR HAND!
REEEEENCH
SHOW ME MERCY!
MERCY IS A HUMAN QUALITY. I AM A MONSTER.
REMEMBER?
CHOK

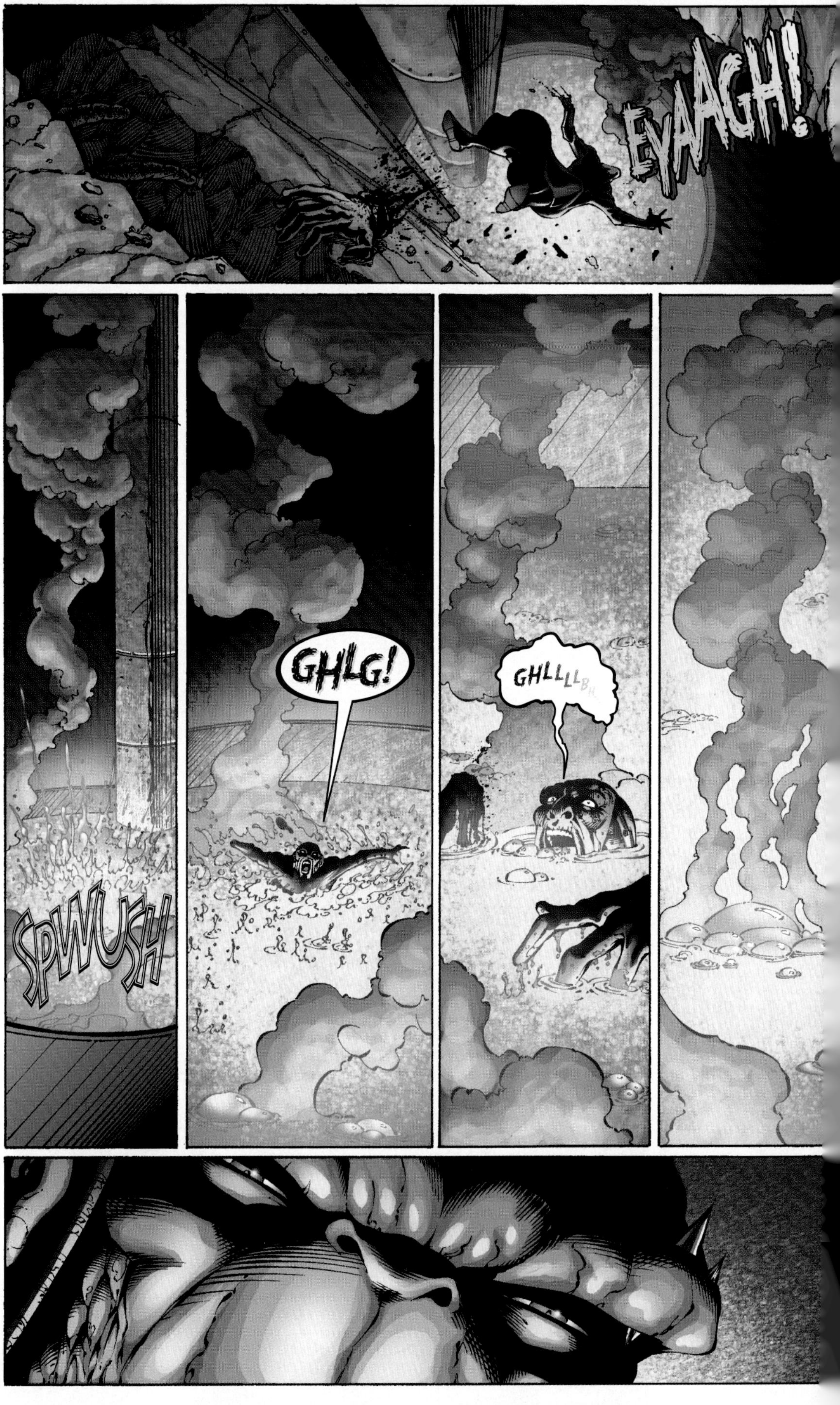
EYAAGH!
SPWUSH
GHLG!
GHLLLLBH

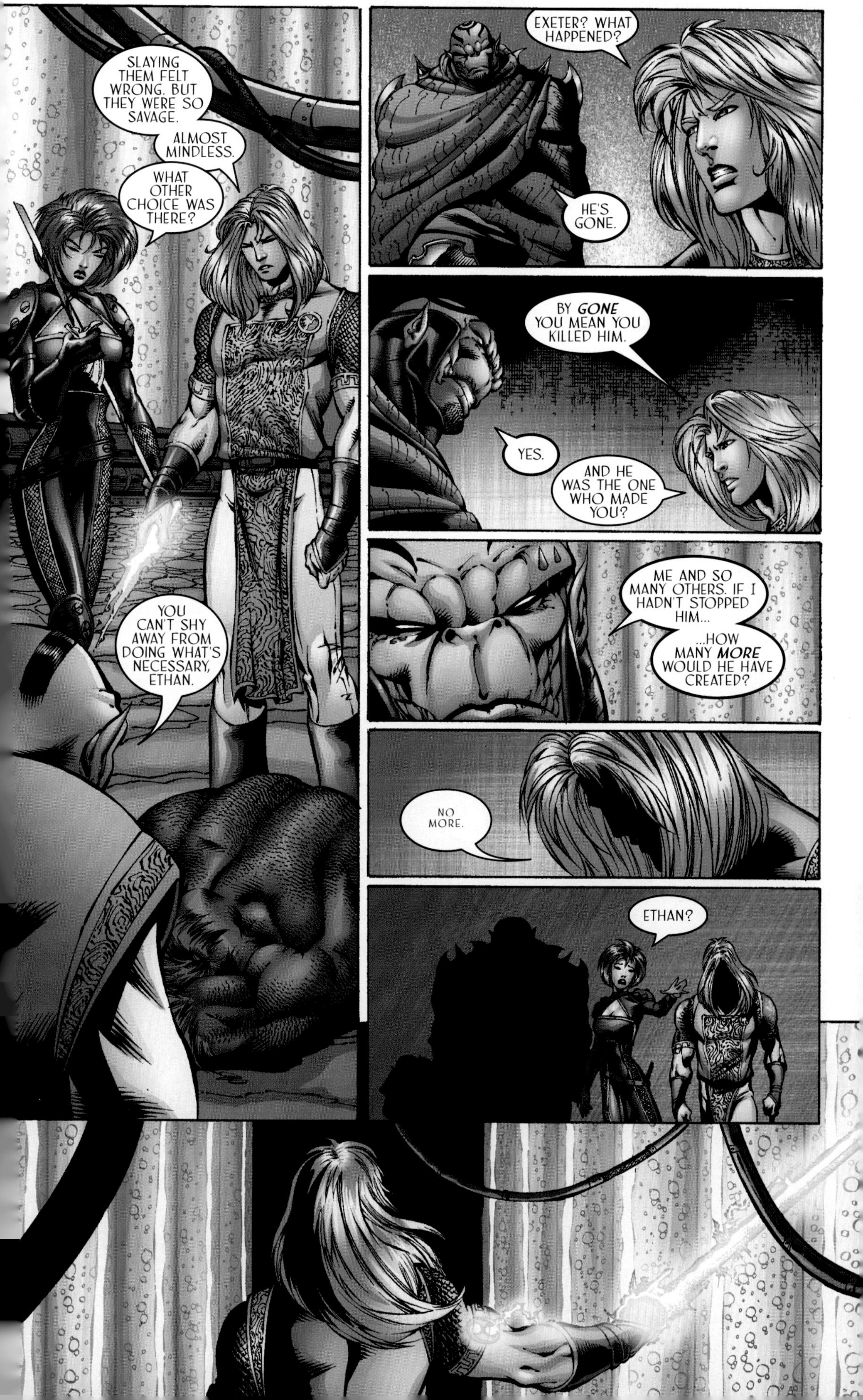
SLAYING THEM FELT WRONG. BUT THEY WERE SO SAVAGE.
ALMOST MINDLESS.
WHAT OTHER CHOICE WAS THERE?
YOU CAN'T SHY AWAY FROM DOING WHAT'S NECESSARY, ETHAN.
EXETER? WHAT HAPPENED?
HE'S GONE.
BY GONE YOU MEAN YOU KILLED HIM.
YES.
AND HE WAS THE ONE WHO MADE YOU?
ME AND SO MANY OTHERS. IF I HADN'T STOPPED HIM...
...HOW MANY MORE WOULD HE HAVE CREATED?
NO MORE.
ETHAN?

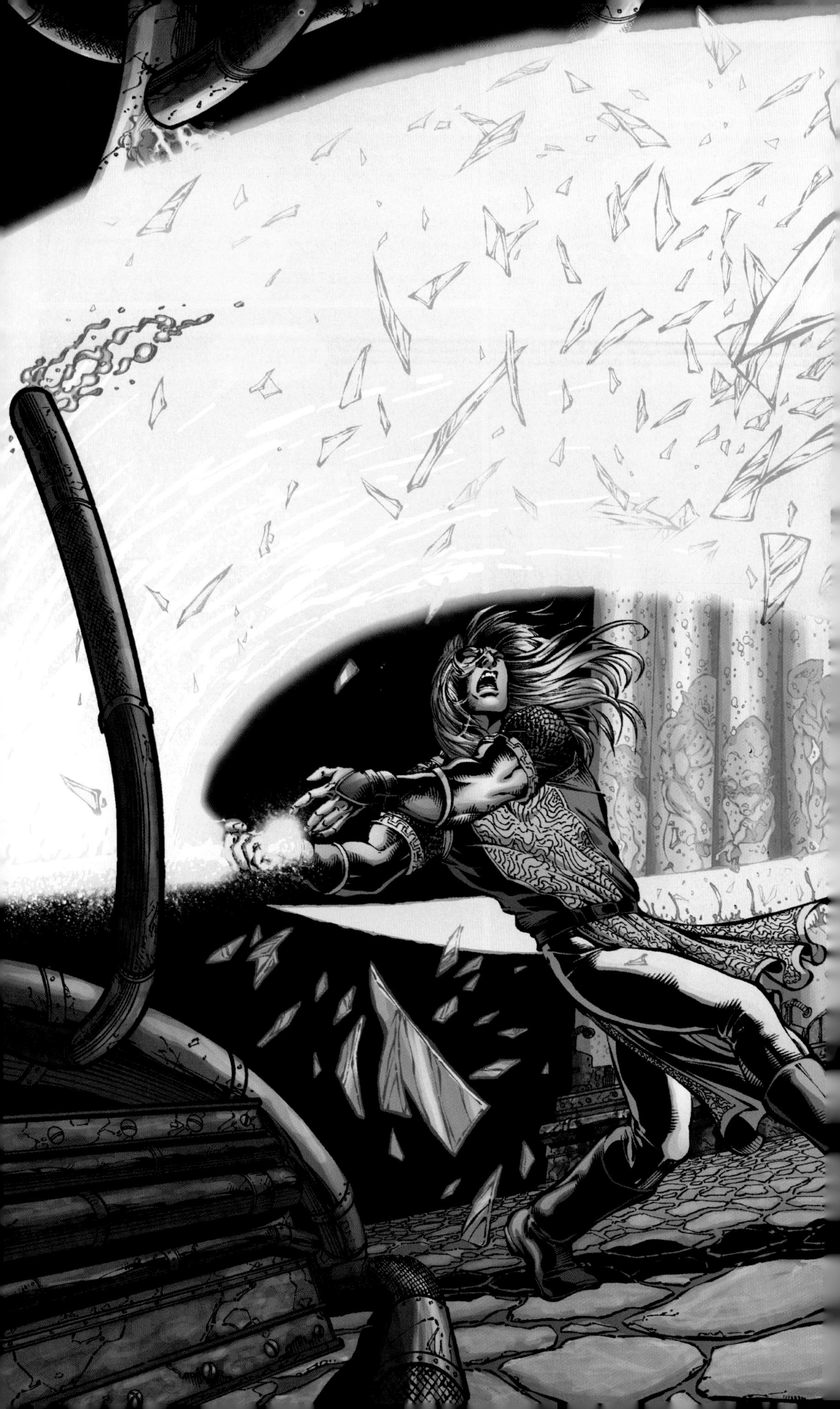

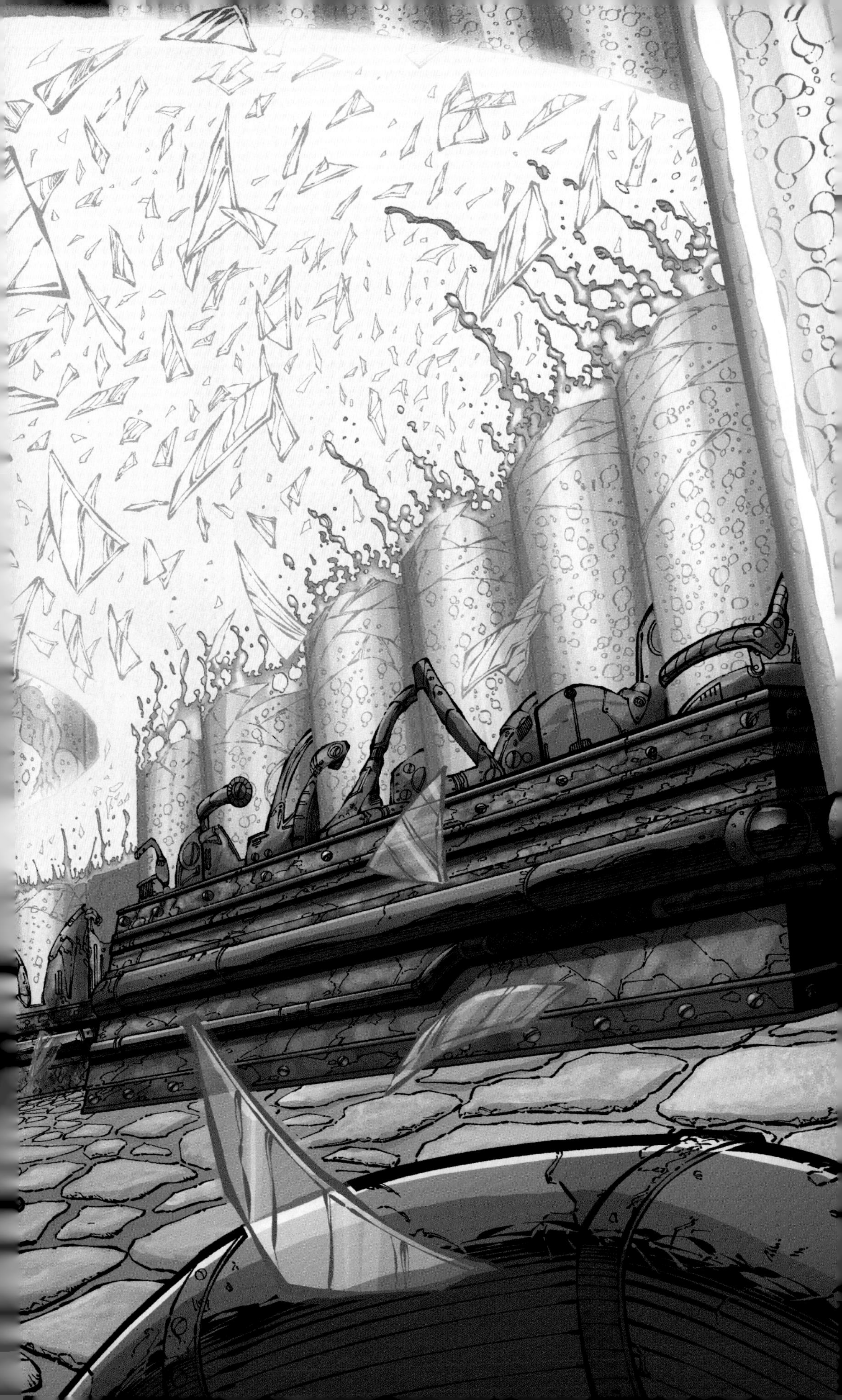

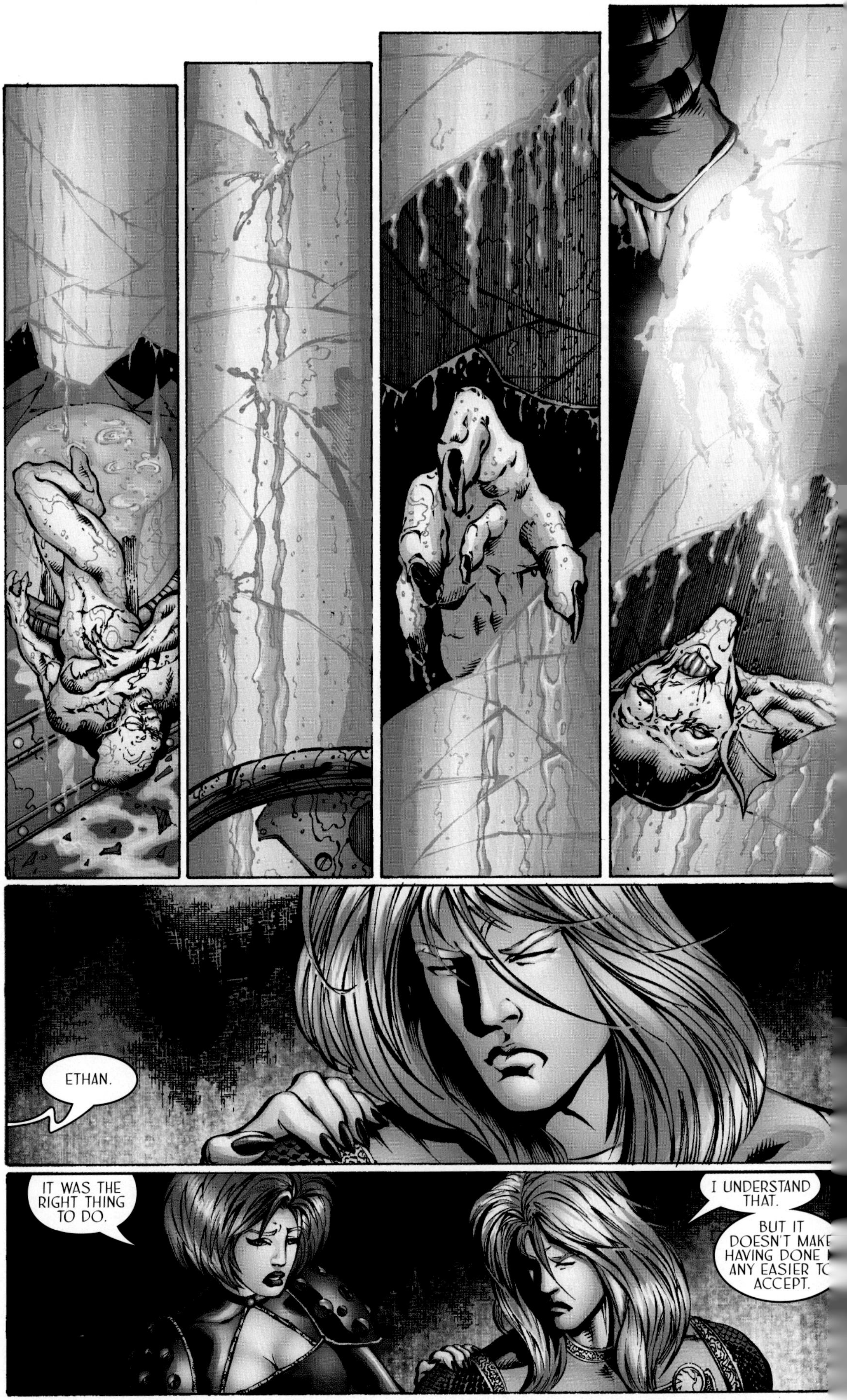
ETHAN.
IT WAS THE RIGHT THING TO DO.
I UNDERSTAND THAT.
BUT IT DOESN'T MAKE HAVING DONE ANY EASIER TO ACCEPT.

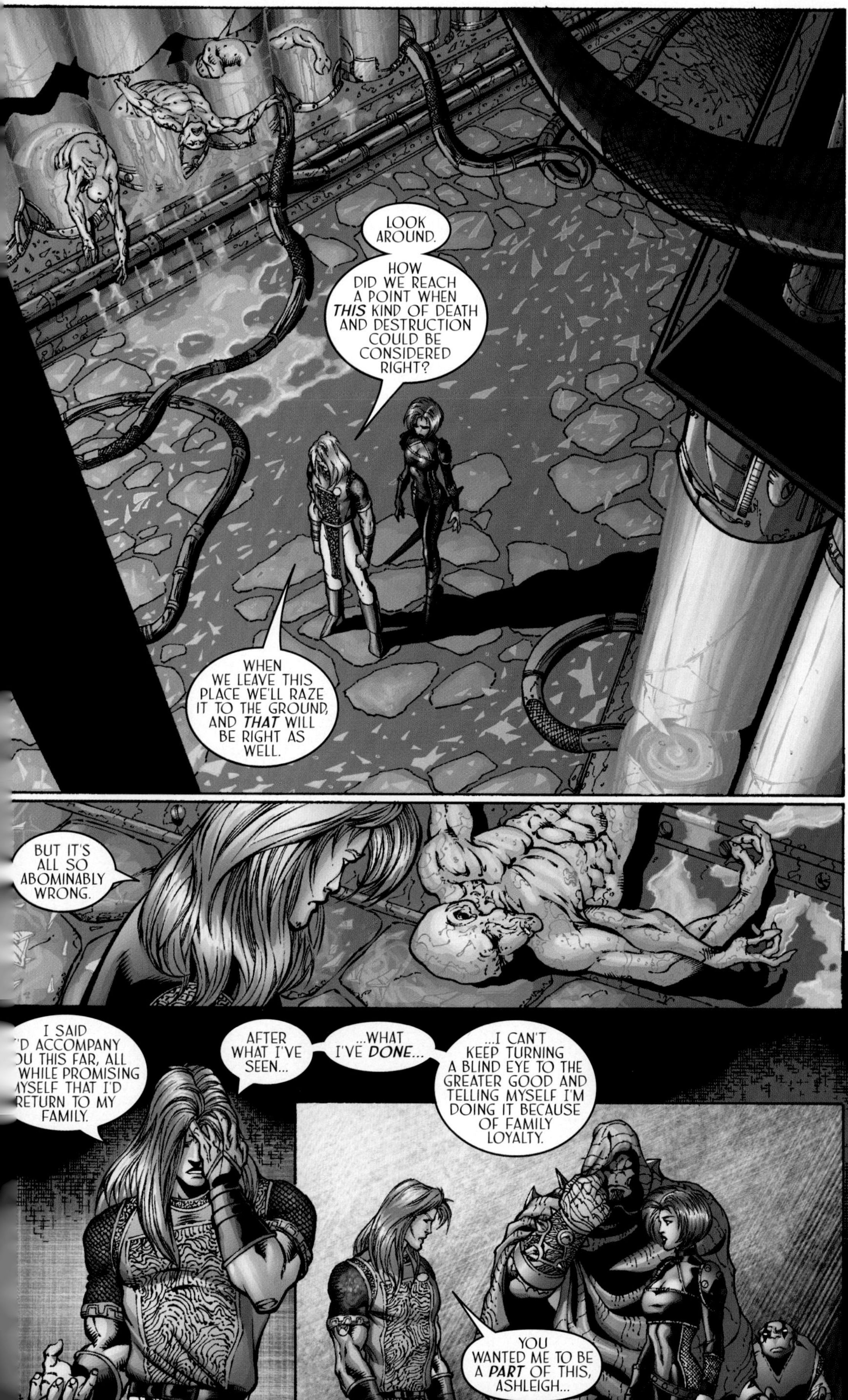
LOOK AROUND.
HOW DID WE REACH A POINT WHEN THIS KIND OF DEATH AND DESTRUCTION COULD BE CONSIDERED RIGHT?
WHEN WE LEAVE THIS PLACE WE'LL RAZE IT TO THE GROUND, AND THAT WILL BE RIGHT AS WELL.
BUT IT'S ALL SO ABOMINABLY WRONG.
I SAID I'D ACCOMPANY YOU THIS FAR, ALL THE WHILE PROMISING MYSELF THAT I'D RETURN TO MY FAMILY.
AFTER WHAT I'VE SEEN...
...WHAT I'VE DONE...
...I CAN'T KEEP TURNING A BLIND EYE TO THE GREATER GOOD AND TELLING MYSELF I'M DOING IT BECAUSE OF FAMILY LOYALTY.
YOU WANTED ME TO BE A PART OF THIS, ASHLEIGH...

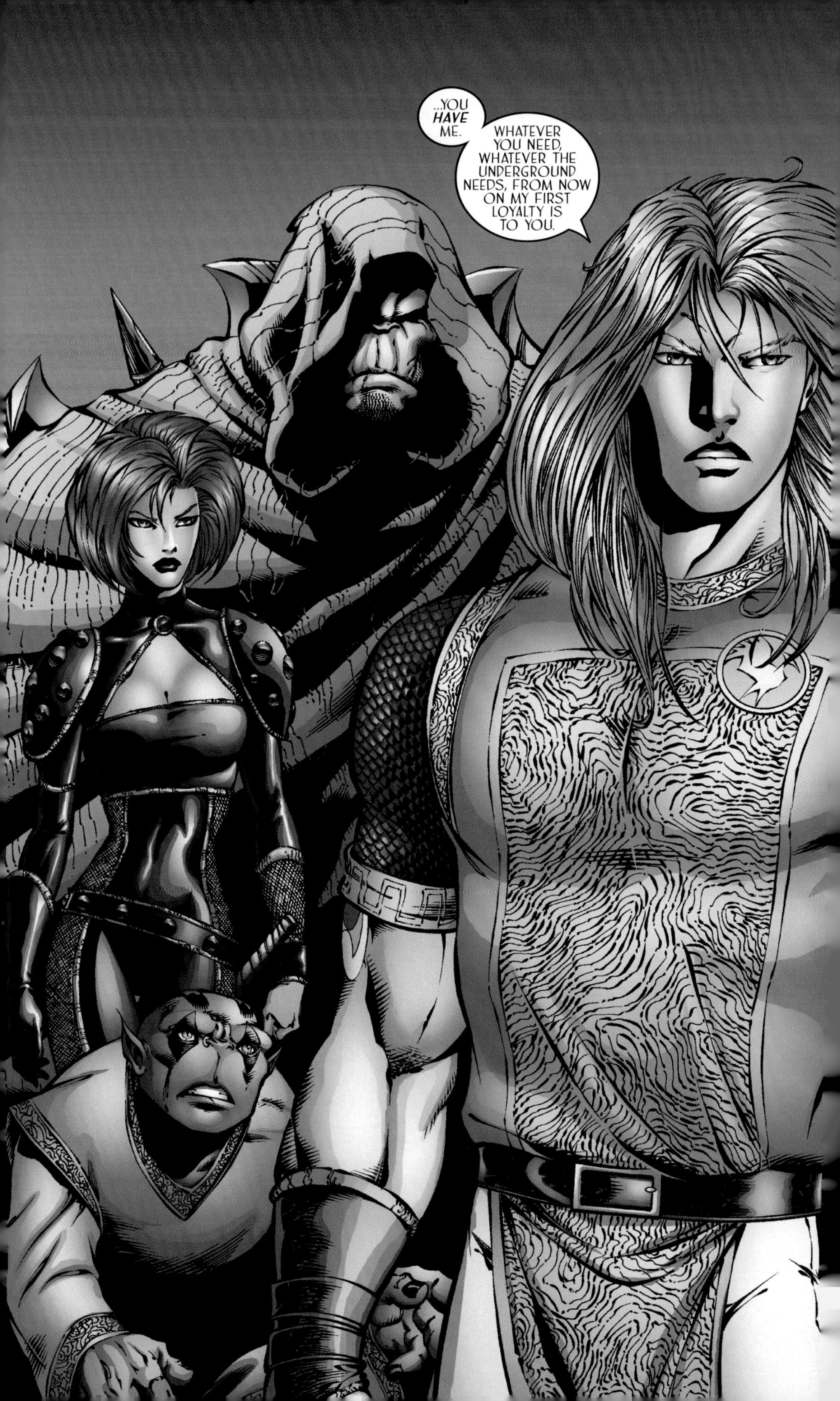
...YOU HAVE ME.
WHATEVER YOU NEED, WHATEVER THE UNDERGROUND NEEDS, FROM NOW ON MY FIRST LOYALTY IS TO YOU.

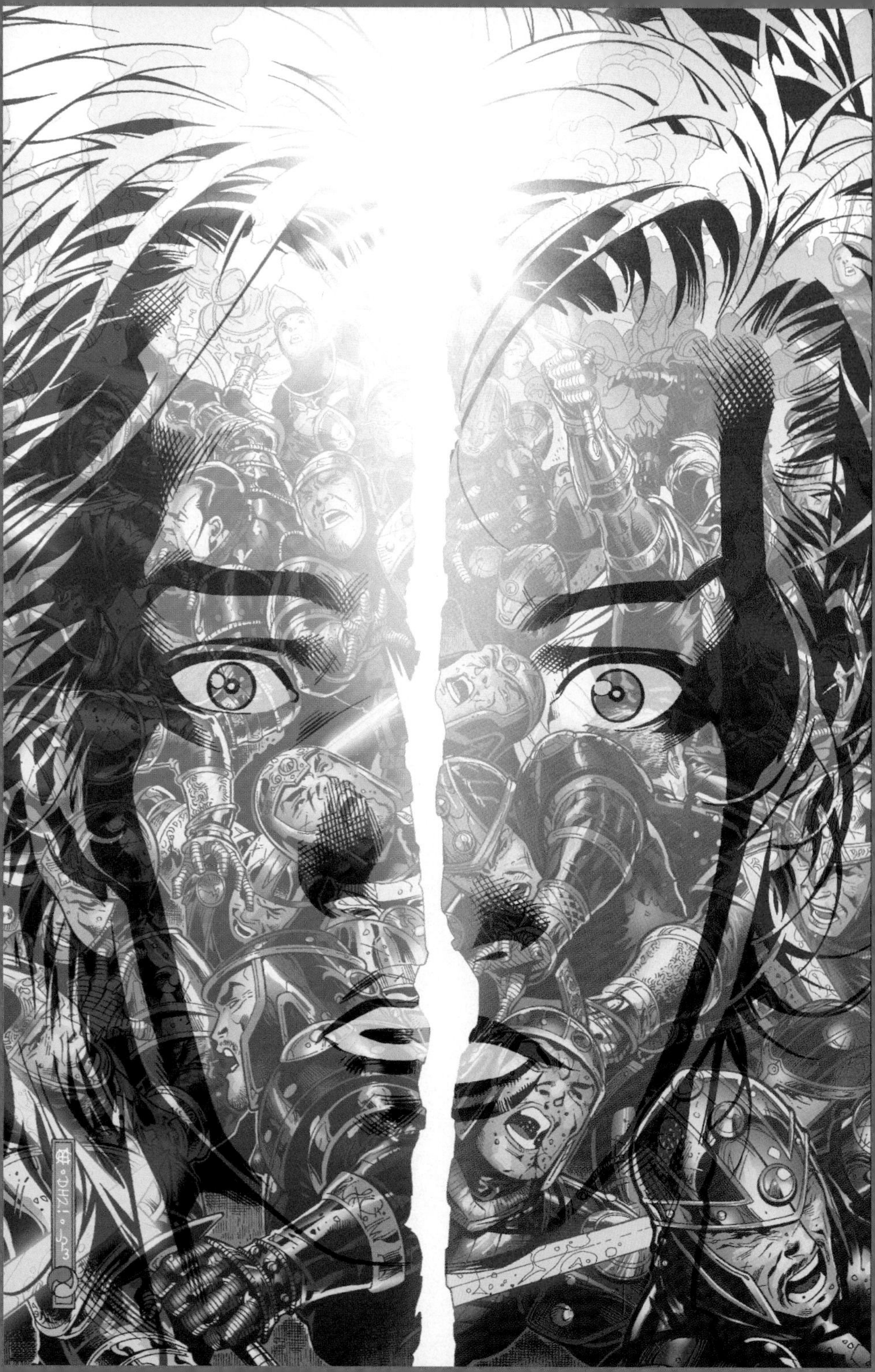

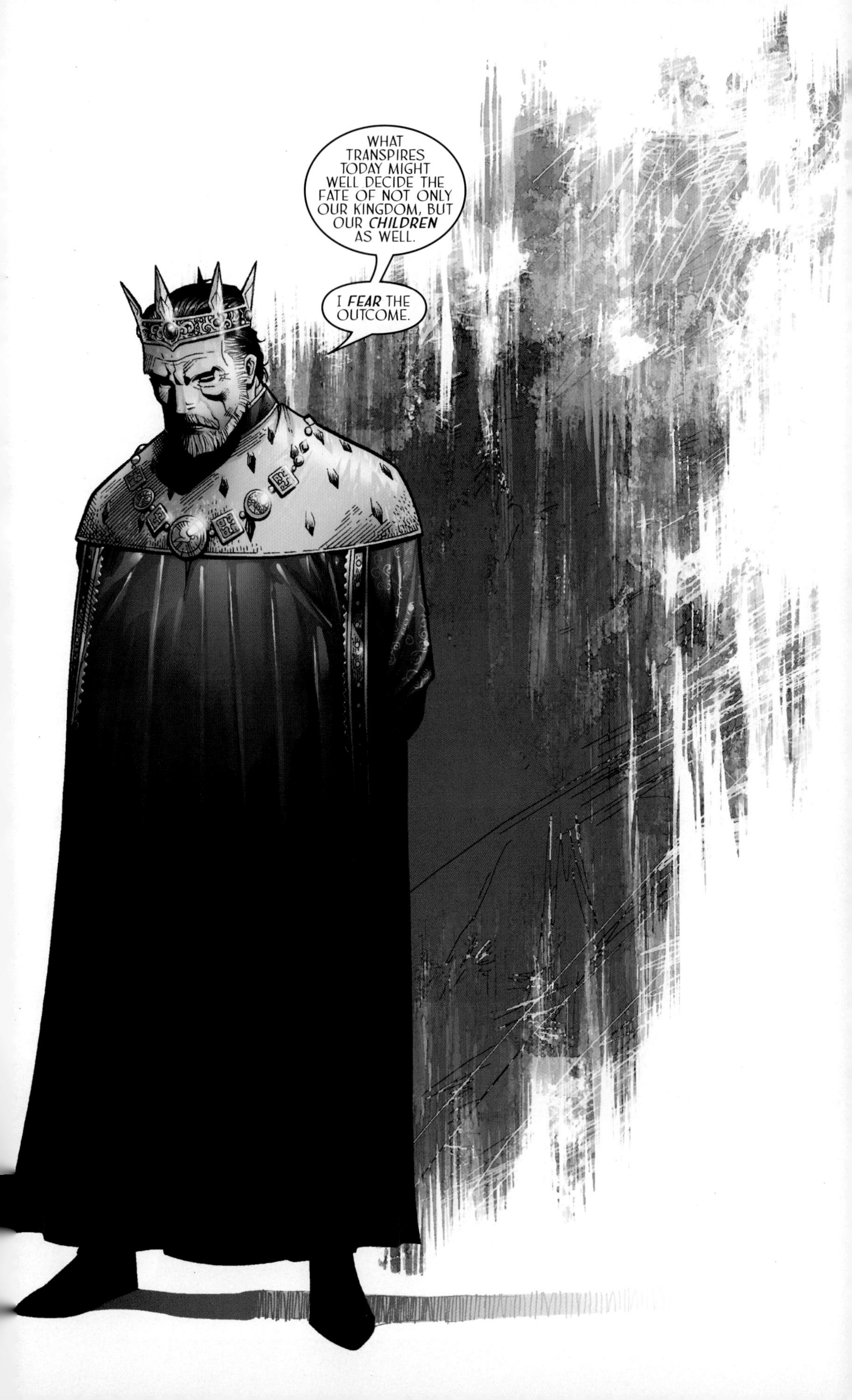
WHAT TRANSPIRES TODAY MIGHT WELL DECIDE THE FATE OF NOT ONLY OUR KINGDOM, BUT OUR *CHILDREN* AS WELL.
I *FEAR* THE OUTCOME.

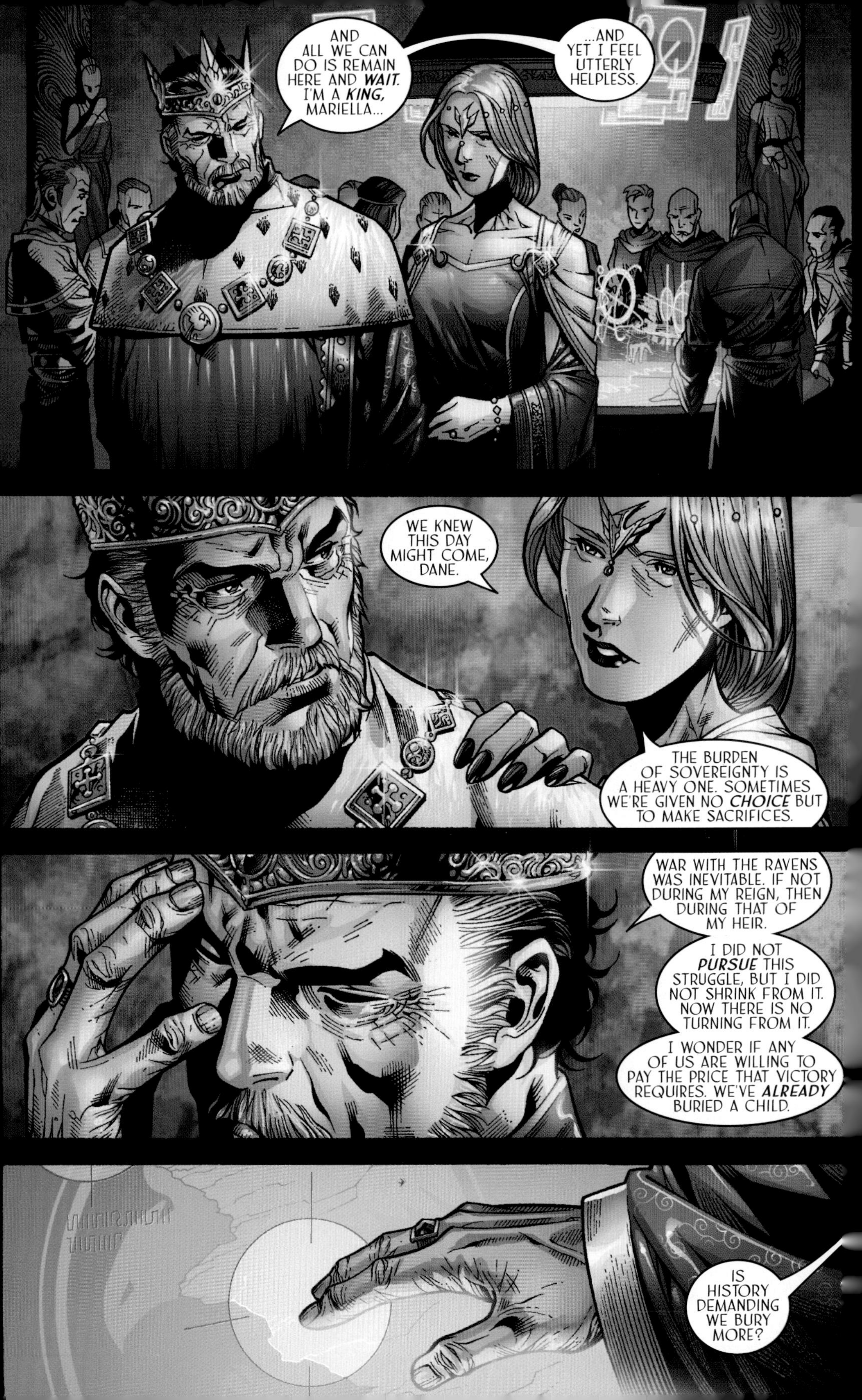

AND ALL WE CAN DO IS REMAIN HERE AND WAIT. I'M A KING, MARIELLA...
...AND YET I FEEL UTTERLY HELPLESS.
WE KNEW THIS DAY MIGHT COME, DANE.
THE BURDEN OF SOVEREIGNTY IS A HEAVY ONE. SOMETIMES WE'RE GIVEN NO CHOICE BUT TO MAKE SACRIFICES.
WAR WITH THE RAVENS WAS INEVITABLE. IF NOT DURING MY REIGN, THEN DURING THAT OF MY HEIR.
I DID NOT PURSUE THIS STRUGGLE, BUT I DID NOT SHRINK FROM IT. NOW THERE IS NO TURNING FROM IT.
I WONDER IF ANY OF US ARE WILLING TO PAY THE PRICE THAT VICTORY REQUIRES. WE'VE ALREADY BURIED A CHILD.
IS HISTORY DEMANDING WE BURY MORE?

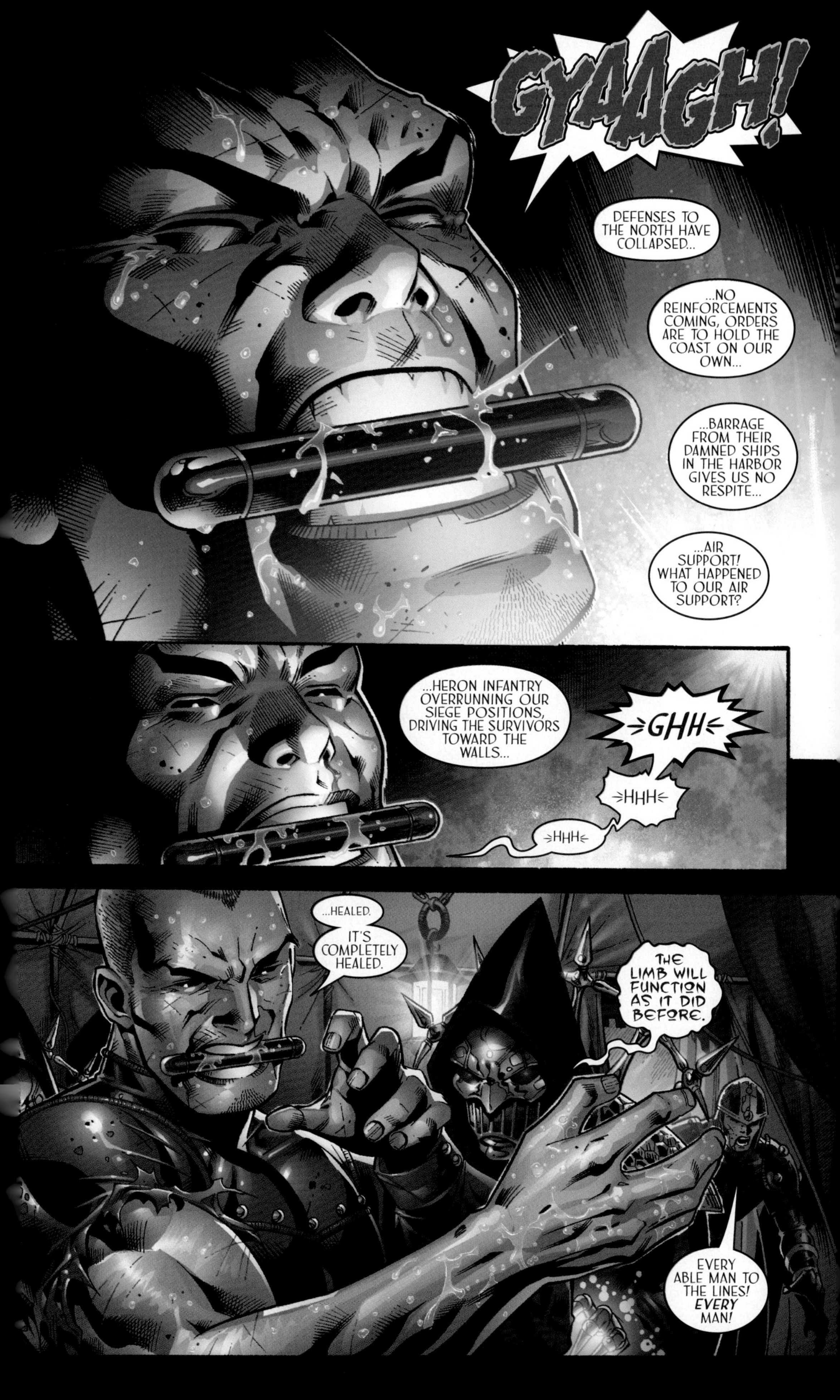
GYAAGH!
DEFENSES TO THE NORTH HAVE COLLAPSED...
...NO REINFORCEMENTS COMING, ORDERS ARE TO HOLD THE COAST ON OUR OWN...
...BARRAGE FROM THEIR DAMNED SHIPS IN THE HARBOR GIVES US NO RESPITE...
...AIR SUPPORT! WHAT HAPPENED TO OUR AIR SUPPORT?
...HERON INFANTRY OVERRUNNING OUR SIEGE POSITIONS, DRIVING THE SURVIVORS TOWARD THE WALLS...
GHH
HHH
HHH
...HEALED.
IT'S COMPLETELY HEALED.
THE LIMB WILL FUNCTION AS IT DID BEFORE.
EVERY ABLE MAN TO THE LINES! *EVERY* MAN!

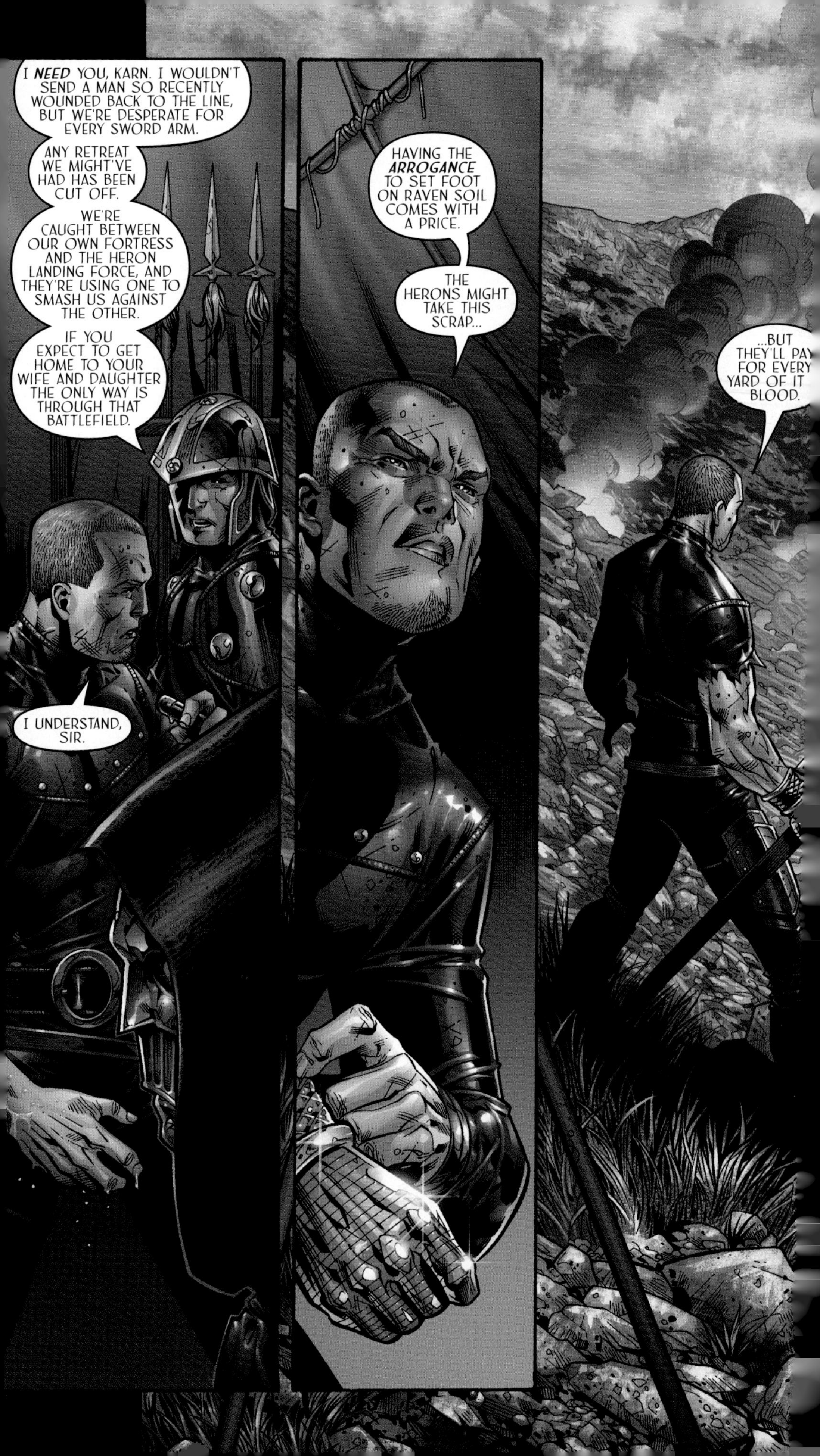

I **NEED** YOU, KARN. I WOULDN'T SEND A MAN SO RECENTLY WOUNDED BACK TO THE LINE, BUT WE'RE DESPERATE FOR EVERY SWORD ARM.
ANY RETREAT WE MIGHT'VE HAD HAS BEEN CUT OFF.
WE'RE CAUGHT BETWEEN OUR OWN FORTRESS AND THE HERON LANDING FORCE, AND THEY'RE USING ONE TO SMASH US AGAINST THE OTHER.
IF YOU EXPECT TO GET HOME TO YOUR WIFE AND DAUGHTER THE ONLY WAY IS THROUGH THAT BATTLEFIELD.
I UNDERSTAND, SIR.
HAVING THE ***ARROGANCE*** TO SET FOOT ON RAVEN SOIL COMES WITH A PRICE.
THE HERONS MIGHT TAKE THIS SCRAP...
...BUT THEY'LL PAY FOR EVERY YARD OF IT BLOOD.

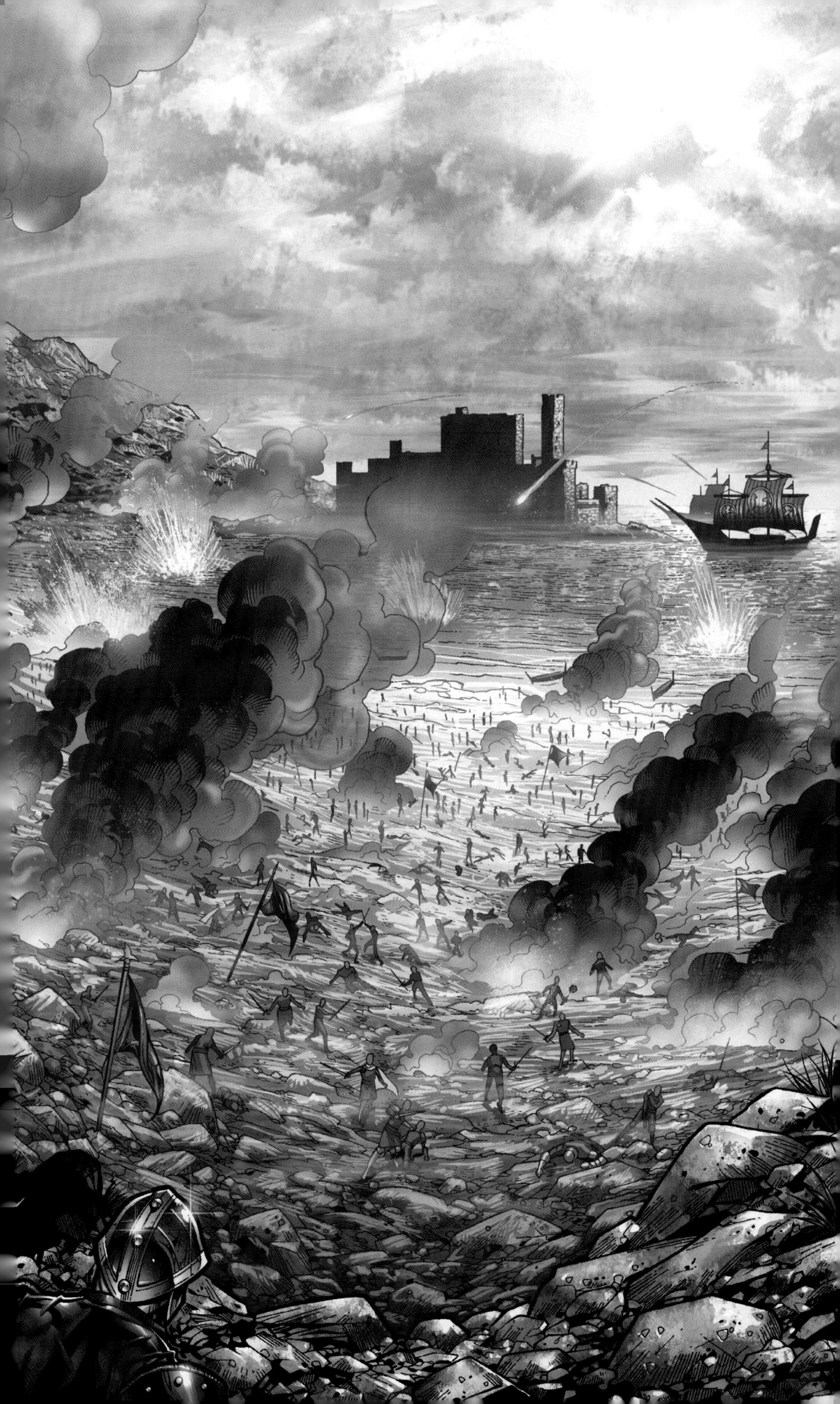

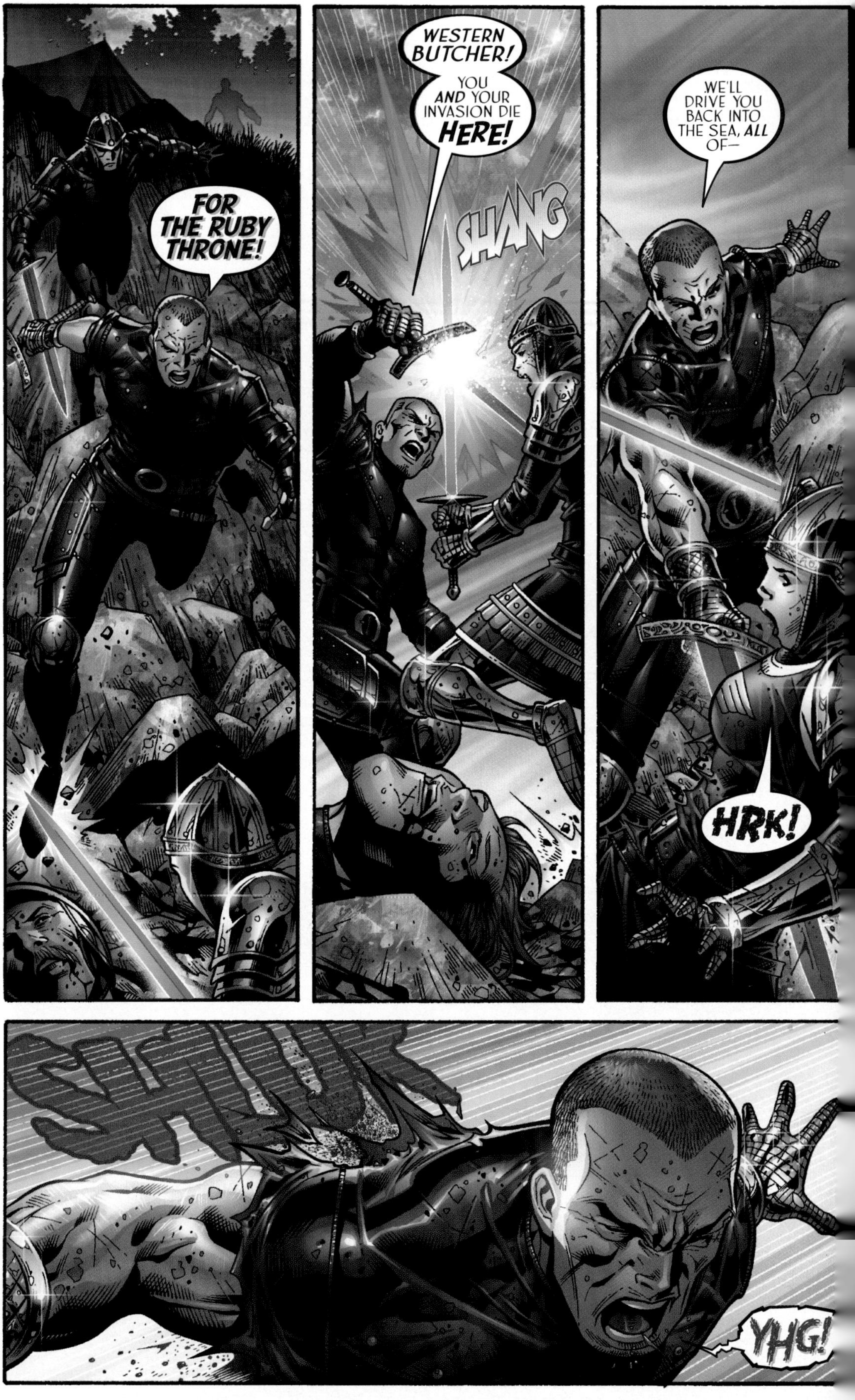
FOR THE RUBY THRONE!
WESTERN BUTCHER!
YOU AND YOUR INVASION DIE HERE!
SHANG
WE'LL DRIVE YOU BACK INTO THE SEA, ALL OF—
HRK!
YHG!

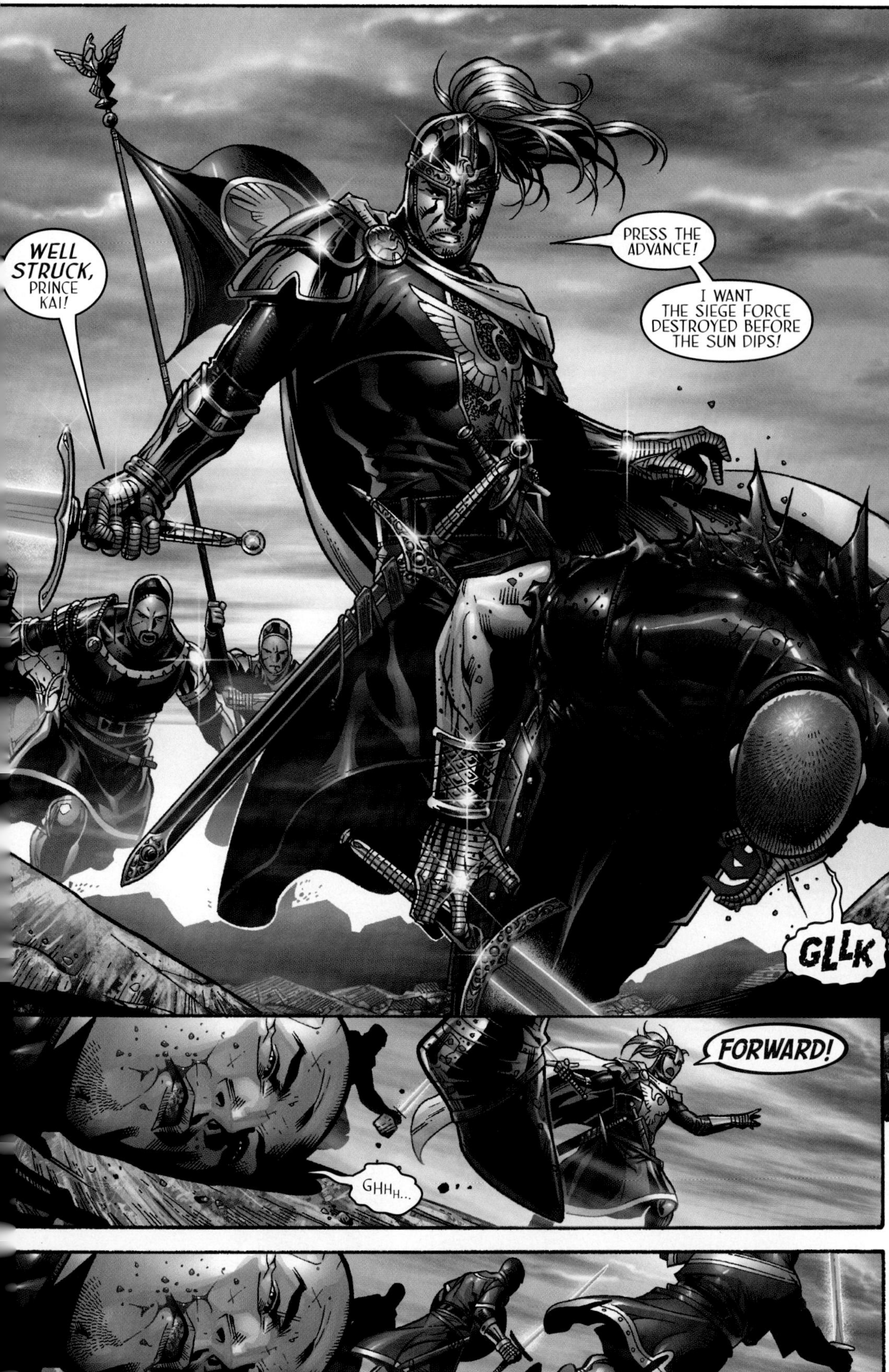
WELL STRUCK, PRINCE KAI!
PRESS THE ADVANCE!
I WANT THE SIEGE FORCE DESTROYED BEFORE THE SUN DIPS!
GLLK
FORWARD!
GHHH...

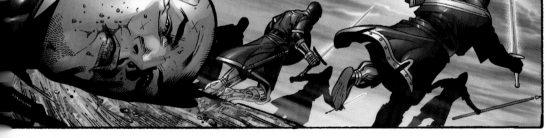

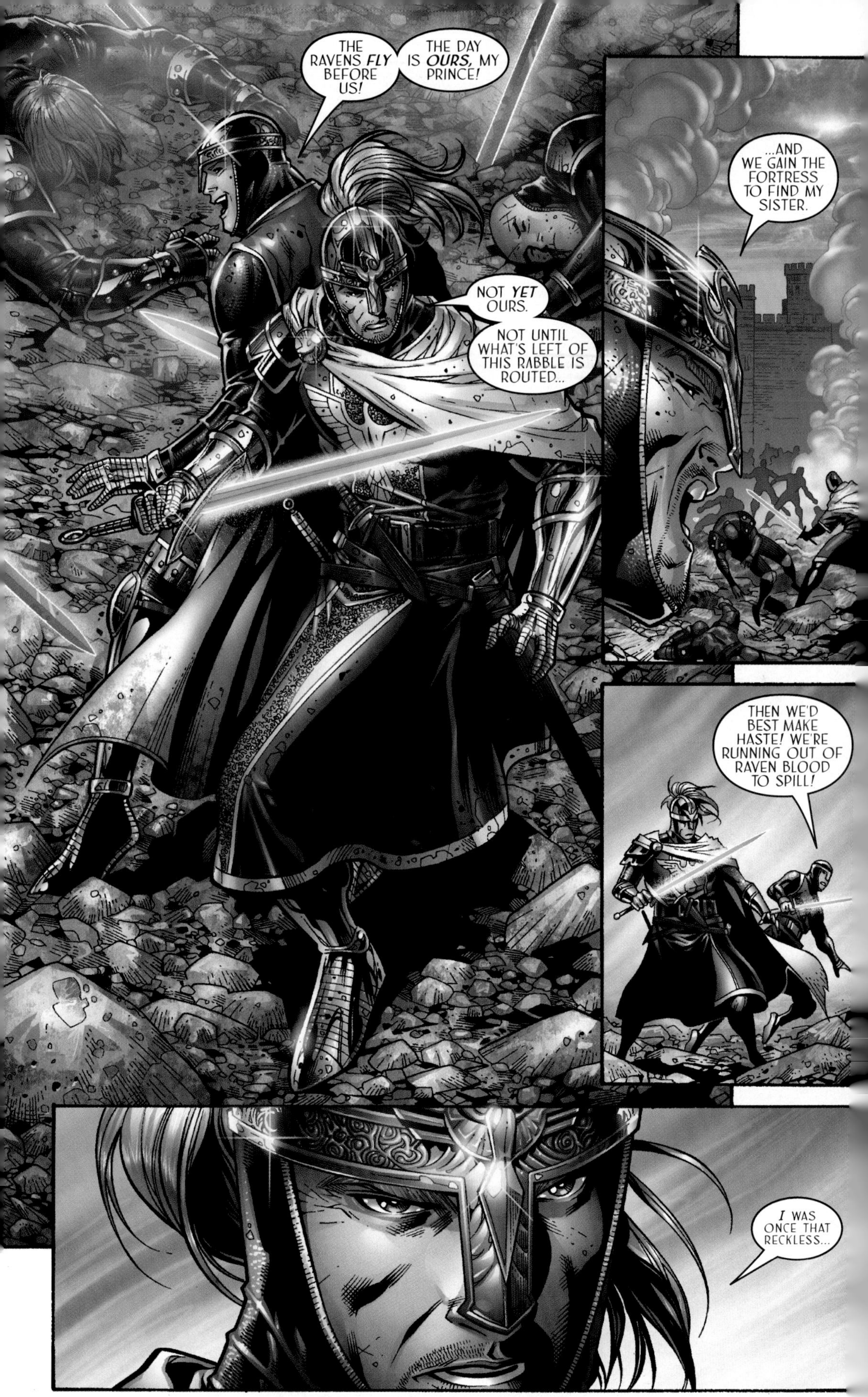
THE RAVENS FLY BEFORE US!
THE DAY IS OURS, MY PRINCE!
NOT YET OURS.
NOT UNTIL WHAT'S LEFT OF THIS RABBLE IS ROUTED...
...AND WE GAIN THE FORTRESS TO FIND MY SISTER.
THEN WE'D BEST MAKE HASTE! WE'RE RUNNING OUT OF RAVEN BLOOD TO SPILL!
I WAS ONCE THAT RECKLESS...

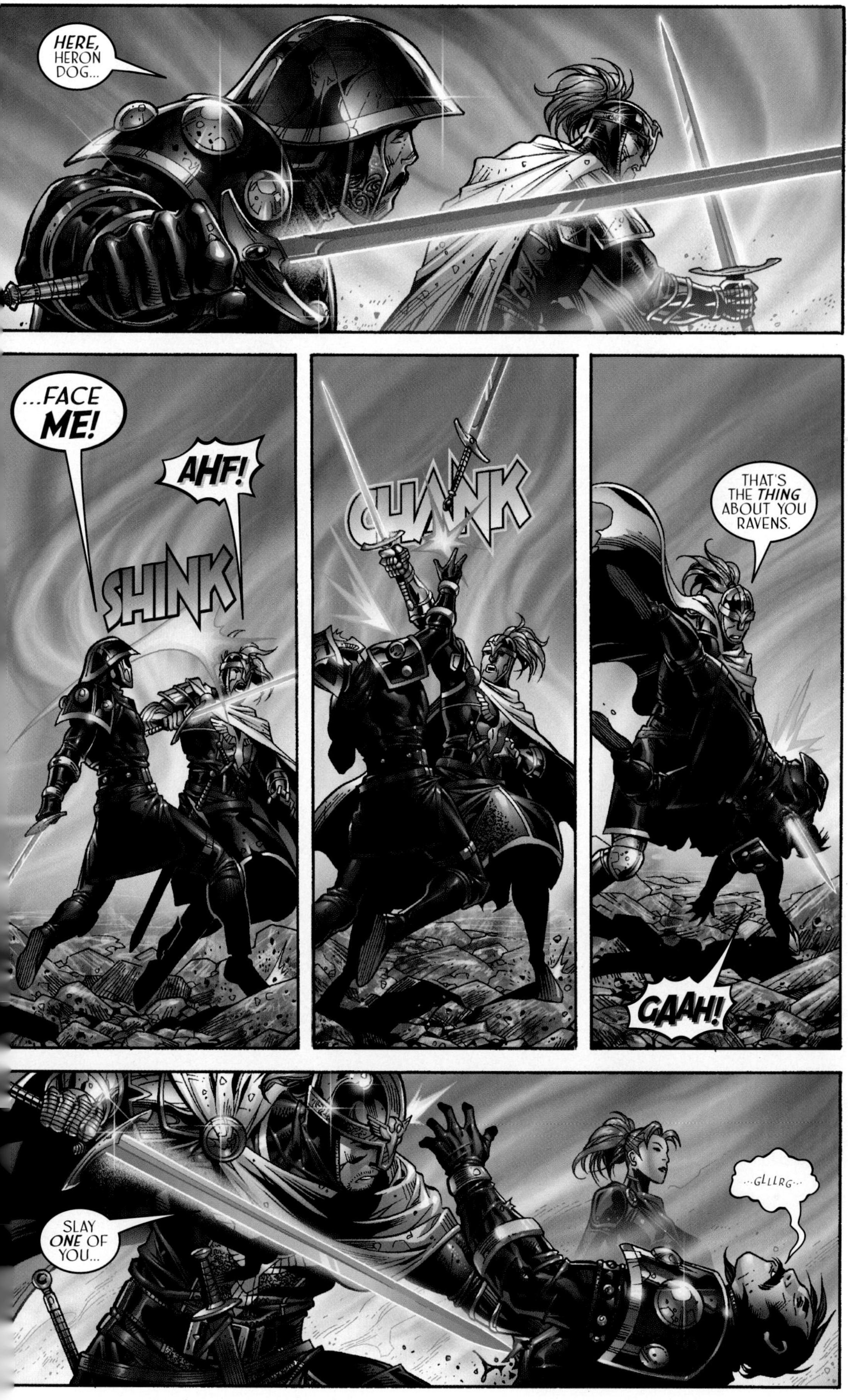
HERE, HERON DOG...
...FACE ME!
SHINK
AHF!
CLANK
THAT'S THE THING ABOUT YOU RAVENS.
GAAH!
SLAY ONE OF YOU...
...GLLLRG...

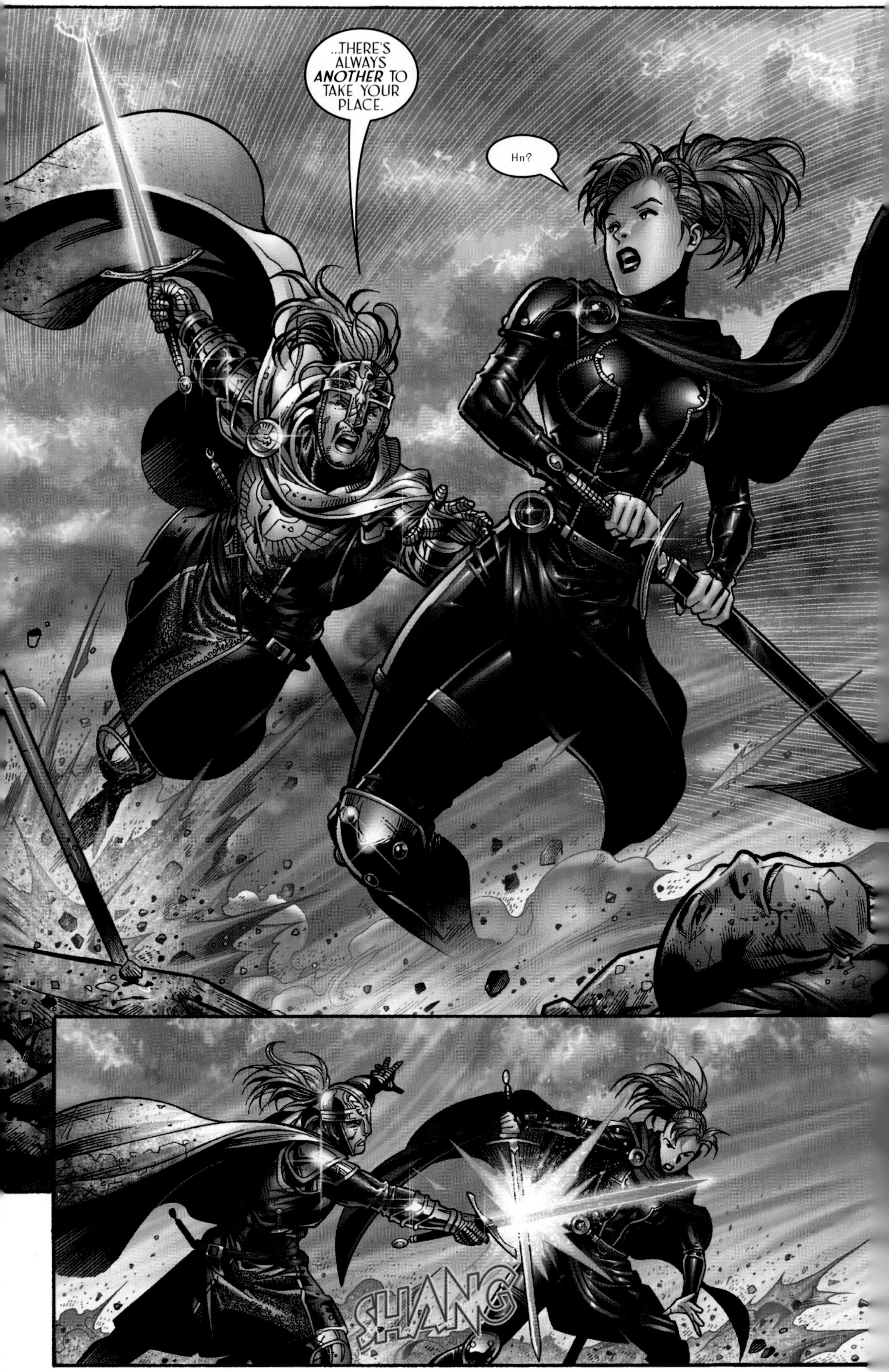
...THERE'S ALWAYS *ANOTHER* TO TAKE YOUR PLACE.
Hn?
SHANG

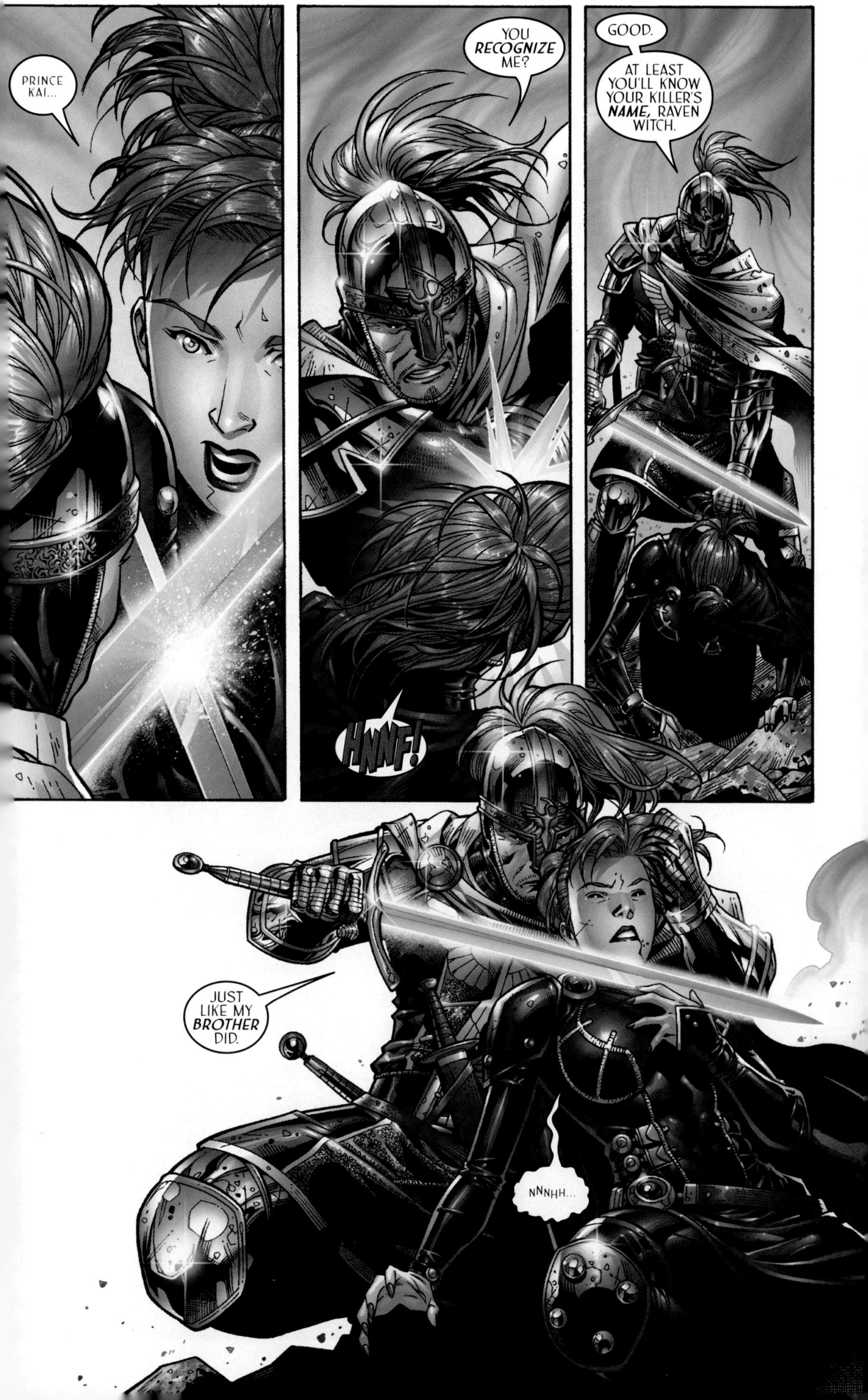
PRINCE KAI...
YOU RECOGNIZE ME?
HNNF!
GOOD.
AT LEAST YOU'LL KNOW YOUR KILLER'S NAME, RAVEN WITCH.
JUST LIKE MY BROTHER DID.
NNNHH...

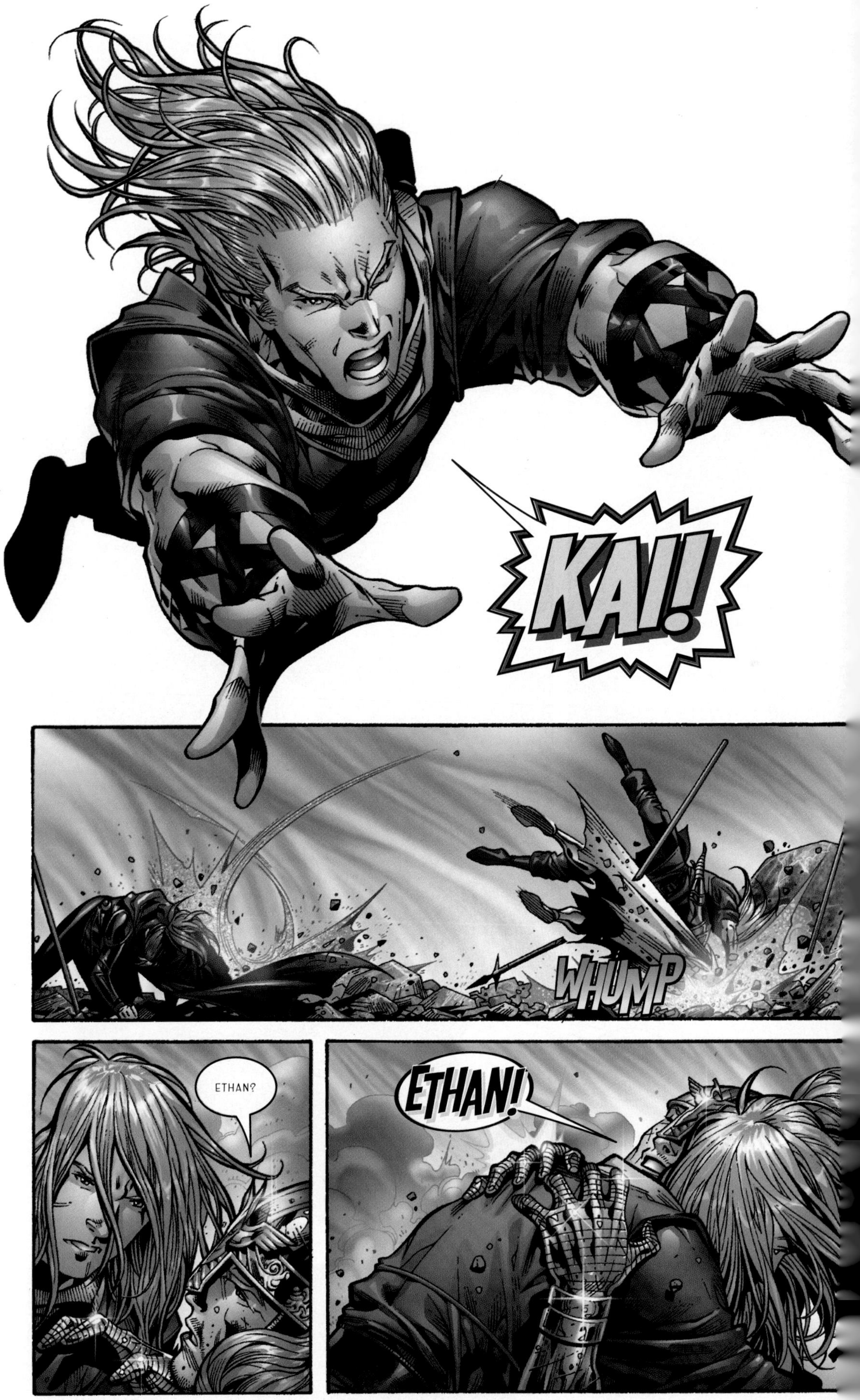
KAI!
WHUMP
ETHAN?
ETHAN!

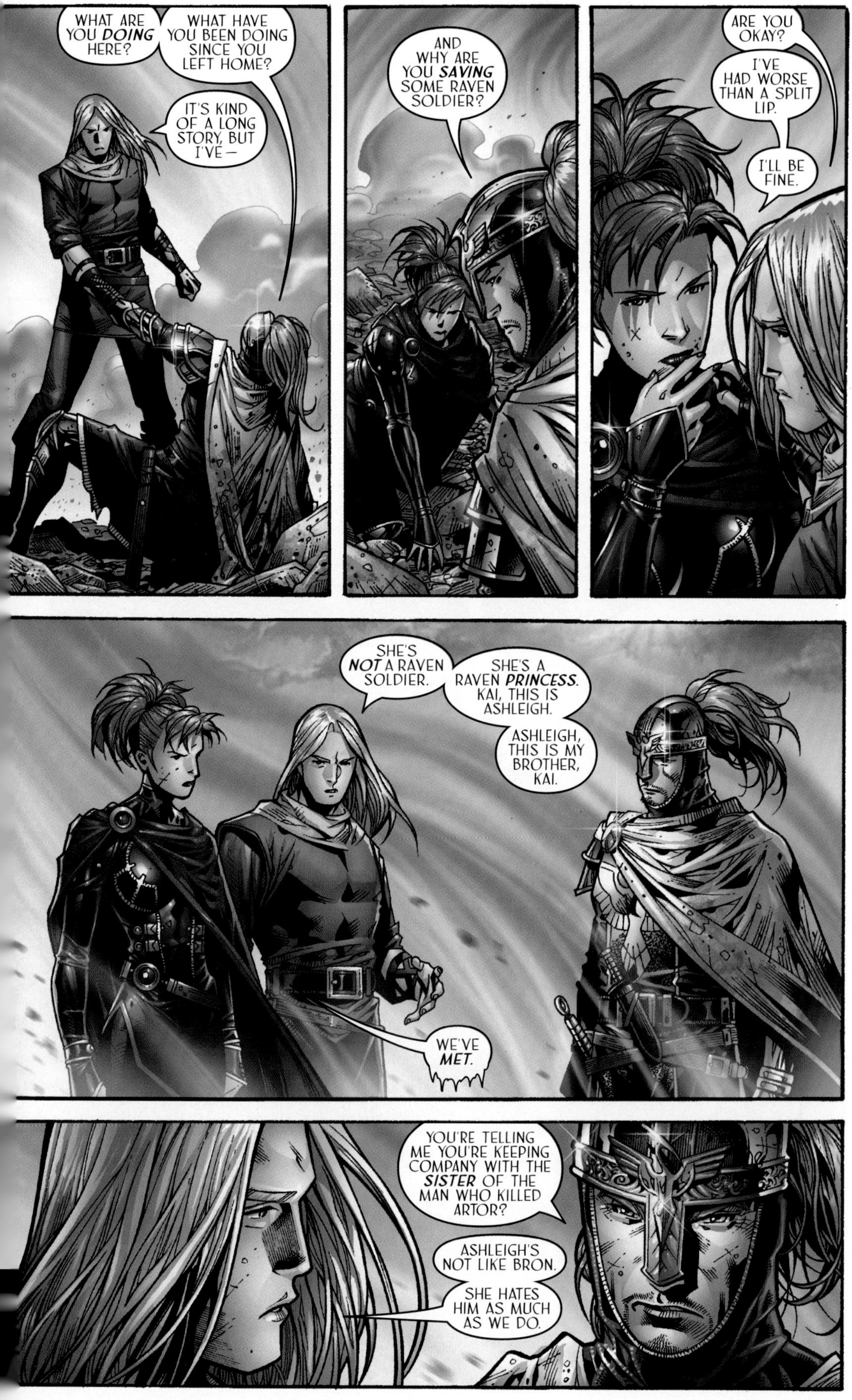

WHAT ARE YOU DOING HERE?
WHAT HAVE YOU BEEN DOING SINCE YOU LEFT HOME?
IT'S KIND OF A LONG STORY, BUT I'VE—
AND WHY ARE YOU SAVING SOME RAVEN SOLDIER?
ARE YOU OKAY?
I'VE HAD WORSE THAN A SPLIT LIP.
I'LL BE FINE.
SHE'S NOT A RAVEN SOLDIER.
SHE'S A RAVEN PRINCESS. KAI, THIS IS ASHLEIGH.
ASHLEIGH, THIS IS MY BROTHER, KAI.
WE'VE MET.
YOU'RE TELLING ME YOU'RE KEEPING COMPANY WITH THE SISTER OF THE MAN WHO KILLED ARTOR?
ASHLEIGH'S NOT LIKE BRON.
SHE HATES HIM AS MUCH AS WE DO.

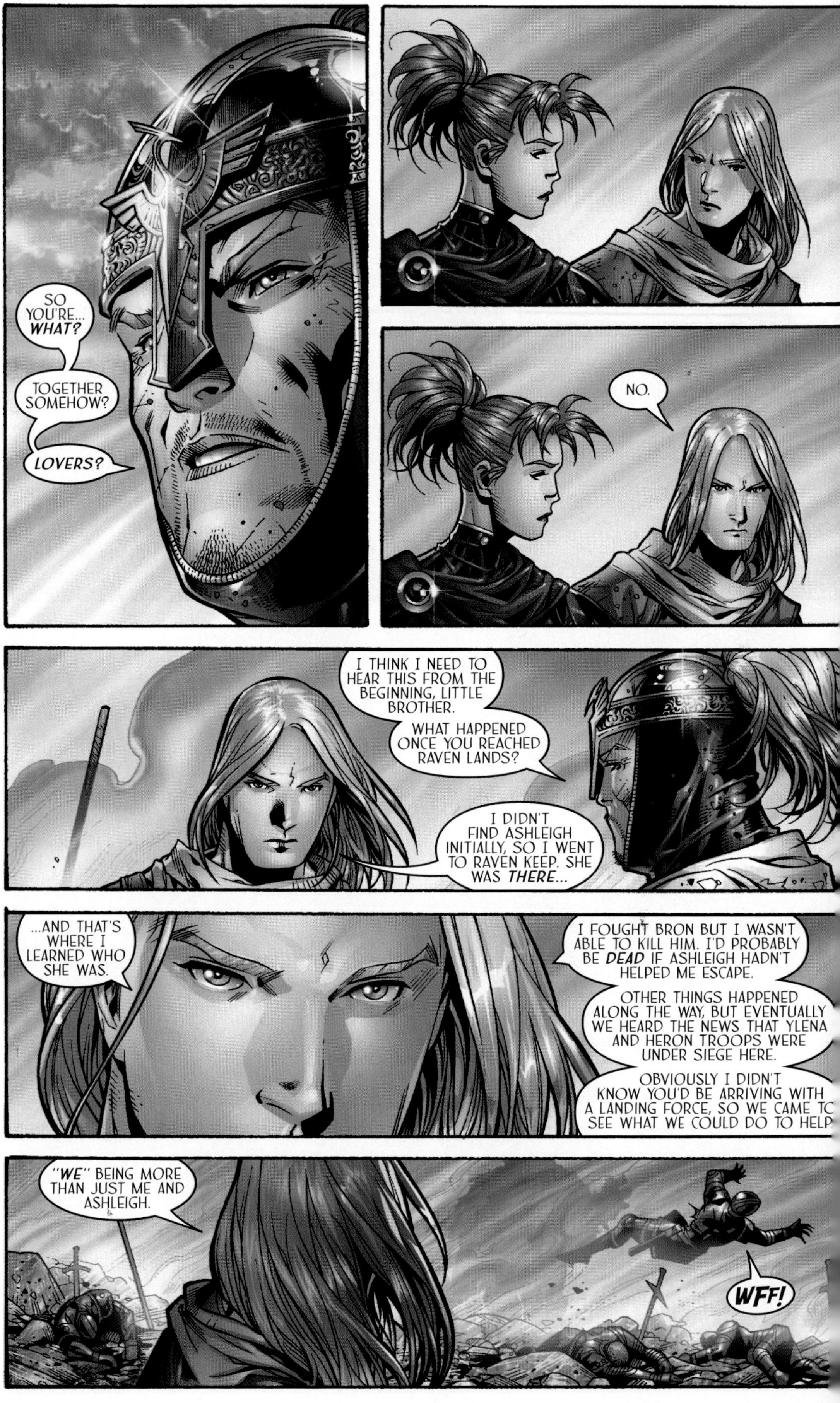

SO YOU'RE... WHAT?
TOGETHER SOMEHOW?
LOVERS?
NO.
I THINK I NEED TO HEAR THIS FROM THE BEGINNING, LITTLE BROTHER.
WHAT HAPPENED ONCE YOU REACHED RAVEN LANDS?
I DIDN'T FIND ASHLEIGH INITIALLY, SO I WENT TO RAVEN KEEP. SHE WAS THERE...
...AND THAT'S WHERE I LEARNED WHO SHE WAS.
I FOUGHT BRON BUT I WASN'T ABLE TO KILL HIM. I'D PROBABLY BE DEAD IF ASHLEIGH HADN'T HELPED ME ESCAPE.
OTHER THINGS HAPPENED ALONG THE WAY, BUT EVENTUALLY WE HEARD THE NEWS THAT YLENA AND HERON TROOPS WERE UNDER SIEGE HERE.
OBVIOUSLY I DIDN'T KNOW YOU'D BE ARRIVING WITH A LANDING FORCE, SO WE CAME TO SEE WHAT WE COULD DO TO HELP.
"WE" BEING MORE THAN JUST ME AND ASHLEIGH.
WFF!

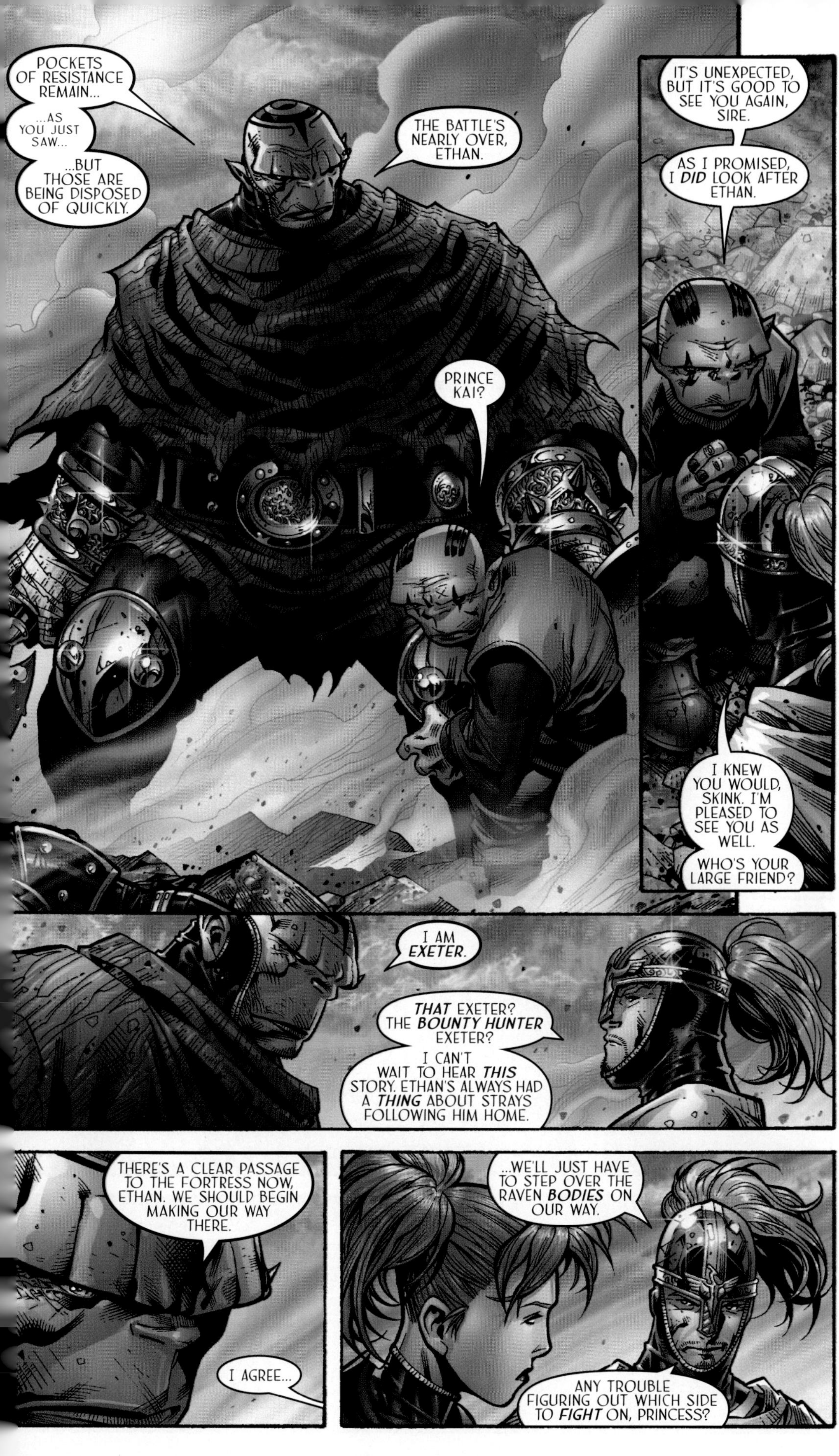
POCKETS OF RESISTANCE REMAIN...
...AS YOU JUST SAW...
...BUT THOSE ARE BEING DISPOSED OF QUICKLY.
THE BATTLE'S NEARLY OVER, ETHAN.
PRINCE KAI?
IT'S UNEXPECTED, BUT IT'S GOOD TO SEE YOU AGAIN, SIRE.
AS I PROMISED, I *DID* LOOK AFTER ETHAN.
I KNEW YOU WOULD, SKINK. I'M PLEASED TO SEE YOU AS WELL.
WHO'S YOUR LARGE FRIEND?
I AM ***EXETER***.
***THAT*** EXETER? THE ***BOUNTY HUNTER*** EXETER?
I CAN'T WAIT TO HEAR ***THIS*** STORY. ETHAN'S ALWAYS HAD A ***THING*** ABOUT STRAYS FOLLOWING HIM HOME.
THERE'S A CLEAR PASSAGE TO THE FORTRESS NOW, ETHAN. WE SHOULD BEGIN MAKING OUR WAY THERE.
I AGREE...
...WE'LL JUST HAVE TO STEP OVER THE RAVEN ***BODIES*** ON OUR WAY.
ANY TROUBLE FIGURING OUT WHICH SIDE TO ***FIGHT*** ON, PRINCESS?

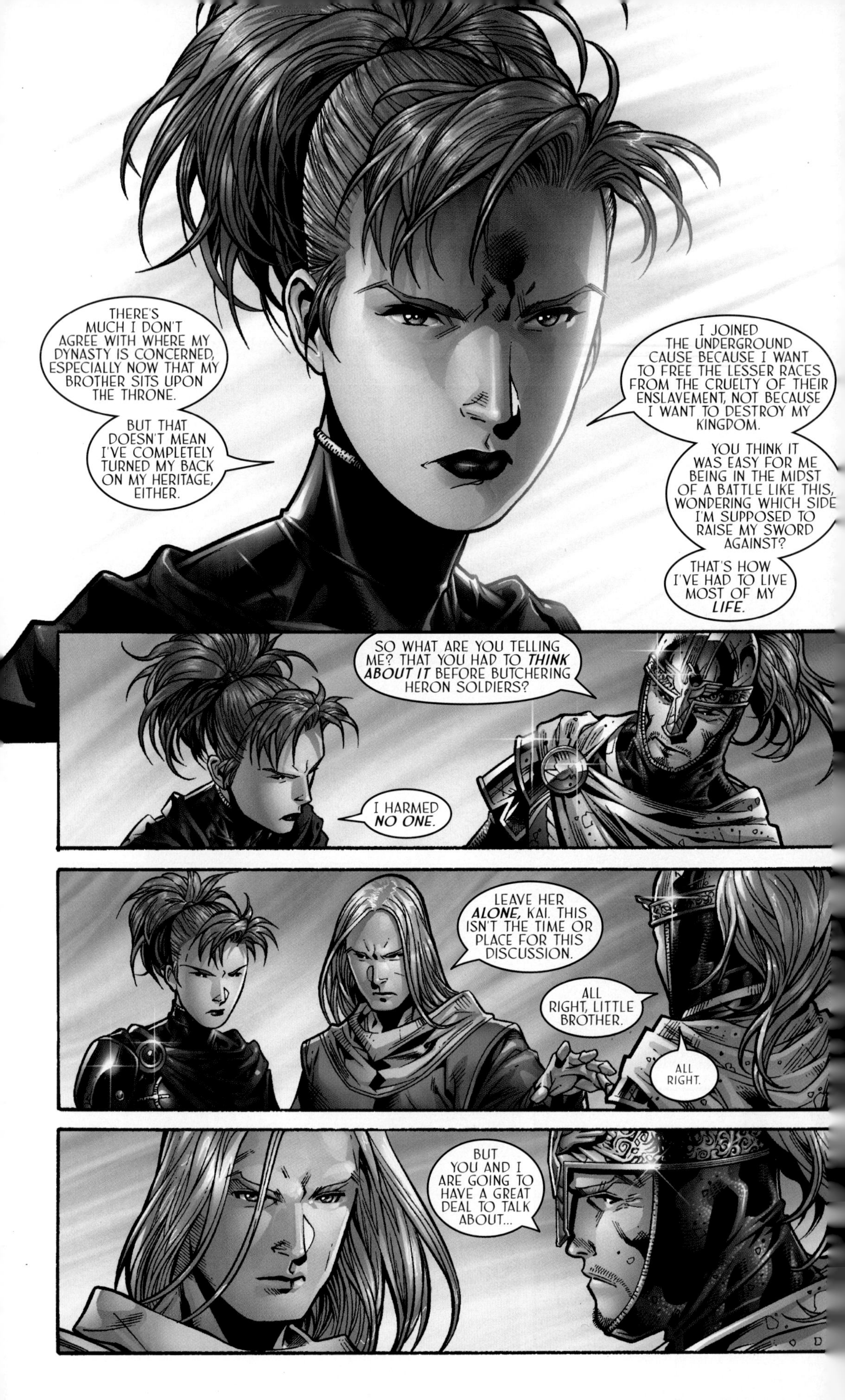

THERE'S MUCH I DON'T AGREE WITH WHERE MY DYNASTY IS CONCERNED, ESPECIALLY NOW THAT MY BROTHER SITS UPON THE THRONE.
BUT THAT DOESN'T MEAN I'VE COMPLETELY TURNED MY BACK ON MY HERITAGE, EITHER.
I JOINED THE UNDERGROUND CAUSE BECAUSE I WANT TO FREE THE LESSER RACES FROM THE CRUELTY OF THEIR ENSLAVEMENT, NOT BECAUSE I WANT TO DESTROY MY KINGDOM.
YOU THINK IT WAS EASY FOR ME BEING IN THE MIDST OF A BATTLE LIKE THIS, WONDERING WHICH SIDE I'M SUPPOSED TO RAISE MY SWORD AGAINST?
THAT'S HOW I'VE HAD TO LIVE MOST OF MY *LIFE*.
SO WHAT ARE YOU TELLING ME? THAT YOU HAD TO *THINK ABOUT IT* BEFORE BUTCHERING HERON SOLDIERS?
I HARMED *NO ONE*.
LEAVE HER *ALONE,* KAI. THIS ISN'T THE TIME OR PLACE FOR THIS DISCUSSION.
ALL RIGHT, LITTLE BROTHER.
ALL RIGHT.
BUT YOU AND I ARE GOING TO HAVE A GREAT DEAL TO TALK ABOUT...

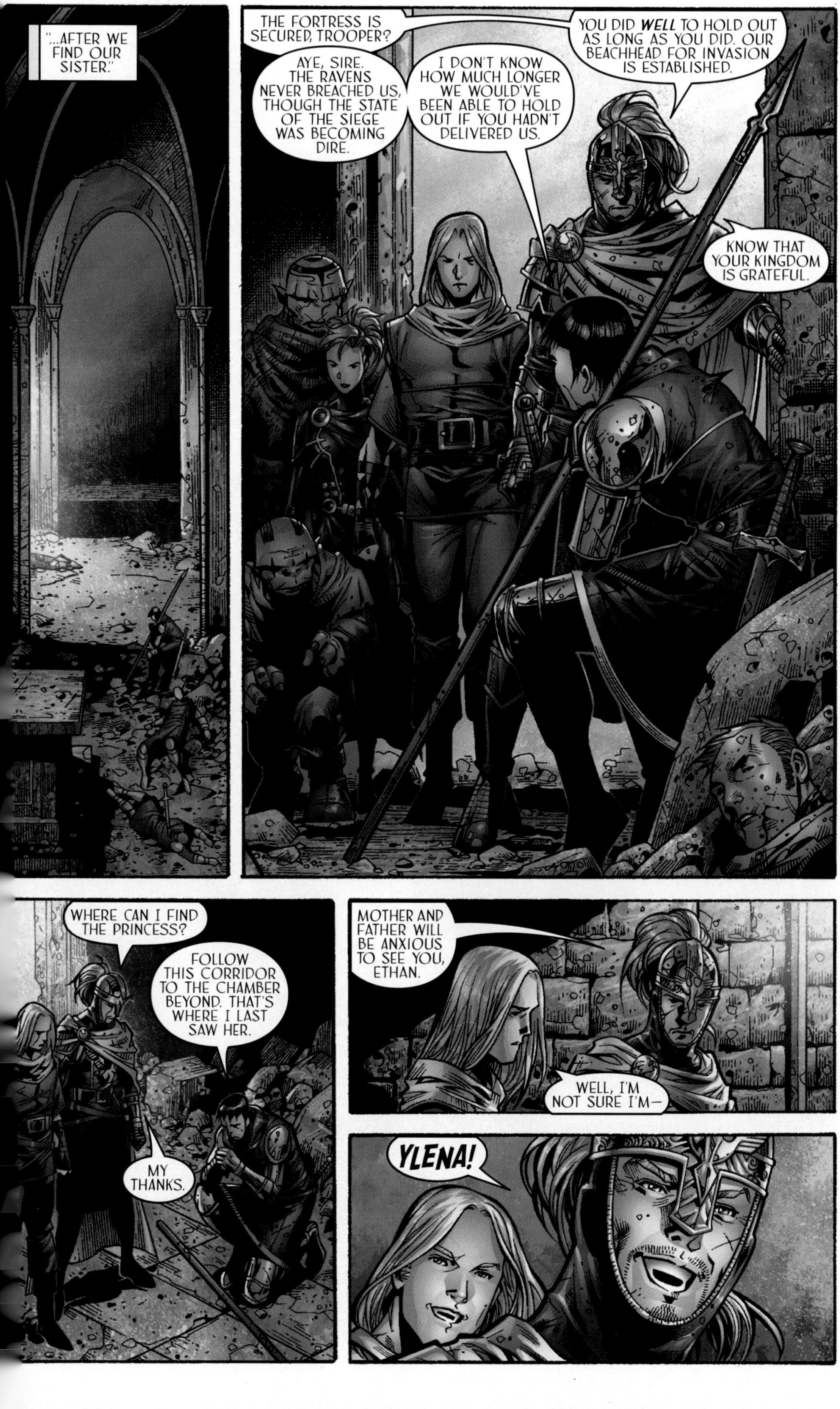
"...AFTER WE FIND OUR SISTER."
THE FORTRESS IS SECURED, TROOPER?
AYE, SIRE. THE RAVENS NEVER BREACHED US, THOUGH THE STATE OF THE SIEGE WAS BECOMING DIRE.
I DON'T KNOW HOW MUCH LONGER WE WOULD'VE BEEN ABLE TO HOLD OUT IF YOU HADN'T DELIVERED US.
YOU DID WELL TO HOLD OUT AS LONG AS YOU DID. OUR BEACHHEAD FOR INVASION IS ESTABLISHED.
KNOW THAT YOUR KINGDOM IS GRATEFUL.
WHERE CAN I FIND THE PRINCESS?
FOLLOW THIS CORRIDOR TO THE CHAMBER BEYOND. THAT'S WHERE I LAST SAW HER.
MY THANKS.
MOTHER AND FATHER WILL BE ANXIOUS TO SEE YOU, ETHAN.
WELL, I'M NOT SURE I'M—
YLENA!

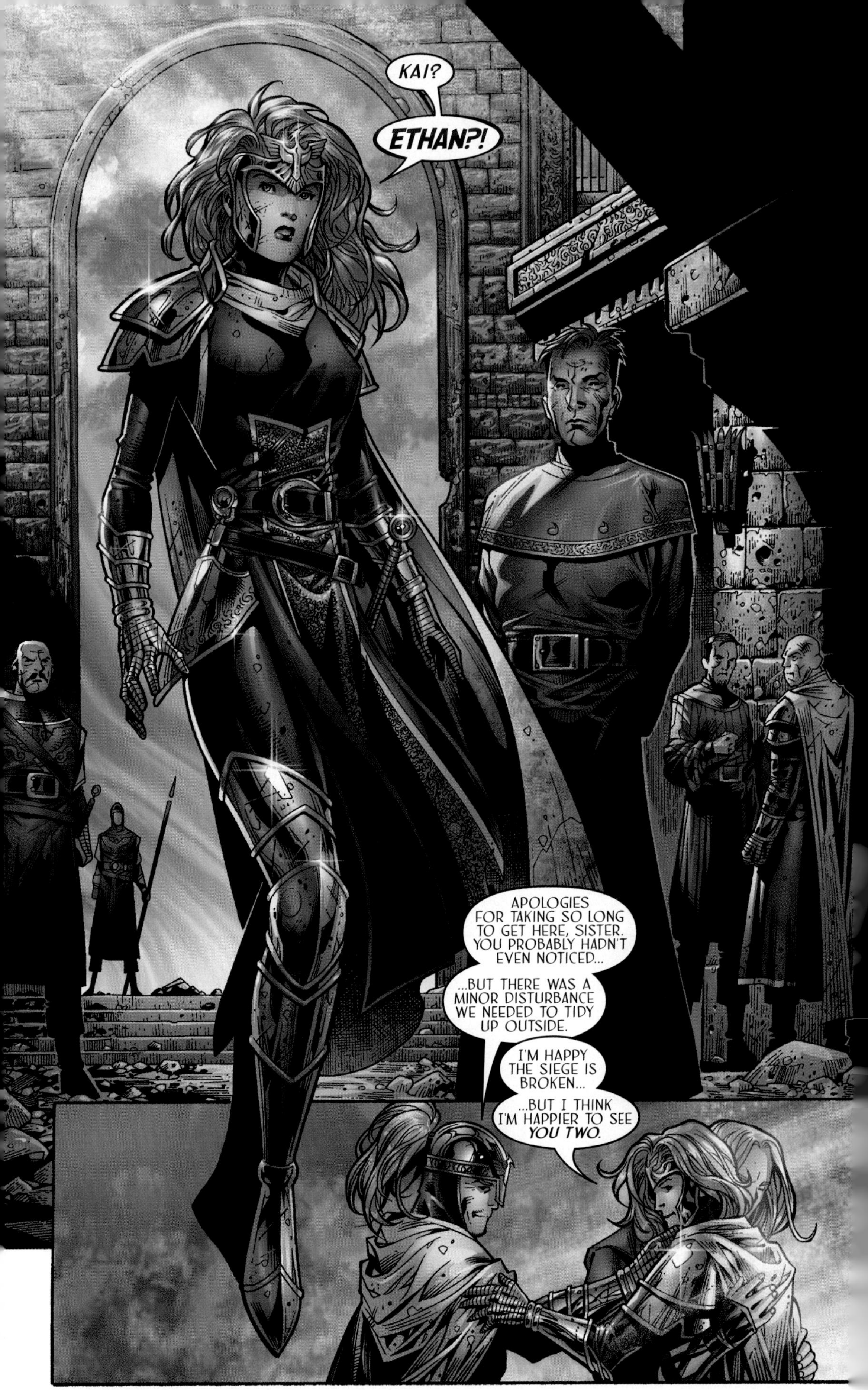
KAI?
ETHAN?!
APOLOGIES FOR TAKING SO LONG TO GET HERE, SISTER. YOU PROBABLY HADN'T EVEN NOTICED...
...BUT THERE WAS A MINOR DISTURBANCE WE NEEDED TO TIDY UP OUTSIDE.
I'M HAPPY THE SIEGE IS BROKEN...
...BUT I THINK I'M HAPPIER TO SEE *YOU TWO*.

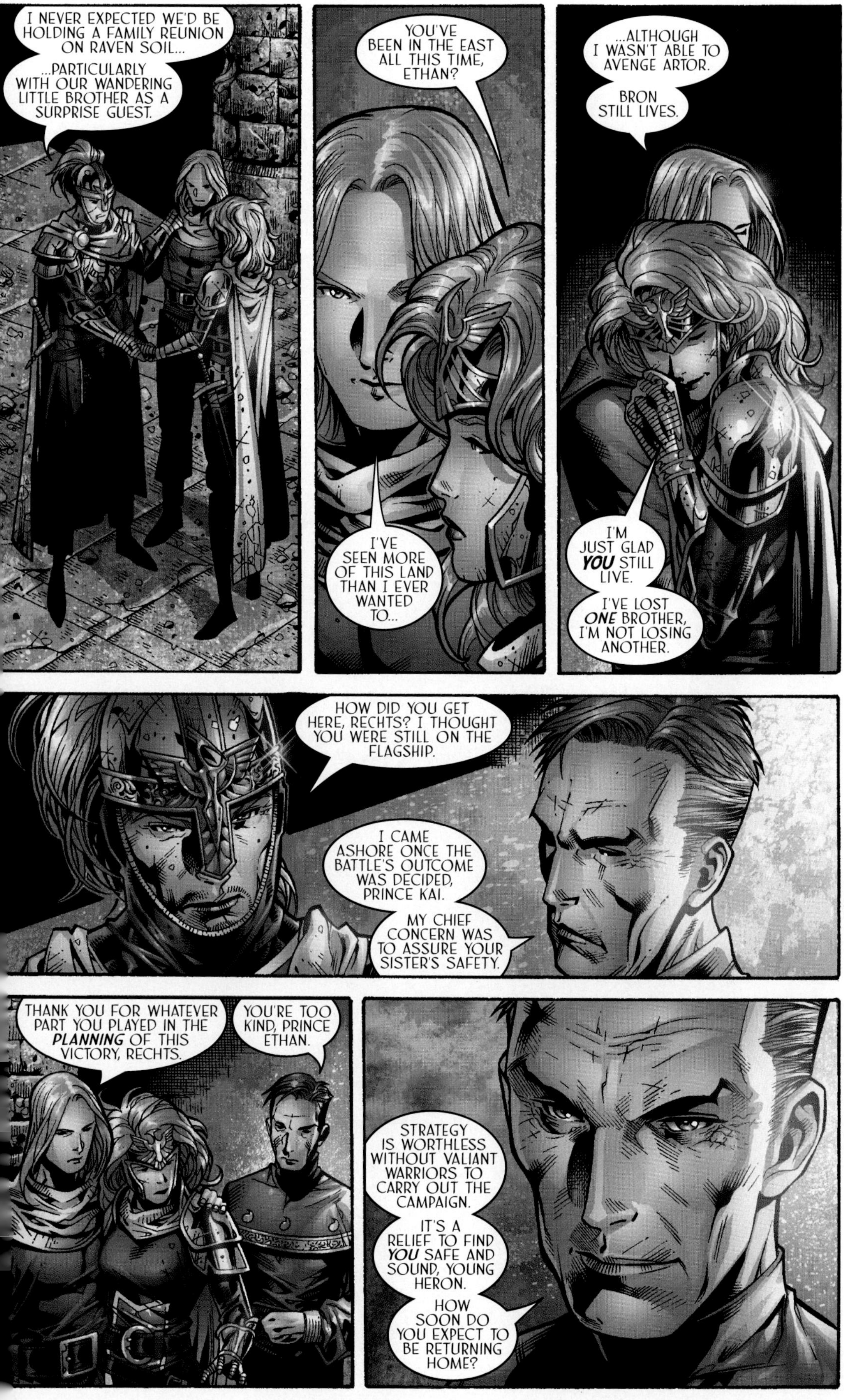

I NEVER EXPECTED WE'D BE HOLDING A FAMILY REUNION ON RAVEN SOIL...
...PARTICULARLY WITH OUR WANDERING LITTLE BROTHER AS A SURPRISE GUEST.
YOU'VE BEEN IN THE EAST ALL THIS TIME, ETHAN?
I'VE SEEN MORE OF THIS LAND THAN I EVER WANTED TO...
...ALTHOUGH I WASN'T ABLE TO AVENGE ARTOR.
BRON STILL LIVES.
I'M JUST GLAD *YOU* STILL LIVE.
I'VE LOST *ONE* BROTHER, I'M NOT LOSING ANOTHER.
HOW DID YOU GET HERE, RECHTS? I THOUGHT YOU WERE STILL ON THE FLAGSHIP.
I CAME ASHORE ONCE THE BATTLE'S OUTCOME WAS DECIDED, PRINCE KAI.
MY CHIEF CONCERN WAS TO ASSURE YOUR SISTER'S SAFETY.
THANK YOU FOR WHATEVER PART YOU PLAYED IN THE *PLANNING* OF THIS VICTORY, RECHTS.
YOU'RE TOO KIND, PRINCE ETHAN.
STRATEGY IS WORTHLESS WITHOUT VALIANT WARRIORS TO CARRY OUT THE CAMPAIGN.
IT'S A RELIEF TO FIND *YOU* SAFE AND SOUND, YOUNG HERON.
HOW SOON DO YOU EXPECT TO BE RETURNING HOME?

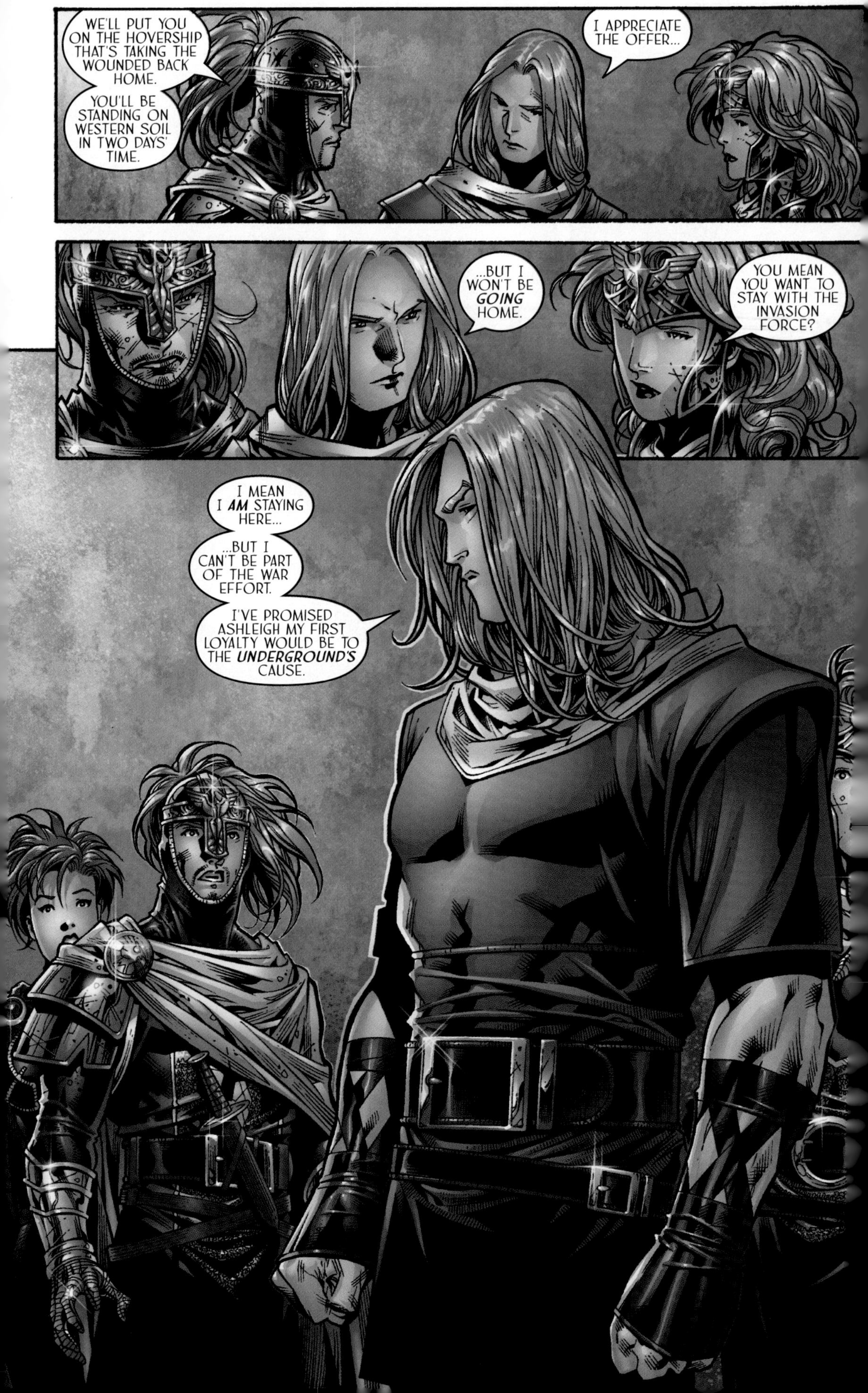
WE'LL PUT YOU ON THE HOVERSHIP THAT'S TAKING THE WOUNDED BACK HOME.
YOU'LL BE STANDING ON WESTERN SOIL IN TWO DAYS' TIME.
I APPRECIATE THE OFFER...
...BUT I WON'T BE *GOING* HOME.
YOU MEAN YOU WANT TO STAY WITH THE INVASION FORCE?
I MEAN I *AM* STAYING HERE...
...BUT I CAN'T BE PART OF THE WAR EFFORT.
I'VE PROMISED ASHLEIGH MY FIRST LOYALTY WOULD BE TO THE *UNDERGROUND'S* CAUSE.

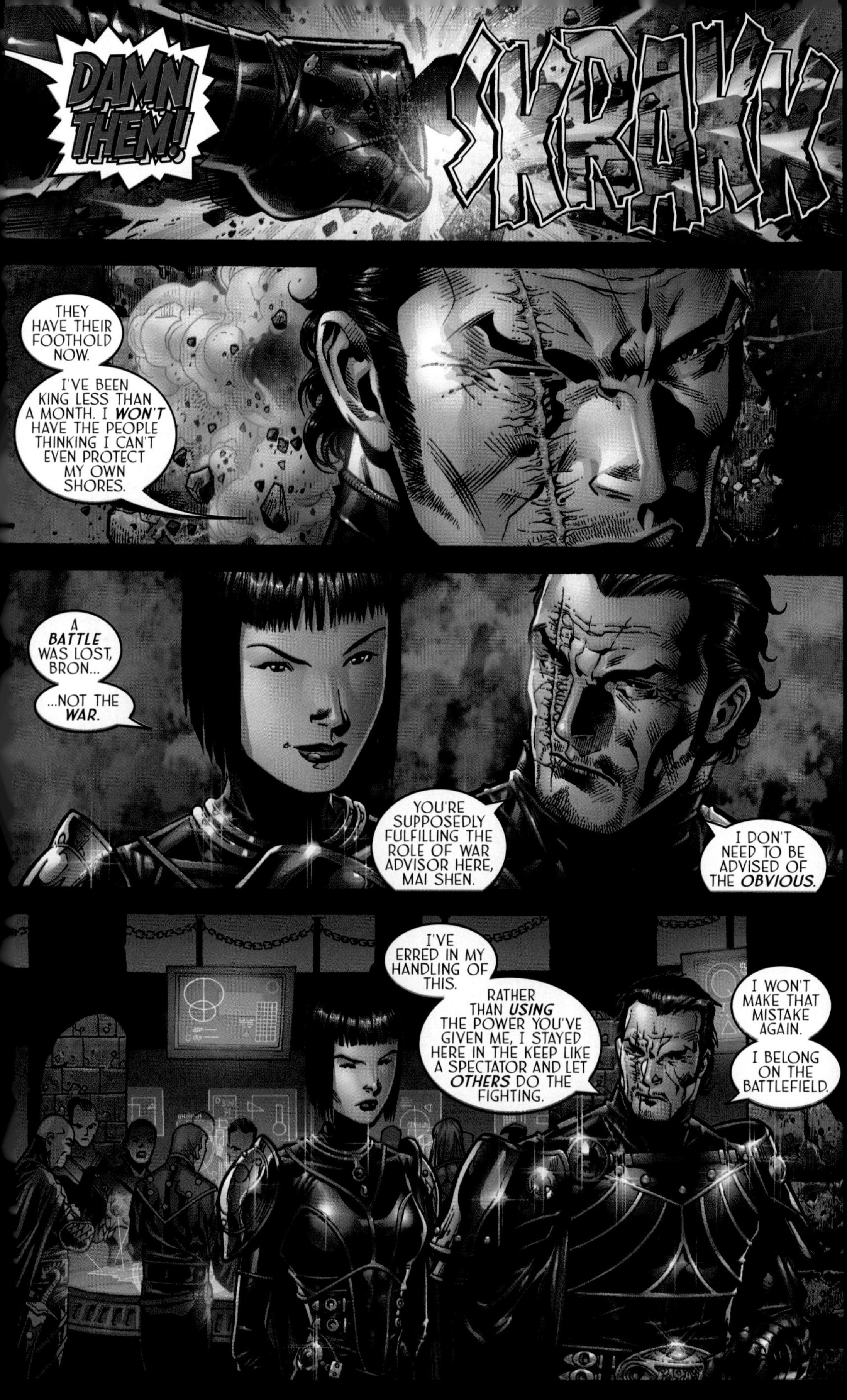
DAMN THEM!
SKRANK
THEY HAVE THEIR FOOTHOLD NOW.
I'VE BEEN KING LESS THAN A MONTH. I WON'T HAVE THE PEOPLE THINKING I CAN'T EVEN PROTECT MY OWN SHORES.
A BATTLE WAS LOST, BRON...
...NOT THE WAR.
YOU'RE SUPPOSEDLY FULFILLING THE ROLE OF WAR ADVISOR HERE, MAI SHEN.
I DON'T NEED TO BE ADVISED OF THE OBVIOUS.
I'VE ERRED IN MY HANDLING OF THIS.
RATHER THAN USING THE POWER YOU'VE GIVEN ME, I STAYED HERE IN THE KEEP LIKE A SPECTATOR AND LET OTHERS DO THE FIGHTING.
I WON'T MAKE THAT MISTAKE AGAIN.
I BELONG ON THE BATTLEFIELD.

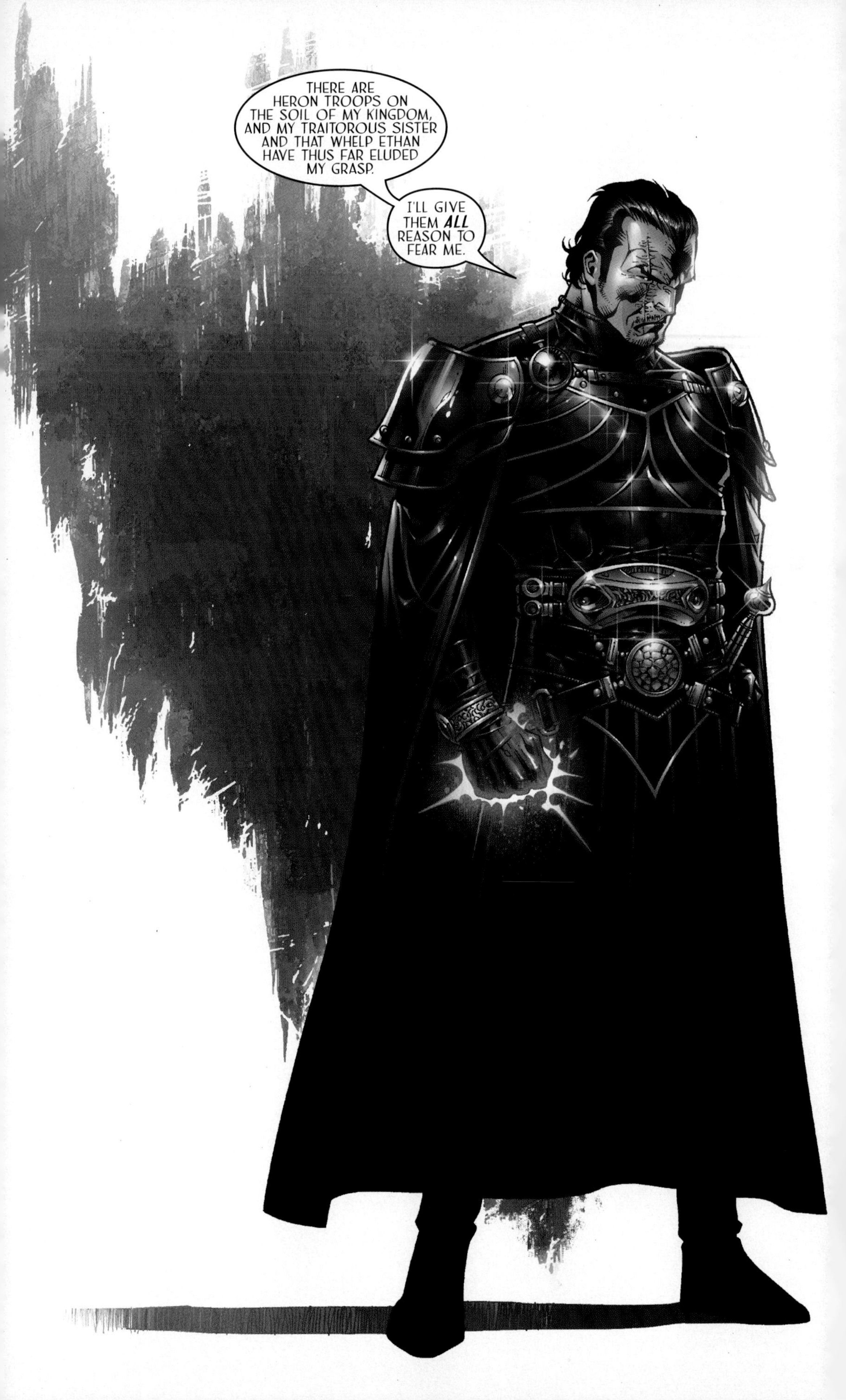
THERE ARE HERON TROOPS ON THE SOIL OF MY KINGDOM, AND MY TRAITOROUS SISTER AND THAT WHELP ETHAN HAVE THUS FAR ELUDED MY GRASP.
I'LL GIVE THEM ***ALL*** REASON TO FEAR ME.

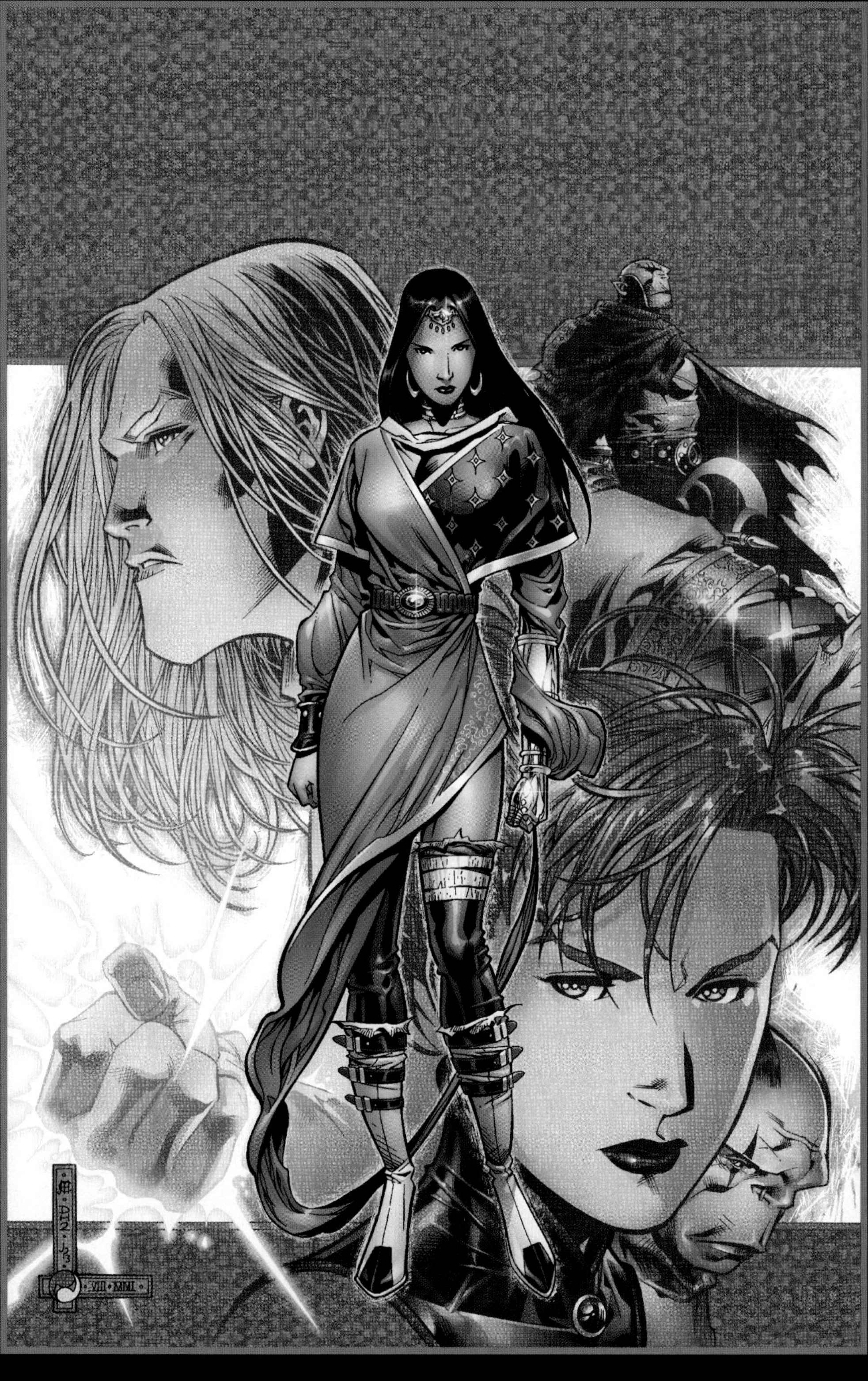

SCION • CHAPTER NINETEEN

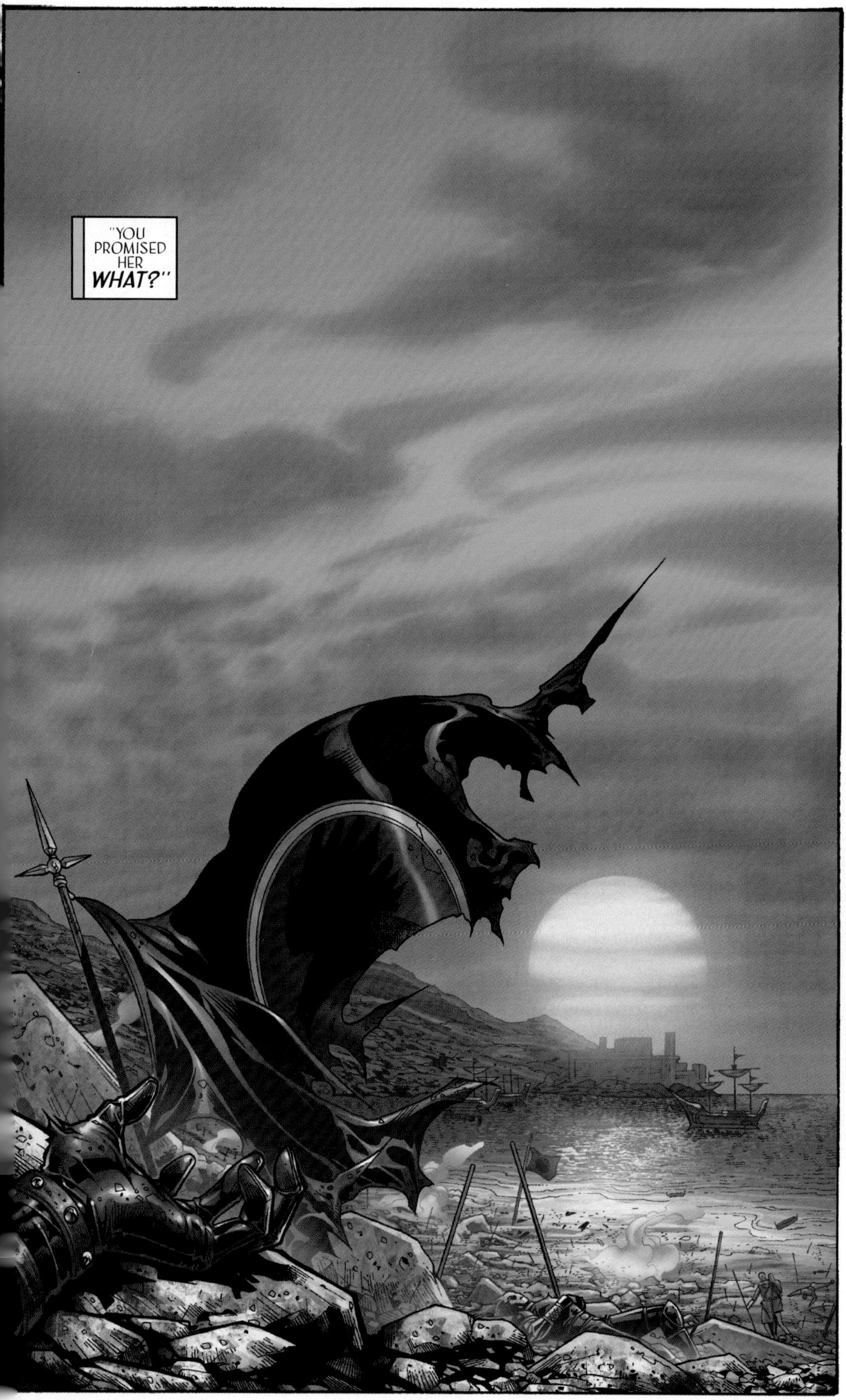
"YOU PROMISED HER *WHAT?*"

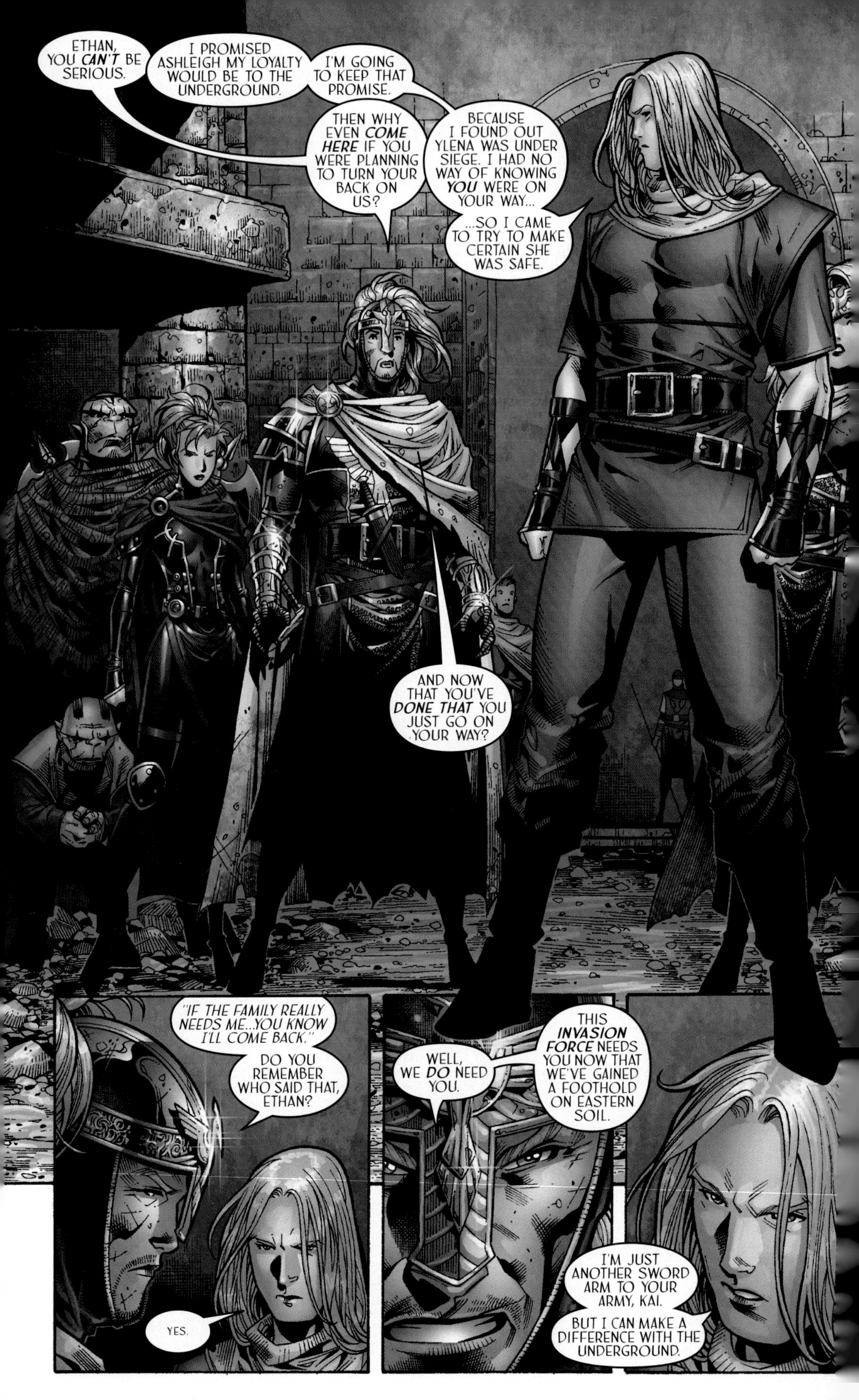

ETHAN, YOU CAN'T BE SERIOUS.
I PROMISED ASHLEIGH MY LOYALTY WOULD BE TO THE UNDERGROUND.
I'M GOING TO KEEP THAT PROMISE.
THEN WHY EVEN COME HERE IF YOU WERE PLANNING TO TURN YOUR BACK ON US?
BECAUSE I FOUND OUT YLENA WAS UNDER SIEGE. I HAD NO WAY OF KNOWING YOU WERE ON YOUR WAY...
...SO I CAME TO TRY TO MAKE CERTAIN SHE WAS SAFE.
AND NOW THAT YOU'VE DONE THAT YOU JUST GO ON YOUR WAY?
"IF THE FAMILY REALLY NEEDS ME...YOU KNOW I'LL COME BACK."
DO YOU REMEMBER WHO SAID THAT, ETHAN?
YES.
WELL, WE DO NEED YOU.
THIS INVASION FORCE NEEDS YOU NOW THAT WE'VE GAINED A FOOTHOLD ON EASTERN SOIL.
I'M JUST ANOTHER SWORD ARM TO YOUR ARMY, KAI.
BUT I CAN MAKE A DIFFERENCE WITH THE UNDERGROUND.

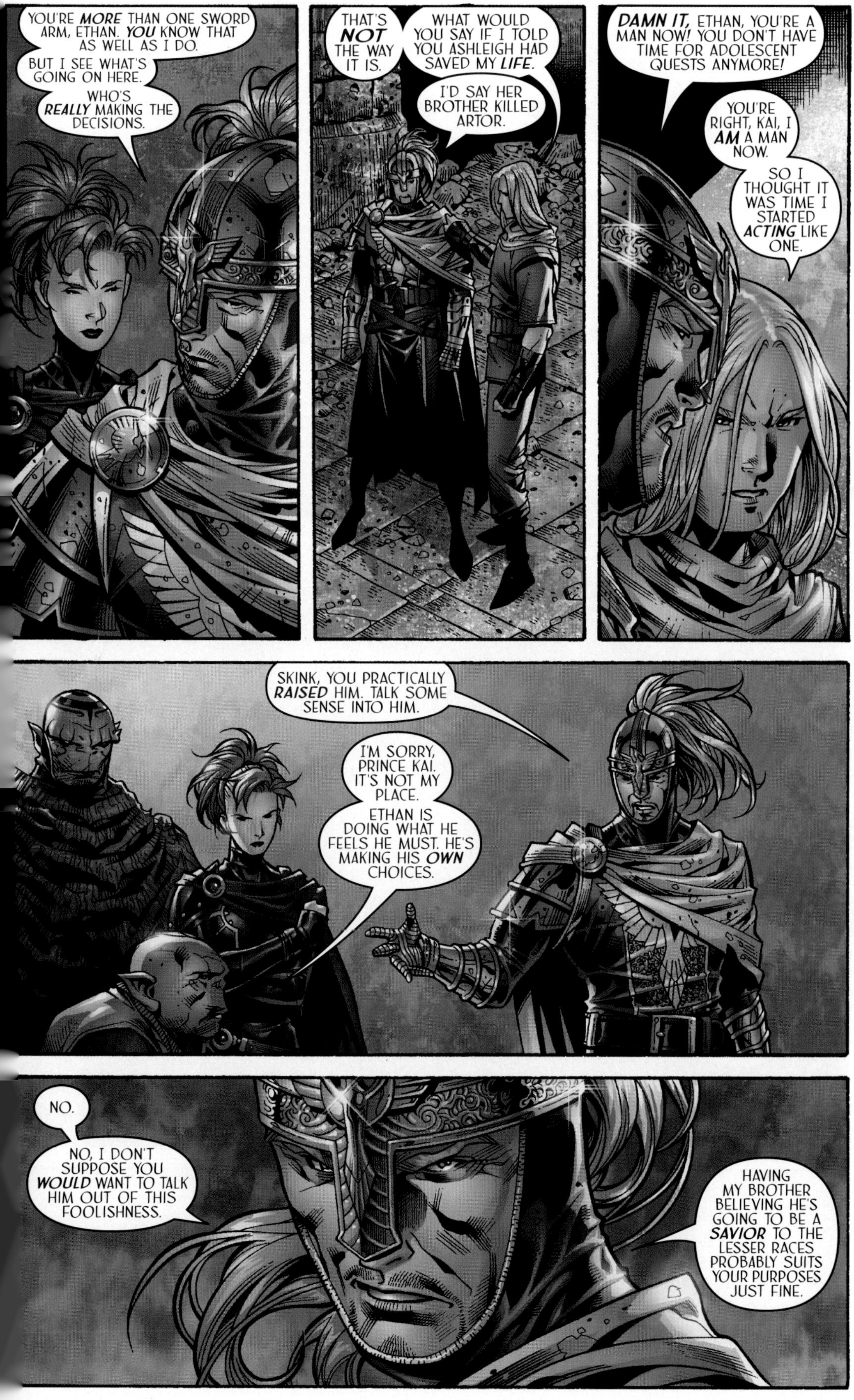
YOU'RE MORE THAN ONE SWORD ARM, ETHAN. YOU KNOW THAT AS WELL AS I DO.
BUT I SEE WHAT'S GOING ON HERE.
WHO'S REALLY MAKING THE DECISIONS.
THAT'S NOT THE WAY IT IS.
WHAT WOULD YOU SAY IF I TOLD YOU ASHLEIGH HAD SAVED MY LIFE.
I'D SAY HER BROTHER KILLED ARTOR.
DAMN IT, ETHAN, YOU'RE A MAN NOW! YOU DON'T HAVE TIME FOR ADOLESCENT QUESTS ANYMORE!
YOU'RE RIGHT, KAI, I AM A MAN NOW.
SO I THOUGHT IT WAS TIME I STARTED ACTING LIKE ONE.
SKINK, YOU PRACTICALLY RAISED HIM. TALK SOME SENSE INTO HIM.
I'M SORRY, PRINCE KAI. IT'S NOT MY PLACE.
ETHAN IS DOING WHAT HE FEELS HE MUST. HE'S MAKING HIS OWN CHOICES.
NO.
NO, I DON'T SUPPOSE YOU WOULD WANT TO TALK HIM OUT OF THIS FOOLISHNESS.
HAVING MY BROTHER BELIEVING HE'S GOING TO BE A SAVIOR TO THE LESSER RACES PROBABLY SUITS YOUR PURPOSES JUST FINE.

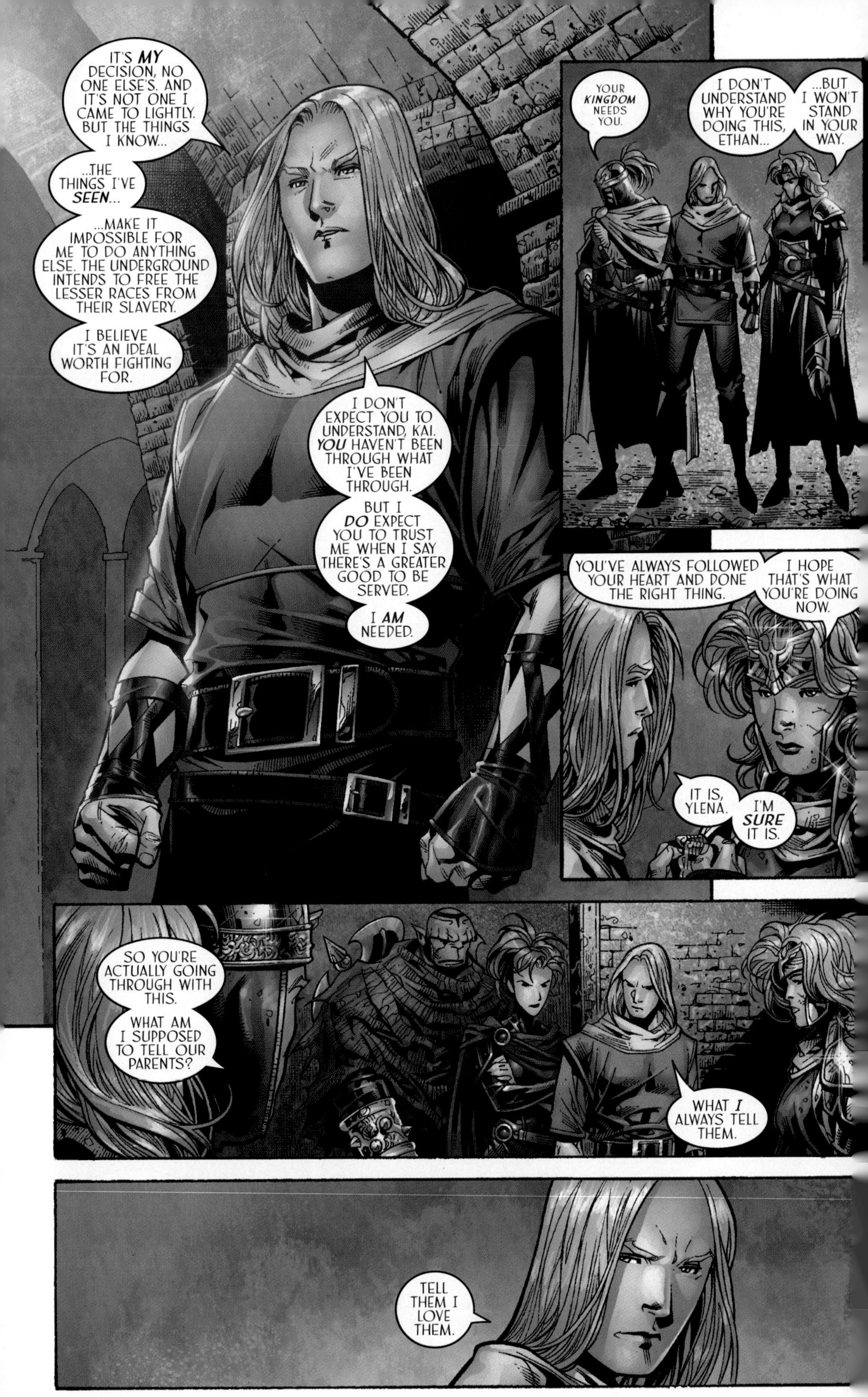

IT'S MY DECISION, NO ONE ELSE'S. AND IT'S NOT ONE I CAME TO LIGHTLY. BUT THE THINGS I KNOW...
...THE THINGS I'VE SEEN...
...MAKE IT IMPOSSIBLE FOR ME TO DO ANYTHING ELSE. THE UNDERGROUND INTENDS TO FREE THE LESSER RACES FROM THEIR SLAVERY.
I BELIEVE IT'S AN IDEAL WORTH FIGHTING FOR.
I DON'T EXPECT YOU TO UNDERSTAND, KAI. YOU HAVEN'T BEEN THROUGH WHAT I'VE BEEN THROUGH.
BUT I DO EXPECT YOU TO TRUST ME WHEN I SAY THERE'S A GREATER GOOD TO BE SERVED.
I AM NEEDED.
YOUR KINGDOM NEEDS YOU.
I DON'T UNDERSTAND WHY YOU'RE DOING THIS, ETHAN...
...BUT I WON'T STAND IN YOUR WAY.
YOU'VE ALWAYS FOLLOWED YOUR HEART AND DONE THE RIGHT THING.
I HOPE THAT'S WHAT YOU'RE DOING NOW.
IT IS, YLENA.
I'M SURE IT IS.
SO YOU'RE ACTUALLY GOING THROUGH WITH THIS.
WHAT AM I SUPPOSED TO TELL OUR PARENTS?
WHAT I ALWAYS TELL THEM.
TELL THEM I LOVE THEM.

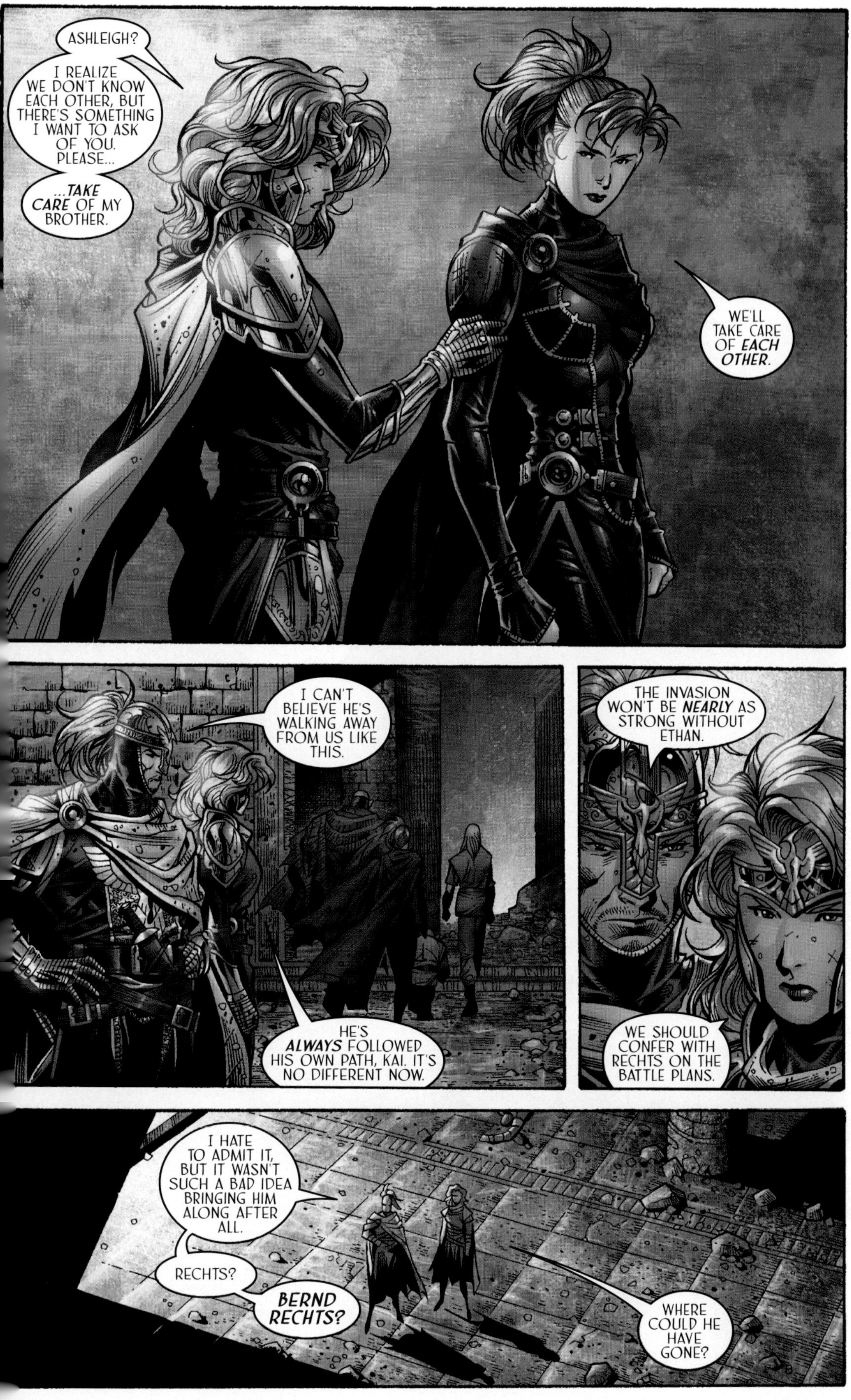
ASHLEIGH?
I REALIZE WE DON'T KNOW EACH OTHER, BUT THERE'S SOMETHING I WANT TO ASK OF YOU. PLEASE...
...TAKE CARE OF MY BROTHER.
WE'LL TAKE CARE OF EACH OTHER.
I CAN'T BELIEVE HE'S WALKING AWAY FROM US LIKE THIS.
HE'S ALWAYS FOLLOWED HIS OWN PATH, KAI. IT'S NO DIFFERENT NOW.
THE INVASION WON'T BE NEARLY AS STRONG WITHOUT ETHAN.
WE SHOULD CONFER WITH RECHTS ON THE BATTLE PLANS.
I HATE TO ADMIT IT, BUT IT WASN'T SUCH A BAD IDEA BRINGING HIM ALONG AFTER ALL.
RECHTS?
BERND RECHTS?
WHERE COULD HE HAVE GONE?

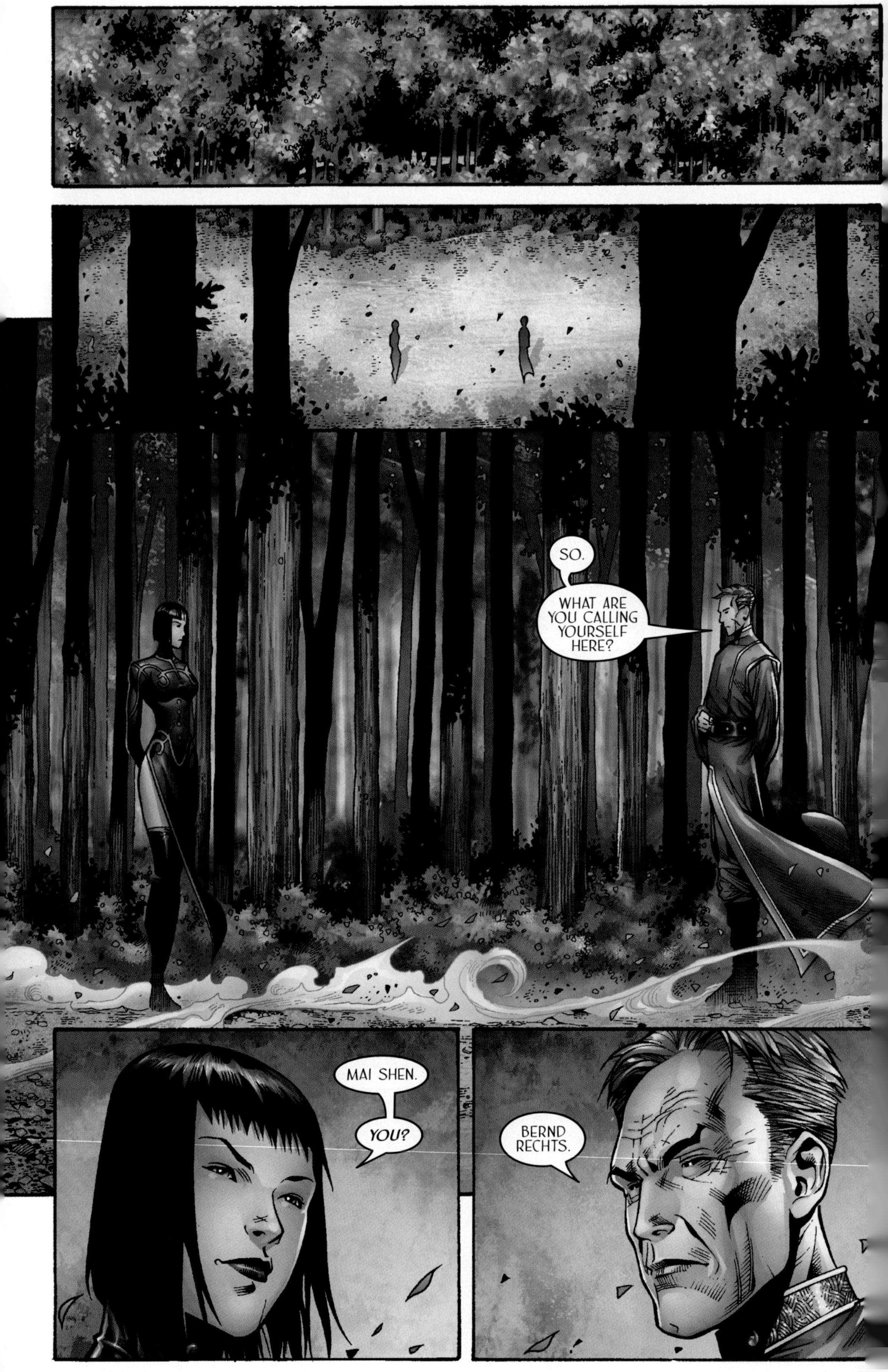
SO.
WHAT ARE YOU CALLING YOURSELF HERE?
MAI SHEN.
*YOU?*
BERND RECHTS.

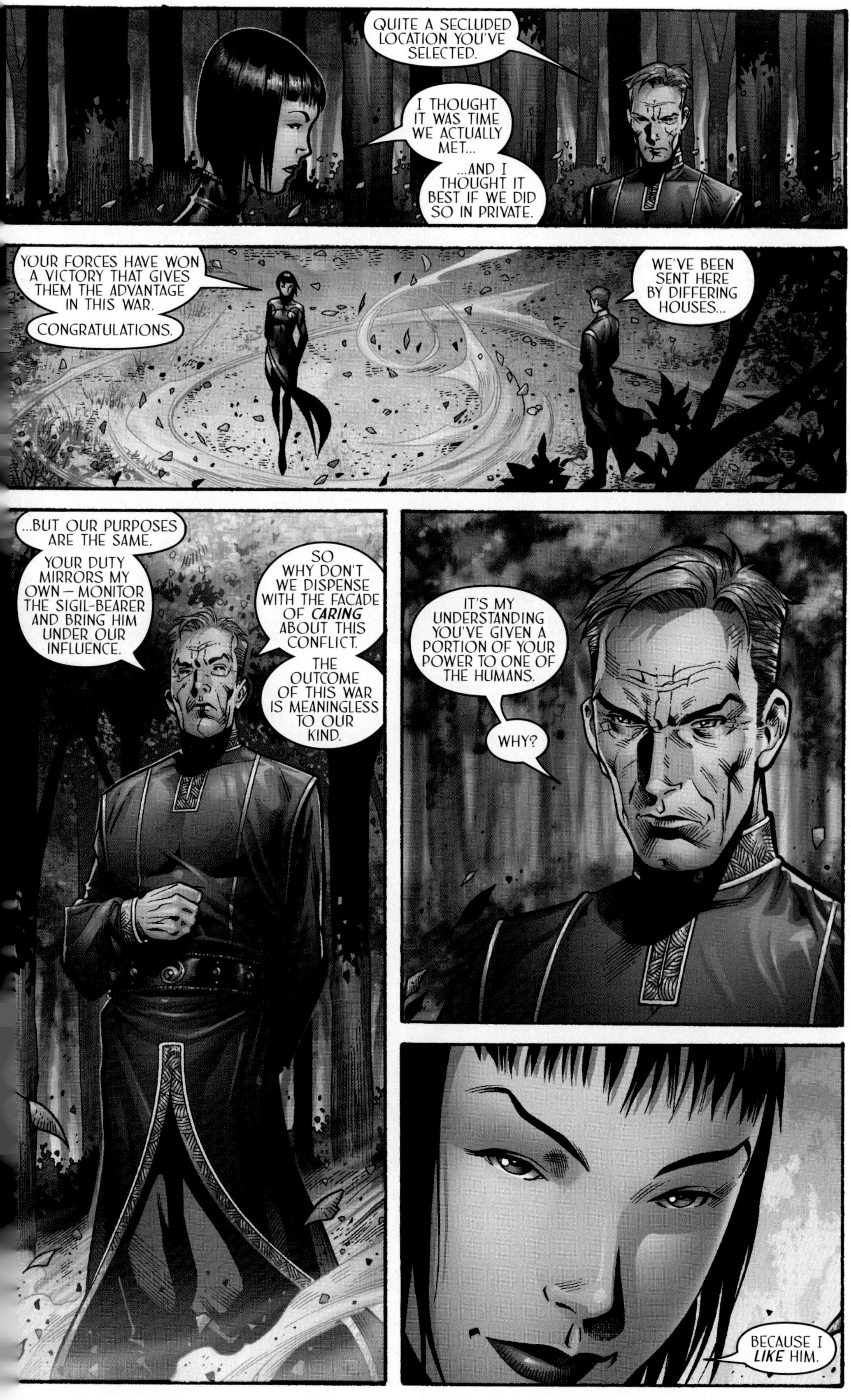
QUITE A SECLUDED LOCATION YOU'VE SELECTED.
I THOUGHT IT WAS TIME WE ACTUALLY MET...
...AND I THOUGHT IT BEST IF WE DID SO IN PRIVATE.
YOUR FORCES HAVE WON A VICTORY THAT GIVES THEM THE ADVANTAGE IN THIS WAR.
CONGRATULATIONS.
WE'VE BEEN SENT HERE BY DIFFERING HOUSES...
...BUT OUR PURPOSES ARE THE SAME.
YOUR DUTY MIRRORS MY OWN—MONITOR THE SIGIL-BEARER AND BRING HIM UNDER OUR INFLUENCE.
SO WHY DON'T WE DISPENSE WITH THE FACADE OF *CARING* ABOUT THIS CONFLICT.
THE OUTCOME OF THIS WAR IS MEANINGLESS TO OUR KIND.
IT'S MY UNDERSTANDING YOU'VE GIVEN A PORTION OF YOUR POWER TO ONE OF THE HUMANS.
WHY?
BECAUSE I *LIKE* HIM.

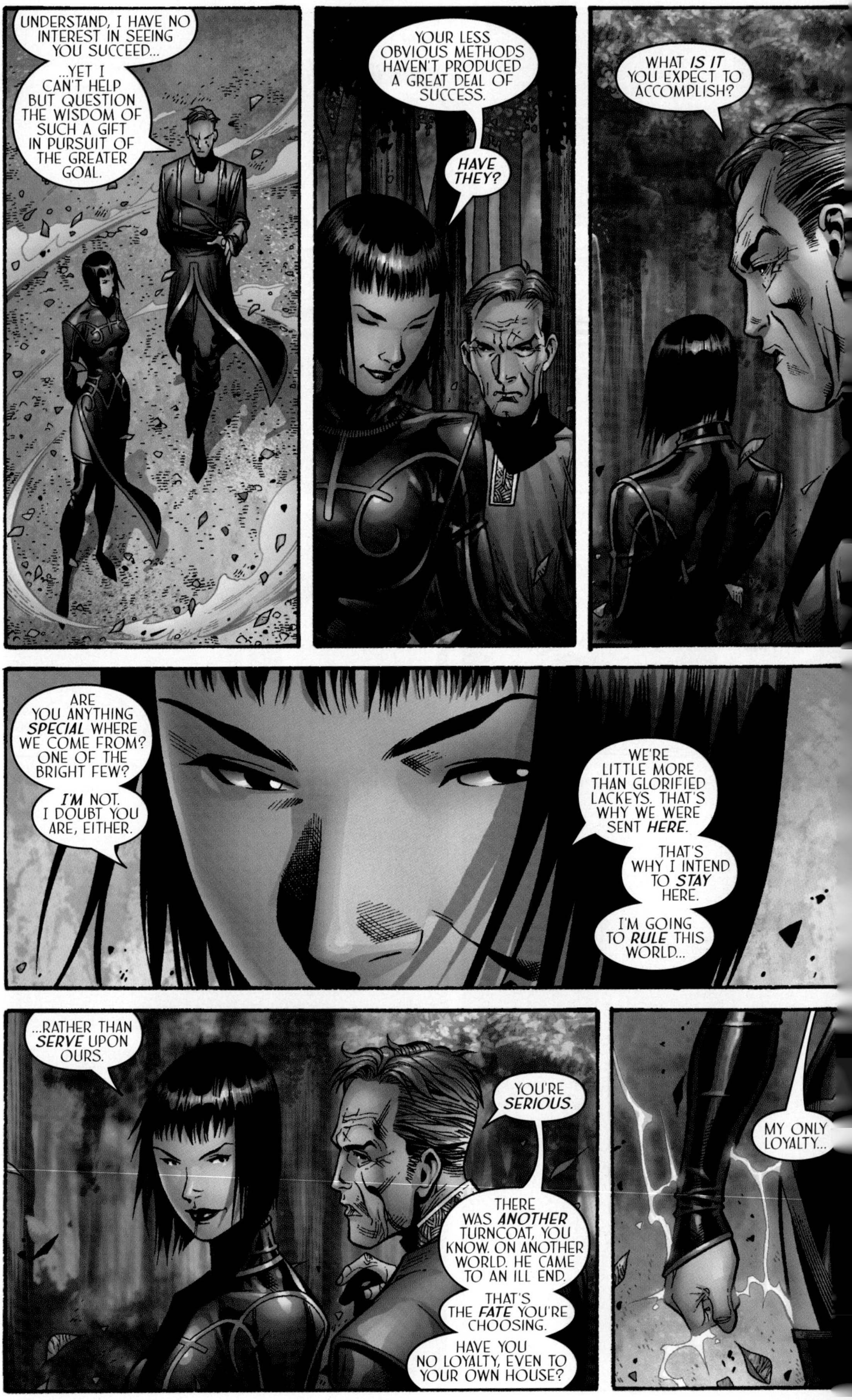
UNDERSTAND, I HAVE NO INTEREST IN SEEING YOU SUCCEED...
...YET I CAN'T HELP BUT QUESTION THE WISDOM OF SUCH A GIFT IN PURSUIT OF THE GREATER GOAL.
YOUR LESS OBVIOUS METHODS HAVEN'T PRODUCED A GREAT DEAL OF SUCCESS.
HAVE THEY?
WHAT IS IT YOU EXPECT TO ACCOMPLISH?
ARE YOU ANYTHING SPECIAL WHERE WE COME FROM? ONE OF THE BRIGHT FEW?
I'M NOT. I DOUBT YOU ARE, EITHER.
WE'RE LITTLE MORE THAN GLORIFIED LACKEYS. THAT'S WHY WE WERE SENT HERE.
THAT'S WHY I INTEND TO STAY HERE.
I'M GOING TO RULE THIS WORLD...
...RATHER THAN SERVE UPON OURS.
YOU'RE SERIOUS.
THERE WAS ANOTHER TURNCOAT, YOU KNOW. ON ANOTHER WORLD. HE CAME TO AN ILL END.
THAT'S THE FATE YOU'RE CHOOSING.
HAVE YOU NO LOYALTY, EVEN TO YOUR OWN HOUSE?
MY ONLY LOYALTY...

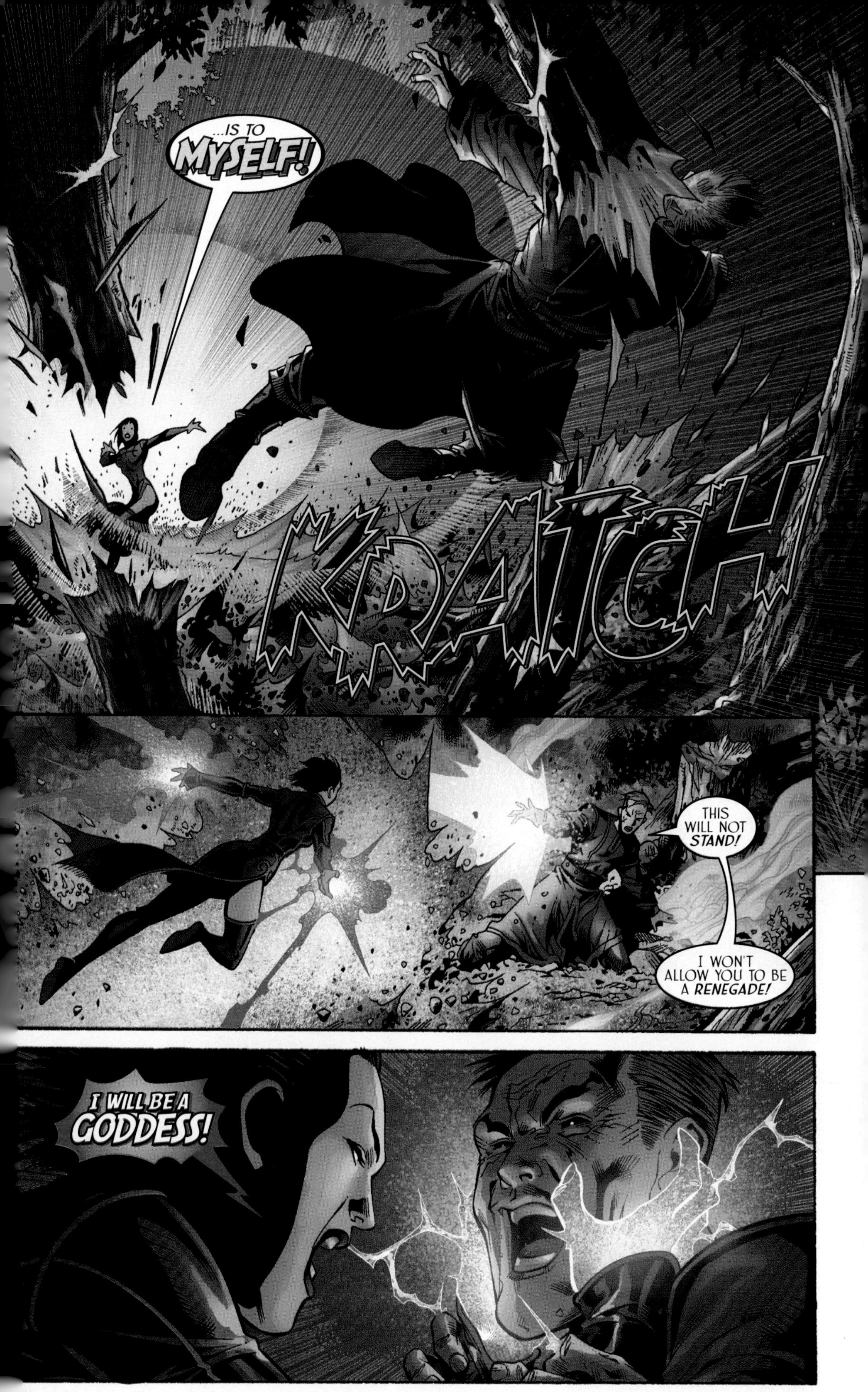
...IS TO MYSELF!
KRATCH
THIS WILL NOT STAND!
I WON'T ALLOW YOU TO BE A RENEGADE!
I WILL BE A GODDESS!

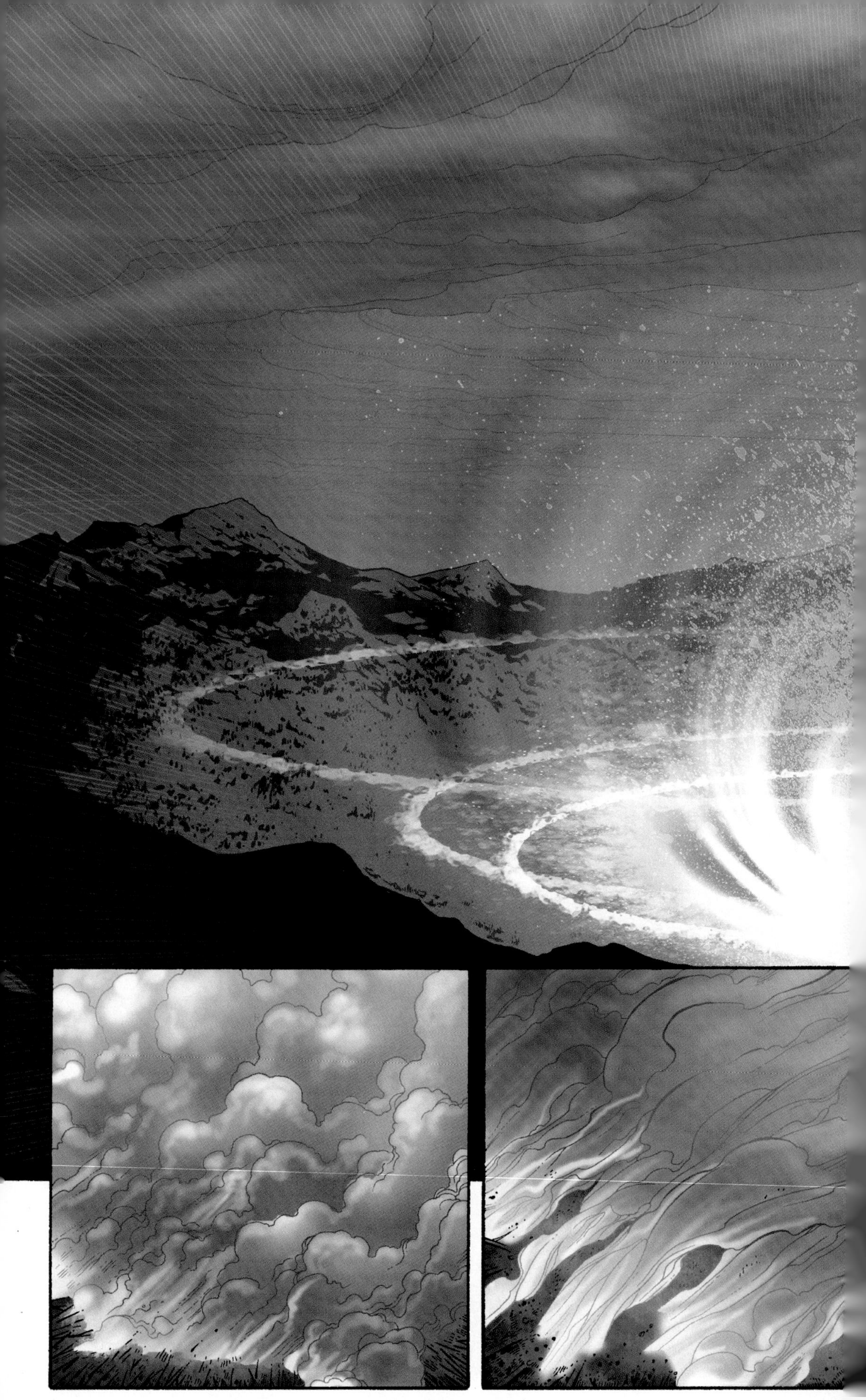

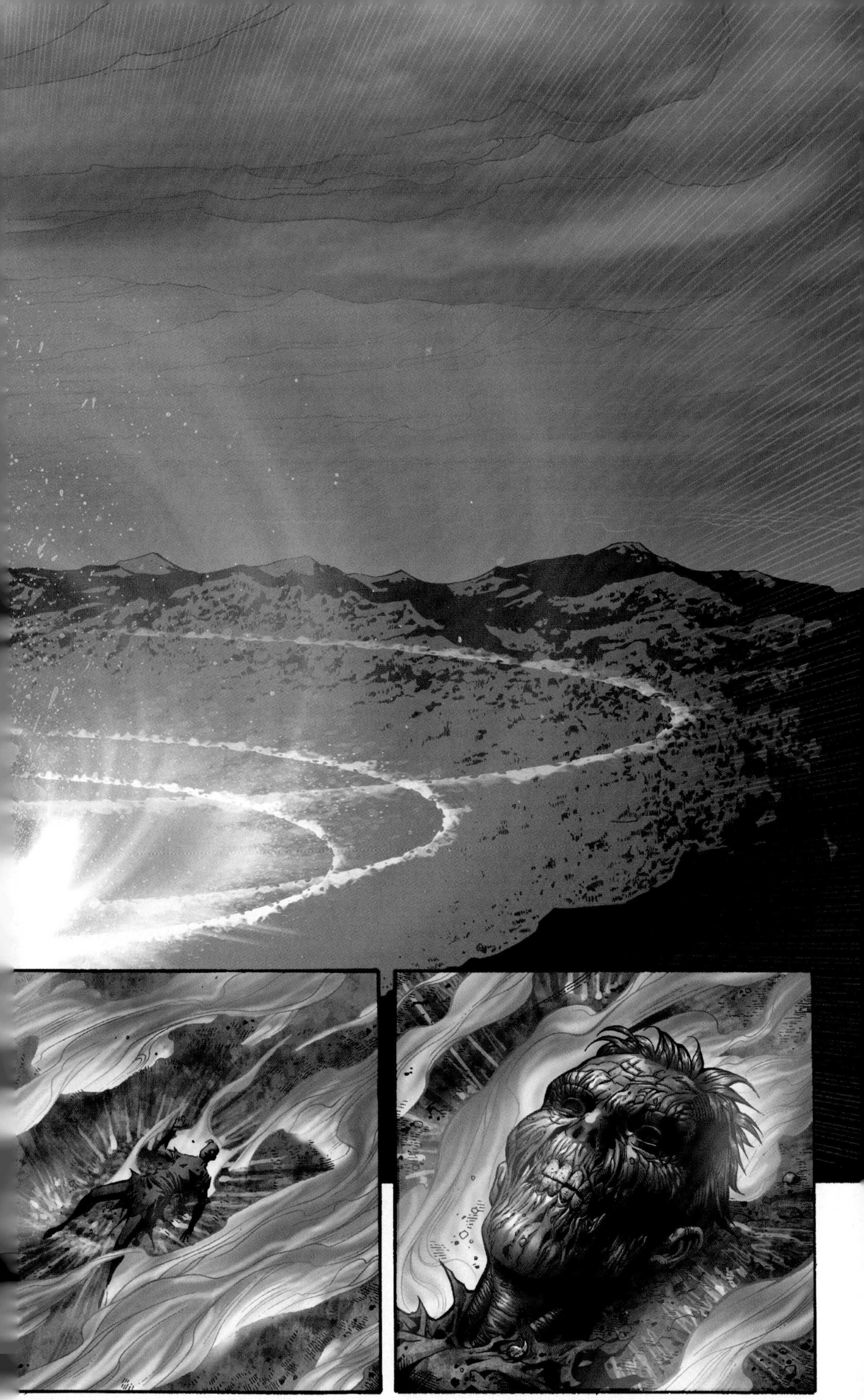

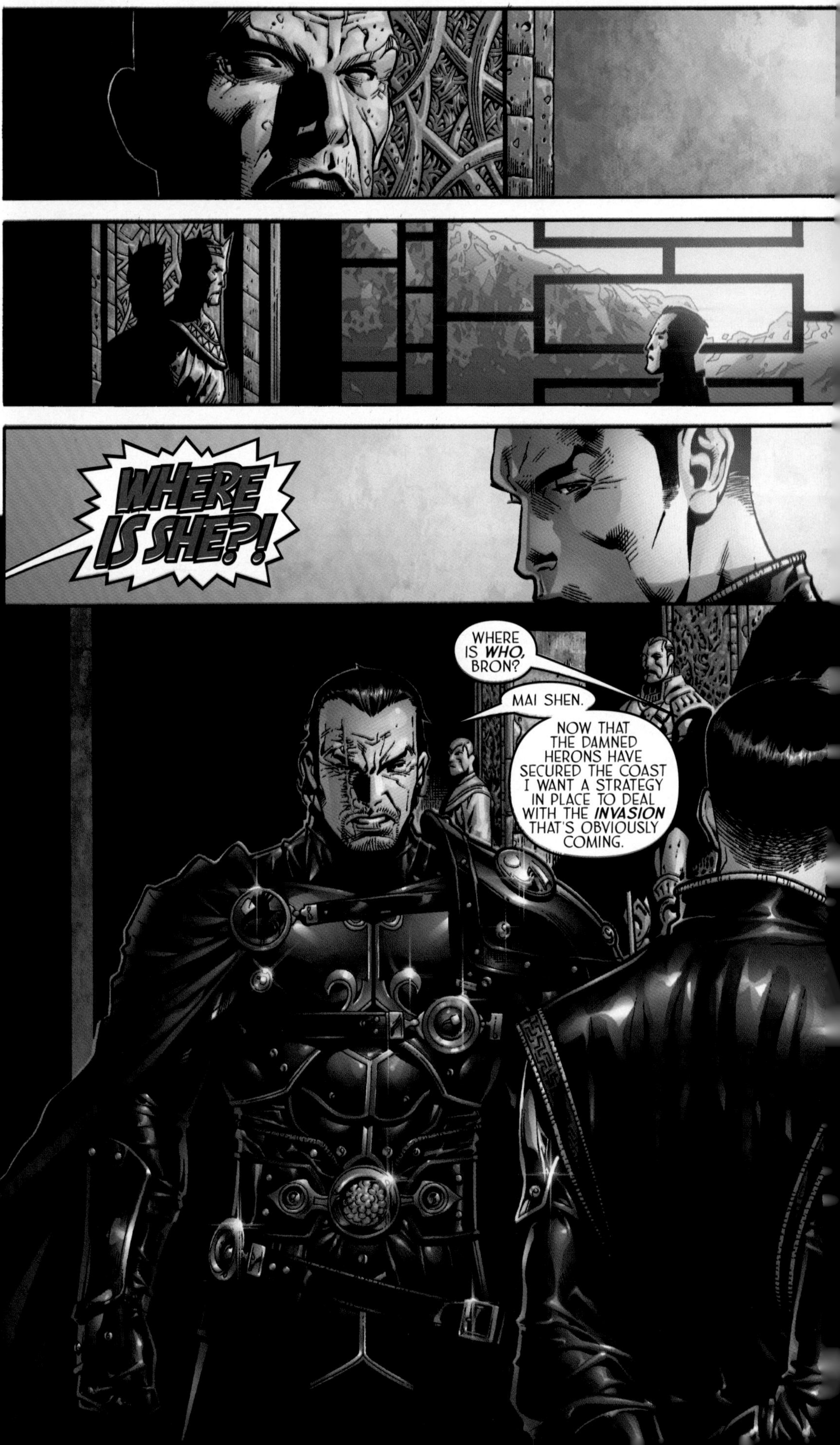
WHERE IS SHE?!
WHERE IS WHO, BRON?
MAI SHEN.
NOW THAT THE DAMNED HERONS HAVE SECURED THE COAST I WANT A STRATEGY IN PLACE TO DEAL WITH THE INVASION THAT'S OBVIOUSLY COMING.

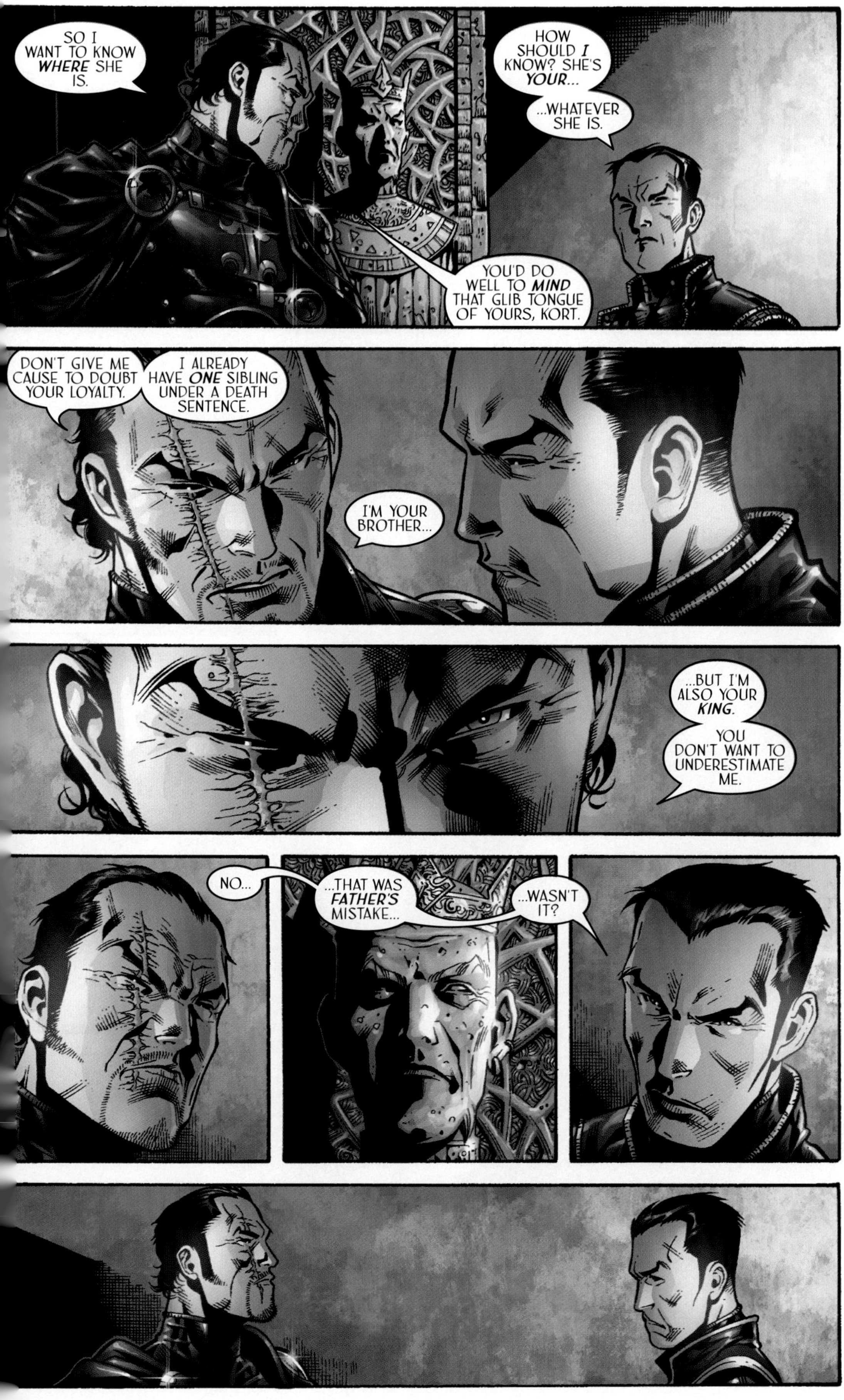

SO I WANT TO KNOW WHERE SHE IS.
HOW SHOULD I KNOW? SHE'S YOUR...
...WHATEVER SHE IS.
YOU'D DO WELL TO MIND THAT GLIB TONGUE OF YOURS, KORT.
DON'T GIVE ME CAUSE TO DOUBT YOUR LOYALTY.
I ALREADY HAVE ONE SIBLING UNDER A DEATH SENTENCE.
I'M YOUR BROTHER...
...BUT I'M ALSO YOUR KING.
YOU DON'T WANT TO UNDERESTIMATE ME.
NO...
...THAT WAS FATHER'S MISTAKE...
...WASN'T IT?

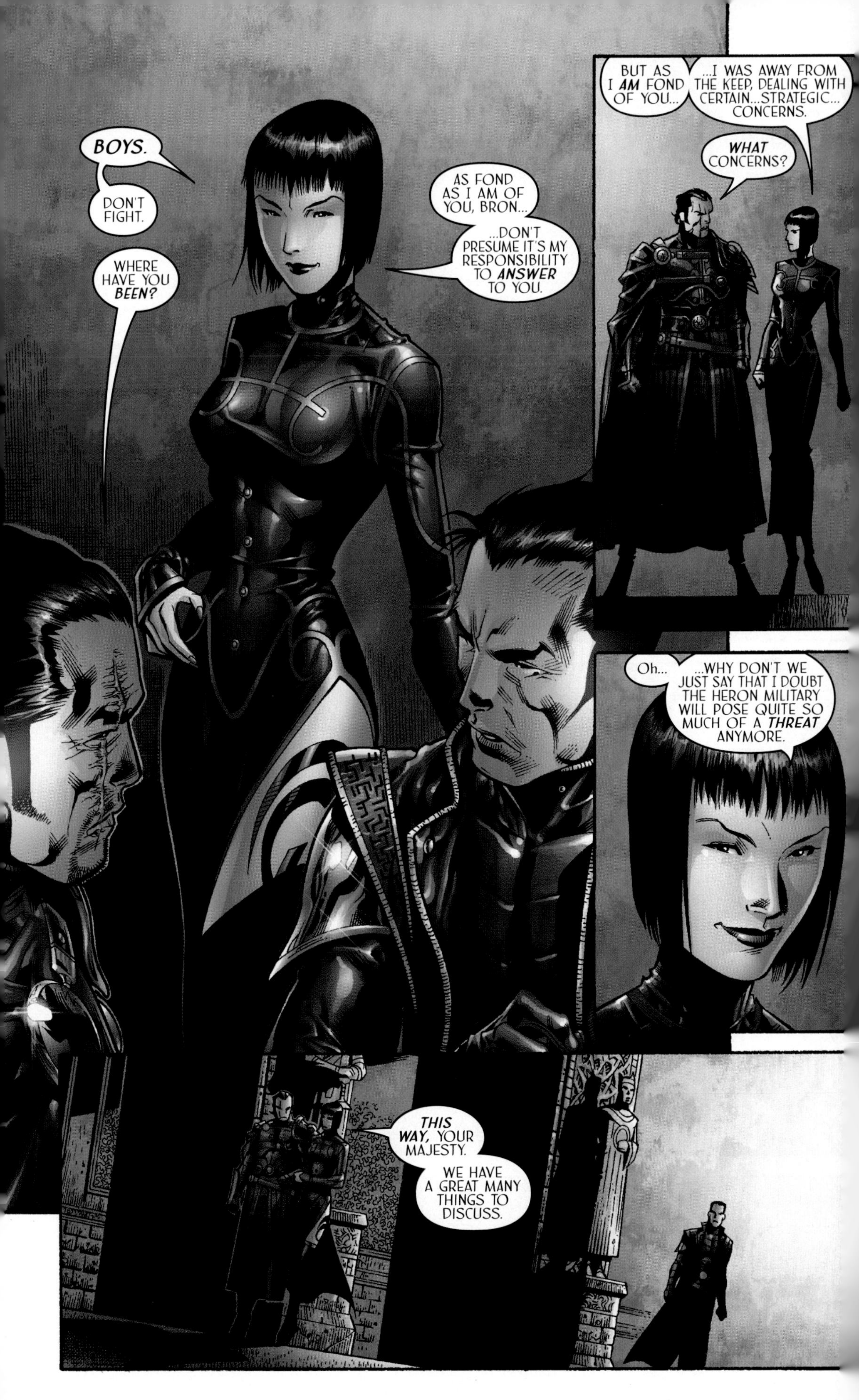
BOYS.
DON'T FIGHT.
WHERE HAVE YOU BEEN?
AS FOND AS I AM OF YOU, BRON...
...DON'T PRESUME IT'S MY RESPONSIBILITY TO ANSWER TO YOU.
BUT AS I AM FOND OF YOU...
...I WAS AWAY FROM THE KEEP, DEALING WITH CERTAIN...STRATEGIC... CONCERNS.
WHAT CONCERNS?
Oh...
...WHY DON'T WE JUST SAY THAT I DOUBT THE HERON MILITARY WILL POSE QUITE SO MUCH OF A THREAT ANYMORE.
THIS WAY, YOUR MAJESTY.
WE HAVE A GREAT MANY THINGS TO DISCUSS.

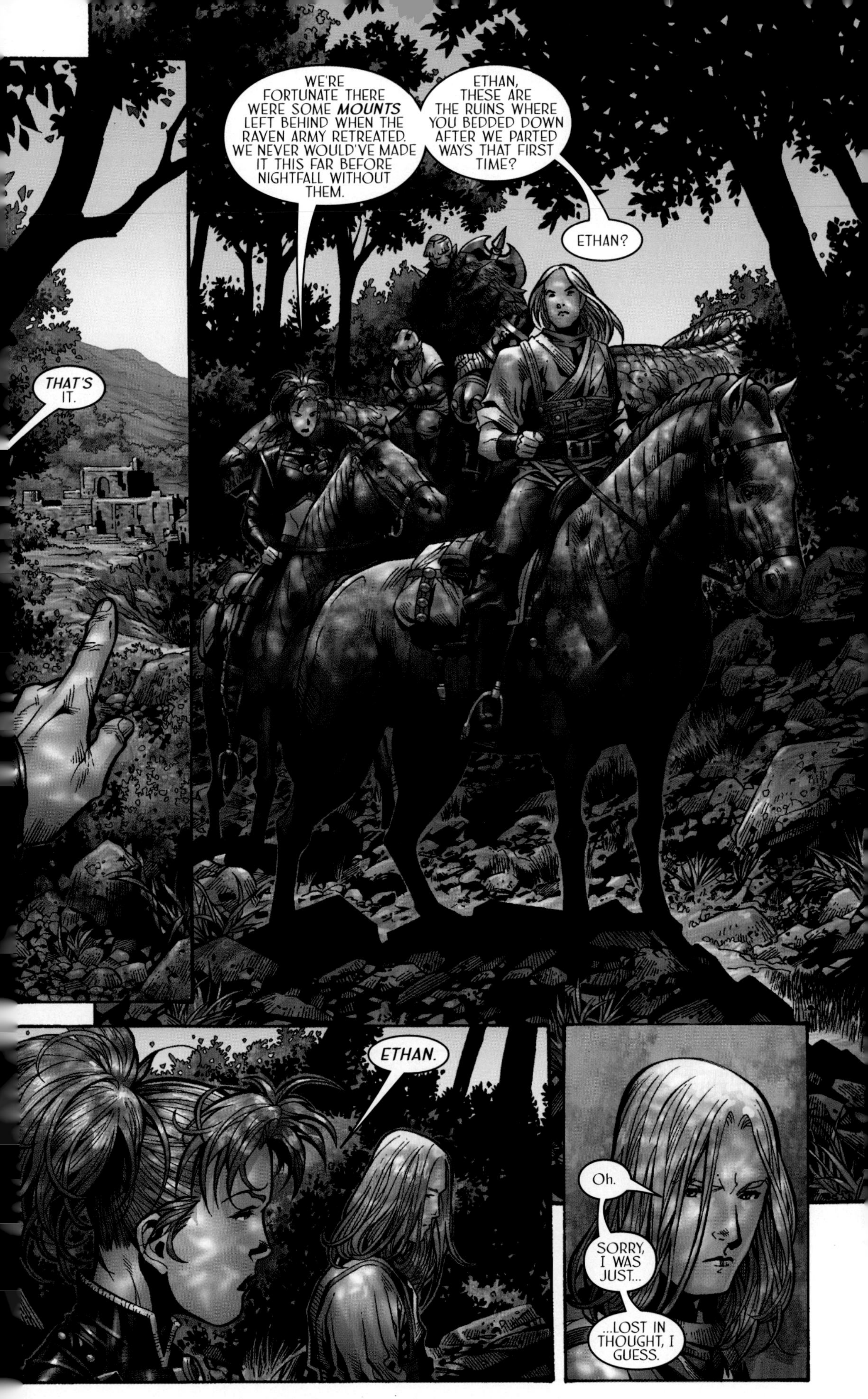

WE'RE FORTUNATE THERE WERE SOME MOUNTS LEFT BEHIND WHEN THE RAVEN ARMY RETREATED. WE NEVER WOULD'VE MADE IT THIS FAR BEFORE NIGHTFALL WITHOUT THEM.
ETHAN, THESE ARE THE RUINS WHERE YOU BEDDED DOWN AFTER WE PARTED WAYS THAT FIRST TIME?
ETHAN?
THAT'S IT.
ETHAN.
Oh.
SORRY, I WAS JUST...
...LOST IN THOUGHT, I GUESS.

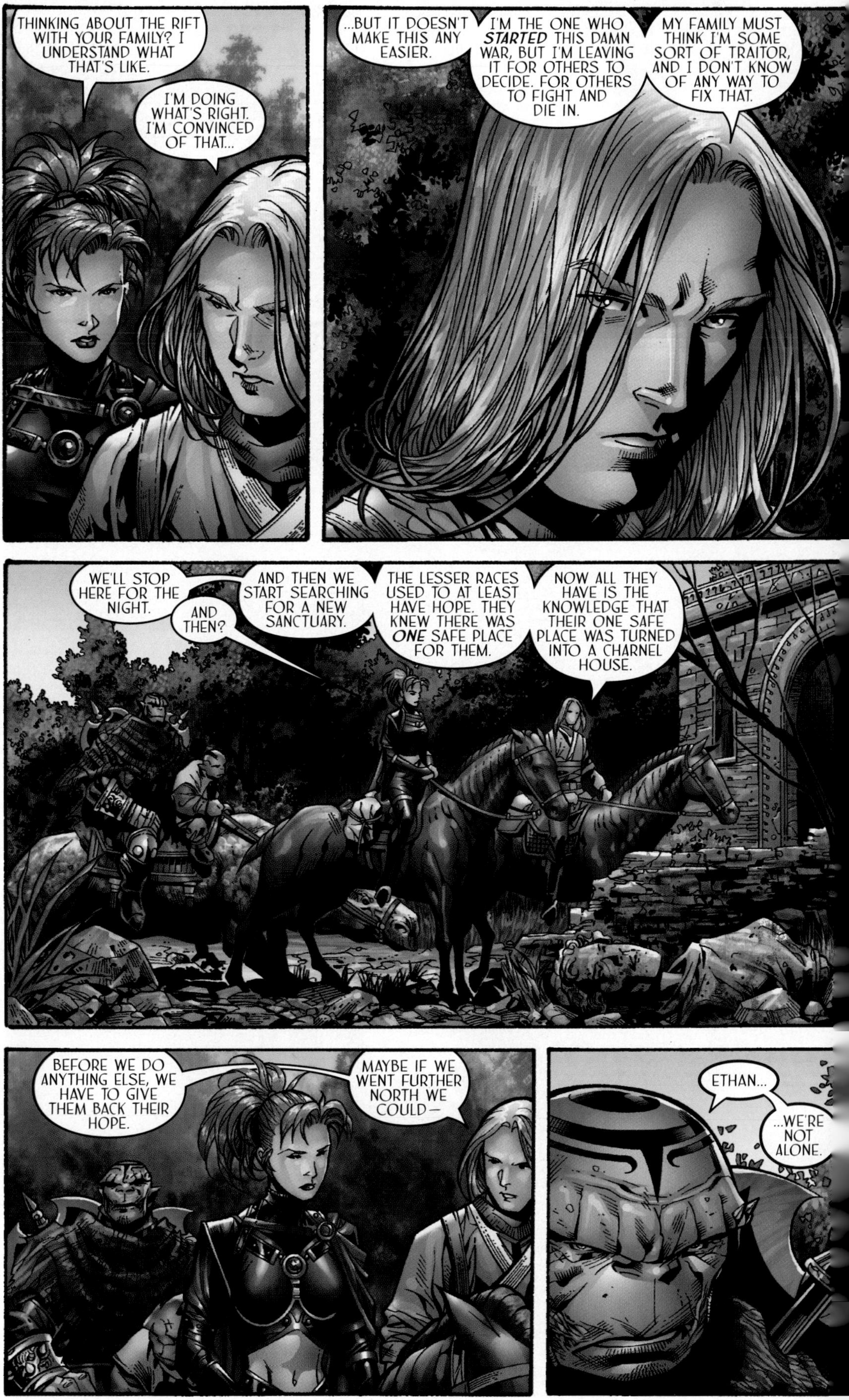
THINKING ABOUT THE RIFT WITH YOUR FAMILY? I UNDERSTAND WHAT THAT'S LIKE.
I'M DOING WHAT'S RIGHT. I'M CONVINCED OF THAT...
...BUT IT DOESN'T MAKE THIS ANY EASIER.
I'M THE ONE WHO STARTED THIS DAMN WAR, BUT I'M LEAVING IT FOR OTHERS TO DECIDE. FOR OTHERS TO FIGHT AND DIE IN.
MY FAMILY MUST THINK I'M SOME SORT OF TRAITOR, AND I DON'T KNOW OF ANY WAY TO FIX THAT.
WE'LL STOP HERE FOR THE NIGHT.
AND THEN?
AND THEN WE START SEARCHING FOR A NEW SANCTUARY.
THE LESSER RACES USED TO AT LEAST HAVE HOPE. THEY KNEW THERE WAS ONE SAFE PLACE FOR THEM.
NOW ALL THEY HAVE IS THE KNOWLEDGE THAT THEIR ONE SAFE PLACE WAS TURNED INTO A CHARNEL HOUSE.
BEFORE WE DO ANYTHING ELSE, WE HAVE TO GIVE THEM BACK THEIR HOPE.
MAYBE IF WE WENT FURTHER NORTH WE COULD—
ETHAN...
...WE'RE NOT ALONE.

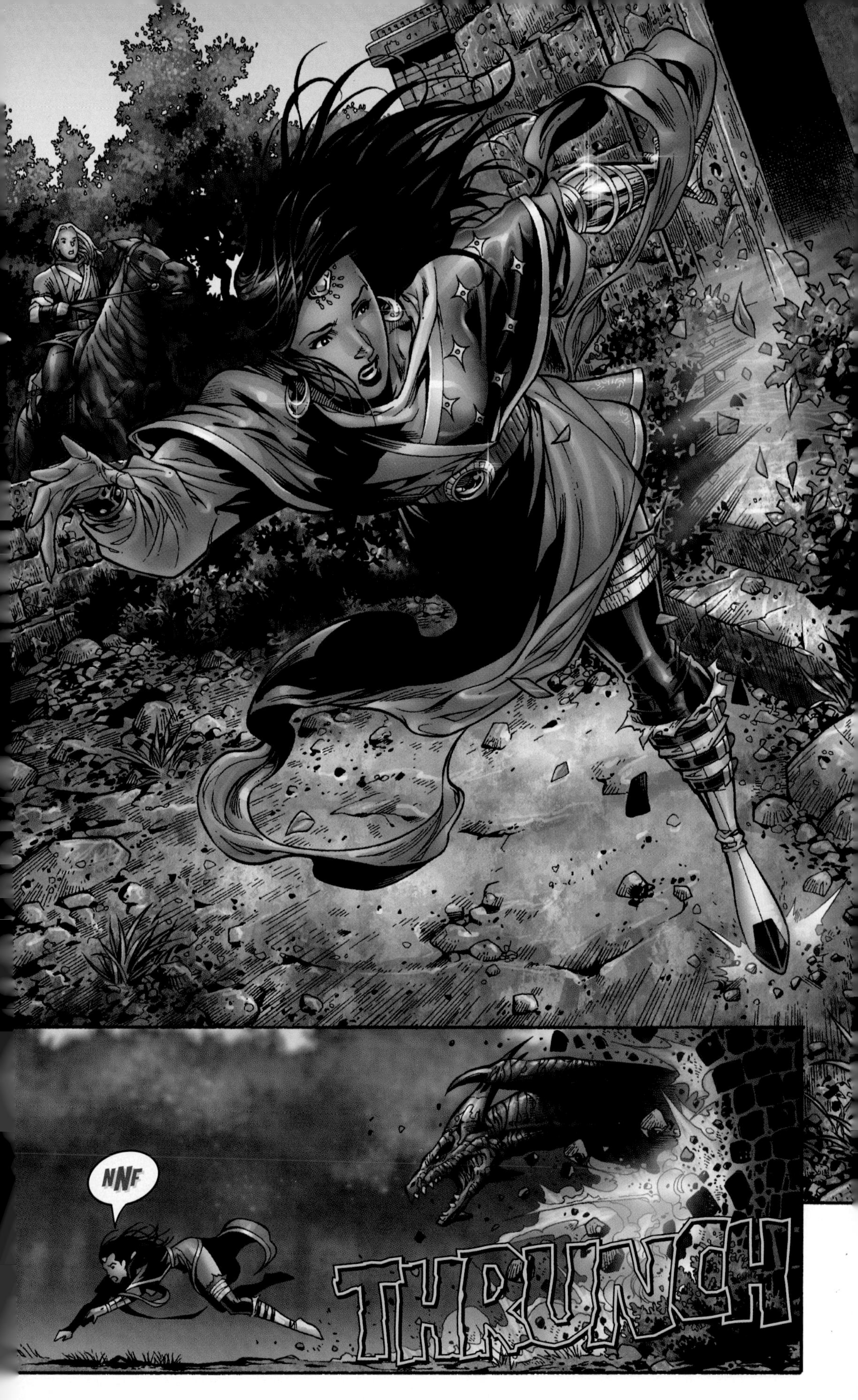
NNF
THRUNCH

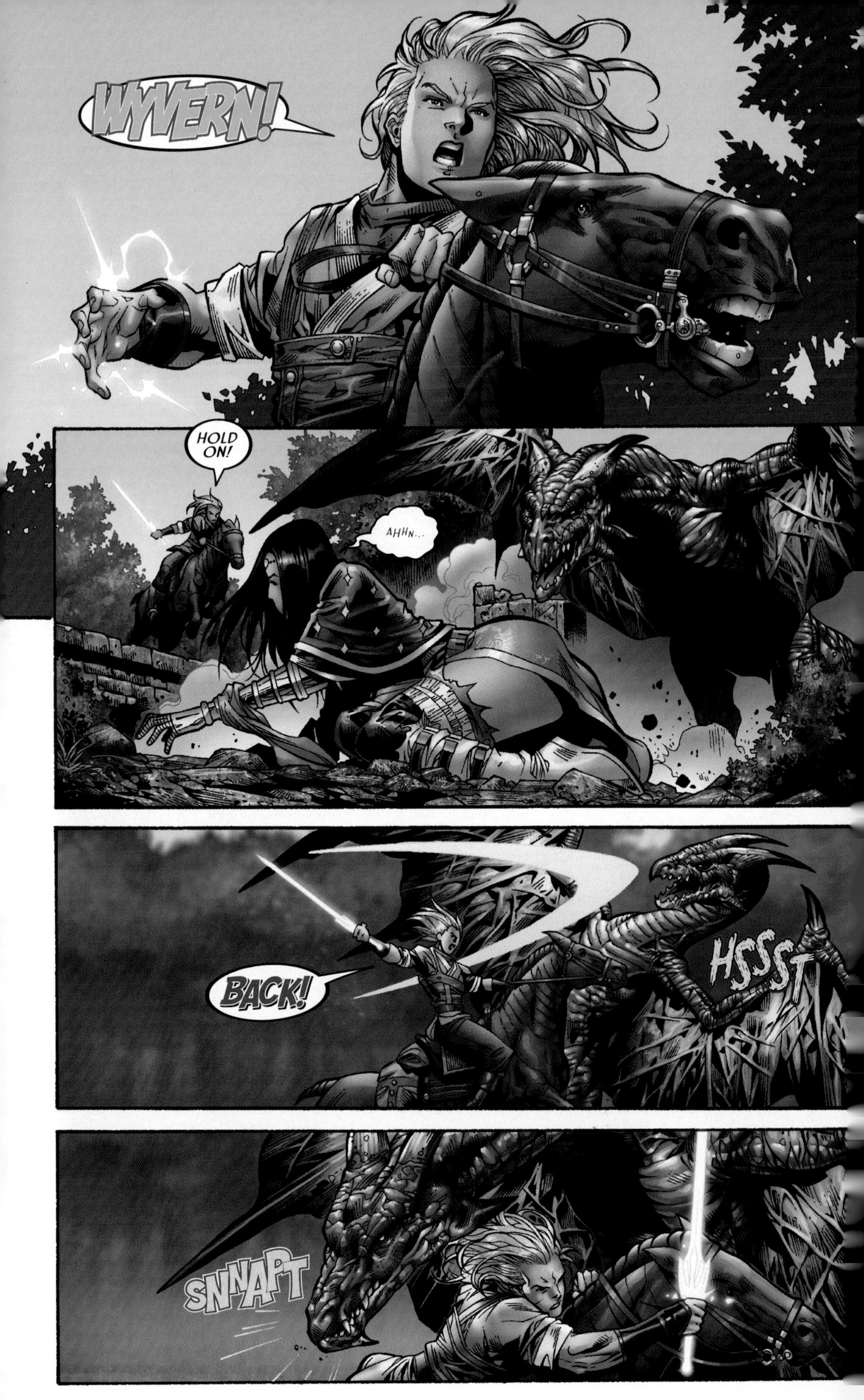
WYVERN!
HOLD ON!
AHHN...
BACK!
HSSST
SNNAPT

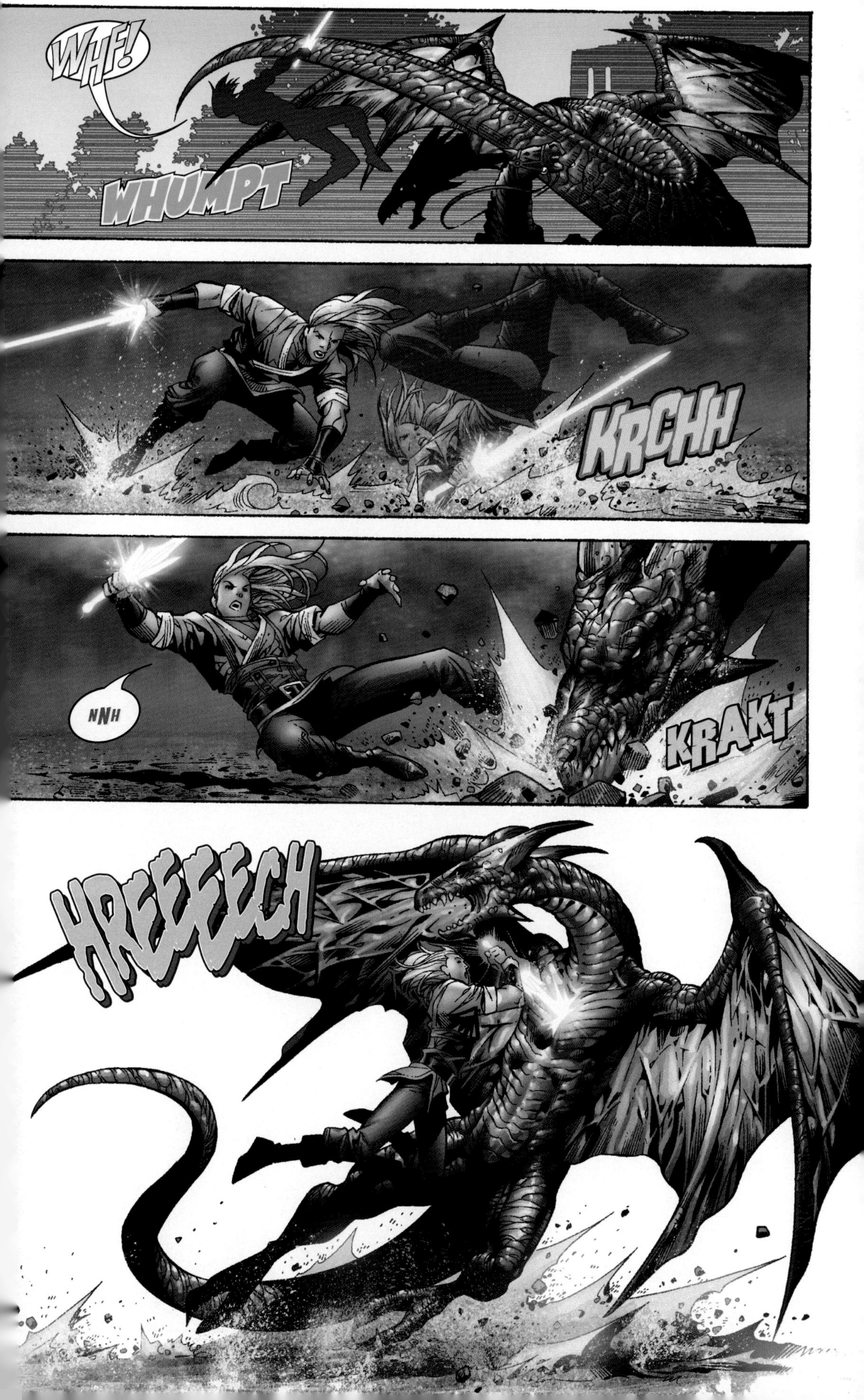
WHF!
WHUMPT
KRCHH
NNH
KRAKT
HREEEECH

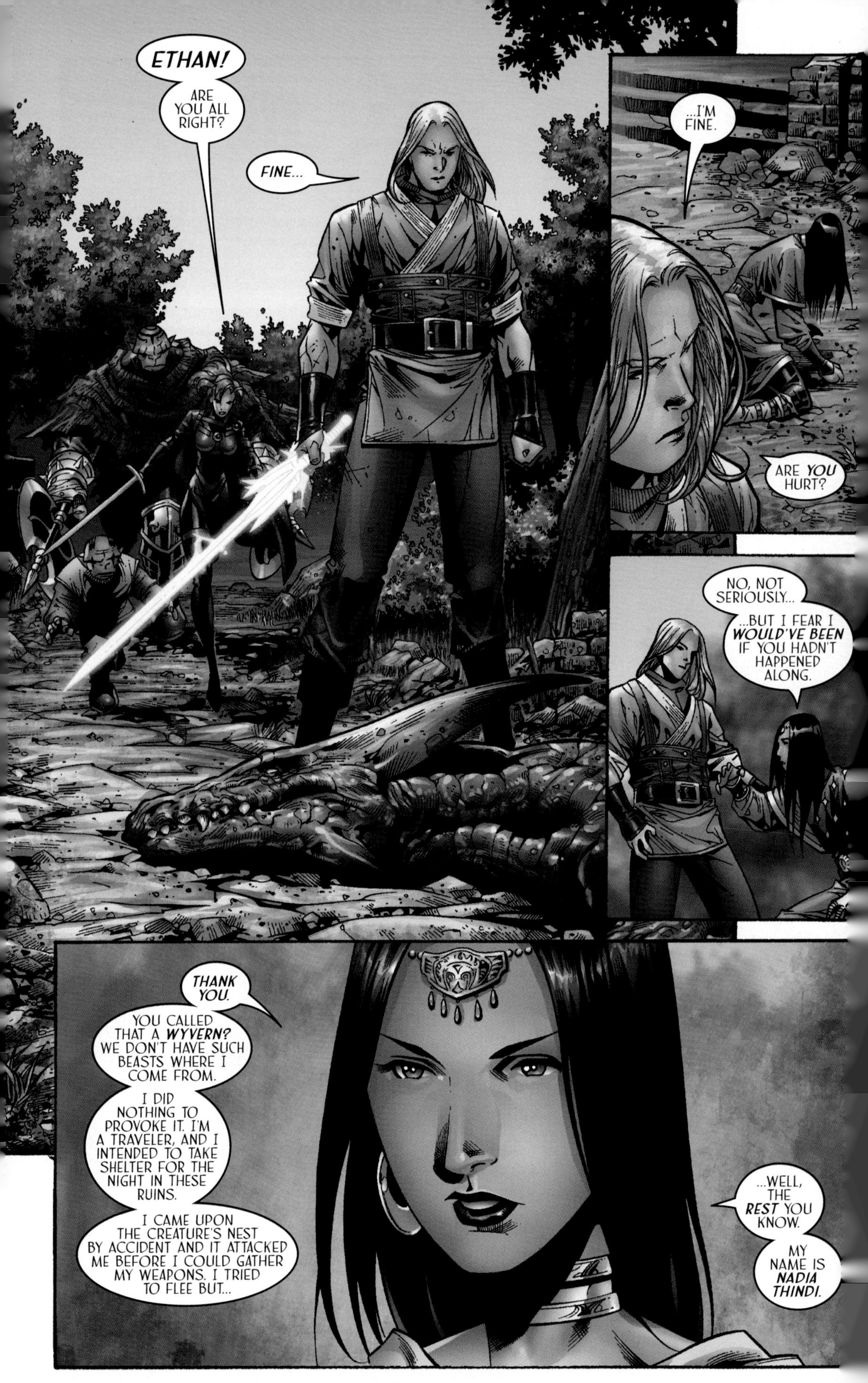
ETHAN!
ARE YOU ALL RIGHT?
FINE...
...I'M FINE.
ARE YOU HURT?
NO, NOT SERIOUSLY...
...BUT I FEAR I WOULD'VE BEEN IF YOU HADN'T HAPPENED ALONG.
THANK YOU.
YOU CALLED THAT A WYVERN? WE DON'T HAVE SUCH BEASTS WHERE I COME FROM.
I DID NOTHING TO PROVOKE IT. I'M A TRAVELER, AND I INTENDED TO TAKE SHELTER FOR THE NIGHT IN THESE RUINS.
I CAME UPON THE CREATURE'S NEST BY ACCIDENT AND IT ATTACKED ME BEFORE I COULD GATHER MY WEAPONS. I TRIED TO FLEE BUT...
...WELL, THE REST YOU KNOW.
MY NAME IS NADIA THINDI.

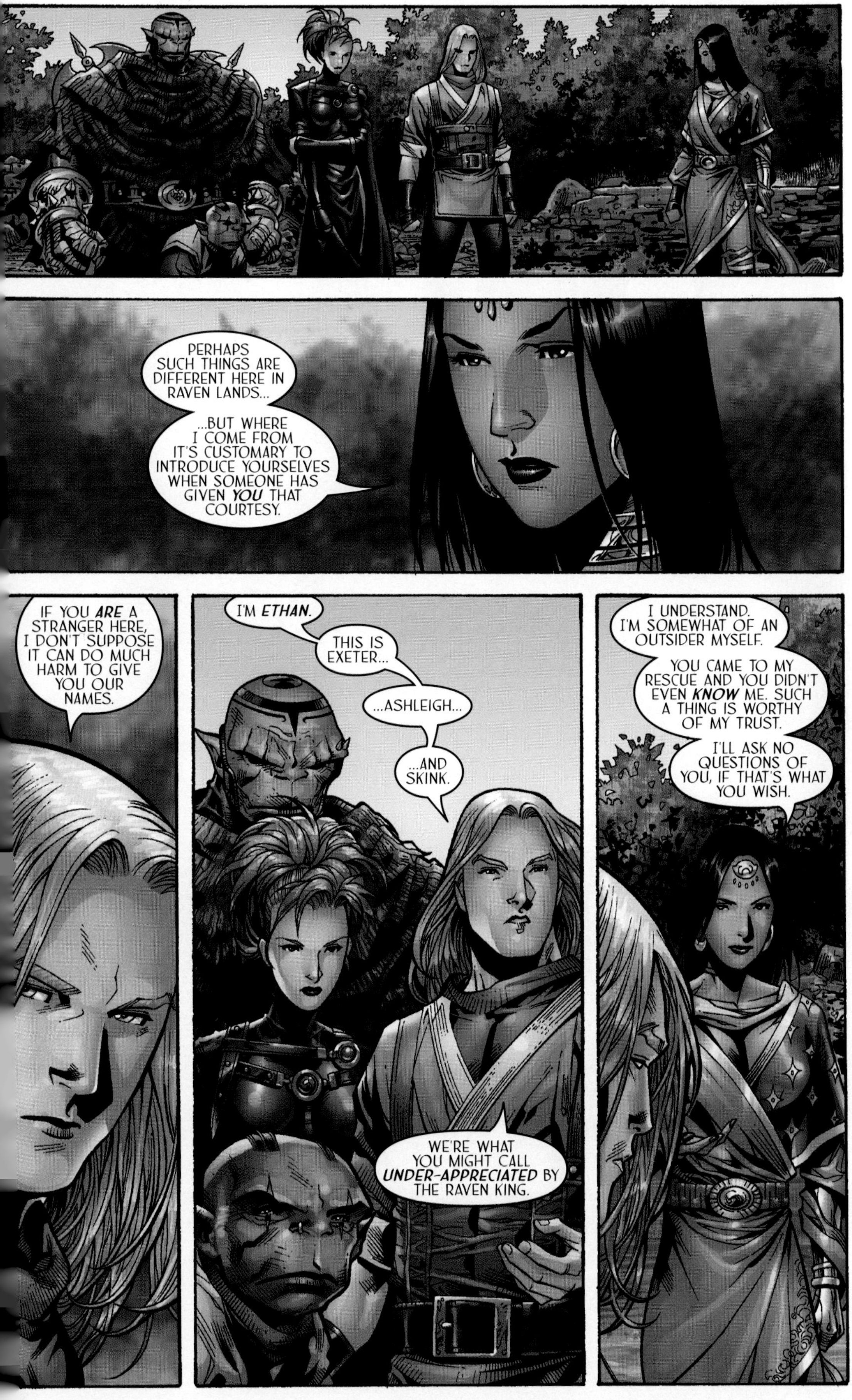

PERHAPS SUCH THINGS ARE DIFFERENT HERE IN RAVEN LANDS...
...BUT WHERE I COME FROM IT'S CUSTOMARY TO INTRODUCE YOURSELVES WHEN SOMEONE HAS GIVEN *YOU* THAT COURTESY.
IF YOU *ARE* A STRANGER HERE, I DON'T SUPPOSE IT CAN DO MUCH HARM TO GIVE YOU OUR NAMES.
I'M *ETHAN*.
THIS IS EXETER...
...ASHLEIGH...
...AND SKINK.
WE'RE WHAT YOU MIGHT CALL *UNDER-APPRECIATED* BY THE RAVEN KING.
I UNDERSTAND. I'M SOMEWHAT OF AN OUTSIDER MYSELF.
YOU CAME TO MY RESCUE AND YOU DIDN'T EVEN *KNOW* ME. SUCH A THING IS WORTHY OF MY TRUST.
I'LL ASK NO QUESTIONS OF YOU, IF THAT'S WHAT YOU WISH.

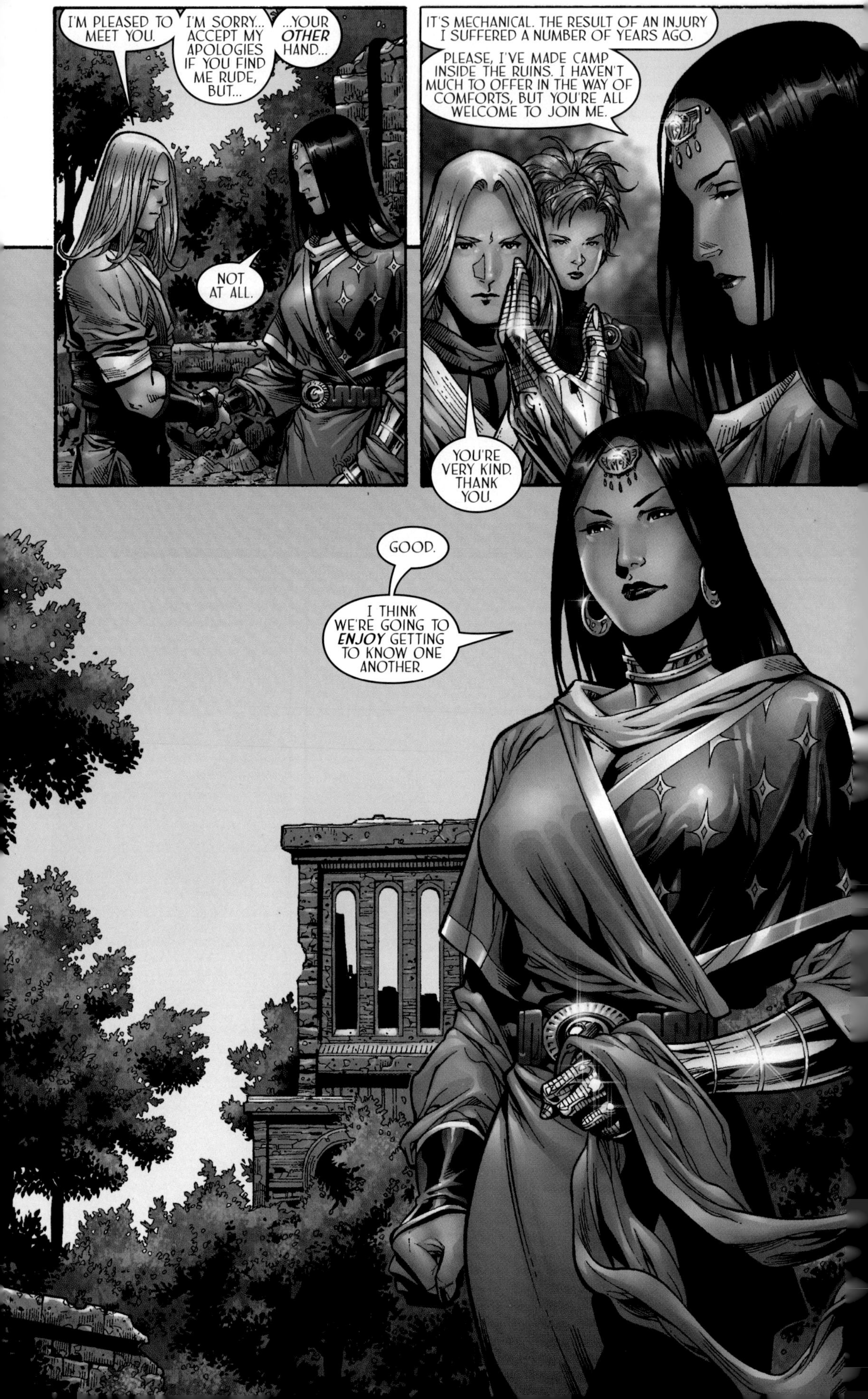
I'M PLEASED TO MEET YOU.
I'M SORRY... ACCEPT MY APOLOGIES IF YOU FIND ME RUDE, BUT...
...YOUR *OTHER* HAND...
NOT AT ALL.
IT'S MECHANICAL. THE RESULT OF AN INJURY I SUFFERED A NUMBER OF YEARS AGO.
PLEASE, I'VE MADE CAMP INSIDE THE RUINS. I HAVEN'T MUCH TO OFFER IN THE WAY OF COMFORTS, BUT YOU'RE ALL WELCOME TO JOIN ME.
YOU'RE VERY KIND. THANK YOU.
GOOD.
I THINK WE'RE GOING TO *ENJOY* GETTING TO KNOW ONE ANOTHER.

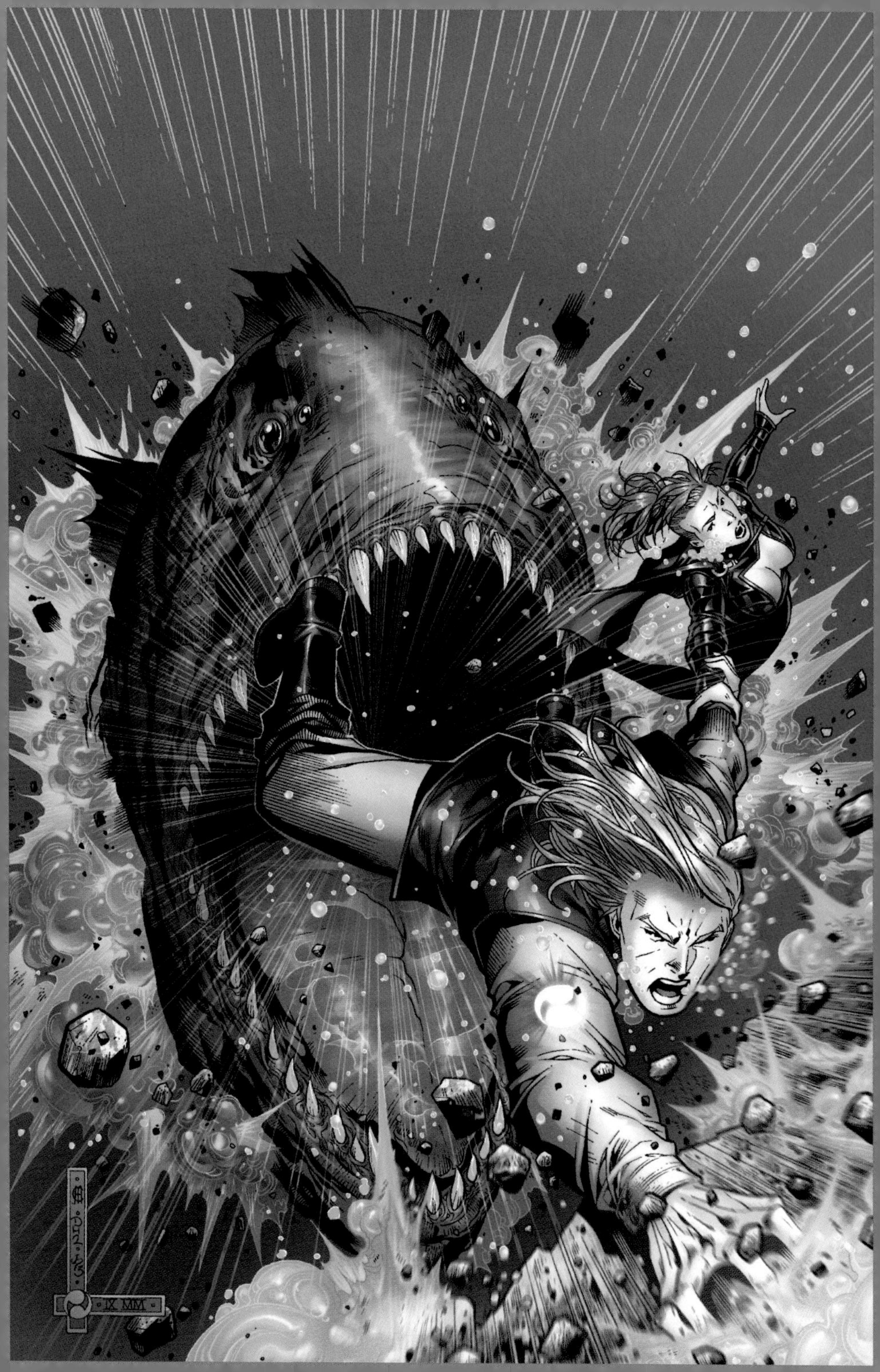
IX MM

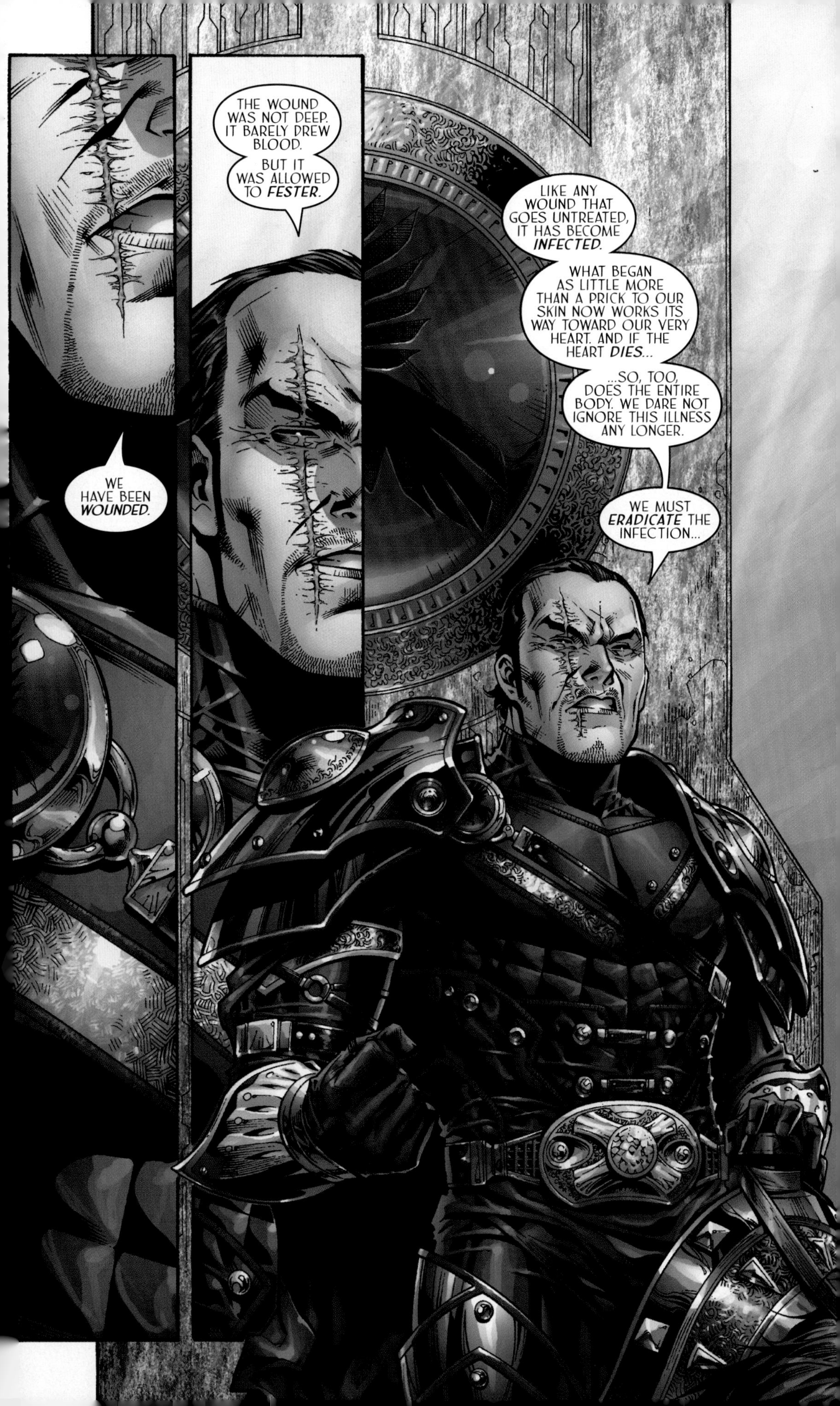
WE HAVE BEEN *WOUNDED.*
THE WOUND WAS NOT DEEP. IT BARELY DREW BLOOD.
BUT IT WAS ALLOWED TO *FESTER.*
LIKE ANY WOUND THAT GOES UNTREATED, IT HAS BECOME *INFECTED.*
WHAT BEGAN AS LITTLE MORE THAN A PRICK TO OUR SKIN NOW WORKS ITS WAY TOWARD OUR VERY HEART. AND IF THE HEART *DIES...*
...SO, TOO, DOES THE ENTIRE BODY. WE DARE NOT IGNORE THIS ILLNESS ANY LONGER.
WE MUST *ERADICATE* THE INFECTION...

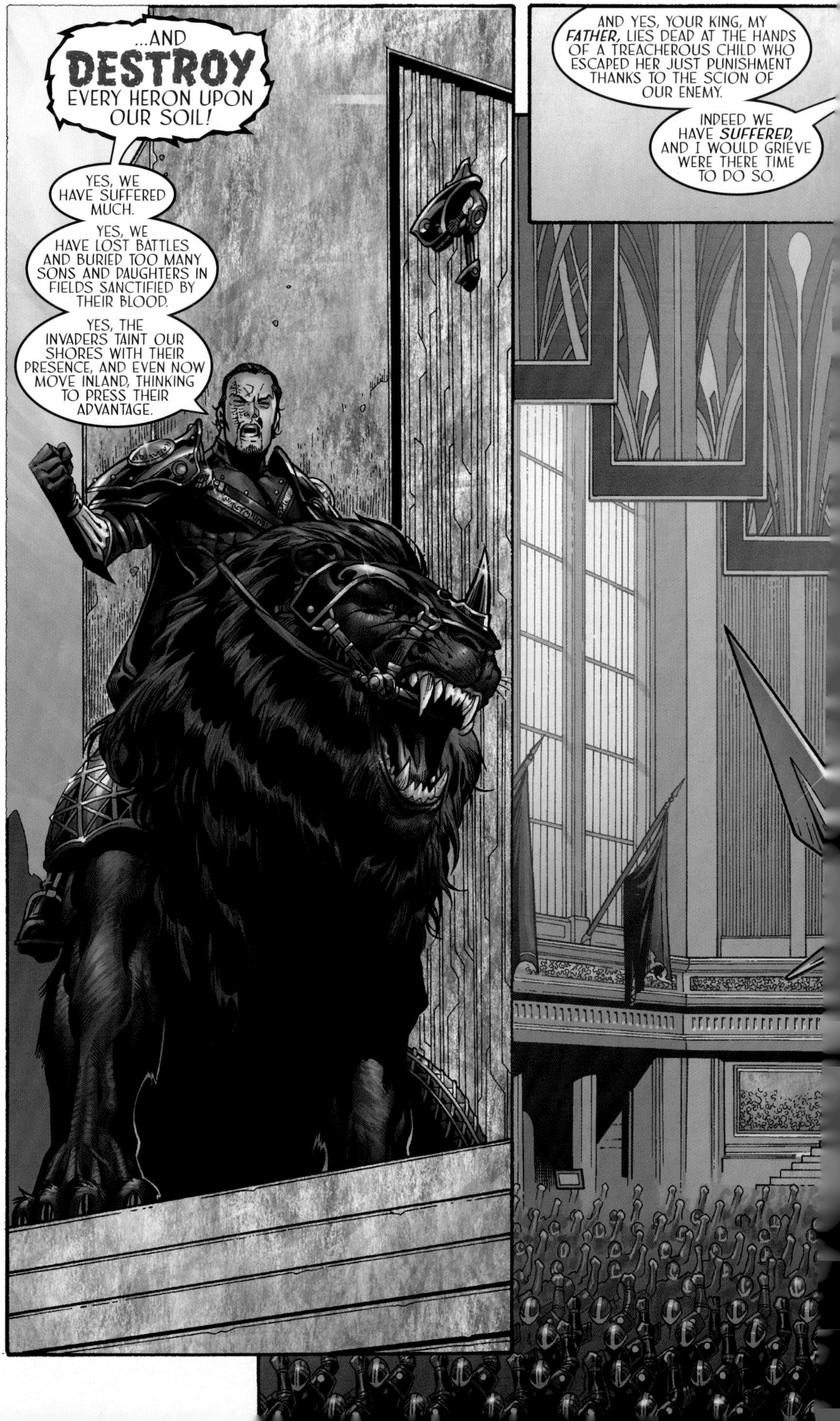
...AND DESTROY EVERY HERON UPON OUR SOIL!
YES, WE HAVE SUFFERED MUCH.
YES, WE HAVE LOST BATTLES AND BURIED TOO MANY SONS AND DAUGHTERS IN FIELDS SANCTIFIED BY THEIR BLOOD.
YES, THE INVADERS TAINT OUR SHORES WITH THEIR PRESENCE, AND EVEN NOW MOVE INLAND, THINKING TO PRESS THEIR ADVANTAGE.
AND YES, YOUR KING, MY FATHER, LIES DEAD AT THE HANDS OF A TREACHEROUS CHILD WHO ESCAPED HER JUST PUNISHMENT THANKS TO THE SCION OF OUR ENEMY.
INDEED WE HAVE SUFFERED, AND I WOULD GRIEVE WERE THERE TIME TO DO SO.

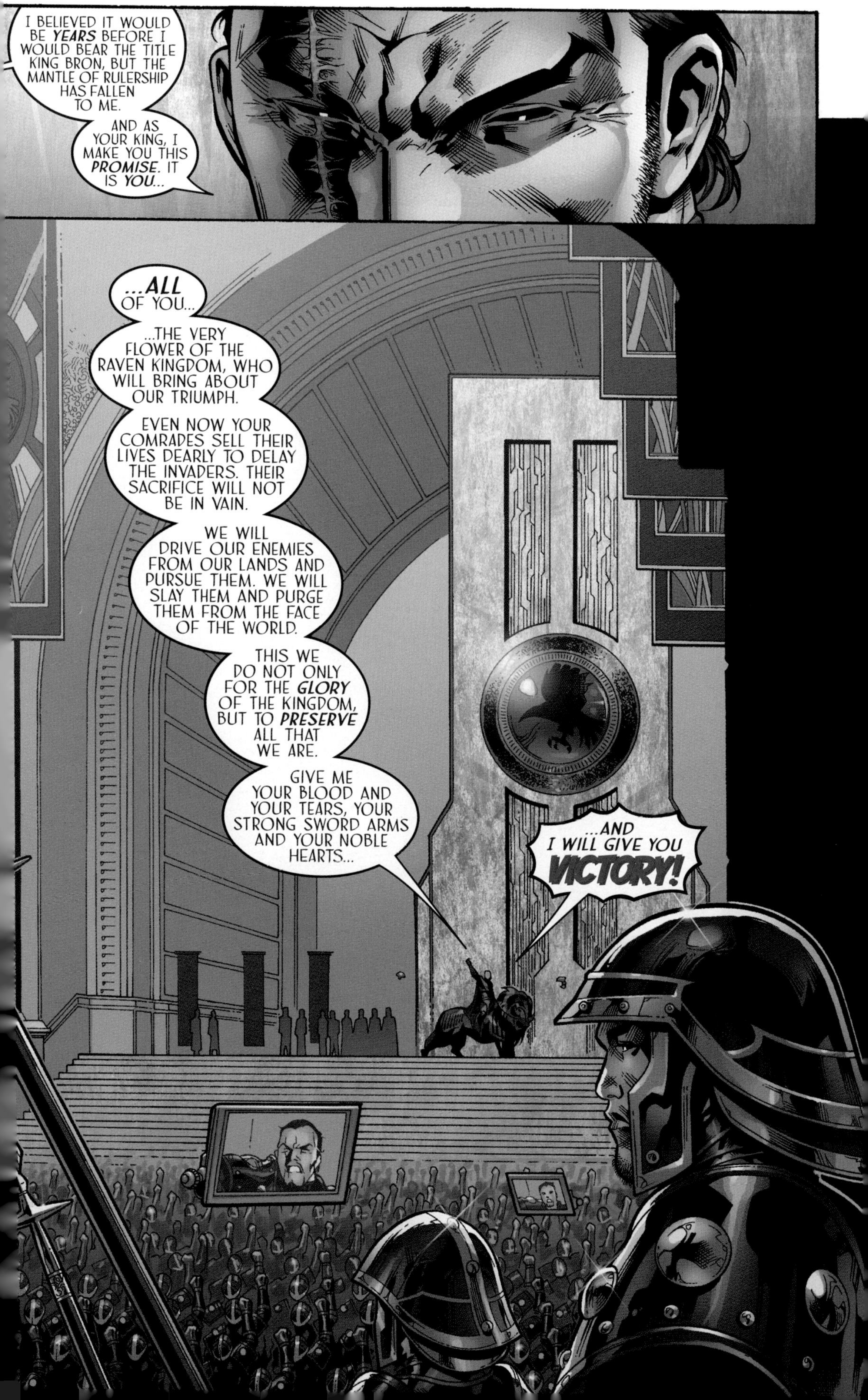
I BELIEVED IT WOULD BE YEARS BEFORE I WOULD BEAR THE TITLE KING BRON, BUT THE MANTLE OF RULERSHIP HAS FALLEN TO ME.
AND AS YOUR KING, I MAKE YOU THIS PROMISE. IT IS YOU...
...ALL OF YOU...
...THE VERY FLOWER OF THE RAVEN KINGDOM, WHO WILL BRING ABOUT OUR TRIUMPH.
EVEN NOW YOUR COMRADES SELL THEIR LIVES DEARLY TO DELAY THE INVADERS. THEIR SACRIFICE WILL NOT BE IN VAIN.
WE WILL DRIVE OUR ENEMIES FROM OUR LANDS AND PURSUE THEM. WE WILL SLAY THEM AND PURGE THEM FROM THE FACE OF THE WORLD.
THIS WE DO NOT ONLY FOR THE GLORY OF THE KINGDOM, BUT TO PRESERVE ALL THAT WE ARE.
GIVE ME YOUR BLOOD AND YOUR TEARS, YOUR STRONG SWORD ARMS AND YOUR NOBLE HEARTS...
...AND I WILL GIVE YOU VICTORY!

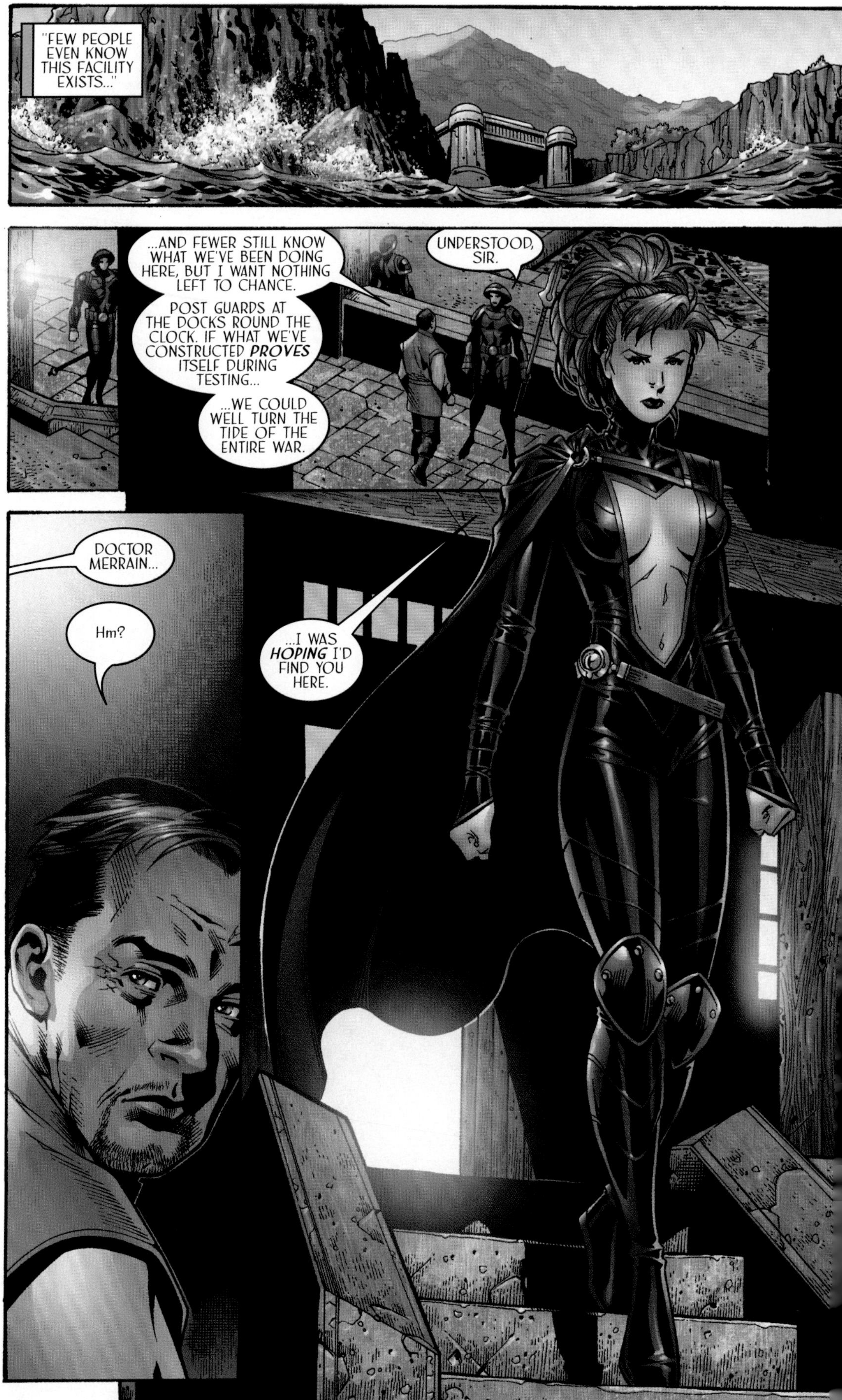
"FEW PEOPLE EVEN KNOW THIS FACILITY EXISTS..."
...AND FEWER STILL KNOW WHAT WE'VE BEEN DOING HERE, BUT I WANT NOTHING LEFT TO CHANCE.
POST GUARDS AT THE DOCKS ROUND THE CLOCK. IF WHAT WE'VE CONSTRUCTED PROVES ITSELF DURING TESTING...
...WE COULD WELL TURN THE TIDE OF THE ENTIRE WAR.
UNDERSTOOD, SIR.
DOCTOR MERRAIN...
Hm?
...I WAS HOPING I'D FIND YOU HERE.

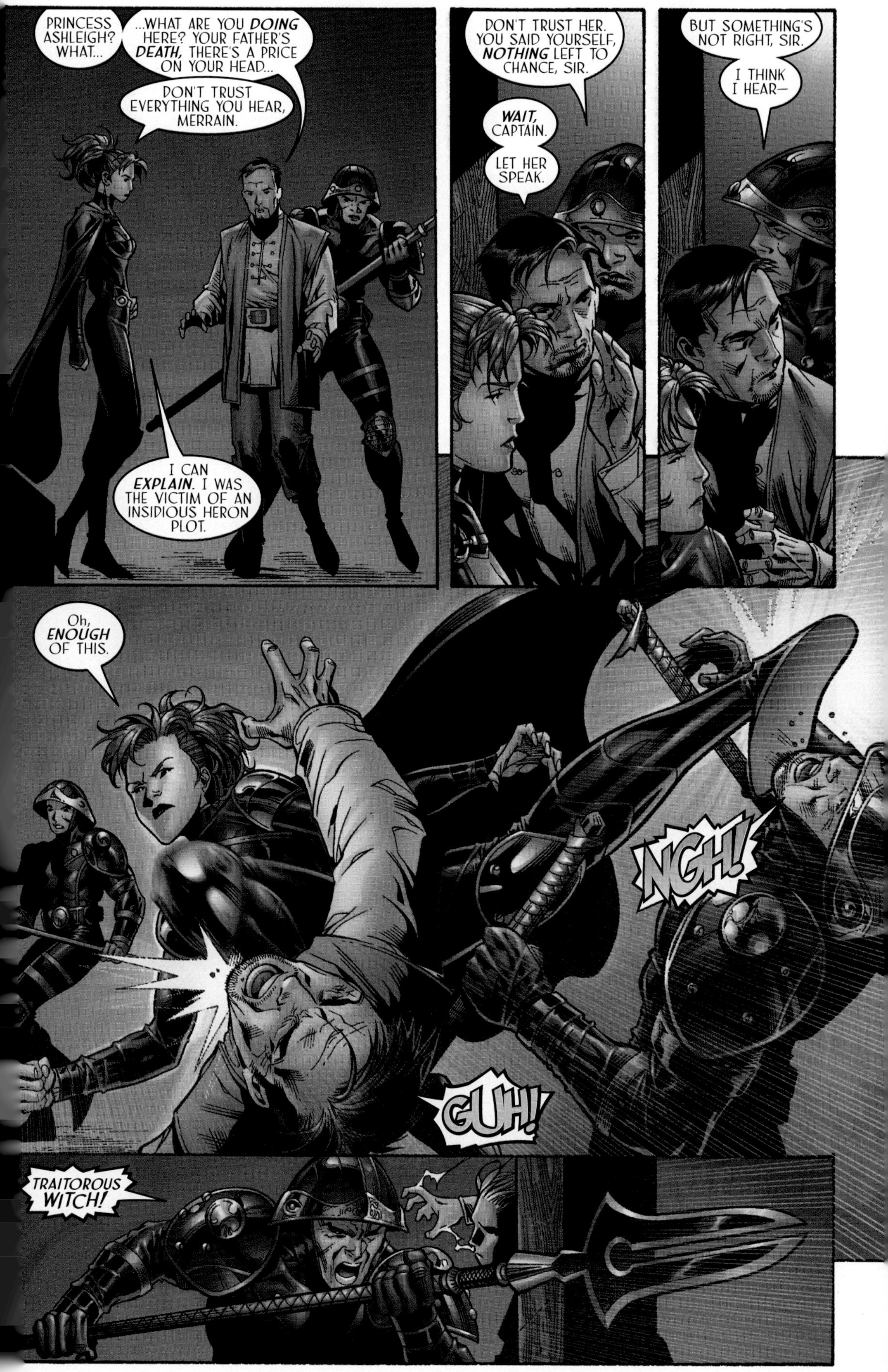

PRINCESS ASHLEIGH? WHAT...
...WHAT ARE YOU DOING HERE? YOUR FATHER'S DEATH, THERE'S A PRICE ON YOUR HEAD...
DON'T TRUST EVERYTHING YOU HEAR, MERRAIN.
I CAN EXPLAIN. I WAS THE VICTIM OF AN INSIDIOUS HERON PLOT.
DON'T TRUST HER. YOU SAID YOURSELF, NOTHING LEFT TO CHANCE, SIR.
WAIT, CAPTAIN.
LET HER SPEAK.
BUT SOMETHING'S NOT RIGHT, SIR.
I THINK I HEAR—
Oh, ENOUGH OF THIS.
NGH!
GUH!
TRAITOROUS WITCH!

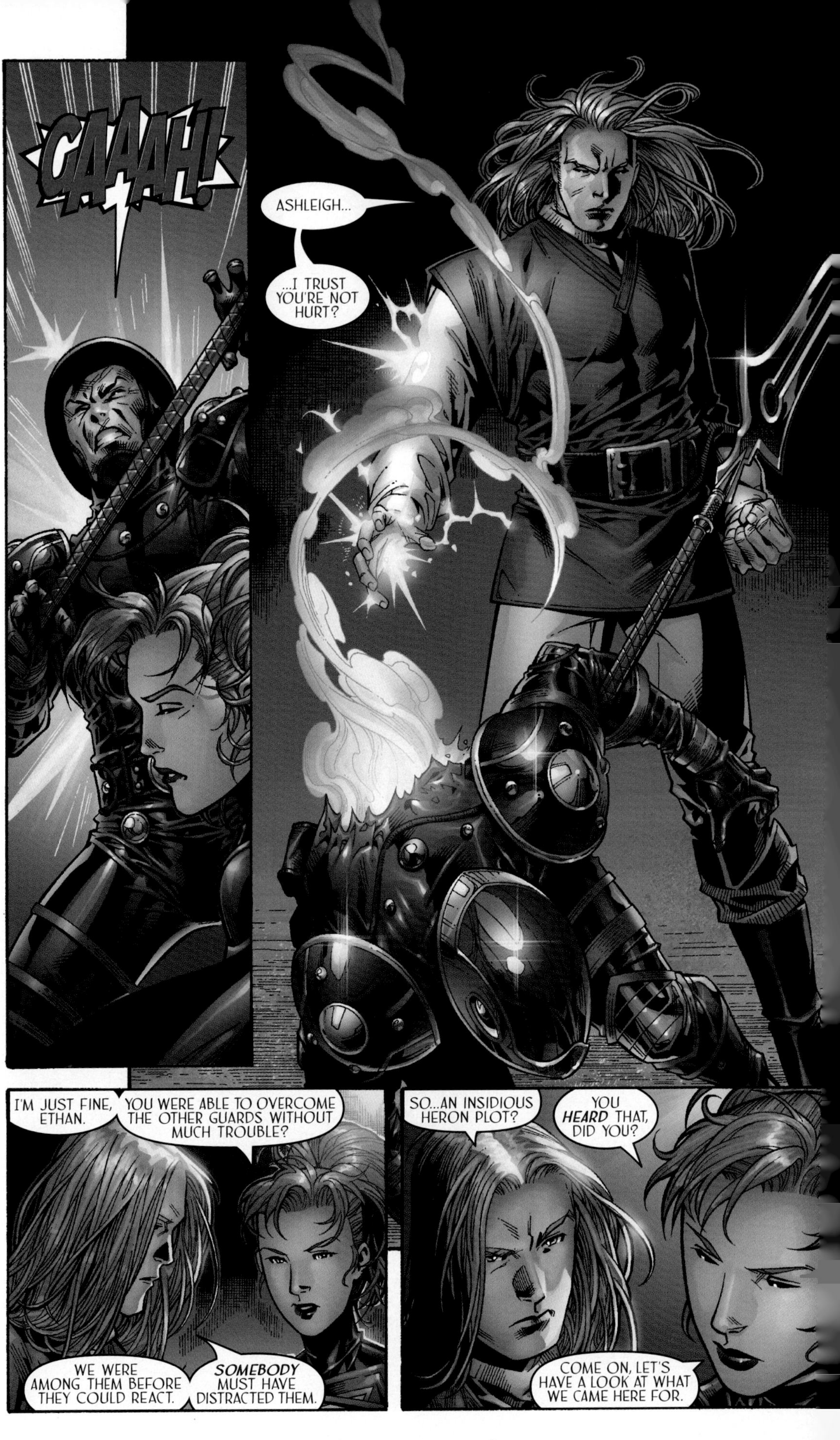
GAAAH!
ASHLEIGH...
...I TRUST YOU'RE NOT HURT?
I'M JUST FINE, ETHAN.
YOU WERE ABLE TO OVERCOME THE OTHER GUARDS WITHOUT MUCH TROUBLE?
WE WERE AMONG THEM BEFORE THEY COULD REACT.
SOMEBODY MUST HAVE DISTRACTED THEM.
SO...AN INSIDIOUS HERON PLOT?
YOU HEARD THAT, DID YOU?
COME ON, LET'S HAVE A LOOK AT WHAT WE CAME HERE FOR.

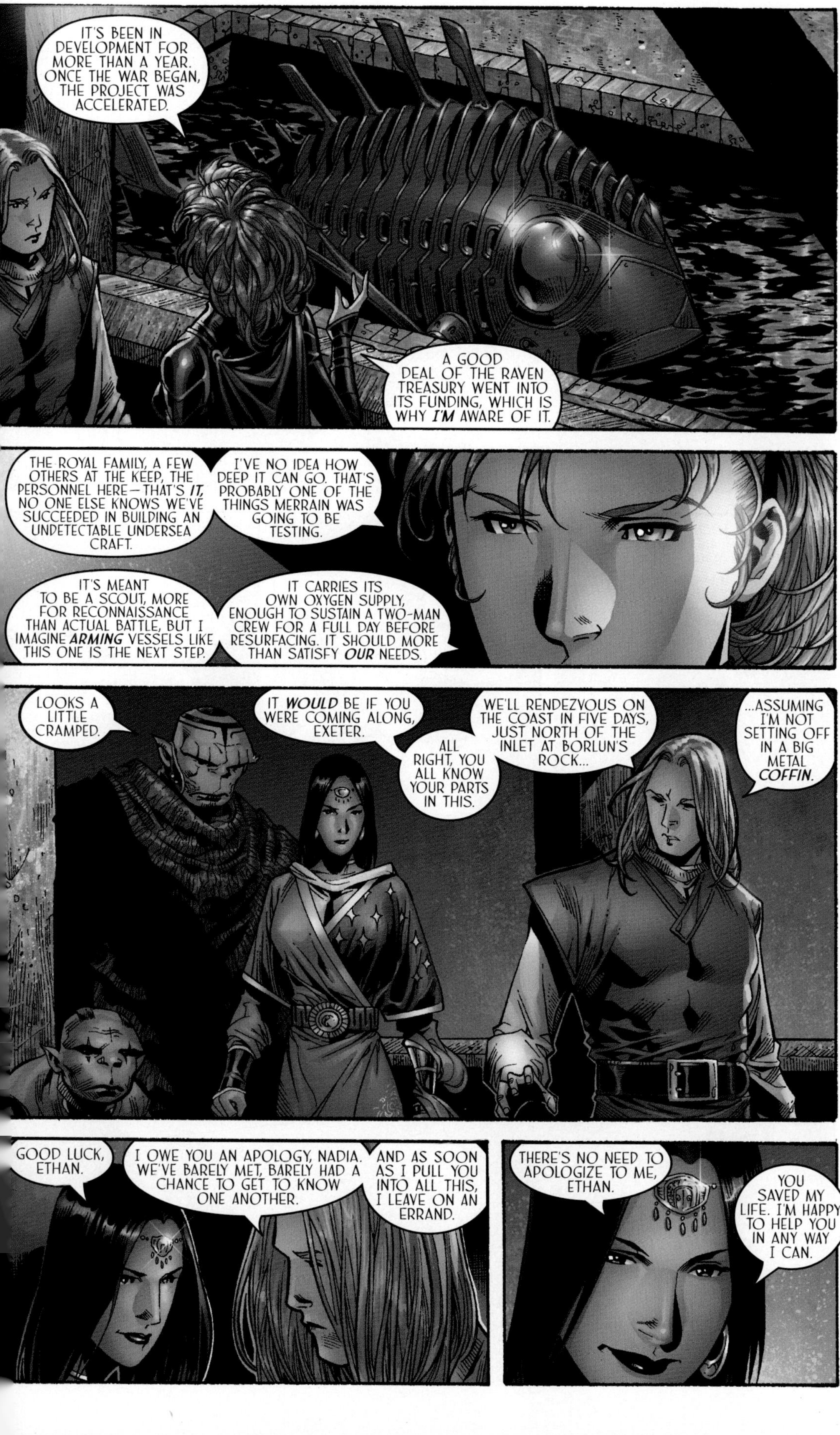
IT'S BEEN IN DEVELOPMENT FOR MORE THAN A YEAR. ONCE THE WAR BEGAN, THE PROJECT WAS ACCELERATED.
A GOOD DEAL OF THE RAVEN TREASURY WENT INTO ITS FUNDING, WHICH IS WHY *I'M* AWARE OF IT.
THE ROYAL FAMILY, A FEW OTHERS AT THE KEEP, THE PERSONNEL HERE—THAT'S *IT,* NO ONE ELSE KNOWS WE'VE SUCCEEDED IN BUILDING AN UNDETECTABLE UNDERSEA CRAFT.
I'VE NO IDEA HOW DEEP IT CAN GO. THAT'S PROBABLY ONE OF THE THINGS MERRAIN WAS GOING TO BE TESTING.
IT'S MEANT TO BE A SCOUT, MORE FOR RECONNAISSANCE THAN ACTUAL BATTLE, BUT I IMAGINE *ARMING* VESSELS LIKE THIS ONE IS THE NEXT STEP.
IT CARRIES ITS OWN OXYGEN SUPPLY, ENOUGH TO SUSTAIN A TWO-MAN CREW FOR A FULL DAY BEFORE RESURFACING. IT SHOULD MORE THAN SATISFY *OUR* NEEDS.
LOOKS A LITTLE CRAMPED.
IT *WOULD* BE IF YOU WERE COMING ALONG, EXETER.
ALL RIGHT, YOU ALL KNOW YOUR PARTS IN THIS.
WE'LL RENDEZVOUS ON THE COAST IN FIVE DAYS, JUST NORTH OF THE INLET AT BORLUN'S ROCK...
...ASSUMING I'M NOT SETTING OFF IN A BIG METAL *COFFIN*.
GOOD LUCK, ETHAN.
I OWE YOU AN APOLOGY, NADIA. WE'VE BARELY MET, BARELY HAD A CHANCE TO GET TO KNOW ONE ANOTHER.
AND AS SOON AS I PULL YOU INTO ALL THIS, I LEAVE ON AN ERRAND.
THERE'S NO NEED TO APOLOGIZE TO ME, ETHAN.
YOU SAVED MY LIFE. I'M HAPPY TO HELP YOU IN ANY WAY I CAN.

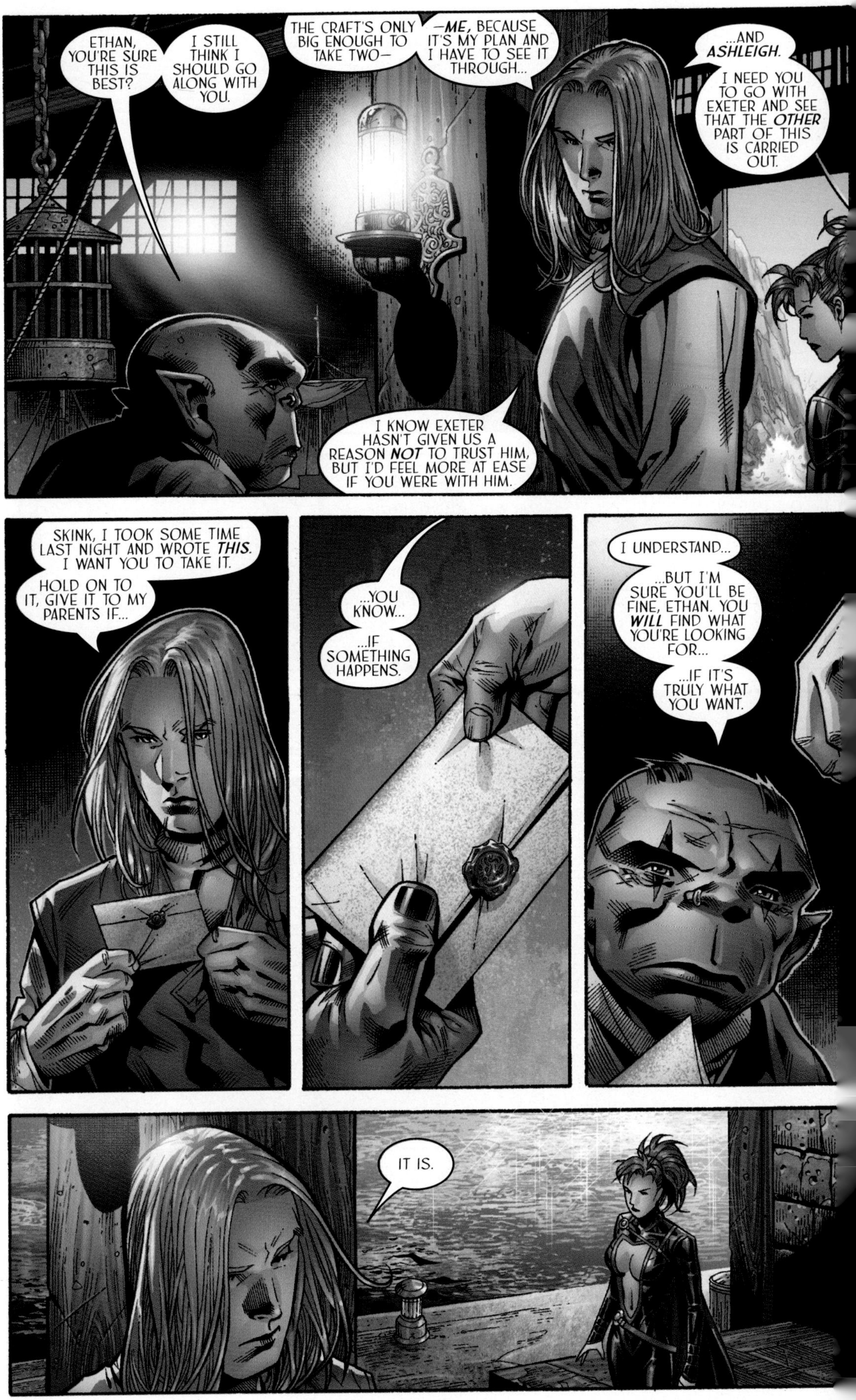
ETHAN, YOU'RE SURE THIS IS BEST?
I STILL THINK I SHOULD GO ALONG WITH YOU.
THE CRAFT'S ONLY BIG ENOUGH TO TAKE TWO—
—ME, BECAUSE IT'S MY PLAN AND I HAVE TO SEE IT THROUGH...
...AND ASHLEIGH.
I NEED YOU TO GO WITH EXETER AND SEE THAT THE OTHER PART OF THIS IS CARRIED OUT.
I KNOW EXETER HASN'T GIVEN US A REASON NOT TO TRUST HIM, BUT I'D FEEL MORE AT EASE IF YOU WERE WITH HIM.
SKINK, I TOOK SOME TIME LAST NIGHT AND WROTE THIS. I WANT YOU TO TAKE IT.
HOLD ON TO IT, GIVE IT TO MY PARENTS IF...
...YOU KNOW...
...IF SOMETHING HAPPENS.
I UNDERSTAND...
...BUT I'M SURE YOU'LL BE FINE, ETHAN. YOU WILL FIND WHAT YOU'RE LOOKING FOR...
...IF IT'S TRULY WHAT YOU WANT.
IT IS.

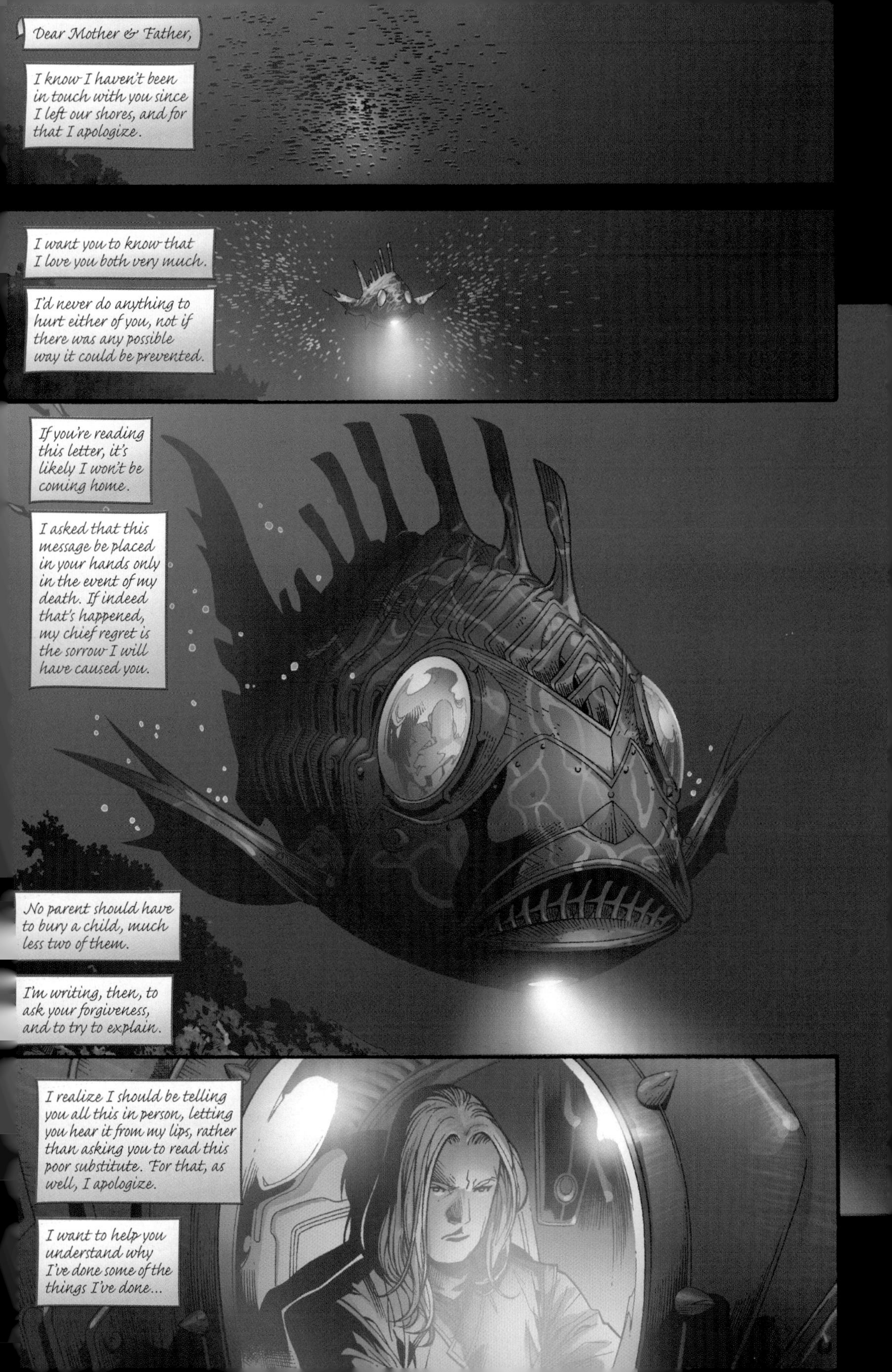
Dear Mother & Father,
I know I haven't been in touch with you since I left our shores, and for that I apologize.
I want you to know that I love you both very much.
I'd never do anything to hurt either of you, not if there was any possible way it could be prevented.
If you're reading this letter, it's likely I won't be coming home.
I asked that this message be placed in your hands only in the event of my death. If indeed that's happened, my chief regret is the sorrow I will have caused you.
No parent should have to bury a child, much less two of them.
I'm writing, then, to ask your forgiveness, and to try to explain.
I realize I should be telling you all this in person, letting you hear it from my lips, rather than asking you to read this poor substitute. For that, as well, I apologize.
I want to help you understand why I've done some of the things I've done...

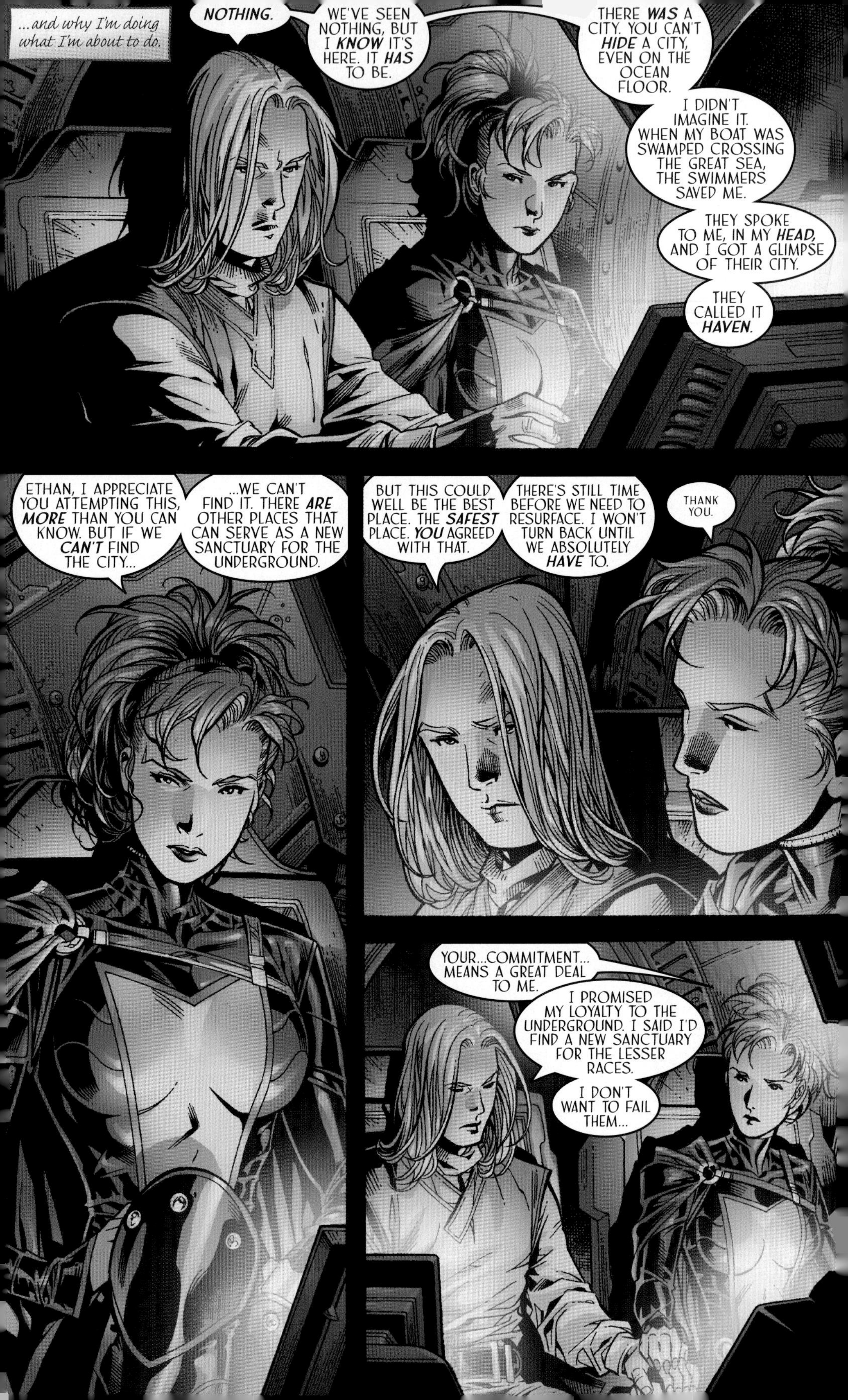

...and why I'm doing what I'm about to do.
NOTHING.
WE'VE SEEN NOTHING, BUT I KNOW IT'S HERE. IT HAS TO BE.
THERE WAS A CITY. YOU CAN'T HIDE A CITY, EVEN ON THE OCEAN FLOOR.
I DIDN'T IMAGINE IT. WHEN MY BOAT WAS SWAMPED CROSSING THE GREAT SEA, THE SWIMMERS SAVED ME.
THEY SPOKE TO ME, IN MY HEAD, AND I GOT A GLIMPSE OF THEIR CITY.
THEY CALLED IT HAVEN.
ETHAN, I APPRECIATE YOU ATTEMPTING THIS, MORE THAN YOU CAN KNOW. BUT IF WE CAN'T FIND THE CITY...
...WE CAN'T FIND IT. THERE ARE OTHER PLACES THAT CAN SERVE AS A NEW SANCTUARY FOR THE UNDERGROUND.
BUT THIS COULD WELL BE THE BEST PLACE. THE SAFEST PLACE. YOU AGREED WITH THAT.
THERE'S STILL TIME BEFORE WE NEED TO RESURFACE. I WON'T TURN BACK UNTIL WE ABSOLUTELY HAVE TO.
THANK YOU.
YOUR...COMMITMENT... MEANS A GREAT DEAL TO ME.
I PROMISED MY LOYALTY TO THE UNDERGROUND. I SAID I'D FIND A NEW SANCTUARY FOR THE LESSER RACES.
I DON'T WANT TO FAIL THEM...

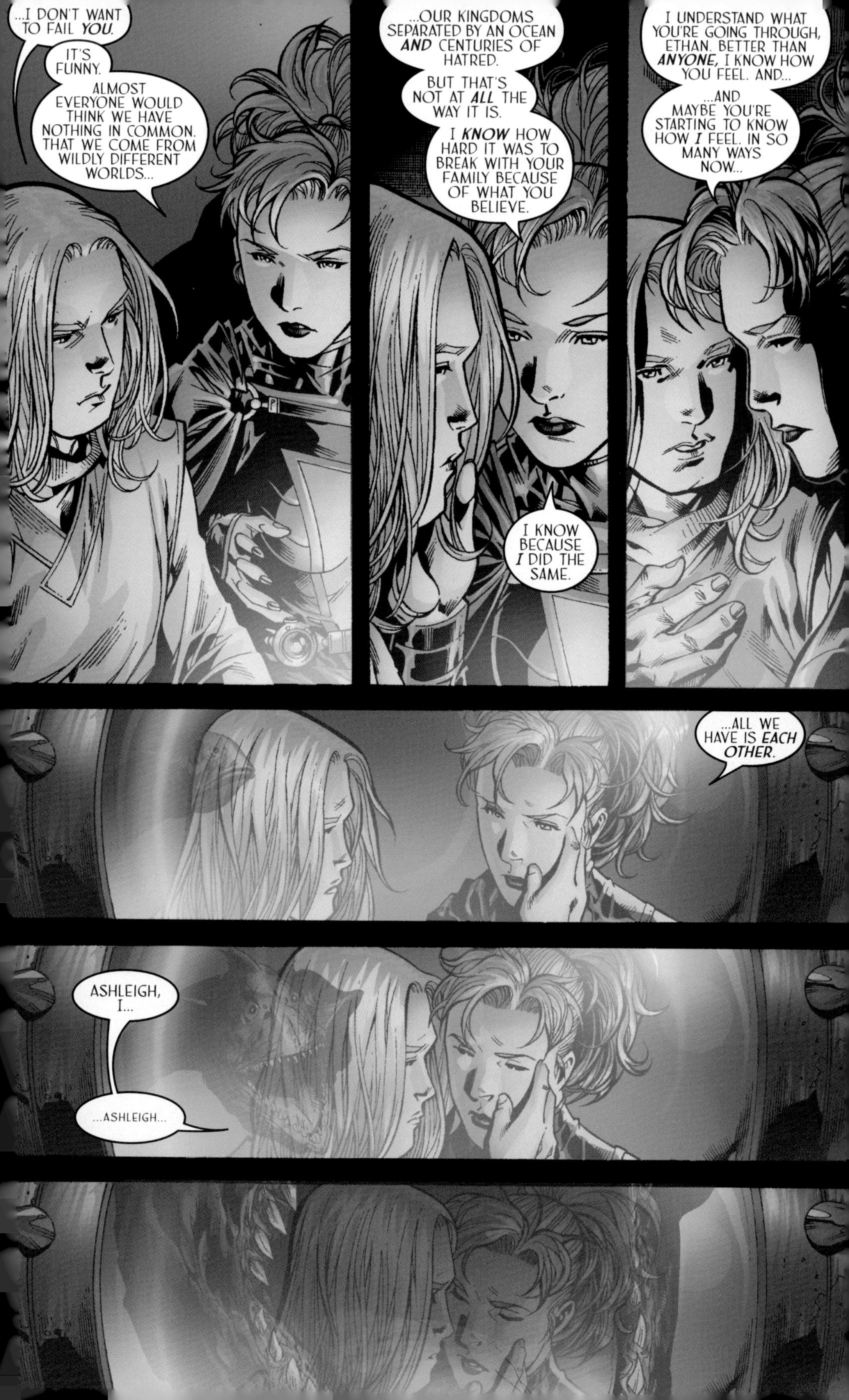
...I DON'T WANT TO FAIL YOU.
IT'S FUNNY.
ALMOST EVERYONE WOULD THINK WE HAVE NOTHING IN COMMON. THAT WE COME FROM WILDLY DIFFERENT WORLDS...
...OUR KINGDOMS SEPARATED BY AN OCEAN AND CENTURIES OF HATRED.
BUT THAT'S NOT AT ALL THE WAY IT IS.
I KNOW HOW HARD IT WAS TO BREAK WITH YOUR FAMILY BECAUSE OF WHAT YOU BELIEVE.
I KNOW BECAUSE I DID THE SAME.
I UNDERSTAND WHAT YOU'RE GOING THROUGH, ETHAN. BETTER THAN ANYONE, I KNOW HOW YOU FEEL. AND...
...AND MAYBE YOU'RE STARTING TO KNOW HOW I FEEL. IN SO MANY WAYS NOW...
...ALL WE HAVE IS EACH OTHER.
ASHLEIGH, I...
...ASHLEIGH...

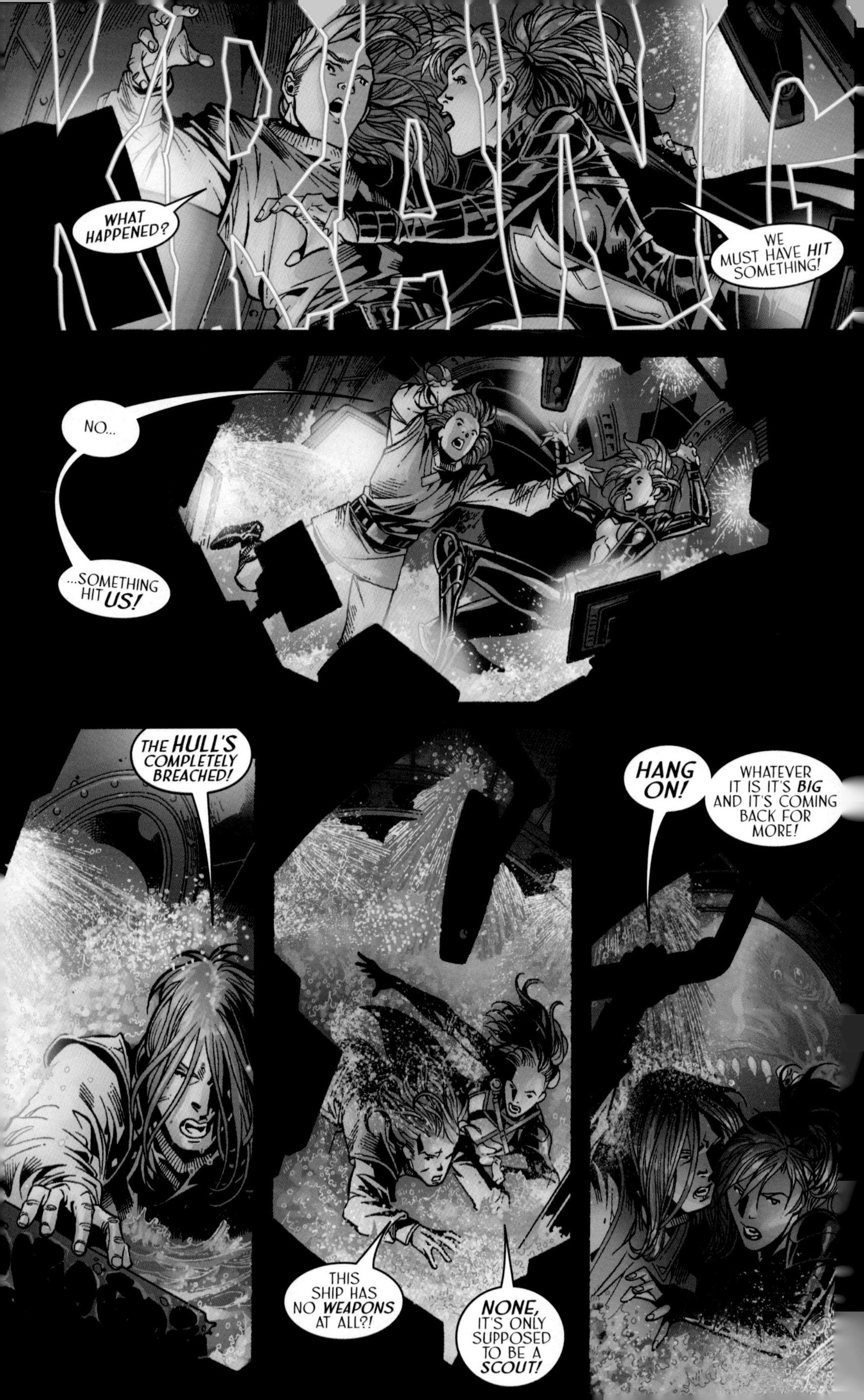
WHAT HAPPENED?
WE MUST HAVE HIT SOMETHING!
NO...
...SOMETHING HIT US!
THE HULL'S COMPLETELY BREACHED!
THIS SHIP HAS NO WEAPONS AT ALL?!
NONE, IT'S ONLY SUPPOSED TO BE A SCOUT!
HANG ON!
WHATEVER IT IS IT'S BIG AND IT'S COMING BACK FOR MORE!

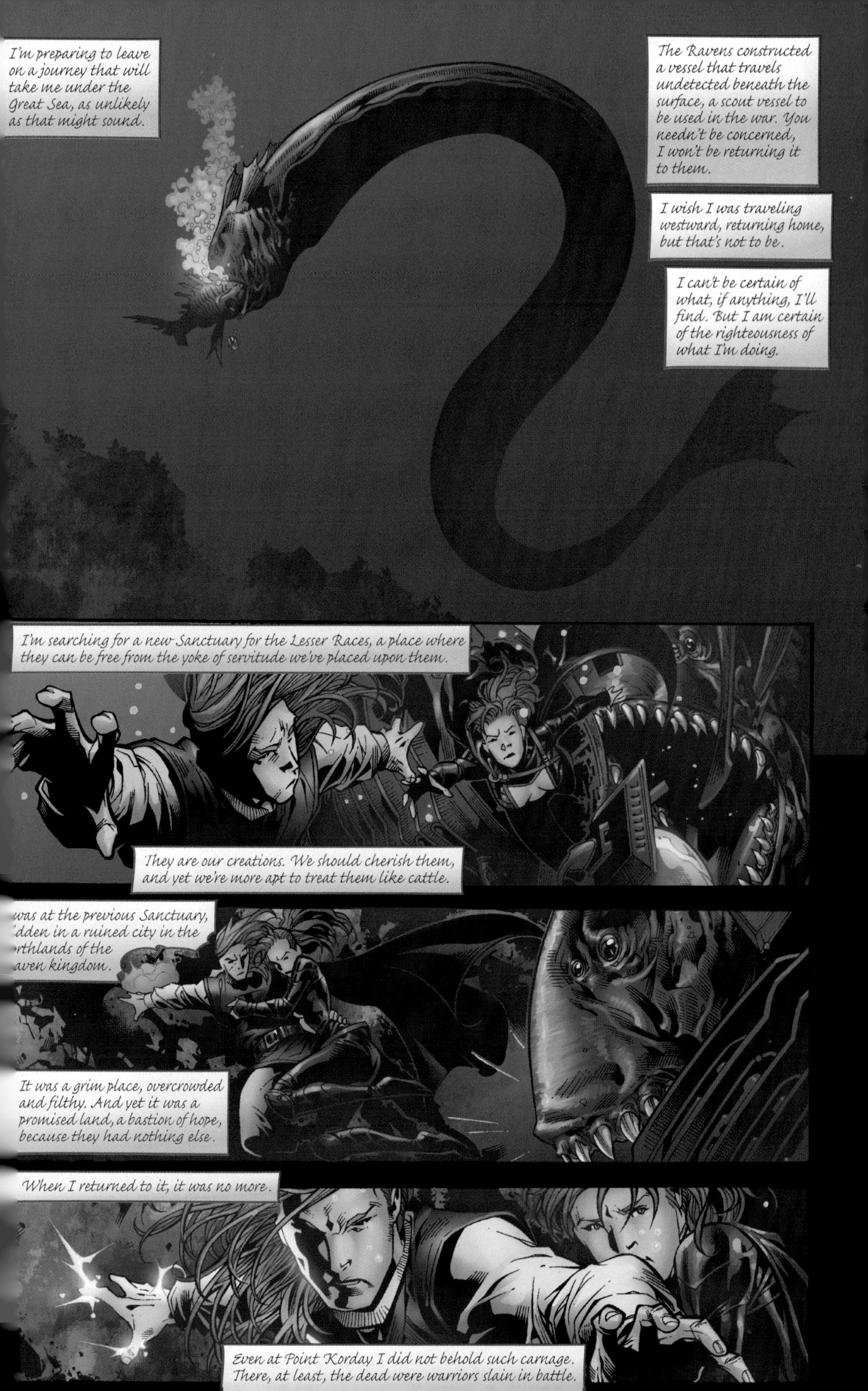
I'm preparing to leave on a journey that will take me under the Great Sea, as unlikely as that might sound.
The Ravens constructed a vessel that travels undetected beneath the surface, a scout vessel to be used in the war. You needn't be concerned, I won't be returning it to them.
I wish I was traveling westward, returning home, but that's not to be.
I can't be certain of what, if anything, I'll find. But I am certain of the righteousness of what I'm doing.
I'm searching for a new Sanctuary for the Lesser Races, a place where they can be free from the yoke of servitude we've placed upon them.
They are our creations. We should cherish them, and yet we're more apt to treat them like cattle.
was at the previous Sanctuary, idden in a ruined city in the rthlands of the aven kingdom.
It was a grim place, overcrowded and filthy. And yet it was a promised land, a bastion of hope, because they had nothing else.
When I returned to it, it was no more.
Even at Point Korday I did not behold such carnage. There, at least, the dead were warriors slain in battle.

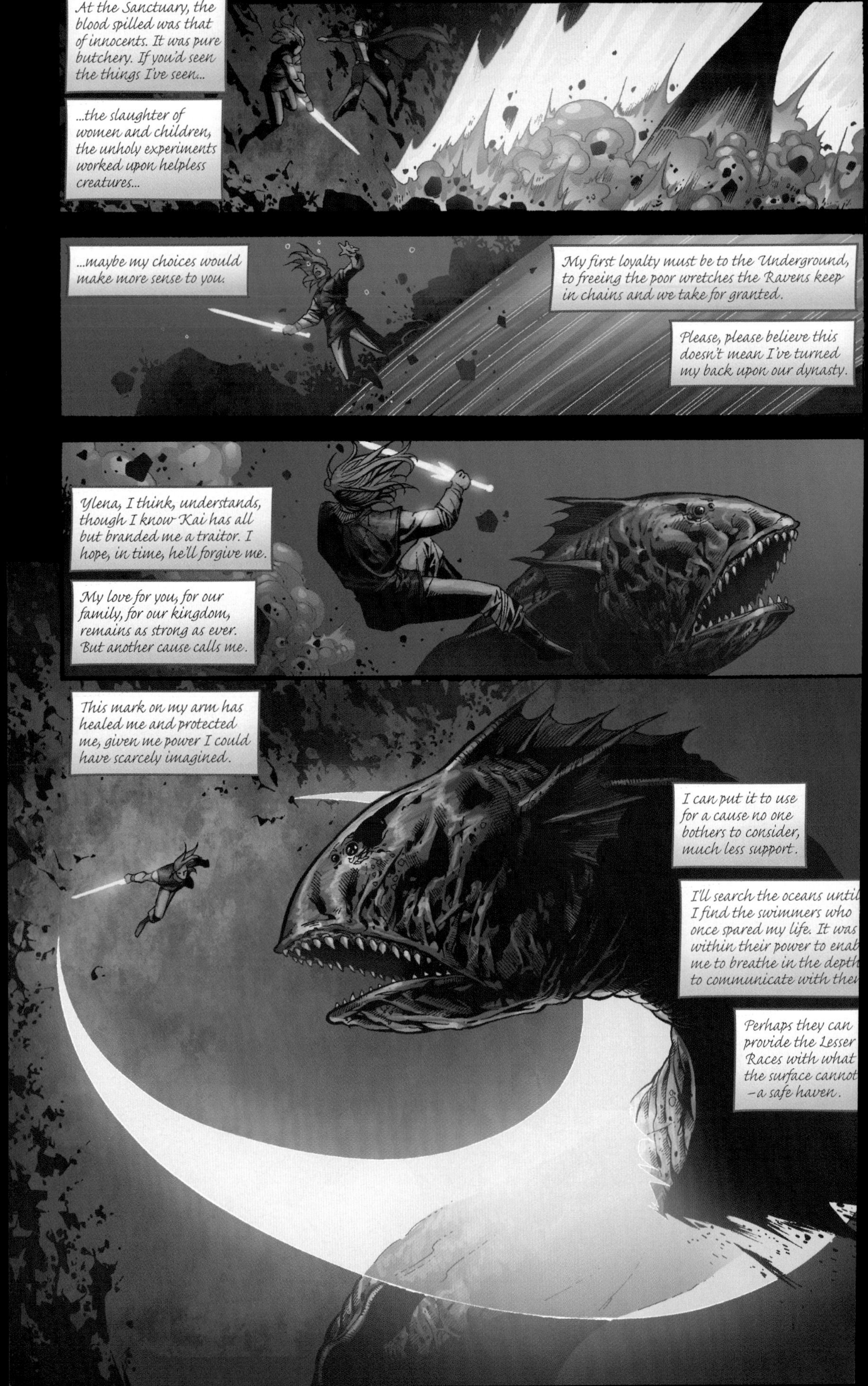
At the Sanctuary, the blood spilled was that of innocents. It was pure butchery. If you'd seen the things I've seen...
...the slaughter of women and children, the unholy experiments worked upon helpless creatures...
...maybe my choices would make more sense to you.
My first loyalty must be to the Underground, to freeing the poor wretches the Ravens keep in chains and we take for granted.
Please, please believe this doesn't mean I've turned my back upon our dynasty.
Ylena, I think, understands, though I know Kai has all but branded me a traitor. I hope, in time, he'll forgive me.
My love for you, for our family, for our kingdom, remains as strong as ever. But another cause calls me.
This mark on my arm has healed me and protected me, given me power I could have scarcely imagined.
I can put it to use for a cause no one bothers to consider, much less support.
I'll search the oceans until I find the swimmers who once spared my life. It was within their power to enab me to breathe in the depth to communicate with the
Perhaps they can provide the Lesser Races with what the surface cannot —a safe haven.

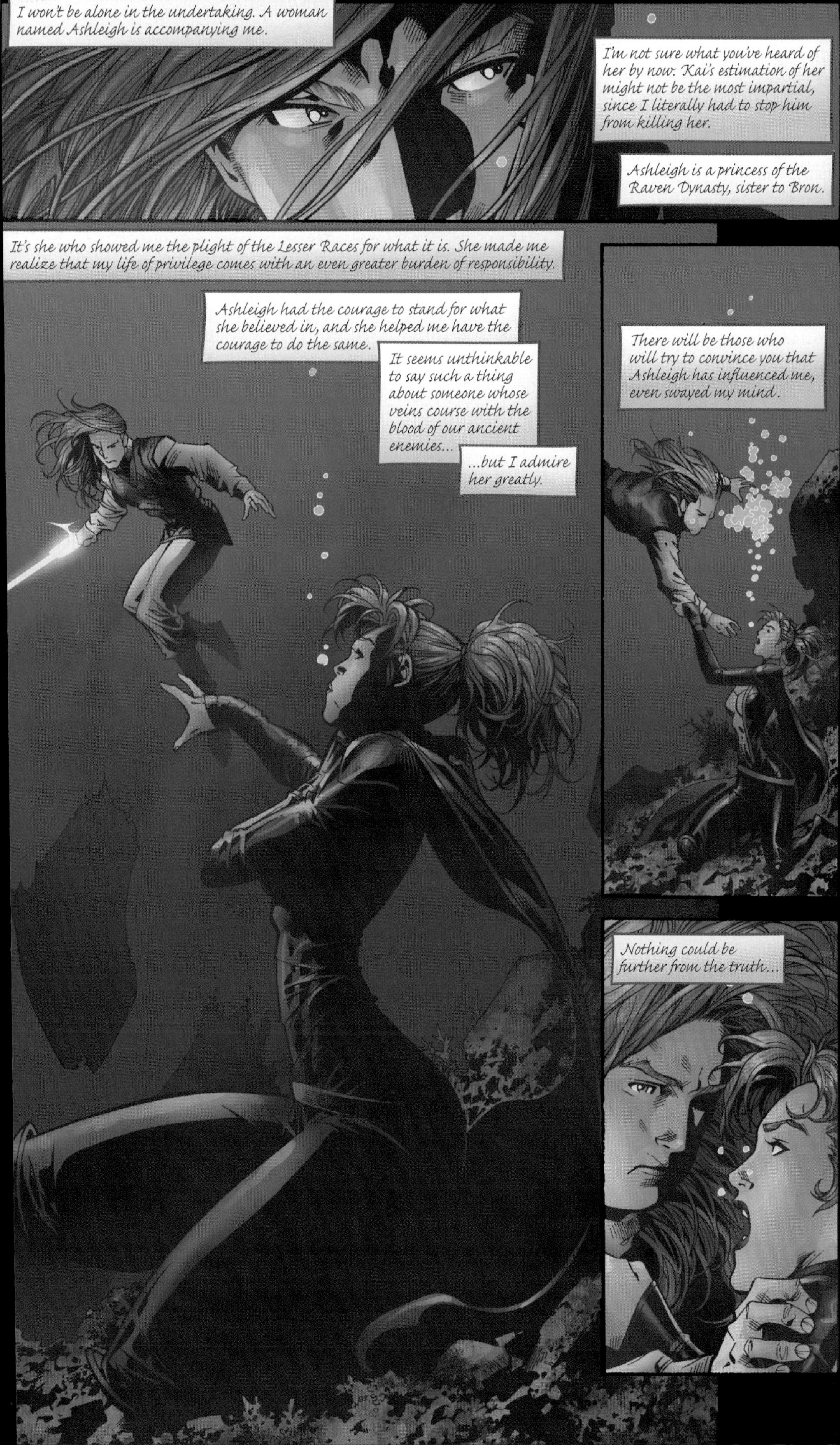
I won't be alone in the undertaking. A woman named Ashleigh is accompanying me.
I'm not sure what you've heard of her by now. Kai's estimation of her might not be the most impartial, since I literally had to stop him from killing her.
Ashleigh is a princess of the Raven Dynasty, sister to Bron.
It's she who showed me the plight of the Lesser Races for what it is. She made me realize that my life of privilege comes with an even greater burden of responsibility.
Ashleigh had the courage to stand for what she believed in, and she helped me have the courage to do the same.
It seems unthinkable to say such a thing about someone whose veins course with the blood of our ancient enemies...
...but I admire her greatly.
There will be those who will try to convince you that Ashleigh has influenced me, even swayed my mind.
Nothing could be further from the truth...

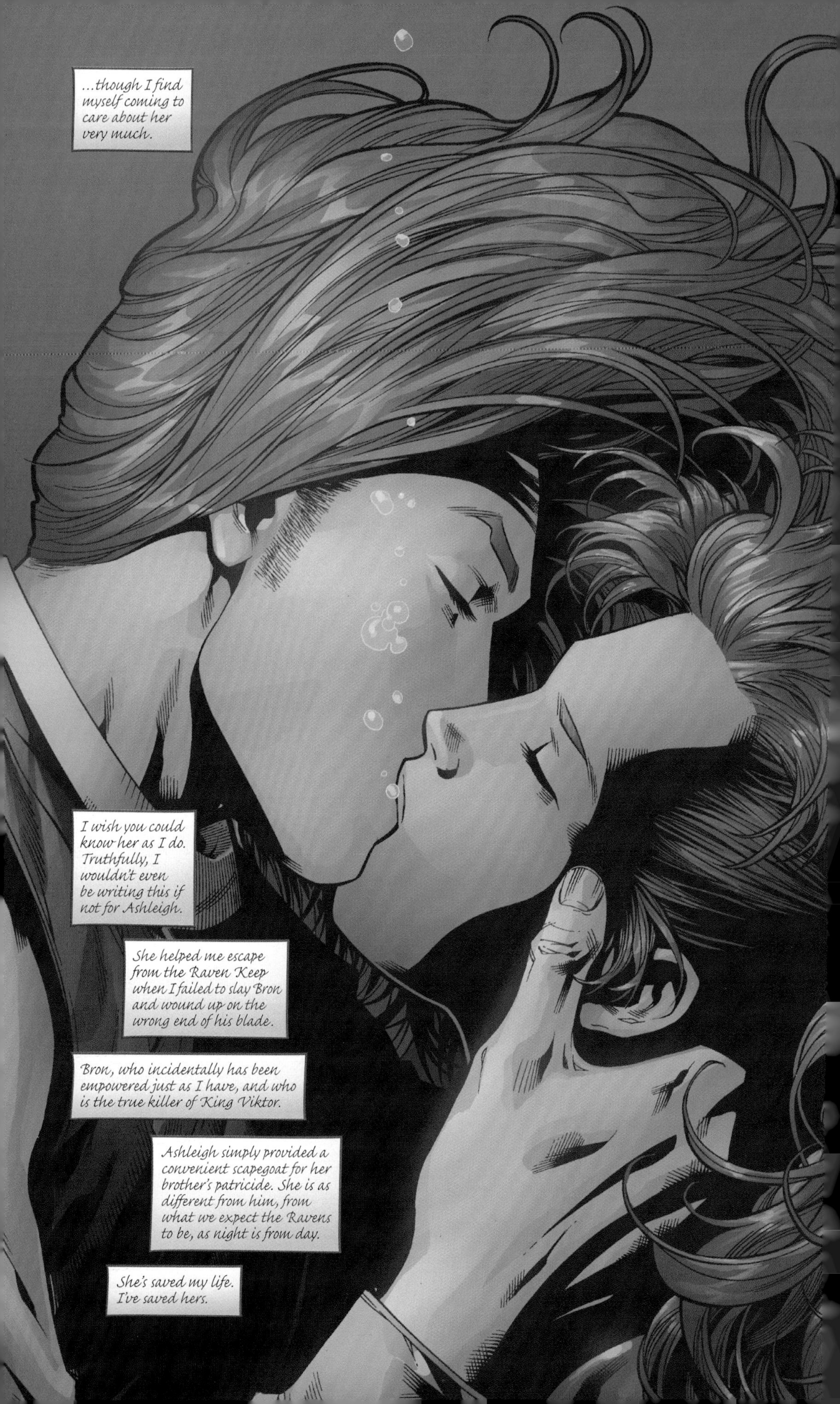
...though I find myself coming to care about her very much.
I wish you could know her as I do. Truthfully, I wouldn't even be writing this if not for Ashleigh.
She helped me escape from the Raven Keep when I failed to slay Bron and wound up on the wrong end of his blade.
Bron, who incidentally has been empowered just as I have, and who is the true killer of King Viktor.
Ashleigh simply provided a convenient scapegoat for her brother's patricide. She is as different from him, from what we expect the Ravens to be, as night is from day.
She's saved my life. I've saved hers.

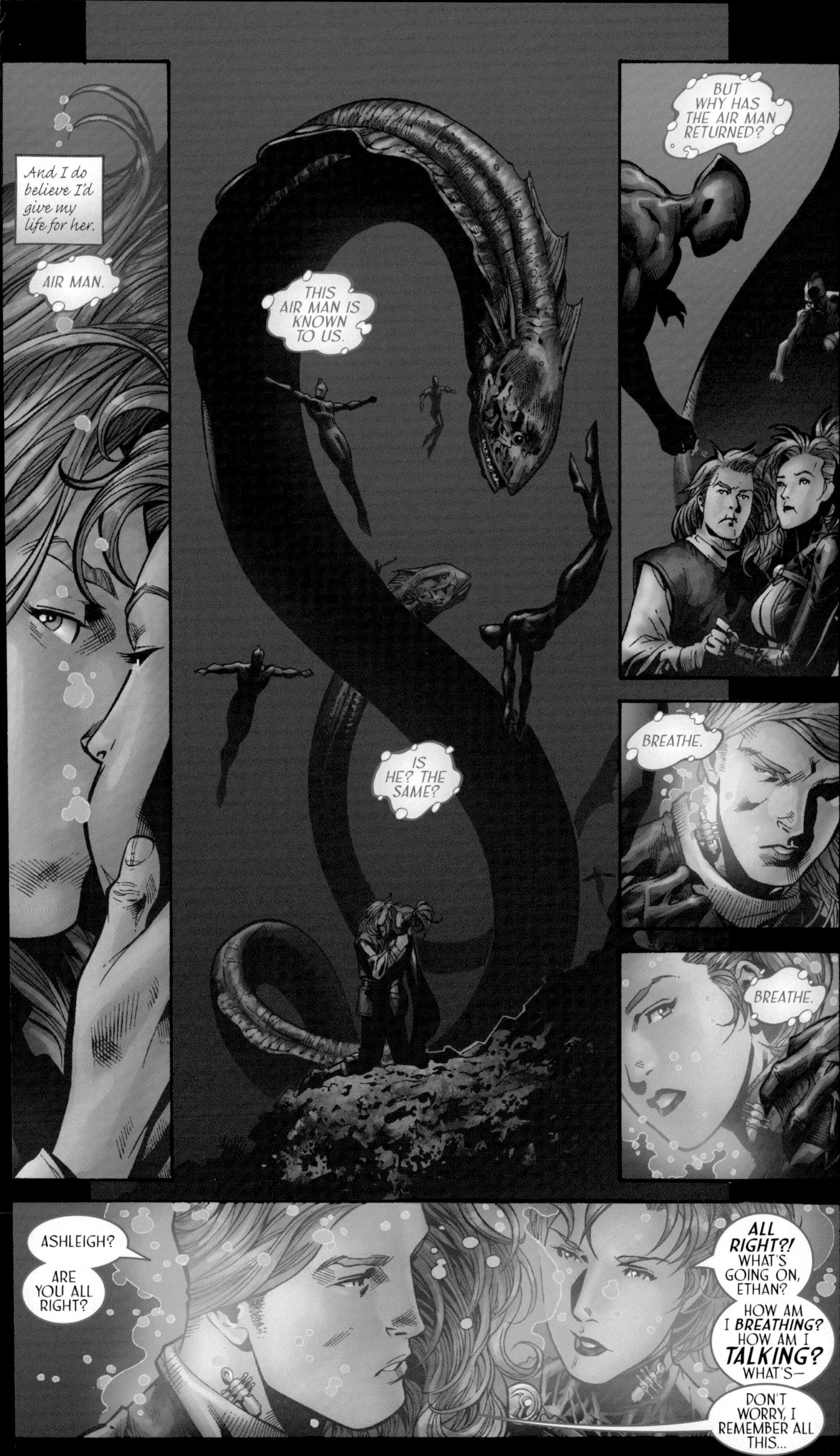
And I do believe I'd give my life for her.
AIR MAN.
THIS AIR MAN IS KNOWN TO US.
IS HE? THE SAME?
BUT WHY HAS THE AIR MAN RETURNED?
BREATHE.
BREATHE.
ASHLEIGH?
ARE YOU ALL RIGHT?
ALL RIGHT?! WHAT'S GOING ON, ETHAN?
HOW AM I BREATHING? HOW AM I TALKING? WHAT'S—
DON'T WORRY, I REMEMBER ALL THIS...

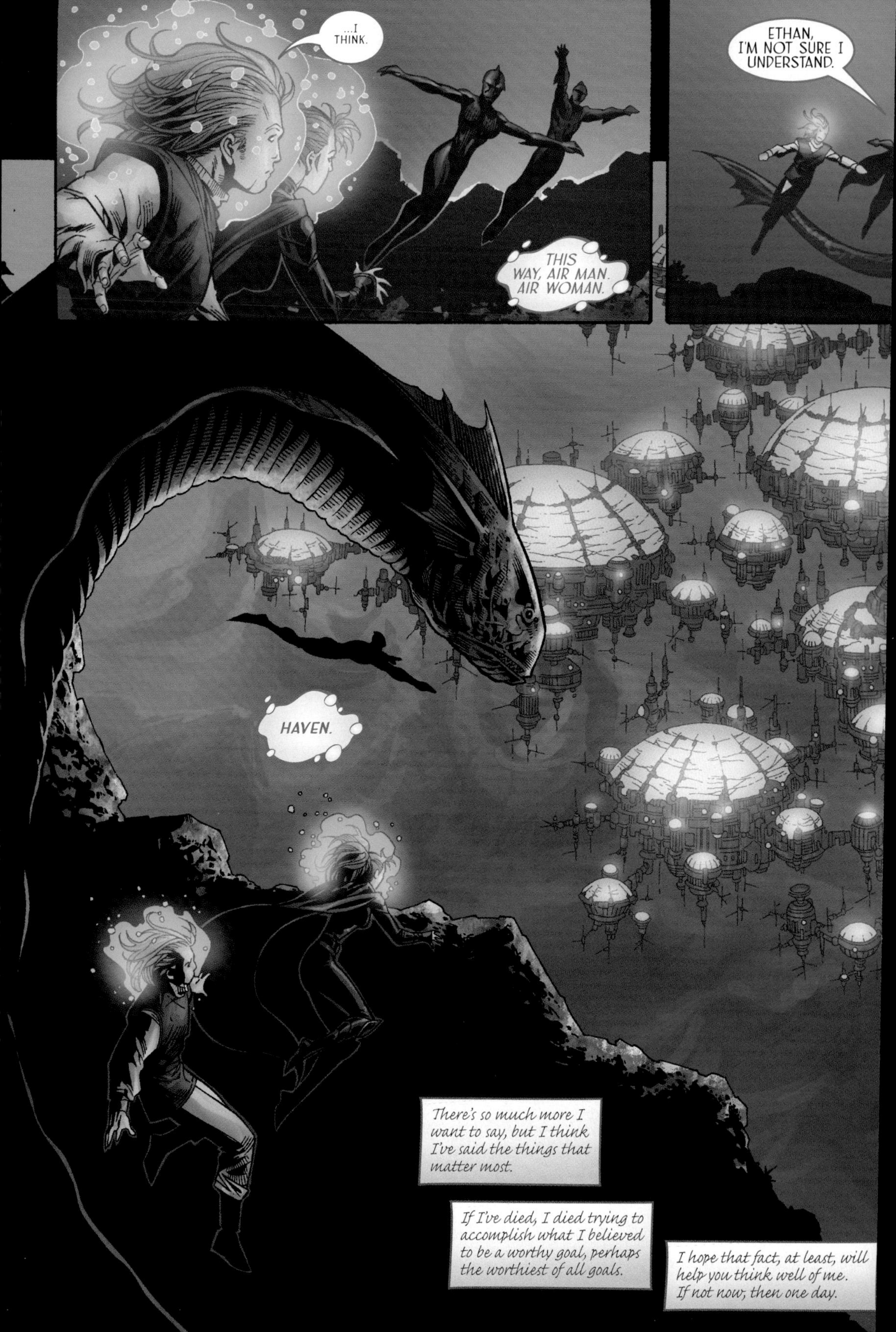
...I THINK.
THIS WAY, AIR MAN. AIR WOMAN.
ETHAN, I'M NOT SURE I UNDERSTAND.
HAVEN.
There's so much more I want to say, but I think I've said the things that matter most.
If I've died, I died trying to accomplish what I believed to be a worthy goal, perhaps the worthiest of all goals.
I hope that fact, at least, will help you think well of me. If not now, then one day.

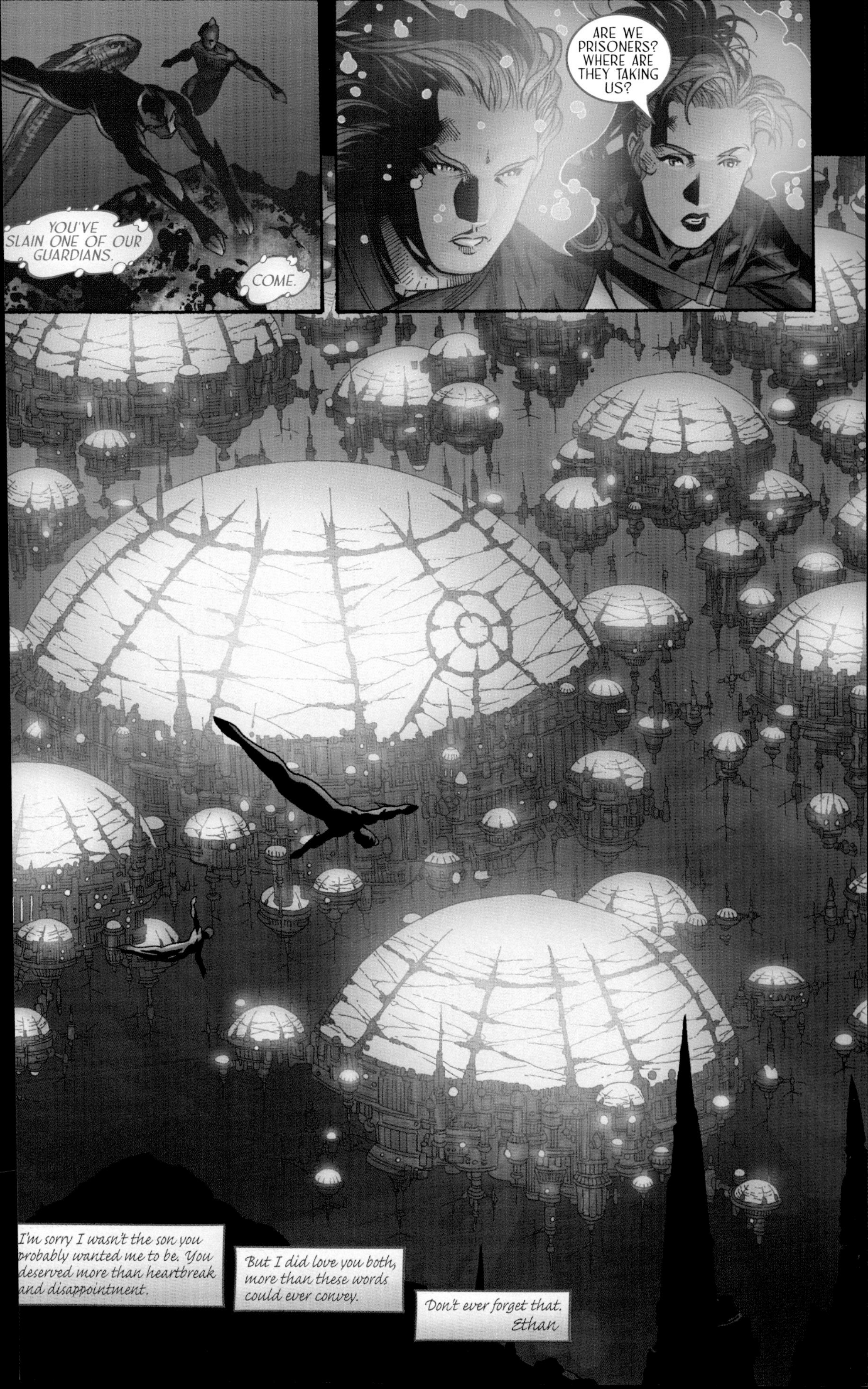
YOU'VE SLAIN ONE OF OUR GUARDIANS.
COME.
ARE WE PRISONERS? WHERE ARE THEY TAKING US?
I'm sorry I wasn't the son you probably wanted me to be. You deserved more than heartbreak and disappointment.
But I did love you both, more than these words could ever convey.
Don't ever forget that.
Ethan

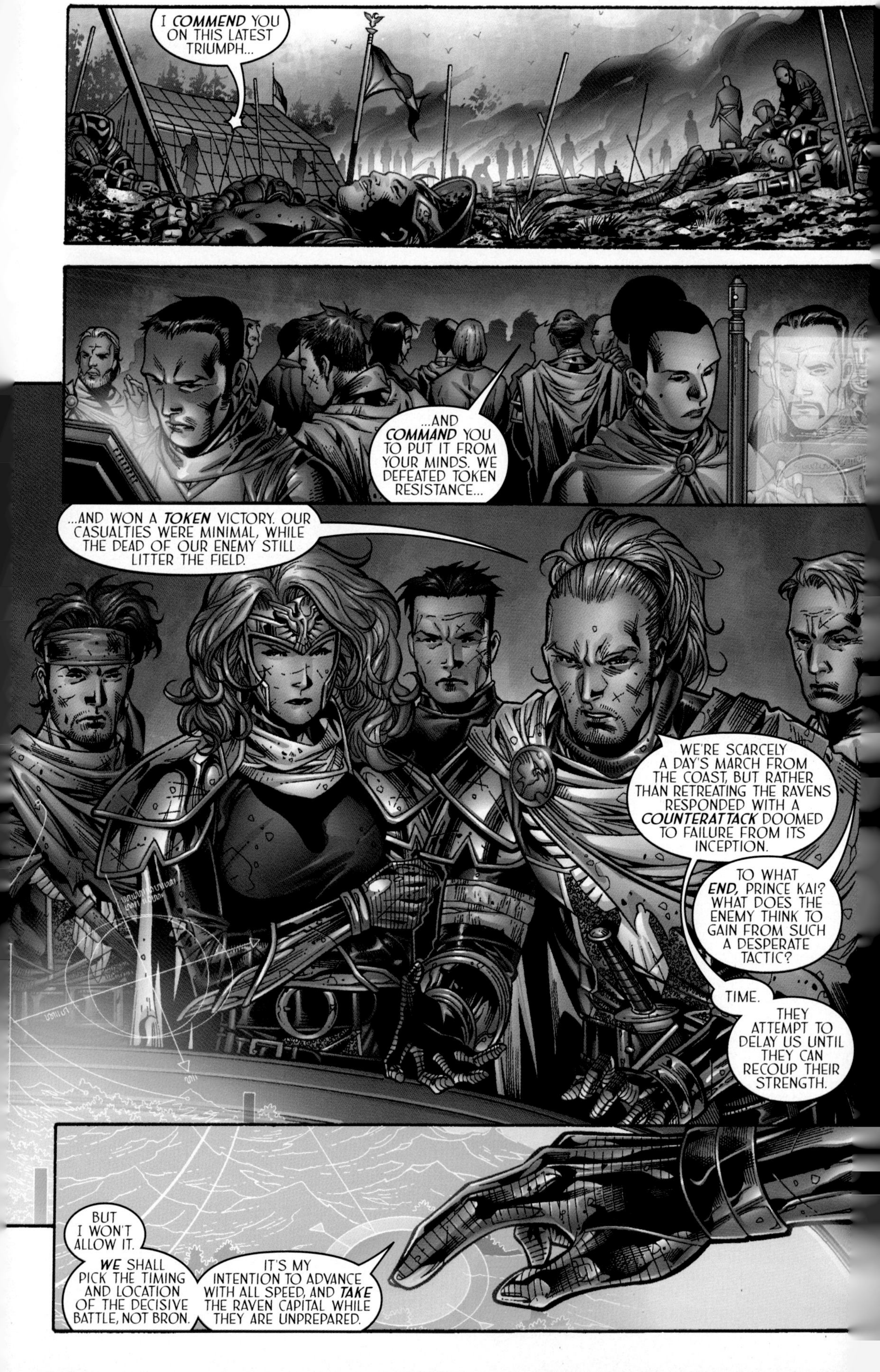

I COMMEND YOU ON THIS LATEST TRIUMPH...
...AND COMMAND YOU TO PUT IT FROM YOUR MINDS. WE DEFEATED TOKEN RESISTANCE...
...AND WON A TOKEN VICTORY. OUR CASUALTIES WERE MINIMAL, WHILE THE DEAD OF OUR ENEMY STILL LITTER THE FIELD.
WE'RE SCARCELY A DAY'S MARCH FROM THE COAST, BUT RATHER THAN RETREATING THE RAVENS RESPONDED WITH A COUNTERATTACK DOOMED TO FAILURE FROM ITS INCEPTION.
TO WHAT END, PRINCE KAI? WHAT DOES THE ENEMY THINK TO GAIN FROM SUCH A DESPERATE TACTIC?
TIME.
THEY ATTEMPT TO DELAY US UNTIL THEY CAN RECOUP THEIR STRENGTH.
BUT I WON'T ALLOW IT.
WE SHALL PICK THE TIMING AND LOCATION OF THE DECISIVE BATTLE, NOT BRON.
IT'S MY INTENTION TO ADVANCE WITH ALL SPEED, AND TAKE THE RAVEN CAPITAL WHILE THEY ARE UNPREPARED.

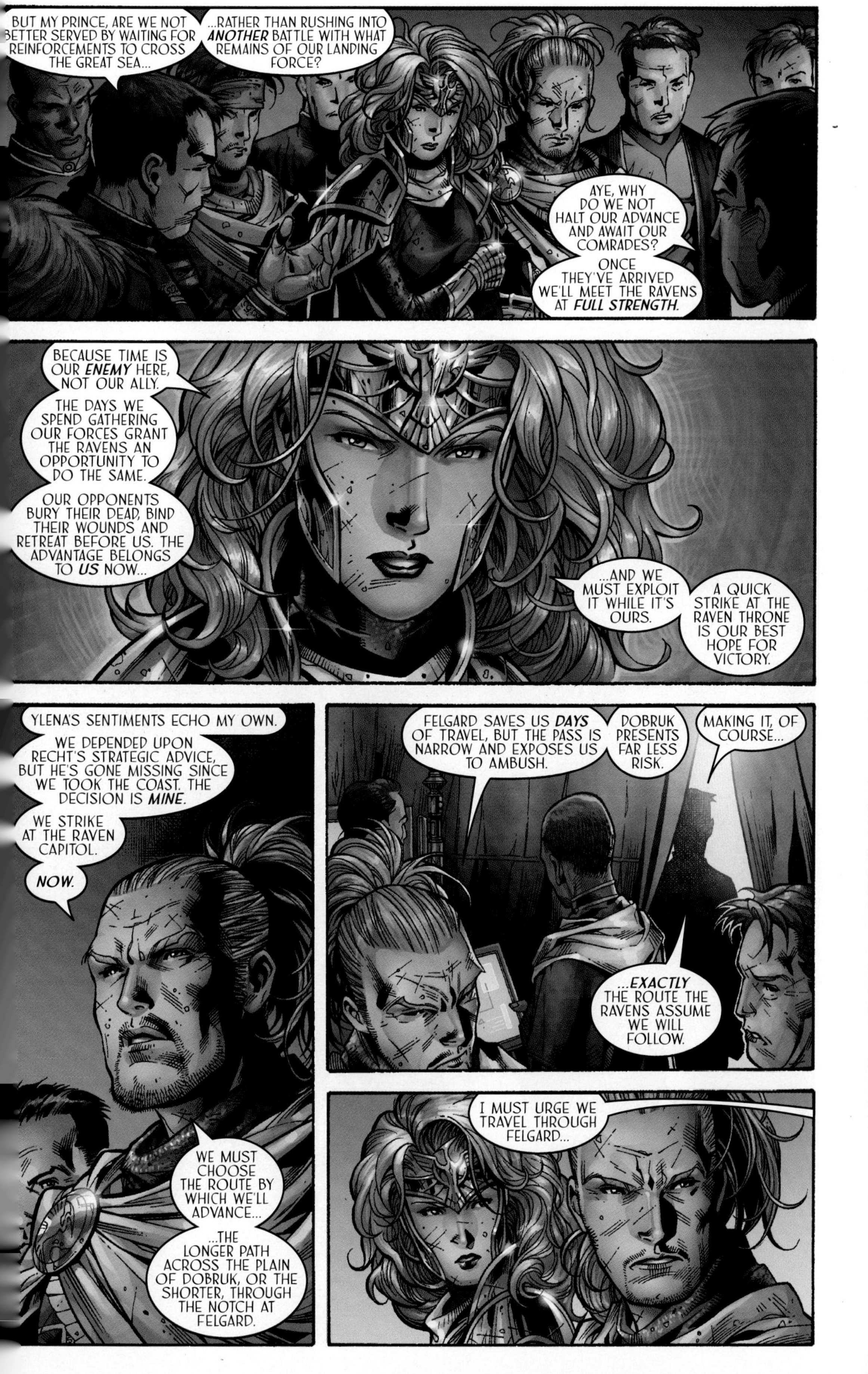

BUT MY PRINCE, ARE WE NOT BETTER SERVED BY WAITING FOR REINFORCEMENTS TO CROSS THE GREAT SEA...
...RATHER THAN RUSHING INTO ANOTHER BATTLE WITH WHAT REMAINS OF OUR LANDING FORCE?
AYE, WHY DO WE NOT HALT OUR ADVANCE AND AWAIT OUR COMRADES?
ONCE THEY'VE ARRIVED WE'LL MEET THE RAVENS AT FULL STRENGTH.
BECAUSE TIME IS OUR ENEMY HERE, NOT OUR ALLY.
THE DAYS WE SPEND GATHERING OUR FORCES GRANT THE RAVENS AN OPPORTUNITY TO DO THE SAME.
OUR OPPONENTS BURY THEIR DEAD, BIND THEIR WOUNDS AND RETREAT BEFORE US. THE ADVANTAGE BELONGS TO US NOW...
...AND WE MUST EXPLOIT IT WHILE IT'S OURS.
A QUICK STRIKE AT THE RAVEN THRONE IS OUR BEST HOPE FOR VICTORY.
YLENA'S SENTIMENTS ECHO MY OWN.
WE DEPENDED UPON RECHT'S STRATEGIC ADVICE, BUT HE'S GONE MISSING SINCE WE TOOK THE COAST. THE DECISION IS MINE.
WE STRIKE AT THE RAVEN CAPITOL.
NOW.
WE MUST CHOOSE THE ROUTE BY WHICH WE'LL ADVANCE...
...THE LONGER PATH ACROSS THE PLAIN OF DOBRUK, OR THE SHORTER, THROUGH THE NOTCH AT FELGARD.
FELGARD SAVES US DAYS OF TRAVEL, BUT THE PASS IS NARROW AND EXPOSES US TO AMBUSH.
DOBRUK PRESENTS FAR LESS RISK.
MAKING IT, OF COURSE...
...EXACTLY THE ROUTE THE RAVENS ASSUME WE WILL FOLLOW.
I MUST URGE WE TRAVEL THROUGH FELGARD...

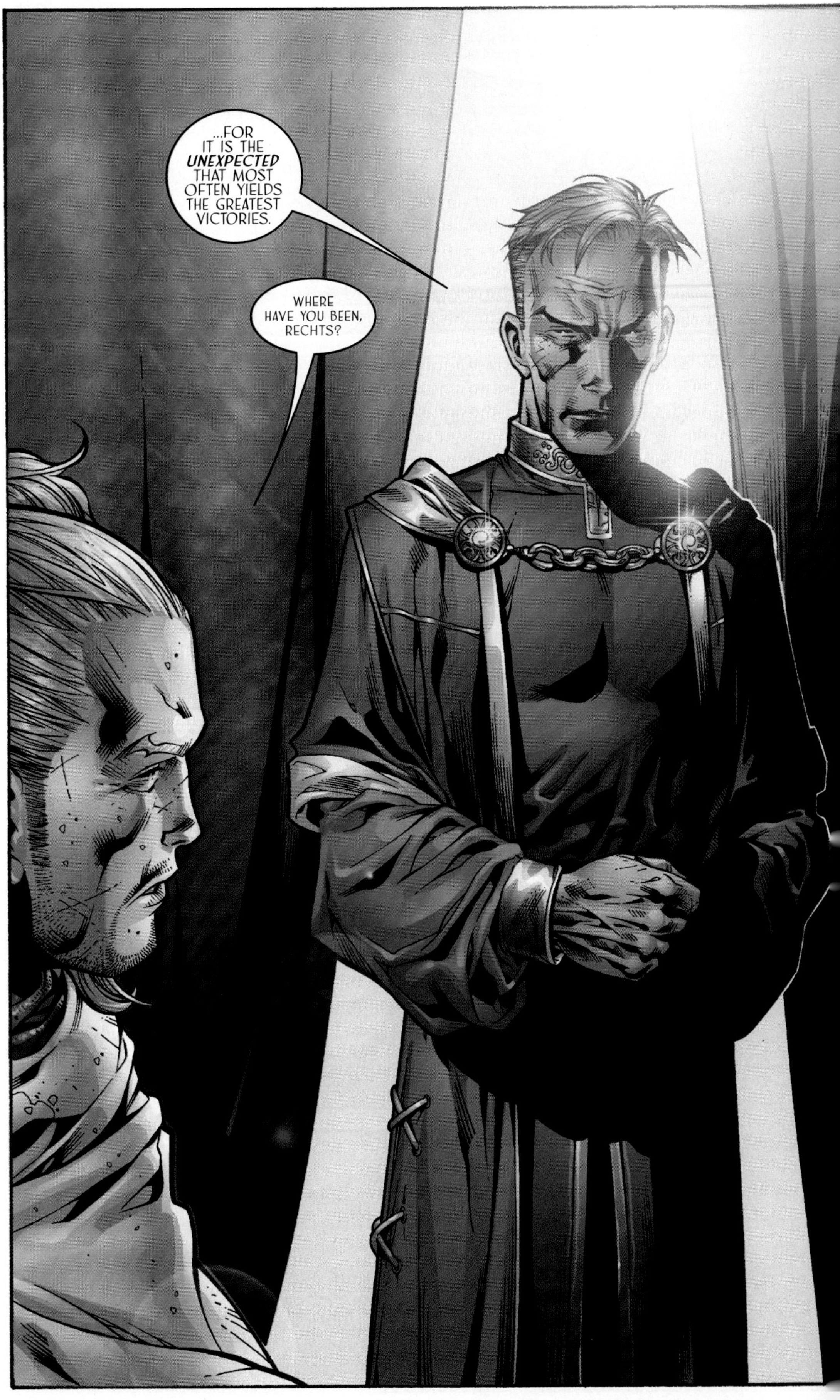
...FOR IT IS THE UNEXPECTED THAT MOST OFTEN YIELDS THE GREATEST VICTORIES.
WHERE HAVE YOU BEEN, RECHTS?

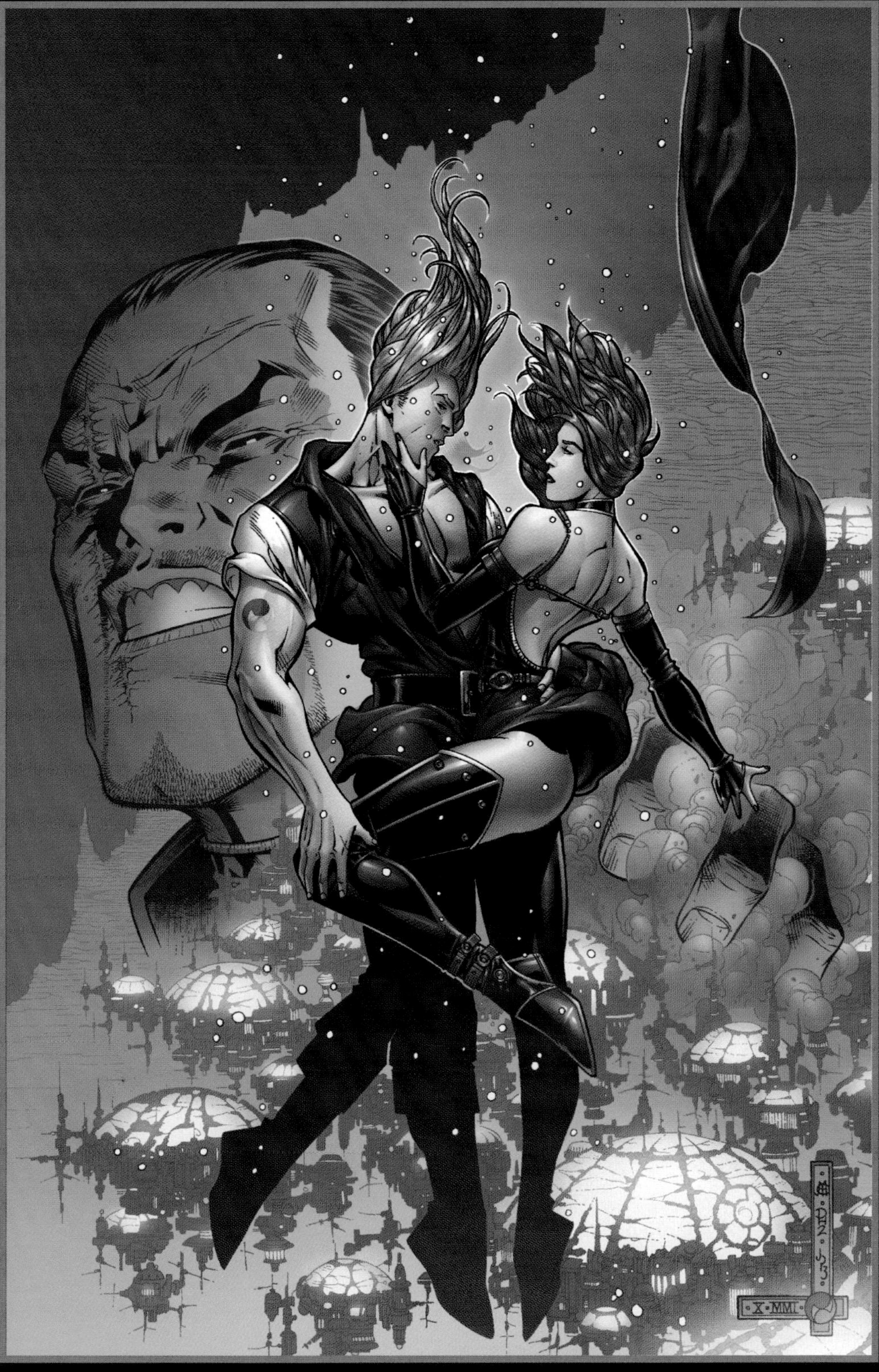

SCION • CHAPTER TWENTY-ONE

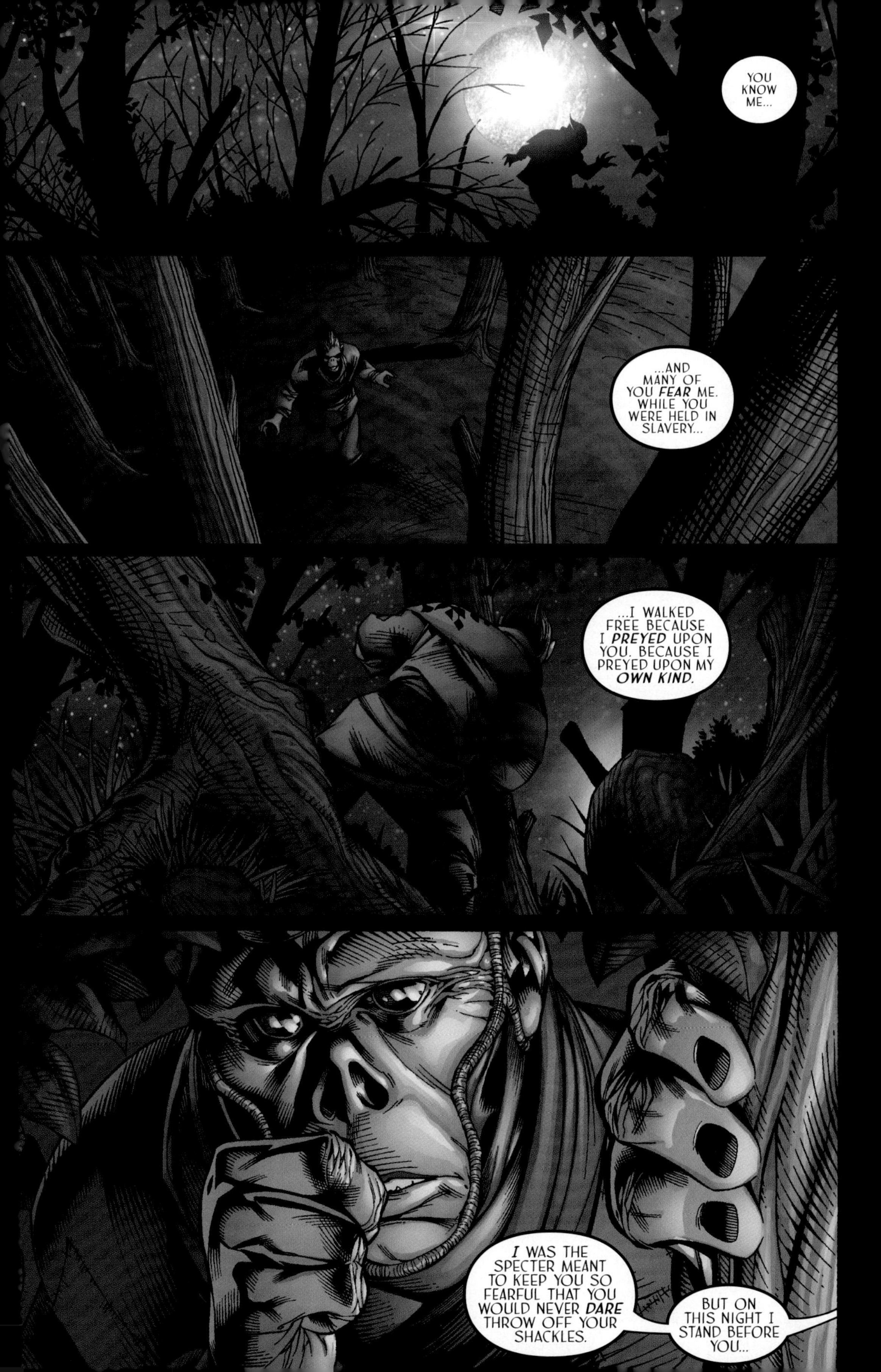
YOU KNOW ME...
...AND MANY OF YOU FEAR ME. WHILE YOU WERE HELD IN SLAVERY...
...I WALKED FREE BECAUSE I PREYED UPON YOU. BECAUSE I PREYED UPON MY OWN KIND.
I WAS THE SPECTER MEANT TO KEEP YOU SO FEARFUL THAT YOU WOULD NEVER DARE THROW OFF YOUR SHACKLES.
BUT ON THIS NIGHT I STAND BEFORE YOU...

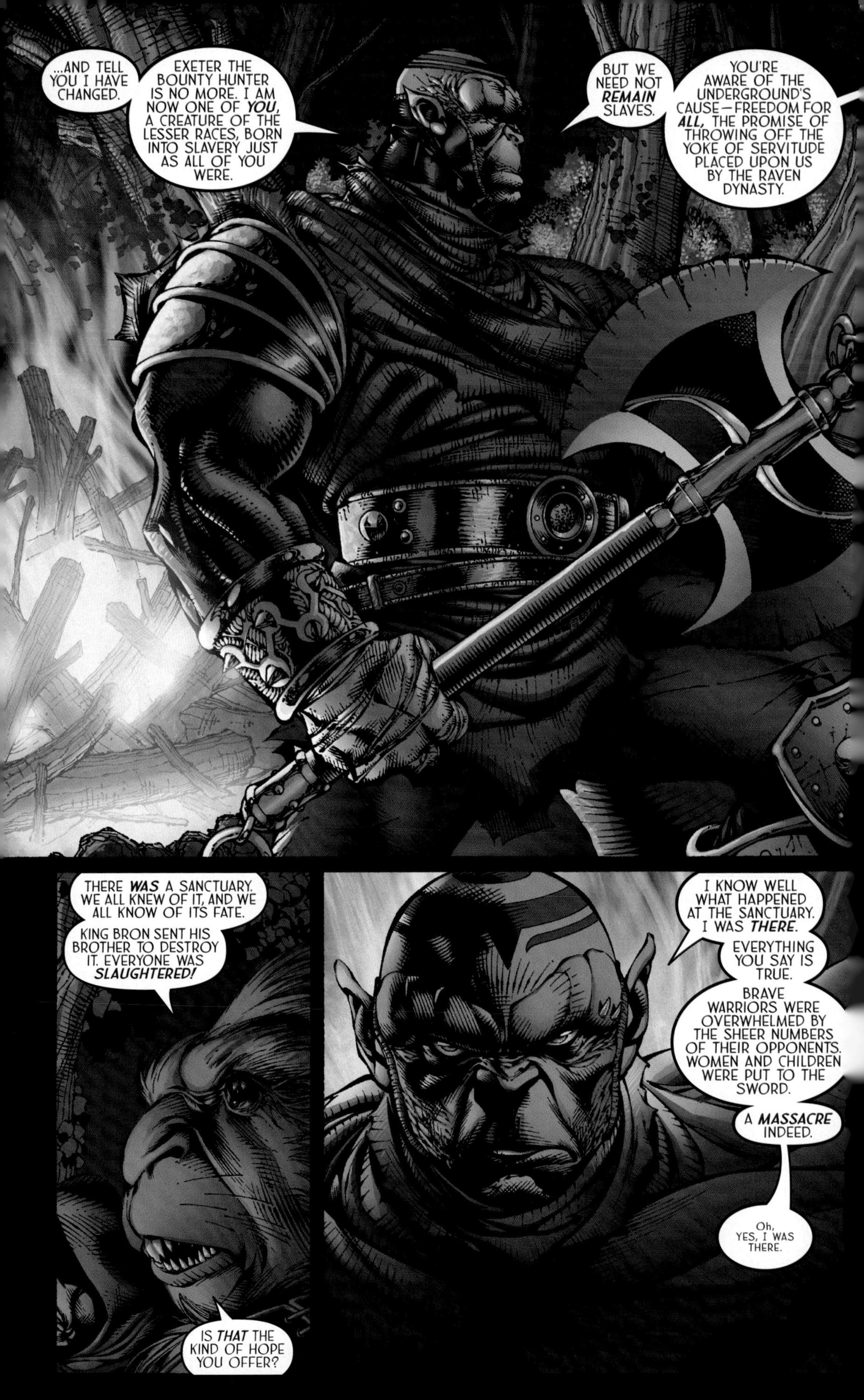
...AND TELL YOU I HAVE CHANGED.
EXETER THE BOUNTY HUNTER IS NO MORE. I AM NOW ONE OF *YOU*, A CREATURE OF THE LESSER RACES, BORN INTO SLAVERY JUST AS ALL OF YOU WERE.
BUT WE NEED NOT *REMAIN* SLAVES.
YOU'RE AWARE OF THE UNDERGROUND'S CAUSE—FREEDOM FOR *ALL*, THE PROMISE OF THROWING OFF THE YOKE OF SERVITUDE PLACED UPON US BY THE RAVEN DYNASTY.
THERE *WAS* A SANCTUARY. WE ALL KNEW OF IT, AND WE ALL KNOW OF ITS FATE.
KING BRON SENT HIS BROTHER TO DESTROY IT. EVERYONE WAS *SLAUGHTERED!*
IS *THAT* THE KIND OF HOPE YOU OFFER?
I KNOW WELL WHAT HAPPENED AT THE SANCTUARY. I WAS *THERE*.
EVERYTHING YOU SAY IS TRUE.
BRAVE WARRIORS WERE OVERWHELMED BY THE SHEER NUMBERS OF THEIR OPPONENTS. WOMEN AND CHILDREN WERE PUT TO THE SWORD.
A *MASSACRE* INDEED.
Oh, YES, I WAS THERE.

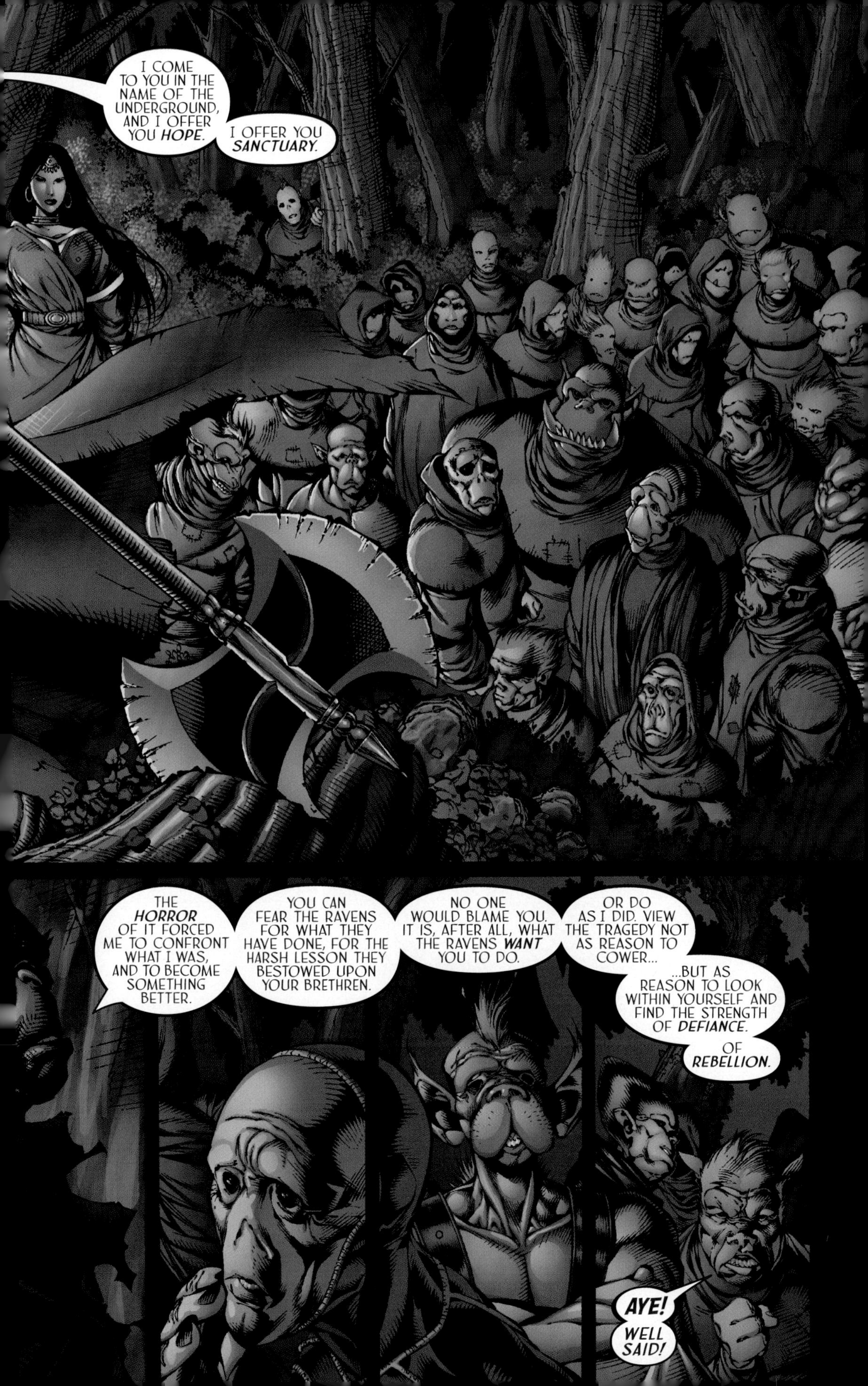
I COME TO YOU IN THE NAME OF THE UNDERGROUND, AND I OFFER YOU HOPE.
I OFFER YOU SANCTUARY.
THE HORROR OF IT FORCED ME TO CONFRONT WHAT I WAS, AND TO BECOME SOMETHING BETTER.
YOU CAN FEAR THE RAVENS FOR WHAT THEY HAVE DONE, FOR THE HARSH LESSON THEY BESTOWED UPON YOUR BRETHREN.
NO ONE WOULD BLAME YOU. IT IS, AFTER ALL, WHAT THE RAVENS WANT YOU TO DO.
OR DO AS I DID. VIEW THE TRAGEDY NOT AS REASON TO COWER...
...BUT AS REASON TO LOOK WITHIN YOURSELF AND FIND THE STRENGTH OF DEFIANCE.
OF REBELLION.
AYE!
WELL SAID!

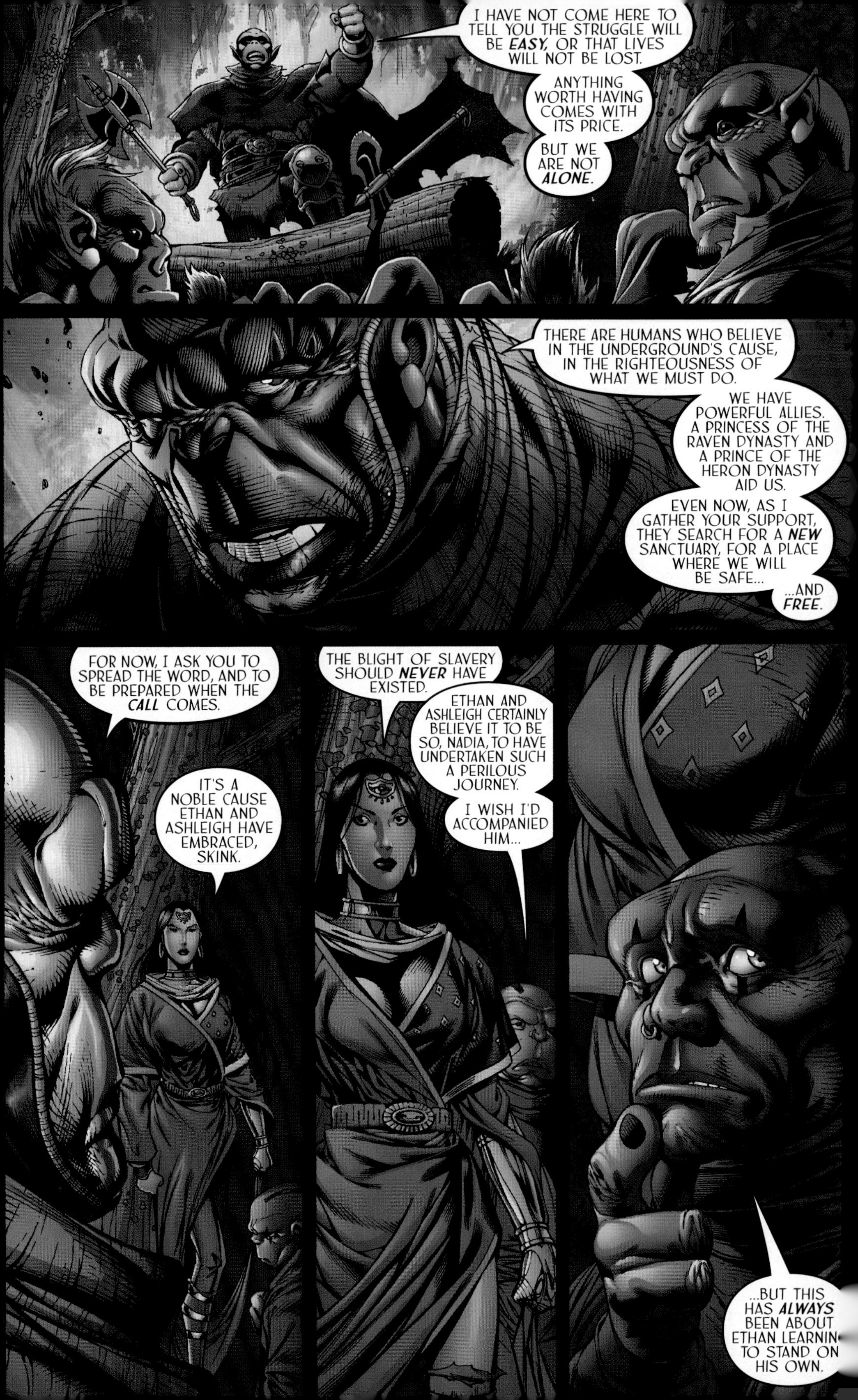
I HAVE NOT COME HERE TO TELL YOU THE STRUGGLE WILL BE EASY, OR THAT LIVES WILL NOT BE LOST.
ANYTHING WORTH HAVING COMES WITH ITS PRICE.
BUT WE ARE NOT ALONE.
THERE ARE HUMANS WHO BELIEVE IN THE UNDERGROUND'S CAUSE, IN THE RIGHTEOUSNESS OF WHAT WE MUST DO.
WE HAVE POWERFUL ALLIES. A PRINCESS OF THE RAVEN DYNASTY AND A PRINCE OF THE HERON DYNASTY AID US.
EVEN NOW, AS I GATHER YOUR SUPPORT, THEY SEARCH FOR A NEW SANCTUARY, FOR A PLACE WHERE WE WILL BE SAFE...
...AND FREE.
FOR NOW, I ASK YOU TO SPREAD THE WORD, AND TO BE PREPARED WHEN THE CALL COMES.
IT'S A NOBLE CAUSE ETHAN AND ASHLEIGH HAVE EMBRACED, SKINK.
THE BLIGHT OF SLAVERY SHOULD NEVER HAVE EXISTED.
ETHAN AND ASHLEIGH CERTAINLY BELIEVE IT TO BE SO, NADIA, TO HAVE UNDERTAKEN SUCH A PERILOUS JOURNEY.
I WISH I'D ACCOMPANIED HIM...
...BUT THIS HAS ALWAYS BEEN ABOUT ETHAN LEARNIN TO STAND ON HIS OWN.

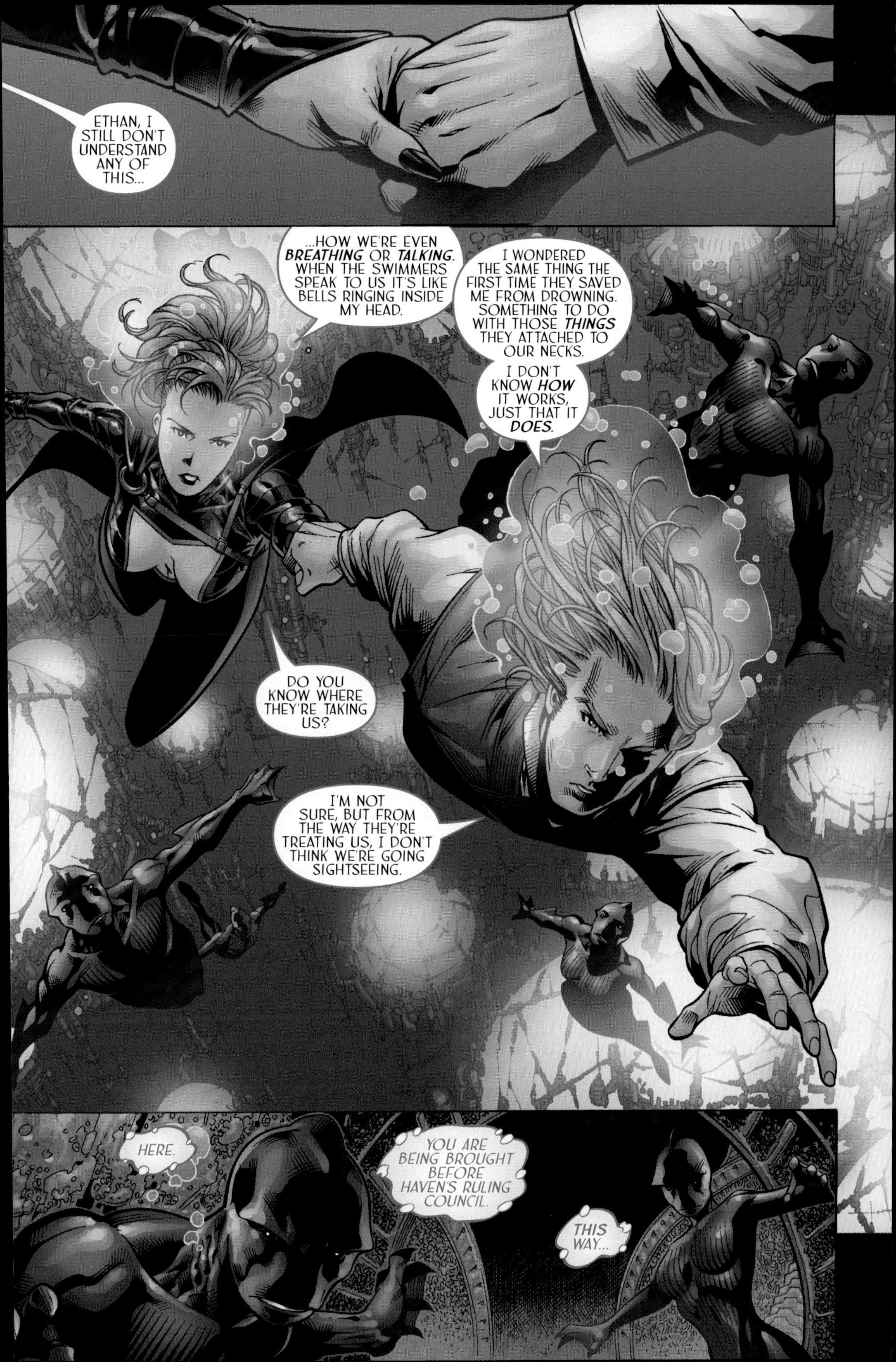
ETHAN, I STILL DON'T UNDERSTAND ANY OF THIS...
...HOW WE'RE EVEN *BREATHING* OR *TALKING*. WHEN THE SWIMMERS SPEAK TO US IT'S LIKE BELLS RINGING INSIDE MY HEAD.
I WONDERED THE SAME THING THE FIRST TIME THEY SAVED ME FROM DROWNING. SOMETHING TO DO WITH THOSE *THINGS* THEY ATTACHED TO OUR NECKS.
I DON'T KNOW *HOW* IT WORKS, JUST THAT IT *DOES*.
DO YOU KNOW WHERE THEY'RE TAKING US?
I'M NOT SURE, BUT FROM THE WAY THEY'RE TREATING US, I DON'T THINK WE'RE GOING SIGHTSEEING.
HERE.
YOU ARE BEING BROUGHT BEFORE HAVEN'S RULING COUNCIL.
THIS WAY...

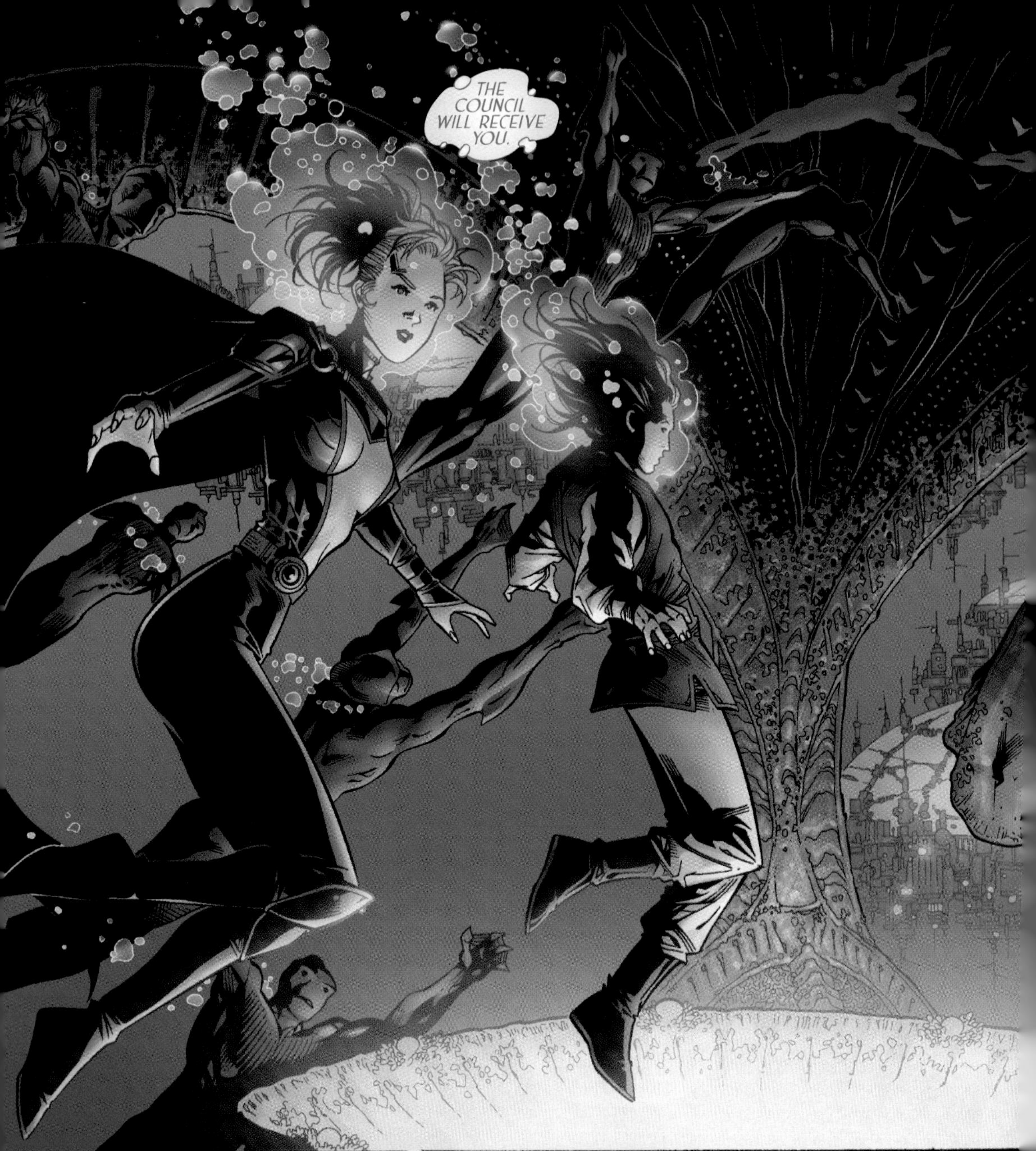
THE COUNCIL WILL RECEIVE YOU.

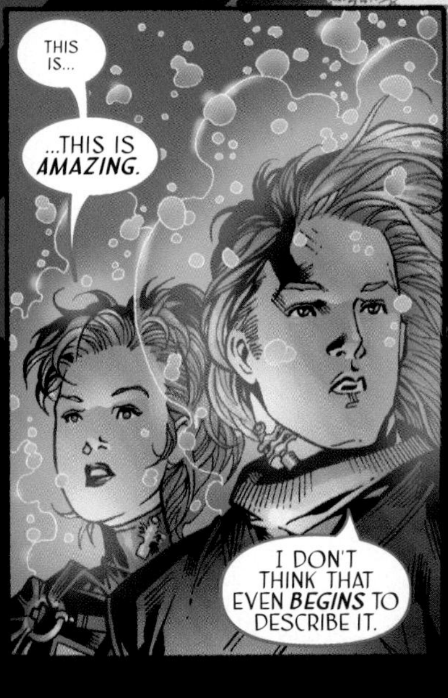
THIS IS...
...THIS IS *AMAZING*.
I DON'T THINK THAT EVEN *BEGINS* TO DESCRIBE IT.

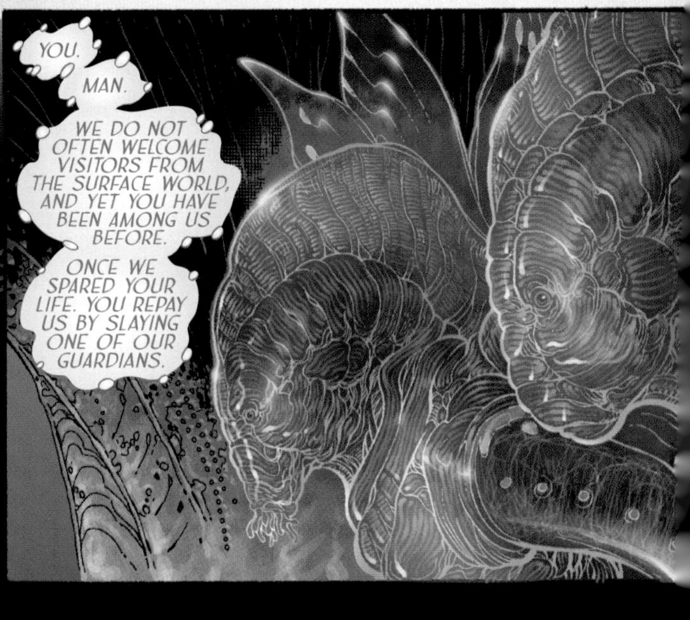
YOU.
MAN.
WE DO NOT OFTEN WELCOME VISITORS FROM THE SURFACE WORLD, AND YET YOU HAVE BEEN AMONG US BEFORE.
ONCE WE SPARED YOUR LIFE. YOU REPAY US BY SLAYING ONE OF OUR GUARDIANS.

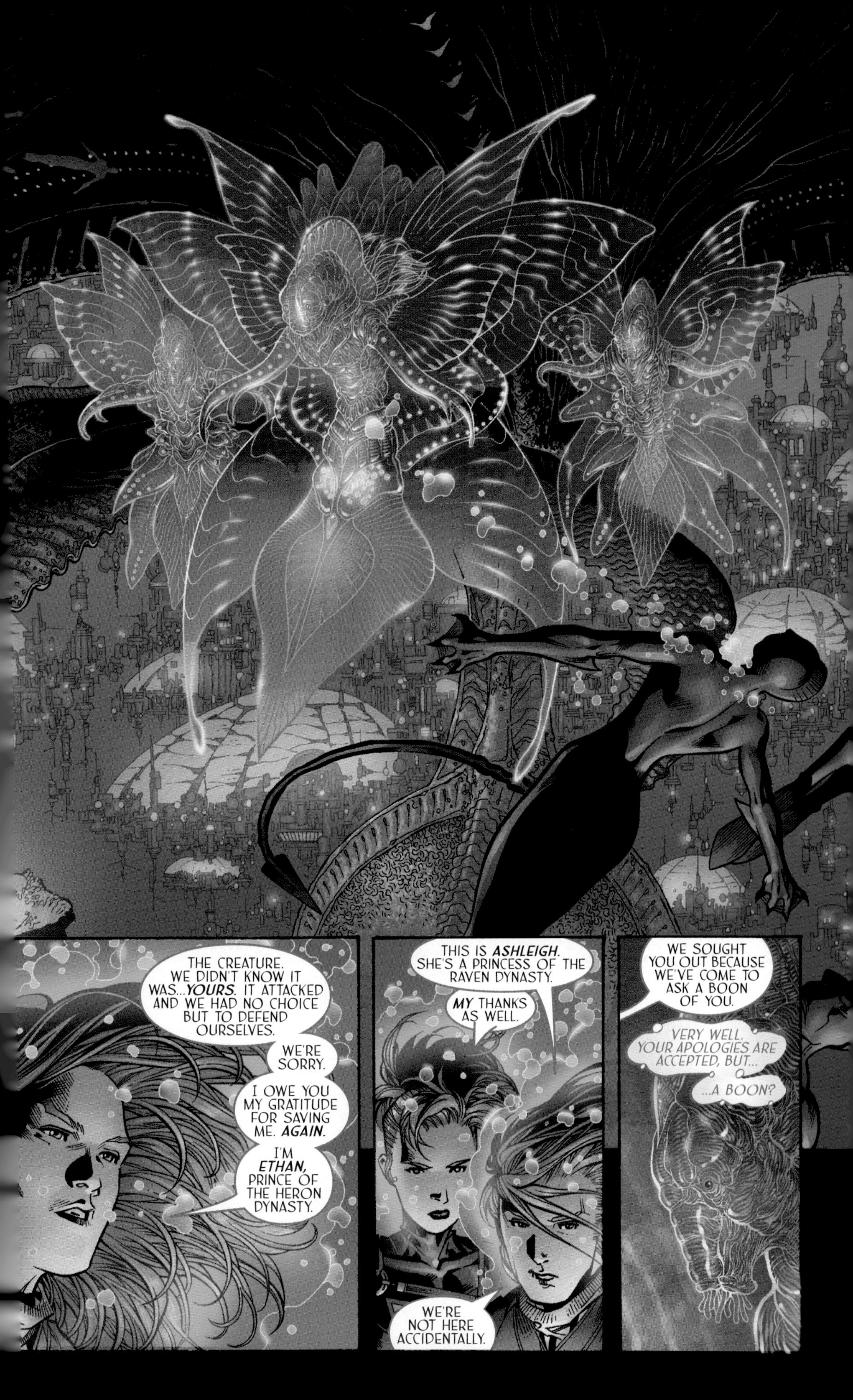
THE CREATURE. WE DIDN'T KNOW IT WAS...YOURS. IT ATTACKED AND WE HAD NO CHOICE BUT TO DEFEND OURSELVES.
WE'RE SORRY.
I OWE YOU MY GRATITUDE FOR SAVING ME. AGAIN.
I'M ETHAN, PRINCE OF THE HERON DYNASTY.
THIS IS ASHLEIGH. SHE'S A PRINCESS OF THE RAVEN DYNASTY.
MY THANKS AS WELL.
WE'RE NOT HERE ACCIDENTALLY.
WE SOUGHT YOU OUT BECAUSE WE'VE COME TO ASK A BOON OF YOU.
VERY WELL. YOUR APOLOGIES ARE ACCEPTED, BUT...
...A BOON?

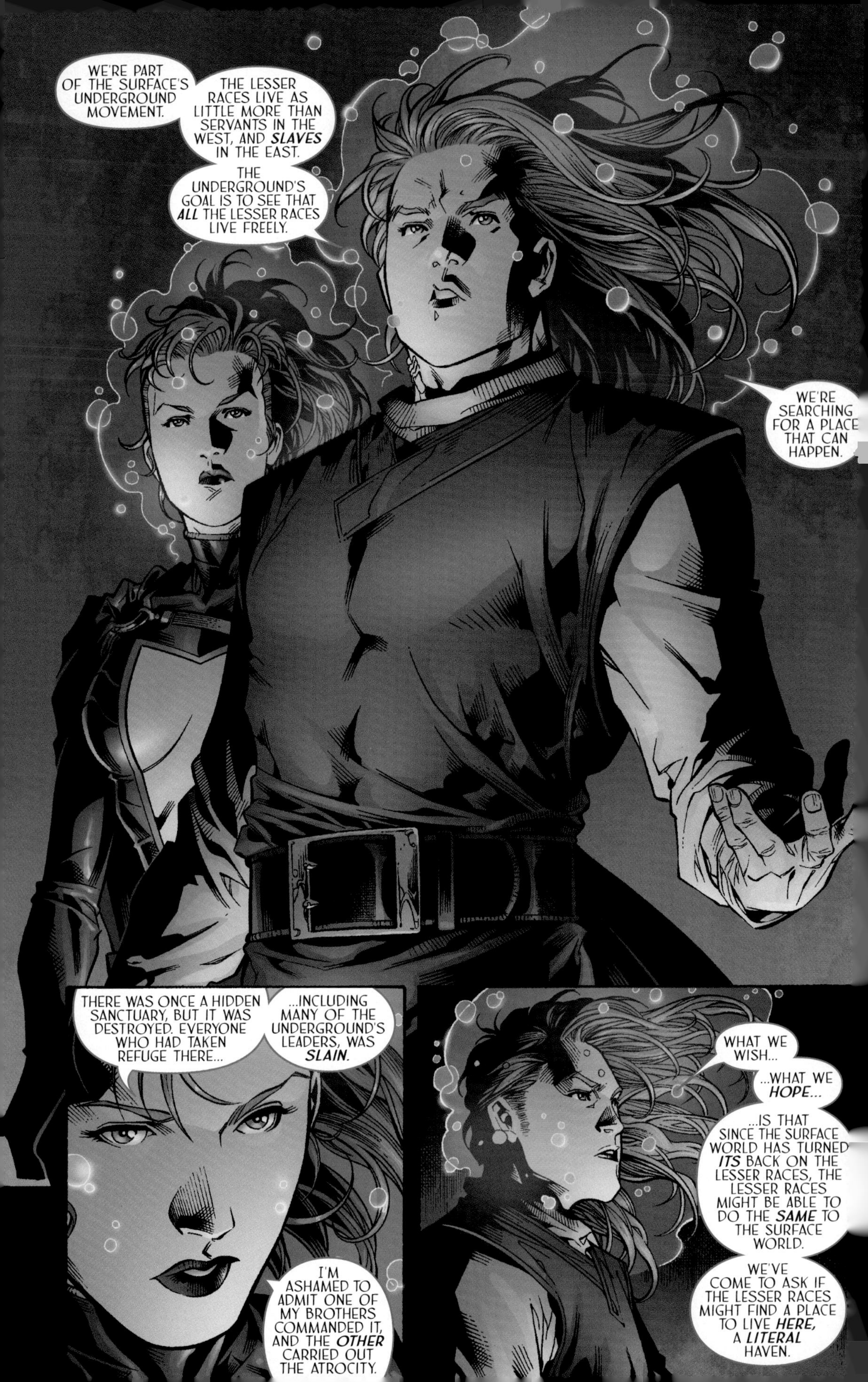

WE'RE PART OF THE SURFACE'S UNDERGROUND MOVEMENT.
THE LESSER RACES LIVE AS LITTLE MORE THAN SERVANTS IN THE WEST, AND *SLAVES* IN THE EAST.
THE UNDERGROUND'S GOAL IS TO SEE THAT *ALL* THE LESSER RACES LIVE FREELY.
WE'RE SEARCHING FOR A PLACE THAT CAN HAPPEN.
THERE WAS ONCE A HIDDEN SANCTUARY, BUT IT WAS DESTROYED. EVERYONE WHO HAD TAKEN REFUGE THERE...
...INCLUDING MANY OF THE UNDERGROUND'S LEADERS, WAS *SLAIN*.
I'M ASHAMED TO ADMIT ONE OF MY BROTHERS COMMANDED IT, AND THE *OTHER* CARRIED OUT THE ATROCITY.
WHAT WE WISH...
...WHAT WE *HOPE*...
...IS THAT SINCE THE SURFACE WORLD HAS TURNED *ITS* BACK ON THE LESSER RACES, THE LESSER RACES MIGHT BE ABLE TO DO THE *SAME* TO THE SURFACE WORLD.
WE'VE COME TO ASK IF THE LESSER RACES MIGHT FIND A PLACE TO LIVE *HERE*, A *LITERAL* HAVEN.

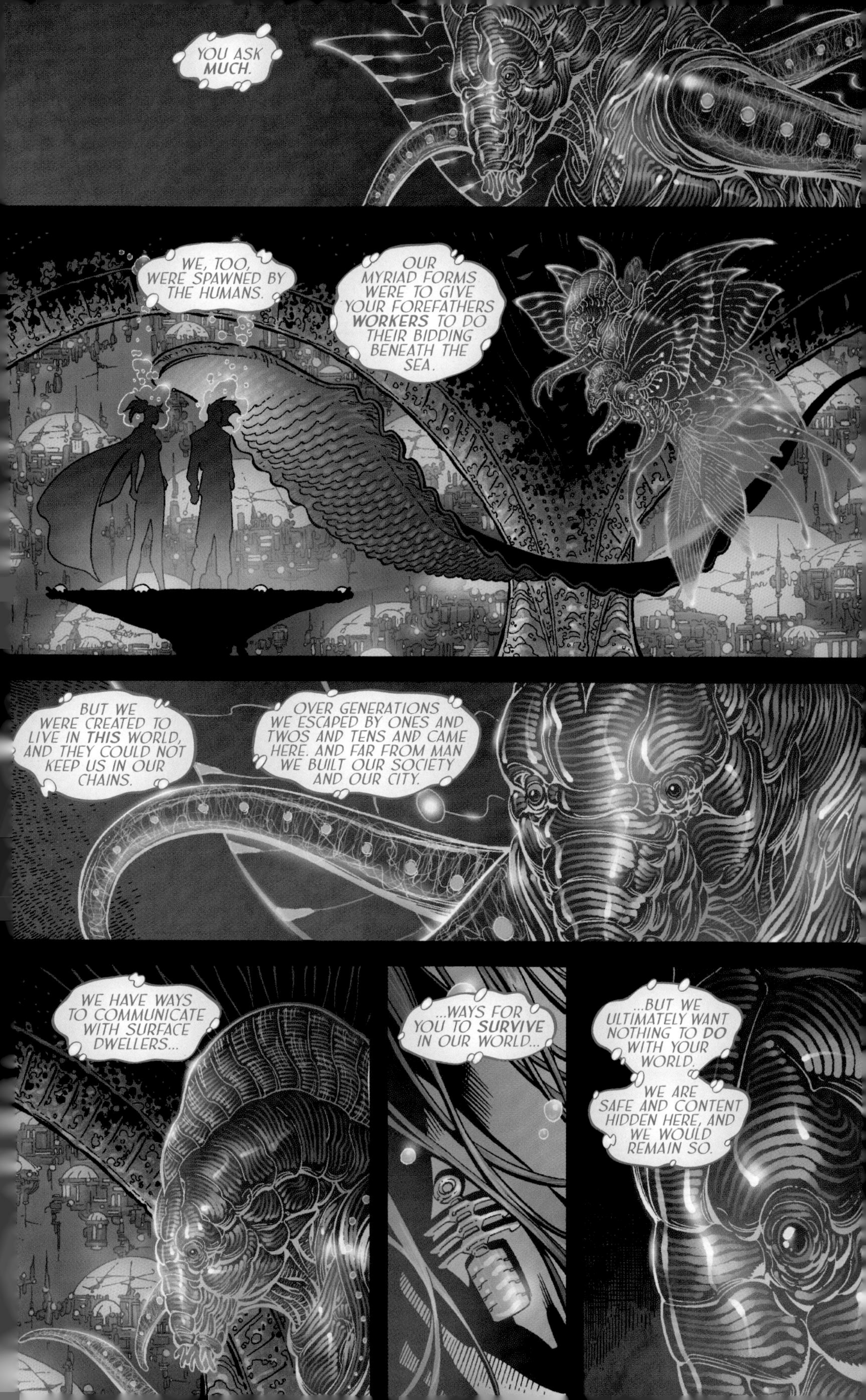
YOU ASK MUCH.
WE, TOO, WERE SPAWNED BY THE HUMANS.
OUR MYRIAD FORMS WERE TO GIVE YOUR FOREFATHERS WORKERS TO DO THEIR BIDDING BENEATH THE SEA.
BUT WE WERE CREATED TO LIVE IN THIS WORLD, AND THEY COULD NOT KEEP US IN OUR CHAINS.
OVER GENERATIONS WE ESCAPED BY ONES AND TWOS AND TENS AND CAME HERE. AND FAR FROM MAN WE BUILT OUR SOCIETY AND OUR CITY.
WE HAVE WAYS TO COMMUNICATE WITH SURFACE DWELLERS...
...WAYS FOR YOU TO SURVIVE IN OUR WORLD...
...BUT WE ULTIMATELY WANT NOTHING TO DO WITH YOUR WORLD.
WE ARE SAFE AND CONTENT HIDDEN HERE, AND WE WOULD REMAIN SO.

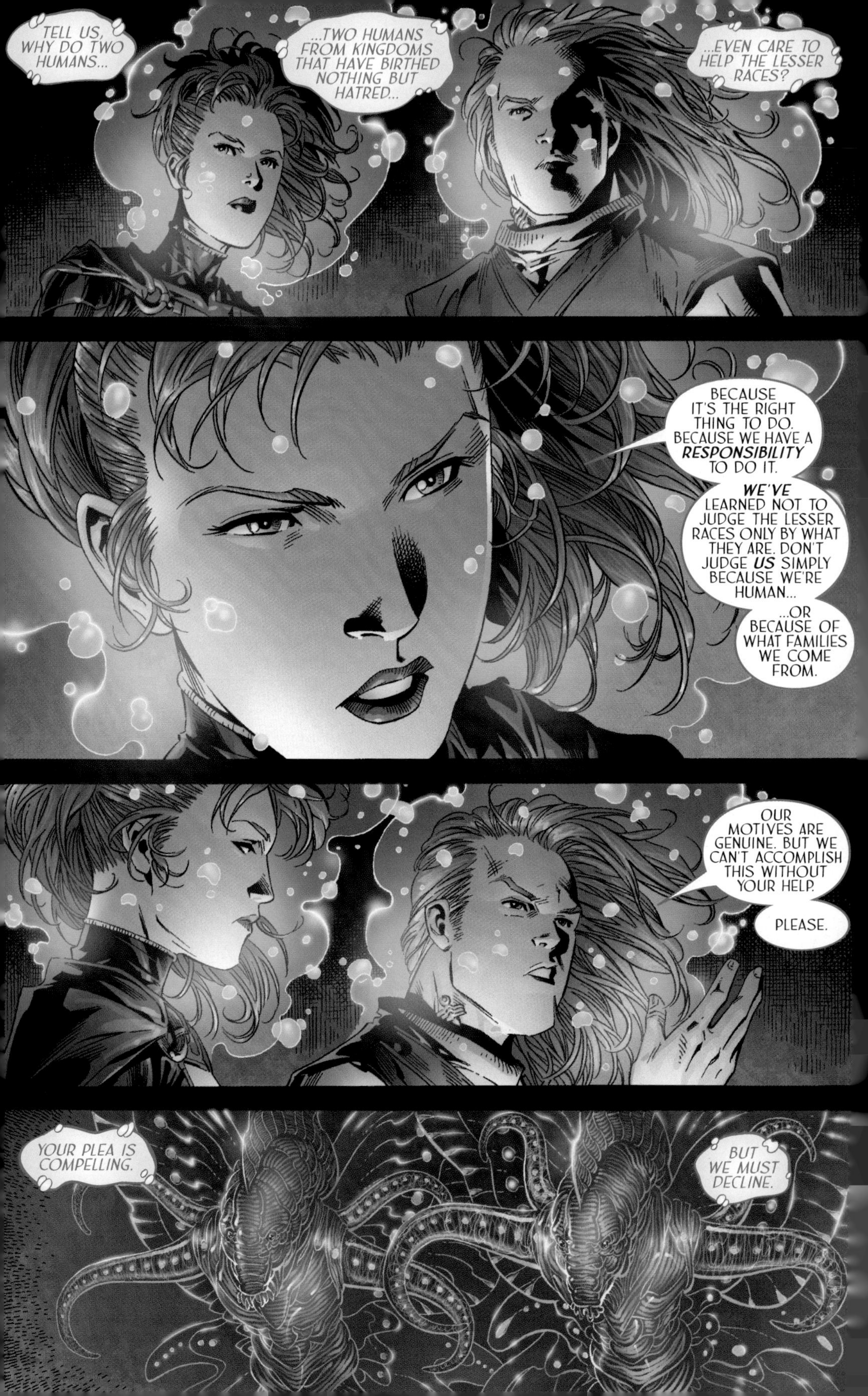
TELL US, WHY DO TWO HUMANS...
...TWO HUMANS FROM KINGDOMS THAT HAVE BIRTHED NOTHING BUT HATRED...
...EVEN CARE TO HELP THE LESSER RACES?
BECAUSE IT'S THE RIGHT THING TO DO. BECAUSE WE HAVE A RESPONSIBILITY TO DO IT.
WE'VE LEARNED NOT TO JUDGE THE LESSER RACES ONLY BY WHAT THEY ARE. DON'T JUDGE US SIMPLY BECAUSE WE'RE HUMAN...
...OR BECAUSE OF WHAT FAMILIES WE COME FROM.
OUR MOTIVES ARE GENUINE. BUT WE CAN'T ACCOMPLISH THIS WITHOUT YOUR HELP.
PLEASE.
YOUR PLEA IS COMPELLING.
BUT WE MUST DECLINE.

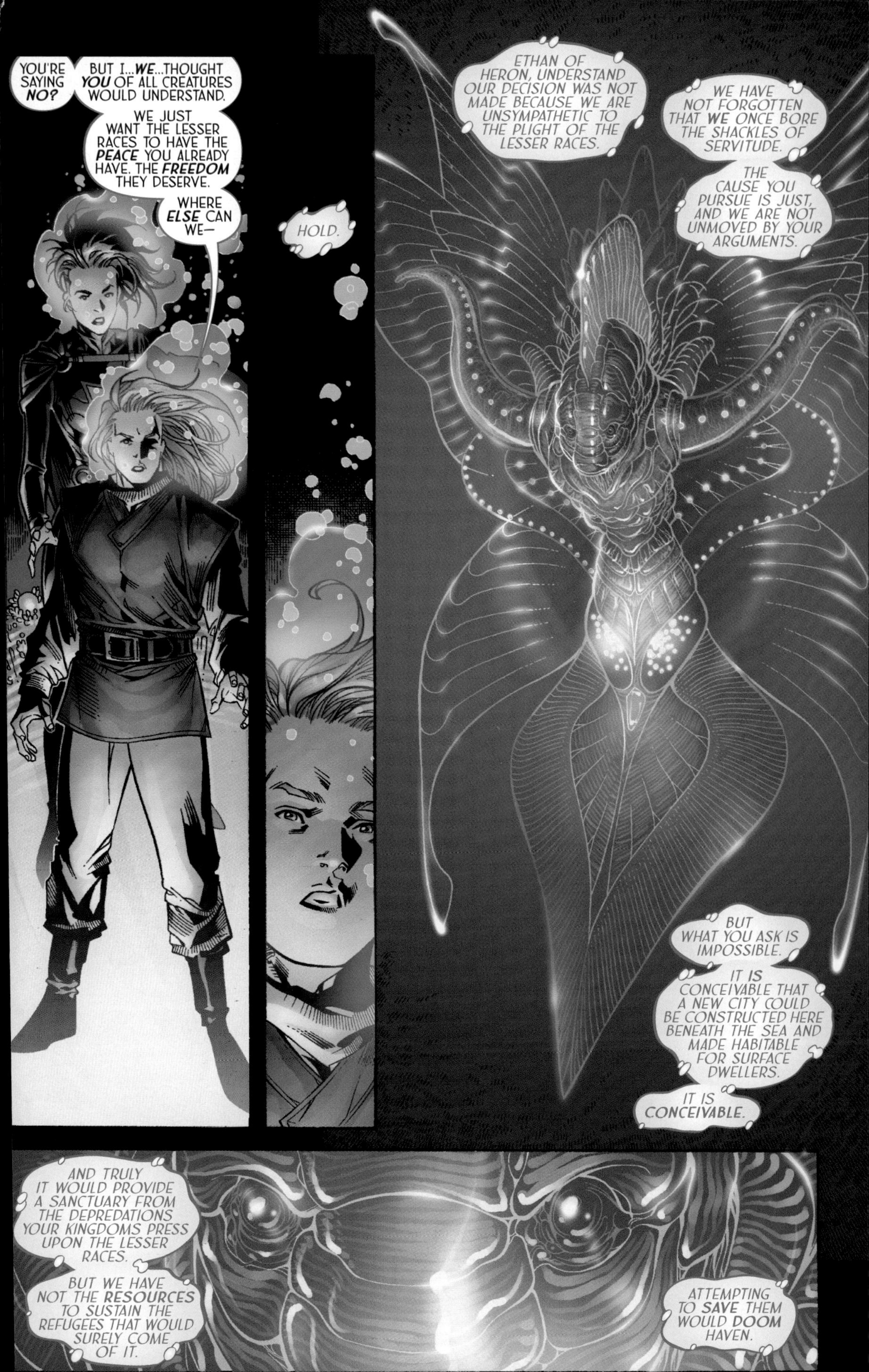
YOU'RE SAYING NO?
BUT I...WE...THOUGHT YOU OF ALL CREATURES WOULD UNDERSTAND.
WE JUST WANT THE LESSER RACES TO HAVE THE PEACE YOU ALREADY HAVE. THE FREEDOM THEY DESERVE.
WHERE ELSE CAN WE—
HOLD.
ETHAN OF HERON, UNDERSTAND OUR DECISION WAS NOT MADE BECAUSE WE ARE UNSYMPATHETIC TO THE PLIGHT OF THE LESSER RACES.
WE HAVE NOT FORGOTTEN THAT WE ONCE BORE THE SHACKLES OF SERVITUDE.
THE CAUSE YOU PURSUE IS JUST, AND WE ARE NOT UNMOVED BY YOUR ARGUMENTS.
BUT WHAT YOU ASK IS IMPOSSIBLE.
IT IS CONCEIVABLE THAT A NEW CITY COULD BE CONSTRUCTED HERE BENEATH THE SEA AND MADE HABITABLE FOR SURFACE DWELLERS.
IT IS CONCEIVABLE.
AND TRULY IT WOULD PROVIDE A SANCTUARY FROM THE DEPREDATIONS YOUR KINGDOMS PRESS UPON THE LESSER RACES.
BUT WE HAVE NOT THE RESOURCES TO SUSTAIN THE REFUGEES THAT WOULD SURELY COME OF IT.
ATTEMPTING TO SAVE THEM WOULD DOOM HAVEN.

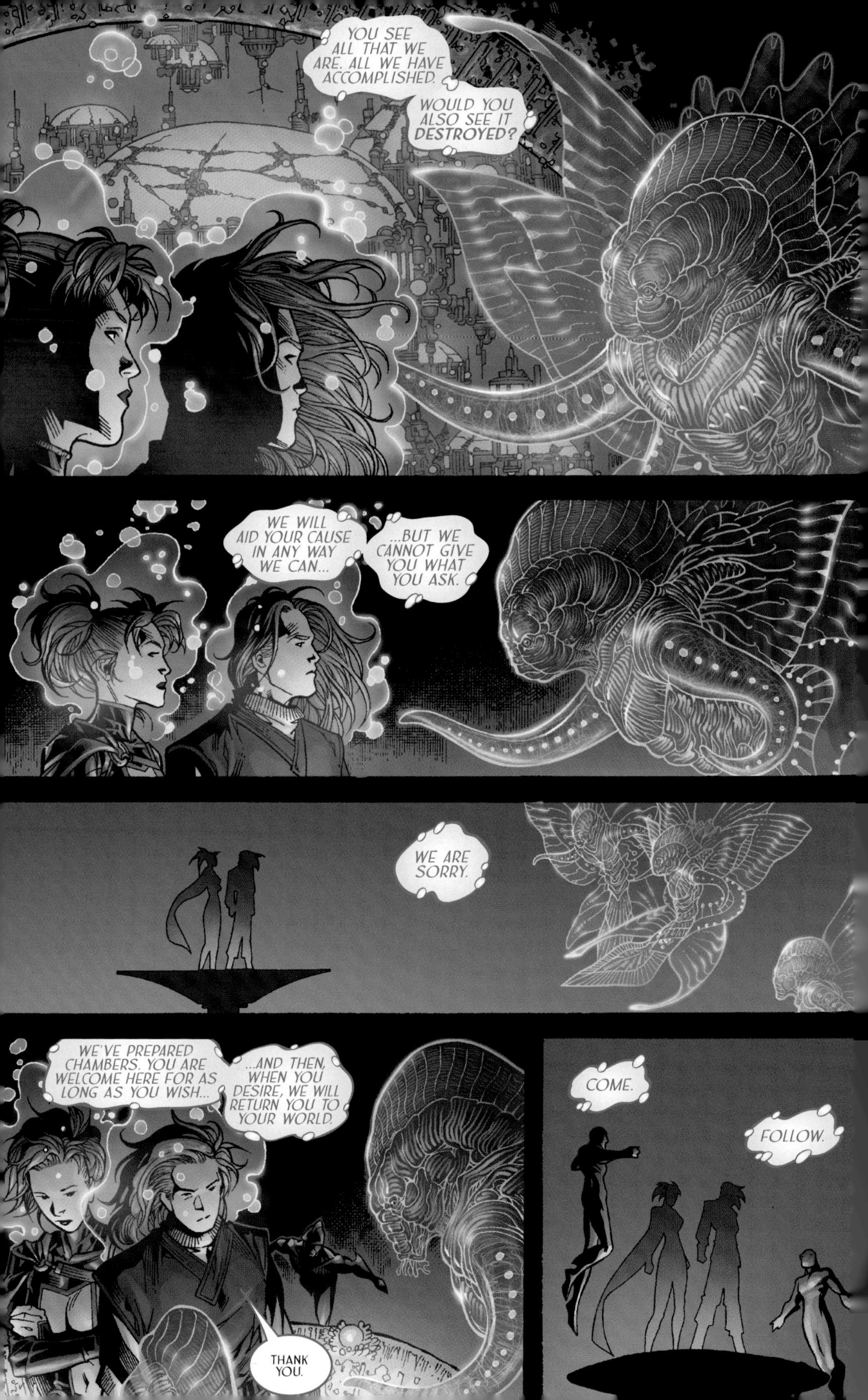
YOU SEE ALL THAT WE ARE. ALL WE HAVE ACCOMPLISHED.
WOULD YOU ALSO SEE IT DESTROYED?
WE WILL AID YOUR CAUSE IN ANY WAY WE CAN...
...BUT WE CANNOT GIVE YOU WHAT YOU ASK.
WE ARE SORRY.
WE'VE PREPARED CHAMBERS. YOU ARE WELCOME HERE FOR AS LONG AS YOU WISH...
...AND THEN, WHEN YOU DESIRE, WE WILL RETURN YOU TO YOUR WORLD.
THANK YOU.
COME.
FOLLOW.

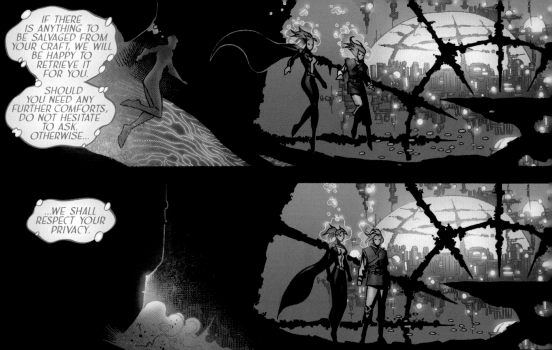

IF THERE IS ANYTHING TO BE SALVAGED FROM YOUR CRAFT, WE WILL BE HAPPY TO RETRIEVE IT FOR YOU.

SHOULD YOU NEED ANY FURTHER COMFORTS, DO NOT HESITATE TO ASK. OTHERWISE...

...WE SHALL RESPECT YOUR PRIVACY.

I'M SORRY, ASHLEIGH.

I REALLY THOUGHT HAVEN WAS THE ANSWER. NOW I CAN SEE THAT WAS...

...NAÏVE.

I'M SORRY I *FAILED* YOU.

ETHAN...

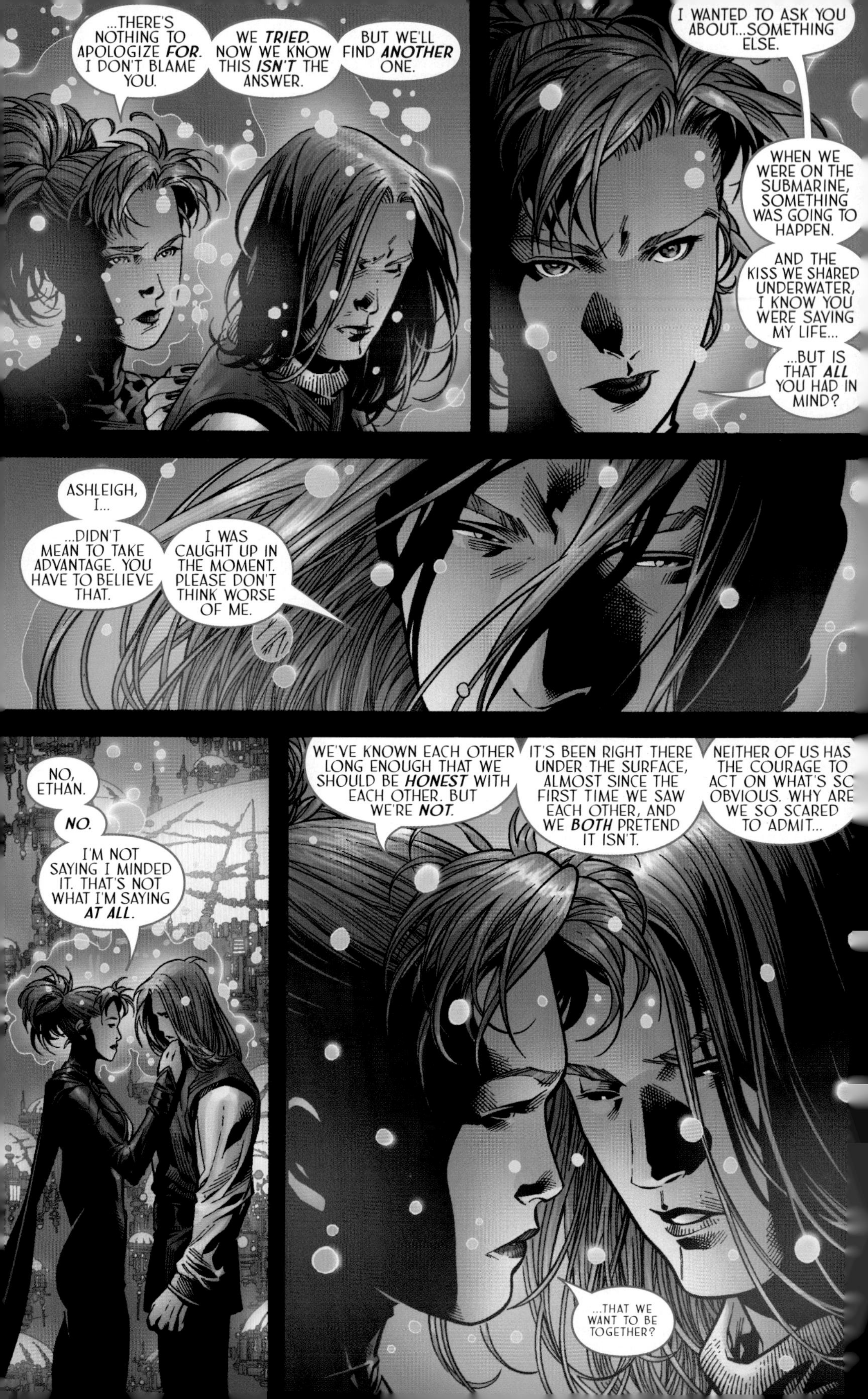
...THERE'S NOTHING TO APOLOGIZE FOR. I DON'T BLAME YOU.
WE TRIED. NOW WE KNOW THIS ISN'T THE ANSWER.
BUT WE'LL FIND ANOTHER ONE.
I WANTED TO ASK YOU ABOUT...SOMETHING ELSE.
WHEN WE WERE ON THE SUBMARINE, SOMETHING WAS GOING TO HAPPEN.
AND THE KISS WE SHARED UNDERWATER, I KNOW YOU WERE SAVING MY LIFE...
...BUT IS THAT ALL YOU HAD IN MIND?
ASHLEIGH, I...
...DIDN'T MEAN TO TAKE ADVANTAGE. YOU HAVE TO BELIEVE THAT.
I WAS CAUGHT UP IN THE MOMENT. PLEASE DON'T THINK WORSE OF ME.
NO, ETHAN.
NO.
I'M NOT SAYING I MINDED IT. THAT'S NOT WHAT I'M SAYING AT ALL.
WE'VE KNOWN EACH OTHER LONG ENOUGH THAT WE SHOULD BE HONEST WITH EACH OTHER. BUT WE'RE NOT.
IT'S BEEN RIGHT THERE UNDER THE SURFACE, ALMOST SINCE THE FIRST TIME WE SAW EACH OTHER, AND WE BOTH PRETEND IT ISN'T.
NEITHER OF US HAS THE COURAGE TO ACT ON WHAT'S SO OBVIOUS. WHY ARE WE SO SCARED TO ADMIT...
...THAT WE WANT TO BE TOGETHER?

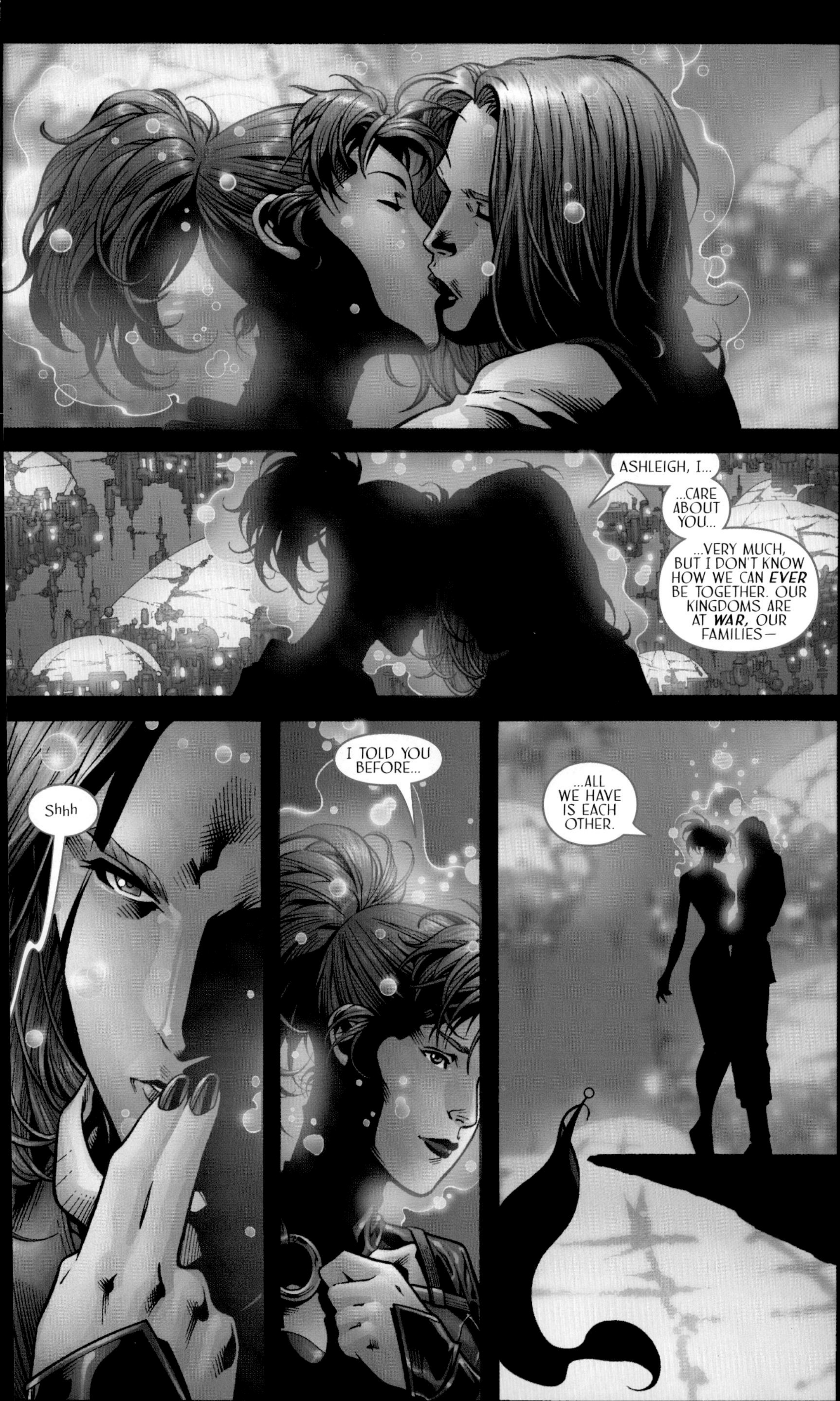
ASHLEIGH, I...
...CARE ABOUT YOU...
...VERY MUCH, BUT I DON'T KNOW HOW WE CAN EVER BE TOGETHER. OUR KINGDOMS ARE AT WAR, OUR FAMILIES—
Shhh
I TOLD YOU BEFORE...
...ALL WE HAVE IS EACH OTHER.

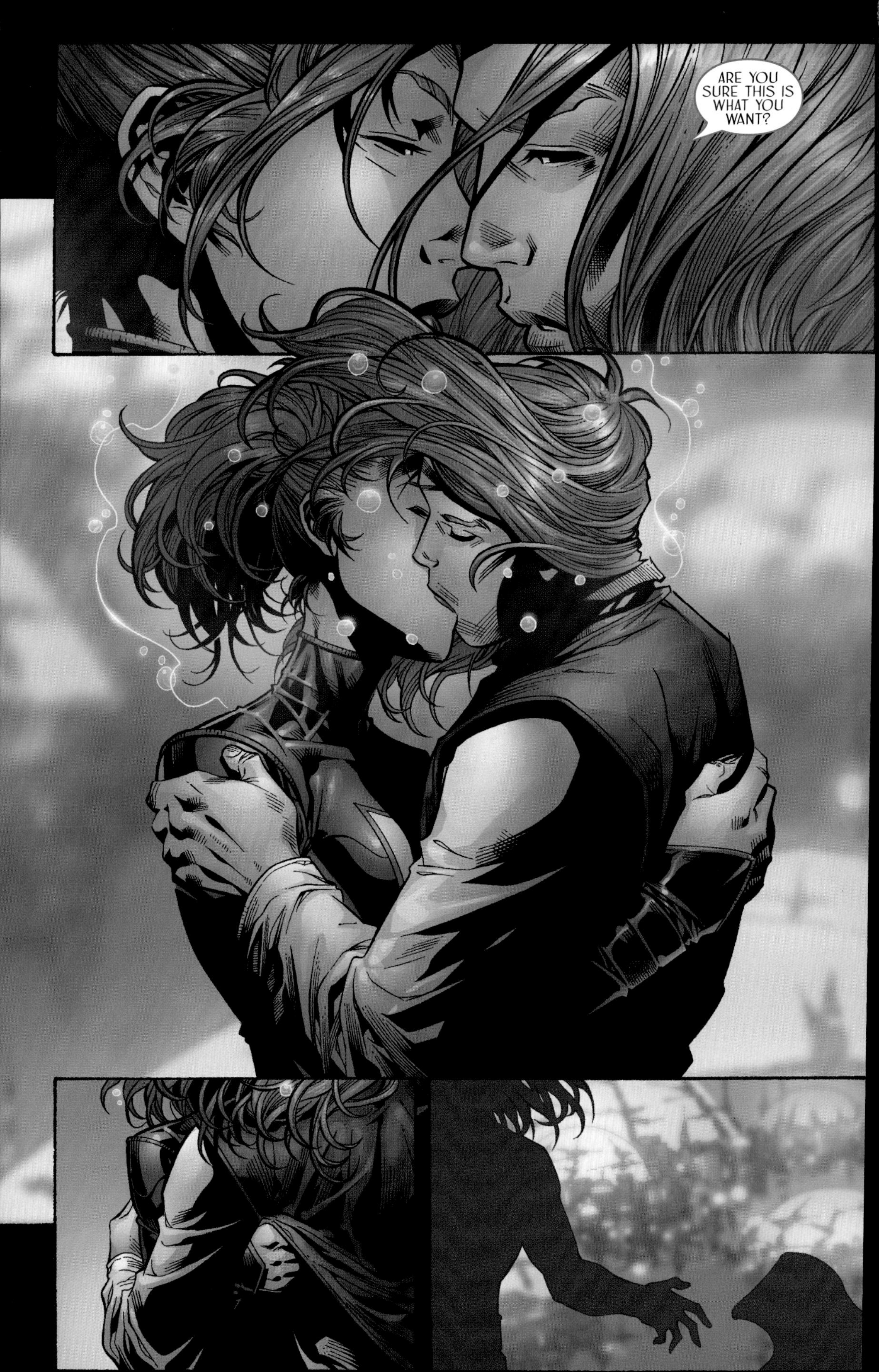
ARE YOU SURE THIS IS WHAT YOU WANT?

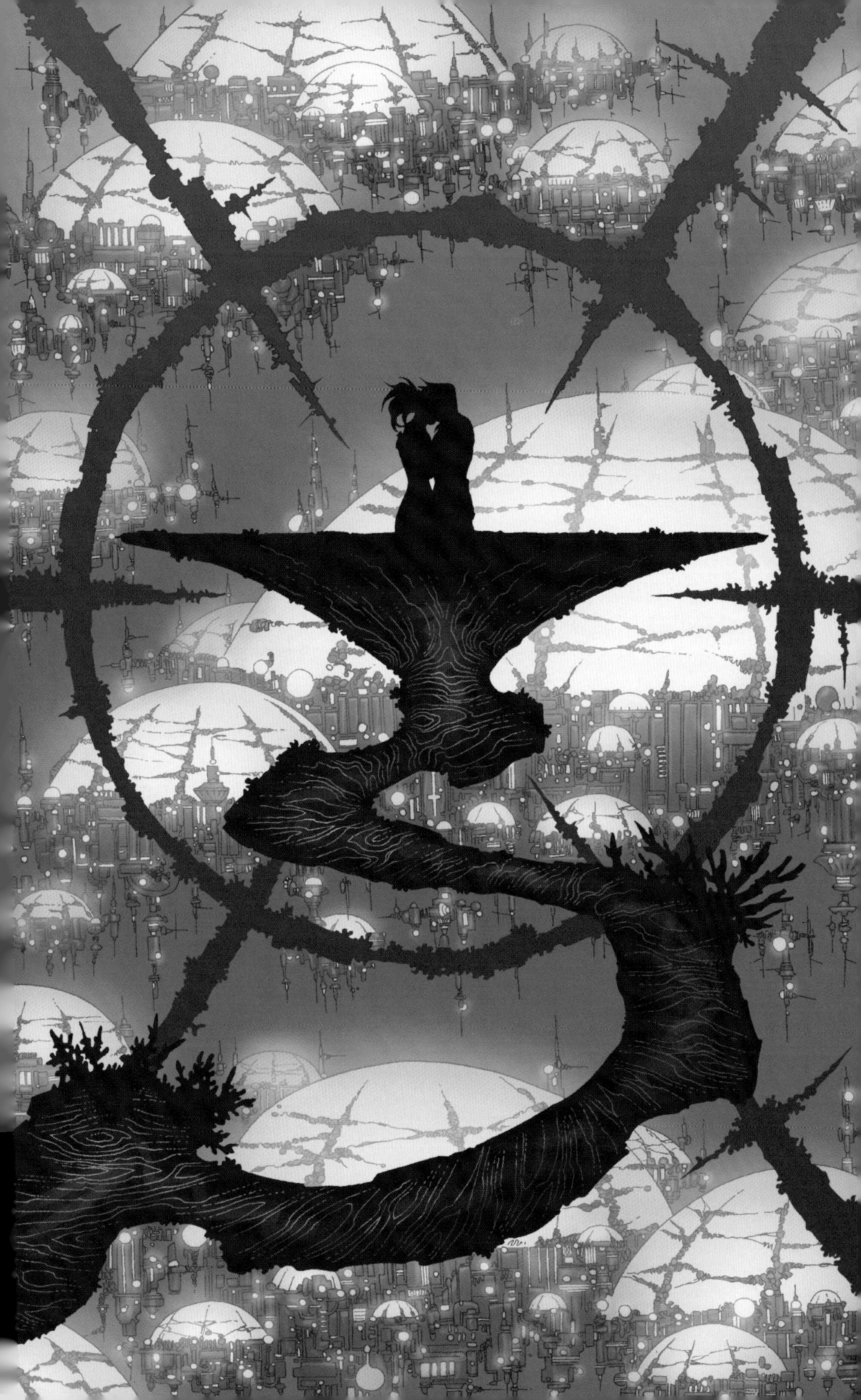

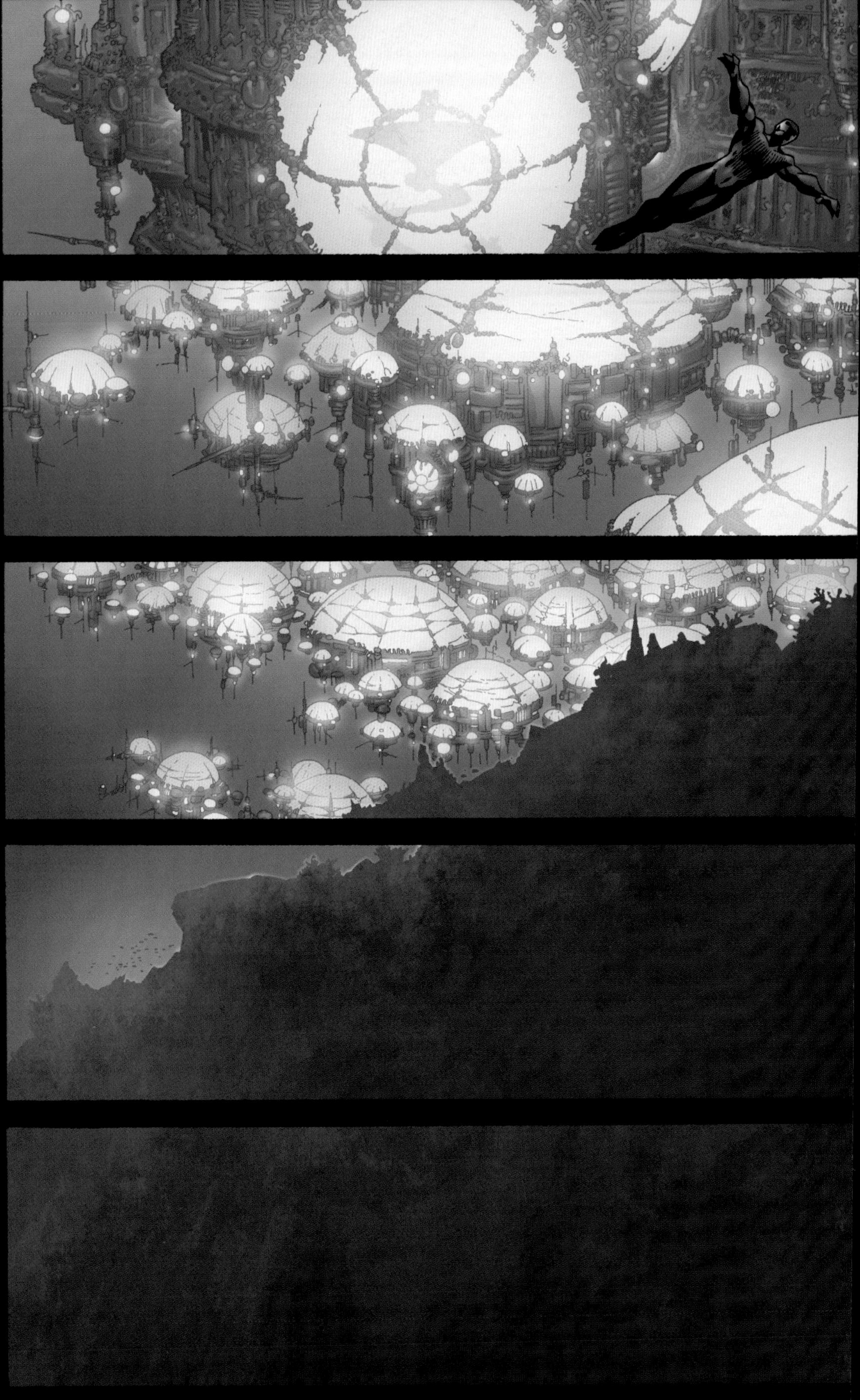

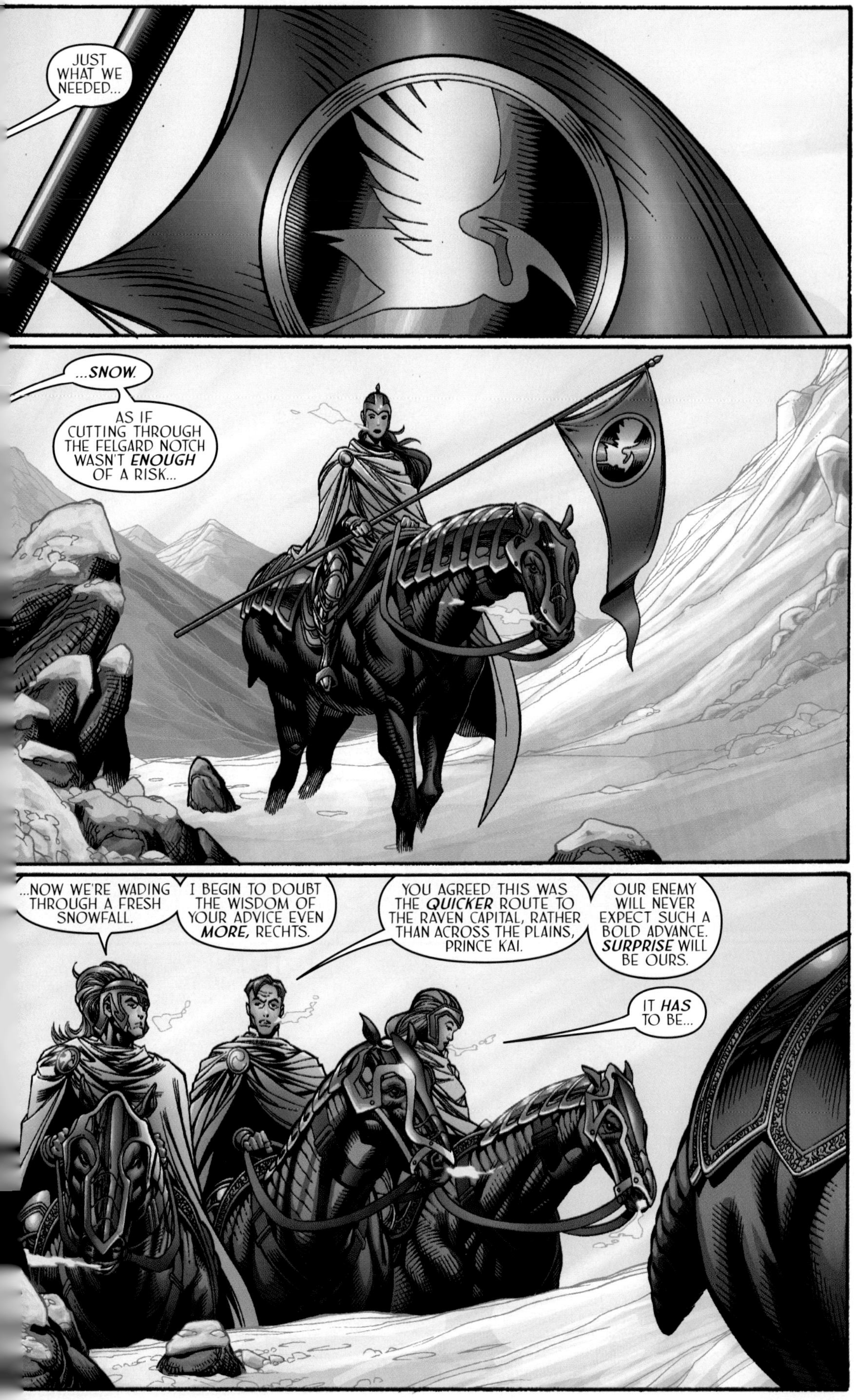
JUST WHAT WE NEEDED...
...SNOW.
AS IF CUTTING THROUGH THE FELGARD NOTCH WASN'T ENOUGH OF A RISK...
...NOW WE'RE WADING THROUGH A FRESH SNOWFALL.
I BEGIN TO DOUBT THE WISDOM OF YOUR ADVICE EVEN MORE, RECHTS.
YOU AGREED THIS WAS THE QUICKER ROUTE TO THE RAVEN CAPITAL, RATHER THAN ACROSS THE PLAINS, PRINCE KAI.
OUR ENEMY WILL NEVER EXPECT SUCH A BOLD ADVANCE. SURPRISE WILL BE OURS.
IT HAS TO BE...

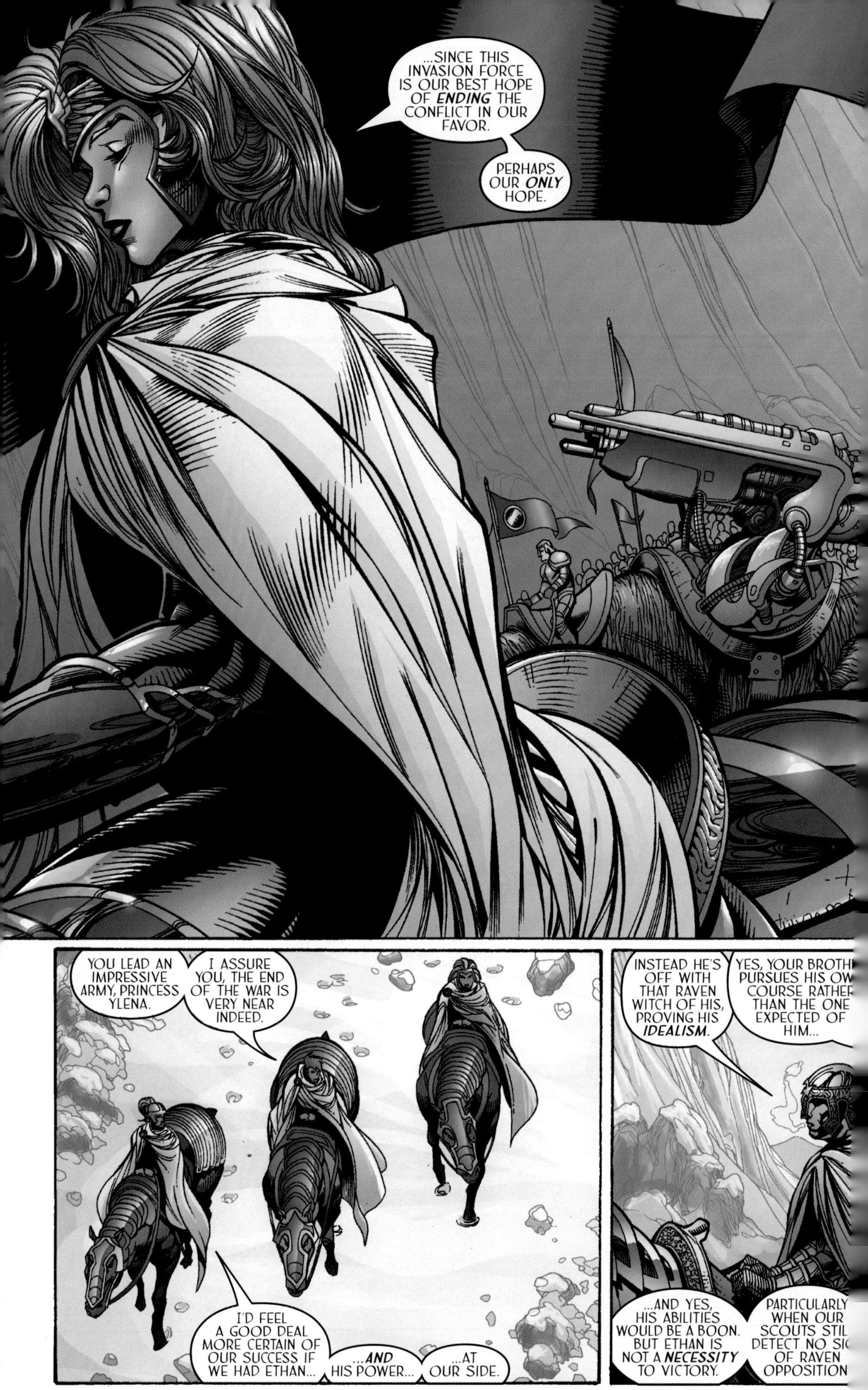
...SINCE THIS INVASION FORCE IS OUR BEST HOPE OF *ENDING* THE CONFLICT IN OUR FAVOR.
PERHAPS OUR *ONLY* HOPE.
YOU LEAD AN IMPRESSIVE ARMY, PRINCESS YLENA.
I ASSURE YOU, THE END OF THE WAR IS VERY NEAR INDEED.
I'D FEEL A GOOD DEAL MORE CERTAIN OF OUR SUCCESS IF WE HAD ETHAN...
*...AND* HIS POWER...
...AT OUR SIDE.
INSTEAD HE'S OFF WITH THAT RAVEN WITCH OF HIS, PROVING HIS *IDEALISM*.
YES, YOUR BROTH PURSUES HIS OW COURSE RATHER THAN THE ONE EXPECTED OF HIM...
...AND YES, HIS ABILITIES WOULD BE A BOON. BUT ETHAN IS NOT A *NECESSITY* TO VICTORY.
PARTICULARLY WHEN OUR SCOUTS STIL DETECT NO SIG OF RAVEN OPPOSITION

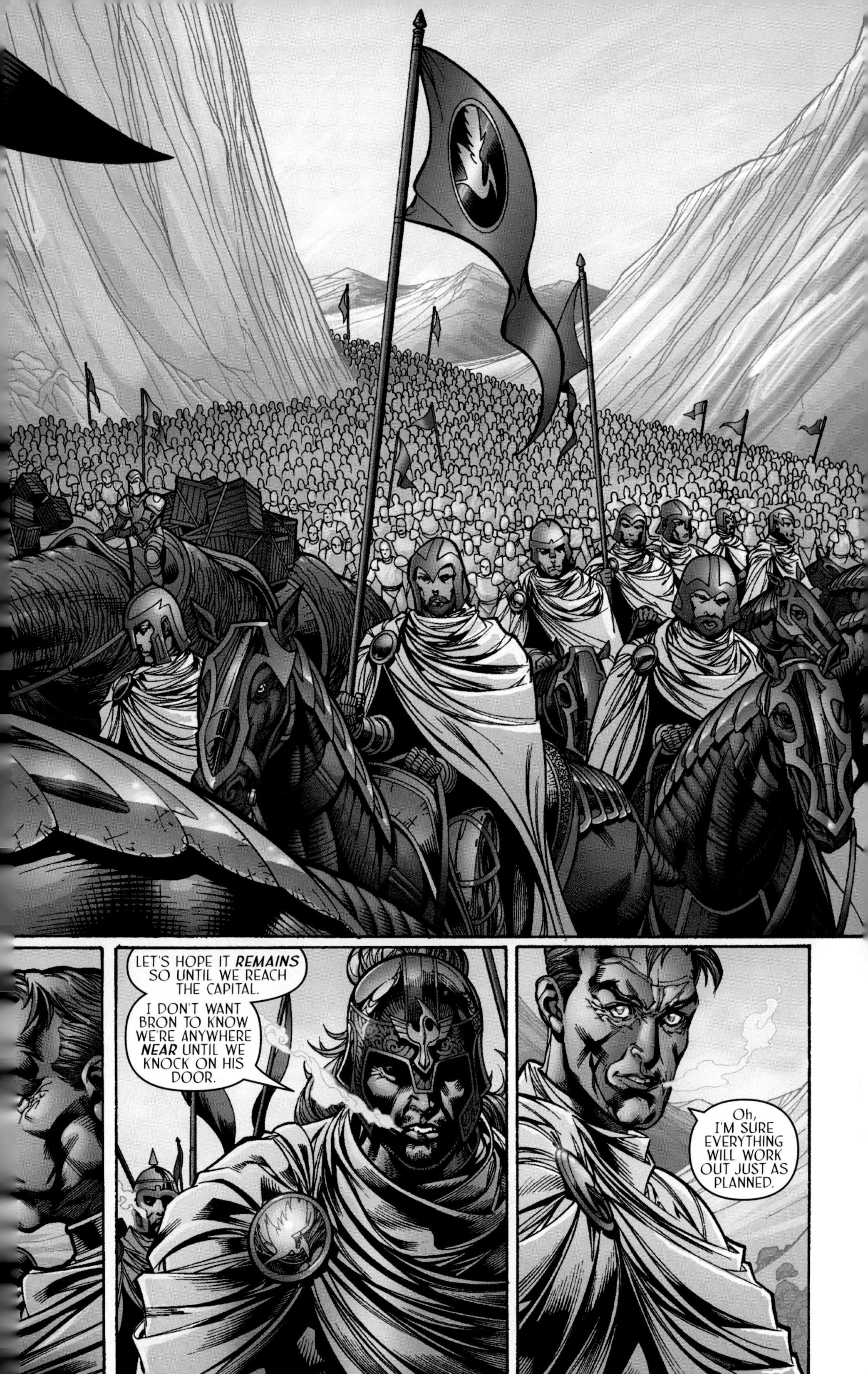
LET'S HOPE IT **REMAINS** SO UNTIL WE REACH THE CAPITAL.
I DON'T WANT BRON TO KNOW WE'RE ANYWHERE **NEAR** UNTIL WE KNOCK ON HIS DOOR.
Oh, I'M SURE EVERYTHING WILL WORK OUT JUST AS PLANNED.

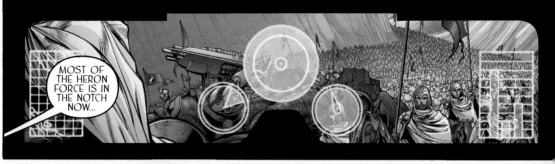

MOST OF THE HERON FORCE IS IN THE NOTCH NOW...

...THEY'LL BE WITHIN RANGE SOON.

LET THEM COME TO *US*, KORT. THE HOLOGRAM GENERATORS WILL MASK OUR PRESENCE UNTIL IT'S *FAR* TOO LATE.

MAI SHEN HAS BEEN NOTICEABLY ABSENT FROM YOUR SIDE OF LATE, BRON.

SHE'S SUPPOSED TO BE OUR *WAR ADVISOR*, SHOULDN'T SHE AT LEAST BE HERE FOR THE ATTACK?

NOT TO WORRY, DEAR BROTHER...

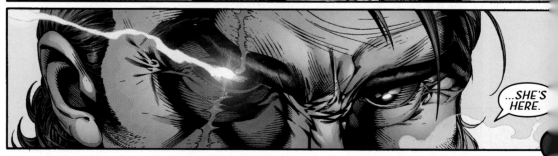

...SHE'S HERE.

# ALSO AVAILABLE

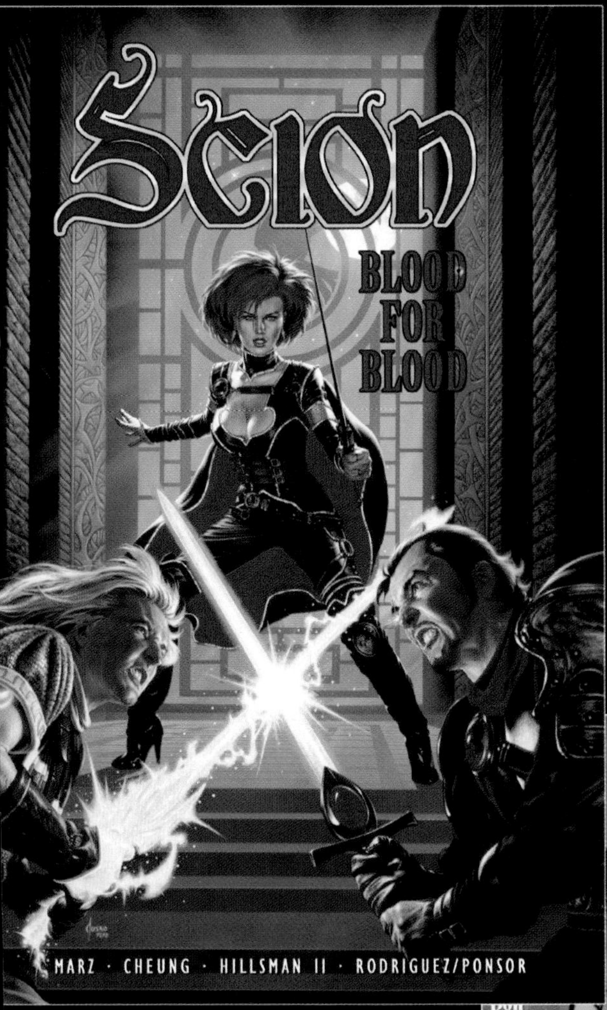
Scion
BLOOD FOR BLOOD
MARZ · CHEUNG · HILLSMAN II · RODRIGUEZ/PONSOR

*Blood for Blood*

TRADE PAPERBACK VOL. 2
208 PAGES $19.95
1-931484-08-3

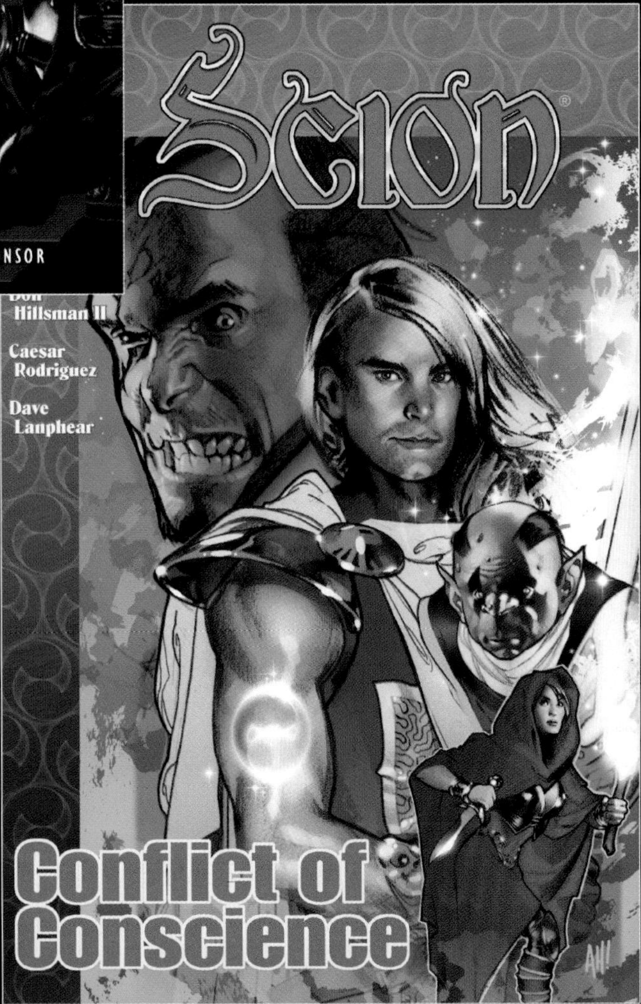
Scion
Hillsman II
Caesar Rodriguez
Dave Lanphear
Conflict of Conscience

*onflict of Conscience*

RADE PAPERBACK VOL. 1
192 PAGES $19.95
1-931484-02-3

# CROSSGEN COMICS

## Graphic Novels

| | | | |
|---|---|---|---|
| **THE FIRST 1** | Two Houses Divided | $19.95 | 1-931484-04-X |
| **THE FIRST 2** | Magnificent Tension | $19.95 | 1-931484-17-1 |
| **MYSTIC 1** | Rite of Passage | $19.95 | 1-931484-00-7 |
| **MYSTIC 2** | The Demon Queen | $19.95 | 1-931484-06-6 |
| **MYSTIC 3** | Seige of Scales | $15.95 | 1-931484-24-4 |
| **MERIDIAN 1** | Flying Solo | $19.95 | 1-931484-03-1 |
| **MERIDIAN 2** | Going to Ground | $19.95 | 1-931484-09-0 |
| **MERIDIAN 3** | Taking the Skies | $15.95 | 1-931484-21-X |
| **SCION 1** | Conflict of Conscience | $19.95 | 1-931484-02-3 |
| **SCION 2** | Blood for Blood | $19.95 | 1-931484-08-2 |
| **SCION 3** | Divided Loyalties | $15.95 | 1-931484-26-0 |
| **SIGIL 1** | Mark of Power | $19.95 | 1-931484-01-5 |
| **SIGIL 2** | The Marked Man | $19.95 | 1-931484-07-4 |
| **SIGIL 3** | The Lizard God | $15.95 | 1-931484-28-7 |
| **CRUX 1** | Atlantis Rising | $15.95 | 1-931484-14-7 |
| **SOJOURN 1** | From the Ashes | $19.95 | 1-931484-15-5 |
| **SOJOURN 2** | The Dragon's Tale | $15.95 | 1-931484-34-1 |
| **RUSE 1** | Enter the Detective | $15.95 | 1-931484-19-8 |
| **CROSSGEN ILLUSTRATED** Volume 1 | | $24.95 | 1-931484-05-8 |